To Ale

BECOMING A

DRUID

Your story will rock!

Mike Mollman

First Edition

Beaver Castle Media

COPYRIGHT 2021 © MIKE MOLLMAN

All rights reserved. No part of this publication may be reproduced, distributed, or transmitted in any form or by any means without the prior written permission of the publisher, except in the case of brief quotations embodied in critical reviews and certain other noncommercial uses permitted by copyright law.

Becoming a Druid

The Protectors of Pretanni Book One

ISBN   978-1-7370524-2-5   *Hardback*

           978-1-7370524-0-1   *Paperback*

           978-1-7370524-1-8   *Ebook*

Table of Contents

Neither really got Fantasy

Both would have been surprised by my desire to write

Each would have given me their unconditional support

Love you always

Mom and Dad

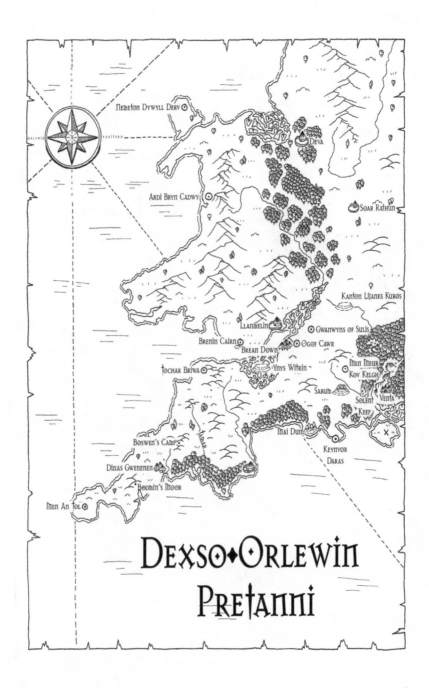

Dexso◆Orlewin
Pretanni

1

Cast Out, Again

Fourteen Days After the Spring Equinox, 819

Master Arthyen, the preeminent animorph among the Pretanni druids and all-around blowhard, is angry at me again.

Why else would he command me to turn into a woodpecker and capture a grub from the largest ash tree in this glade? I choose the great spotted woodpecker and lazily bounce into the air to a dying branch. I spot the telltale holes and start drumming into the wood with enthusiasm. In no time I'm holding a larva as my prize.

"Adequate." He walks away from me as if the instruction bores him.

It should; I've completed every challenge he's thrown at me for the last three months. The old codger has nothing left to teach me. Any reasonable mentor would have assigned me a quest by now.

I toss the remains in his general direction and transform into a screech owl, gliding to the woodland floor behind him. Since he's not paying attention, I let out the screech for which the birds are known.

Arthyen jumps in fright. "No, Gra-mee!" He's always mispronouncing my name, putting emphasis on the end. "Not another owl. You will never understand the intricacies of the forest animals at this rate."

Satisfied that I did more than was asked, I resume my human form. It's a warm spring day with a clear blue sky, the kind that is rarely repeated in this backwater place accurately called "Land's End." Will he waste the whole day with his useless prattle?

He's managed to distance himself from me. From experience, I know he wants me to run and catch up with him so he can feel important. I have a better idea. I transform into an eagle owl and silently glide along, just above him. When he doesn't hear me come running like some child, he thrusts his head around to see where I've gone. I continue to circle him. It's only after he spots my shadow that the old fool pieces it together and scowls.

"You will never appreciate the other animal forms if you continue to fixate on owls."

I land next to him and stare. Owls are so stoic by nature, there's no chance of him reading my disdain while I'm in this form.

He turns his back to me and continues his meandering instruction. "You will miss the beauty of other animal forms like the lynx, the squirrel, and the boar."

I leap into the air and change into a lynx before I touch the ground. He doesn't notice, of course. I run soundlessly toward a hundred-year-old elm. I spring to the base of the tree and I'm a squirrel by the time I reach it. My fluffy tail extends outward to keep my balance. I chitter as I run two rings upward around the trunk. I scurry out along the branch above Master Arthyen's head. I change into a boar.

In retrospect, this is probably a mistake.

Each transformation must involve changing back to my human form before becoming another animal, but I can switch fast enough that I don't even notice it. My hooves slide sideways with every step. I lose my footing and my stomach smashes into the branch. I let out a surprised squeal. Falling on his head would be too much, even for me, so I convert into a tawny owl and spiral down in front of my mentor.

All this morphing has sapped my energy. I'm in need of a nice long nap, perhaps in a sunny pasture. Hopefully, my changing into yet another owl will send him storming off in a huff.

Arthyen snarls his disapproval upon seeing me. He transforms into a massive brown bear and emits a guttural roar. I animorph back into a human and avoid eye contact. I prefer this type of scolding. Later, he won't be able to obsess over whether I remembered his every word.

He rears up onto his hind legs, towering over me. Lowering his head, he hits me with a blast of fetid breath. It's unpleasant, but I stand my ground and wait for him to recover his wits. His forelegs crash back to the ground and his head crashes into my chest with enough force to send me somersaulting backward. I stop at the base of the elm.

I could have been knocked senseless.

I stand up and glare at the clumsy oaf. Instruction is not supposed to include attacking while in animal form. He approaches me, still grunting his displeasure. I advance toward him and swipe with my massive left paw. I don't recall changing into a bear, but this will make for a fair fight. He growls and bites down on my neck. I twist violently and break free. I clamp down on his shoulder and gain leverage along with a mouthful of fur. I force him down on his back and stand over him, refusing to release my hold.

All four of his legs push upward against me until he manages to break free. He rolls over and runs to a rocky outcrop.

I wait. He must transform back first since he was beaten; it is the accepted practice of the animal duel. He vocalizes his anger from above and refuses to yield. I roar in response and start toward him. I will make his defeat clearer.

From the canopy above, a raven touches down between us and fixes me with an impassive gaze. Never have I seen such temerity from a creature so small. I stop and sniff at the odd bird.

It transforms into Boswen, the Lord Protector of our holy site, Men-an-Tol, and the undisputed druidic leader of the Land's End peninsula. His tattered robe gives barely a hint of the white color worn by all druids.

"That is enough," he orders.

"As you command," I say when I regain human form. In my haste, I change back while on all fours. It looks as if I'm trying to kiss his feet.

Arthyen roars in defiance before changing back. "Boswen, it is good that you are here. Don't let his fake deference fool you. I renounce this novice." With every word, his finger jerks toward me. "He will get no further instruction from me."

"What do you have left to teach, you old fool?" I retort.

Boswen silences me with a single upraised eyebrow. I've overstepped again. He turns to Arthyen with great solemnity. "Your words have been heard and the covenant between you and young Grahme is no more."

"I will personally see to it that everyone in Land's End is made aware of this," Arthyen says with glee. "Your failure will be known far and wide, I promise you."

"Is that how you teach your students to act, Arthyen?" Boswen asks.

4

"Say the words, Boswen. I want to see the final blow to this young fool's ego. Tell him that he's forever banned from becoming one of us."

"Arthyen, you are free to take your leave," Boswen says with finality. "Now."

Undaunted, Arthyen basks in his victory before turning into a screech owl and flying away. His victory cries injure me more than any bear attack could.

"Am I to go also, Lord Boswen?" My shame pulls me inward so tightly that I'm convinced I will dissipate from this existence at any moment.

"Yes, you are to go north and east with me to my camp in the woods of Dartmoor. I will finish what Masters Arthyen and Gwalather have started."

"You know of my time with Master Gwalather?"

"I do. And I name you Grahme of the Three Chances, for your fortune is greater than one so prideful has any right to expect."

"Thank you, Lord Protector. I promise to make the most of this chance." I keep my gaze on the ground, afraid to meet his eyes.

"Then stop staring at the ground and keep up, or you shall miss out on your third and final chance." He changes into a gray-faced rook in mid-stride and takes off for the northeast.

Smiling, I follow as a tawny owl. The freedom to soar in the air on a sunny day fills me with unbounded joy. I catch a bit of a thermal and rise even higher in the sky. There will be no more petulance from Arthyen *and* I get to learn from the greatest among us? This is a perfect day.

The old man banks hard to the left and drops in altitude, but I follow him easily. He flies over the River Tamar and trumpets out an alarm call. Below are rooks and jackdaws, busy foraging for their next meal. The air beneath me transforms into a blanket of black wings and murderous intent as the birds rise to attack me, their natural enemy. I can't hope to out-fly them all. I need more speed and more maneuverability. My mind feels fuzzy, no doubt from too many transformations today, but with the encouragement of certain death approaching from below, I'm able to focus and transform once more.

I change back to human and drop half way to the ground before I can assume the shape of a swift. This is exactly why we are taught not to change in midair. I turn right, drop until I'm skimming the ground, and bank back to the left. I've managed to confuse my pursuers as I open up a gap from them. Having lost sight of the owl, they are more than willing to give up the chase. A lassitude falls over me, but I can't rest yet. A swift is not my preferred choice for this journey through shifting winds, so I follow Lord Boswen's lead and become a rook.

Feeling equal parts exhaustion and exhilaration, I give mute praise to the crafty old druid. Already he is more clever than either of my previous instructors.

I accept the challenge, old man.

We sail over the gorse- and heather-covered expanse of the upper moor until we finally reach a narrow ravine. It's filled with moss-covered rocks and old, tortured trees sprouting from wherever soil manages to collect. The gusting wind buffets me hither and yon. *Is it always so bad?* Boswen flairs his wings, changes back into human form, and drops the last few inches onto his feet. He turns and awaits my landing. I had expected him to keep moving, so I have to yank back abruptly on my landing. Changing back to human, I'm unable to keep my balance and I stumble to the unforgiving ground. Again, I'm staring at his feet wrapped in well-worn leather shoes.

"Did you know the significance of my gray beak when I changed into the bird?"

"You chose a rook instead of the raven, which you chose when you entered the glen," I say before I rise. I can't help but let out a huge yawn. Getting to my feet takes most of my remaining energy.

"And after my choice of a bird, you chose the form of its mortal enemy?"

"I did not think of you as my enemy."

"Then you must practice your thinking. Perhaps if you'd listened to your old master, you would know not to upset the natural world without cause. That one mistake could have proven deadly."

"As you say," I grin despite the tongue lashing. *Never again will you catch me unaware.*

"And what is the effect of too many transformations in one day?"

I yawn again. "Each transition saps your energy, both mentally and physically. After too many transitions, the mind fails to remain sharp and the transformation can go badly, resulting in a permanent change, injury, or even death."

"Any other side effects, assuming you avoid those three?"

"It makes you sleepy." My heavy eyelids are evidence of this.

"It does, and it also deadens your appetite. What other signs are there that you have overextended yourself?"

"You fall over in exhaustion?" I'm not sure what the old man wants me to say.

7

"Beyond being tired and exhausted, one would exhibit tremors in the limbs. Raise your arms out in front of you."

I force my hands to stay still, but we both watch as my arms betray me.

"How do your legs feel?"

"Very heavy."

He purses his lips. "You are accomplished as an animorph. What of the other skills of the druids?"

"I am also accomplished at potions and salves."

"So Master Gwalather was also unjustified in releasing you?"

"I should not have struck him, despite his provocation," I admit. "But my skill is undeniable." I dare not say more.

Boswen walks to the fire pit outside his hut. He inspects it before turning back to me. A second hut is filled with firewood and other basic supplies. "I have, or at least I used to have, frequent visitors, so I had need for a good store of dry tinder."

There is obvious sadness in his voice. Not knowing a proper response, I nod my understanding.

"What of the other druid skills?" he asks in a clipped manner. "Runes?"

"I do not see the need to carve ancient elvish letters into tree bark."

He raises an eyebrow at my answer. This is my last chance; I choose to be honest.

"Animal lore?"

"It is the most basic of skills; I can communicate with animals."

"I have seen your animorphing skills and they speak for themselves. What of elemental summoning?"

"I believe druids should commune with the living, not the lifeless substances around us."

"Can you summon an elemental or not?" he asks, aggravated.

"I cannot."

"What of Barding?"

"I do not seek out nor particularly enjoy drunken fools, so my skill is minimal."

"And have you any ability in weather magic?"

"I thought that skill had been lost. Neither Gwalather nor Arthyen would address the subject with me."

"You're lucky neither of them did; they are both beyond useless in the art."

"You know weather magic?" My ears perk up to hear his answer, despite my sluggishness.

"I will teach you weather magic."

I can't hide my smile. The chilly, damp wind from the west picks up, reminding me that the moorland is much colder than the land below. I had no chance to retrieve my wool mantle this morning, and now the wind is numbing me to the bone. I rub my arms to ward off goose bumps. Thick clouds are rolling in from the coast, threatening heavy rain. *If I could control the weather, would I live in such a miserable place?*

Boswen sees me glancing at the clouds. "As in most forms of magic, restraint is usually the proper answer."

He must have read my mind. I yawn again. I have overtaxed myself today.

9

Seeing my waning energy, Boswen extends his hand and pats my shoulder. "You are overly tired from your exertions today."

I nod, torn between the warm fire and the empty hut. A nap would do wonders for me.

"If you were to sleep now, you would wake up half-starved and unable to learn tomorrow."

I continue my mindless nodding. Whatever you say, old man.

"Time is precious, so once more, show me that swift of yours and don't come back until you have eaten your bodyweight in insects."

"But that could take until dinner."

"The folly of your display today will be hammered home quite well, I expect." The audience over, he turns his back to me and tends to the fire.

2

Herbal Skills

A Half Month after *Alban Heruin,*
the Summer Solstice, 819

Boswen can have an acid tongue at times, but he seems willing to answer my questions. That's more than my previous mentors would do.

"Lord Boswen," I start.

"So, what have you done this time, Grahme?"

"Nothing."

"Then what is it you want?"

"Nothing, Lord."

"Then why do you start by using my formal title, if not to ask for forgiveness or a boon?"

"It's only that I wish to ask a question, and I fear that you will judge me stupid."

"You are stupid," he says quickly. "It is my job to change that, so ask whatever questions you will."

I must learn not to ask him questions before our midday meal. He's never agreeable until well after midday.

"I asked my father once why the month ends on the full moon and not the moonless night. He told me it was because that had always been the way of it. In your vast years of learning, have you come across a better answer?"

"Vast years of learning? Hmm. Your father is a farmer, I suspect."

"He was."

"Well, for a farmer, that's the right answer. Part of a druid's job is to give the right answer and not necessarily the complete answer. But as a druid, you should know more. When does the new year begin?"

"Samhain."

"And the first half of the year is known as the dark half, although some mistakenly call it the dark year, correct?"

"Yes, of course."

"And the day, it starts at sundown, no?"

"Yes, it does," I say warily.

"So, the first half of each day begins in darkness and the first half of the year is when we have the least amount of daylight, also favoring darkness. So, too, does the month start as the moonlight starts to wane, namely the day after the full moon. After the night without the moon goddess, the second half of the month begins. Aine's glory then steadily waxes, and, just like the year and the day, the month ends in brightness; in this case, the full moon. This is how we make sense of the world."

"Thank you," I say. Expressing my impatience for his long-winded answer will get me nowhere.

He catches me rolling my eyes, but he flashes me a mischievous grin instead of a reprimand. "Are you ready to meet another member of the Nine?"

"Really? Where are we going? Keynvor Daras? Men Meur Kov Keigh?"

"We are not going to any of the holy sites today, not even our own. But if you look off to the northwest at that merlin, I believe one of the Nine is coming to pay us a call."

"Really? Which one?" I can't keep the excitement out of my voice. We've spent the last five months together and the only other person I've spoken to is the kindly old woman below the moorland who prepares our dinners each night.

"Who, indeed?" His eyes twinkle with mischief. "Perhaps if you can name them?"

"You, Loris, Meraud, ah—"

"And give the holy site they are charged with protecting," he adds.

I frown at him. When I start again, he'll interrupt me and have me include the people's name for each site as well. I won't give him the chance. "Lord Loris is the head druid and protector of Nemeton Dywyll Derw, the Holy Oak Grove of Ynys Mona, and the gift of the elves. You are the protector of Men-an-Tol, the gift of the pixies. Tochar Briwa is Drustan's place and the giant's gift should remind us to always work with nature. Meraud protects Keynvor Daras, the gateway to Lir's and Melusine's watery expanse. Cynbel and his plains druids protect the Giant's Choir: Men Meur Kov Keigh. The Gwanwyns of Sulis are Eghan's abode, and the hot springs provide healing waters to the penitent. All of the great druids find their final resting place at Brenin Cairn and Braden oversees the site."

"Only two left, and you have not yet named our visitor," Boswen taunts. "Let's move out onto the moor so the fool doesn't fly past us."

13

I stumble leaving the camp, but I hardly notice. "Let's see," I pause. The bird is getting very close now. "Hedred is the protector of Ogof Cawr, the underground realm of caves," I say a little too loudly.

Boswen's eyes dance in amusement. Apparently, the last to be named is our visitor. The bird is circling us in a wide arc rather than landing.

This lord must be acquainted with Boswen and his ways of instructing. "And Lord Caradoc is the protector of Ardri Bryn Cadwy, the Tomb of the All King." I manage to get the words out in a flurry. Above us the merlin lets out a short chirp before restarting its lazy descent.

In the intervening time, I ask a question that I've often wondered. "Lord Boswen," I start. He raises one eyebrow at me again, but I continue anyway. "Who was the All King?"

He shrugs. "Nobody knows."

"No man could have ruled when the elder races were still here," I say. "When, in the last eight hundred and nineteen years, did a single man rule all of Pretanni?"

"You should ask Caradoc these questions. If anyone knows, it would be him."

I look back at our humble camp. Why didn't he tell me about this sooner so I could have tried to make our camp presentable? "If he's staying the night, we'll need more wood and water. Should I get them now?"

"Grahme, relax. Caradoc was once a student of mine and he was nearly as hardheaded as you. I doubt time has softened that characteristic overly much. If we need more wood, then Caradoc will collect his share."

The merlin completes two downward circles, dropping to within an arm's length of the ground. The bird changes into a middle-aged druid with long curls of brown hair. On landing, his momentum carries him forward to Boswen. He grasps the old druid's hand and leans in close to whisper a message. Boswen gives no reaction to the news. Caradoc nods his head at me in greeting. Unlike Boswen, his robes are clean and untattered.

"I saw you from a league away," Boswen chuckles.

"One day I will surprise you when I visit."

"How could you tell it was Lord Caradoc?" I ask. "Could you sense him?"

"Only the Sorim can sense another's mind, and even then not while we are in animal form. Since he was upwind, I couldn't smell him like normal. Alas, the secret is that he is a lazy flyer and his half-hearted upstrokes always give him away."

"You and your lies, do you ever tell the truth, you old fox?"

"Only when I have no other choice," Boswen answers, smiling.

"This, I presume, is young Grahme?"

Now that he's focused on me, I struggle to figure out what to do with my arms. They start to sway, so I pull them up across my chest. No good. Now he'll think I'm put off by him. I drop them and interlock my fingers behind my back.

"It is my honor to meet a great one," I say.

"Is this how he speaks to you?" Caradoc asks Boswen.

"Hardly, but then I don't lord the fact that I'm a member of the Nine over him as some do. Shall we get on to business before my protégé faints in your presence?" Boswen asks.

"To business then," Caradoc says. "Loris is quite vexed with you. You have put him in a hard spot."

"He is the Great Druid; does he expect anything less?" Boswen asks.

"Are you talking about Loris, our head druid?" I ask in amazement.

They exchange quick smiles at my interruption.

"How I wish instead it was some insignificant oaf named Loris, but yes, we are," Boswen says.

He changes his stance to let me know that he is conversing with Caradoc now. I risk a rebuke by staying within earshot. It's worth it to hear more about the Council of Nine.

"I miss your insights at Ynys Mona. The weather and conversation somehow feel colder up north when you're not present. Why do you withhold your voice?" Caradoc asks.

Boswen turns to face me. I give him my best innocent expression. "Grahme, we will speak on many topics only some of which are true and none of any interest to an acolyte. Can you prepare a liniment to ease Caradoc's sore shoulders? He would like to apply it himself at dinner so he can rest easy tonight."

"How do you know that Lord Caradoc's shoulders are sore?" I ask. "Gwalather never taught me how to observe so quickly."

"Easy; Caradoc has had bad flying technique since he was your age, and that was quite a long time ago."

"You would probably get more guests," Caradoc says, "if you didn't readily insult them as soon as they arrive."

Boswen smiles at me. "Caradoc is a master of deflecting conversations rather than admitting his faults." He holds up a hand to forestall a reply from Caradoc. "Grahme, please see to the liniment. We will be doing this all night long."

"Yes, Mentor, by dinner." I bow slightly and without another word change into a merlin of my own and fly out over the heather-filled field.

Boswen had not mentioned what herbs to use, but he didn't have to. Gwalather may be a pompous ass, but he knew his herb lore. The elderflower would aid in the bone ache, the willow will reduce the inflammation, and the cotton sedge will restore Lord Caradoc's vigor. That's more than what was requested. A cold breeze from the west ruffles my feathers. It is a harbinger for a harsh change in the weather. Already the fog is building below me. I have only a small sliver of time before the dense fog races over the moor.

I manage the elderflower and willow easily enough. The cotton sedge only grows around the bogs and they collect the fog and hold it tight. I will not be so easily deterred. I select the best young shoots and start my return to camp. Even my keen eyes can barely see the sun poking through the mist. Locating the camp in this fog is an issue I had not considered. I have but a little time to make the poultice. I fly high, higher than the tallest tors since I'd rather not brain myself running into one. Luckily, I spot the tip of an oak breaking through the mist.

There are very few trees on the moor and all of them line the banks of the western River Dart, so I must be nearly to camp. I change to a bat so I can navigate through the unseen trees and boulders. I find the camp, but not the druids. The firewood is damp. I overlooked the need to start a fire, and there's little chance now. I grind the leaves and the sedge. Without fire, I will need a sour component to better release the medicines, but it's too late to hunt for it now.

Disgusted with myself, I grab a bit of soil to thicken it to a balm. I add the flowers last and ready myself for failure. Tiny drops of oil rise to the top of my concoction. The liquid is starting to bloom. I taste the soil; it's slightly sour to the taste. Why hadn't I discovered this before? I can sour cook the herbs. I add more soil and rub the sides of the small cup to produce what heat I can. I thank the many gods for my good fortune. From the sheen on top, I can see that the potency has been released. It's time for dinner, yet still there is no sign of them.

I add a bit more soil to thicken the slurry. With any luck, the sour-cooking will continue. I change into a long-eared bat. I have always found the animal's navigation to be most precise, and their hearing is superior. I soar up and head for Boswen's favorite residents, the moor ponies. They are feeding in the open on this cool, still night.

I hear the druids before I can see their fire. Perhaps I will get a warm meal after all. I land behind them on the tor and wait but an instant. It would never do to spy on two great druids, but I wouldn't want to interrupt them, either.

"I'm afraid you gave too stern of a test to the lad, Boswen, and now I'm left in a difficult spot."

"Perhaps I did. He has not had much time to learn the weather goddess' fickle moods and I fear that I sabotaged him from the start. Perhaps we should go back to the camp."

Now is my moment. I glide down and change back to myself. "If you do, you will find it empty and a mess." I stride confidently into their view. "I apologize for not cleaning up, but it seems that you added a new wrinkle by not telling me where you would be waiting."

Caradoc stares wide-eyed at me. Boswen is clapping as he gazes proudly at me.

"Lord Caradoc, I present you the poultice you require," I say with a bow. "You will need some cloth to hold it in place on a cold, wet evening like tonight."

"And what did you put in this?" Boswen asks, having regained his taskmaster tone.

"I found fresh willow leaves from the eastern slopes of the moor to reduce the swelling, new elder flowers from near the old copper mine tunnels in the southwest for your bone ache, and cotton sedge from around the northern bogs for energy. When I arrived at camp it was too damp for a fire so I sour-cooked the herbs with the soil until the blooming began. I am sorry that I could not do better for you, Lord Caradoc."

Caradoc is dumbfounded. "If this poultice alleviates any part of my pain, I will be amazed. Now tell me, how did you find us?"

He signals for me to sit by the fire, opposite them.

"I couldn't see in this fog so I selected a long-eared bat so I could avoid running into trees or outcrops and hear you."

"No fire and no visibility and yet he still delivers on time?" He faces Boswen. "You must have improved on your instruction."

"He did well," Boswen confirms. "You will give Loris no choice, I assume?"

"He insisted on having a stern test and Grahme has passed easily. You will get your way, as always," Caradoc replies.

"Will I get to meet the head druid?" I ask.

"At some point you undoubtedly will," Boswen says without excitement, "but not any time soon. Since you have clearly passed your test, I will tell you why Caradoc has come." He shakes his head skyward to show his distaste. "It seems Masters Gwalather and

Arthyen have decided to go around me and ask the head druid to expel you from our order."

"Oh." My heart drops into my stomach.

"The move is unprecedented," Caradoc says. "Each lord has total control of his area. Only a vote by the entire Council of Nine could undue a lord's decision."

"Is that why you didn't go to the special council meeting on the summer solstice?" I ask Boswen.

"No. Now if you two don't mind, the Lord Protector of this land would like to finish his speaking without more interruptions." He frowns at both of us, even as Caradoc grins back. "My reasons for not attending the last meeting will remain my own. Loris' pretensions of being master of us all aside, I agreed to have you tested in order to see how well you would use your many skills without my constant direction. Your work is beyond what is expected. But even if you had failed, I would not have allowed you to be dismissed."

"Can I attend you at the next gathering in the fall?" The nine lord druids meet every spring and fall, right after the equinoxes. I joined Lord Boswen well after the spring meeting, but that meeting is only for the Nine anyway. Kantom Lijanks Kuros is the fall site for the council meeting and all druids and students can attend. Several advanced acolytes are given the white robes of a full druid at the event. I have wanted to attend the meeting for years, but Gwalather and Arthyen would not allow it.

"I cannot speak to that now. Unfortunately, Caradoc and I must speak on topics of the Nine. Could you await us at the camp? This shouldn't take long."

"Of course, Master." I keep my voice neutral, though it stings to be sent away again.

"He means that we will start talking unkindly about the other seven once you are out of earshot," Caradoc says.

"As you say," Boswen replies with a laugh.

"I understand. I will take a bit of fire with me, if you don't mind."

I grab a thick branch from the fire. I walk quickly away until I'm out of sight. I take off running to camp and start the fire. I throw extra wood on it and stuff any mess from camp in my hut. I stop and listen closely but the fog has deadened any noise. Master Arthyen taught me long ago that owls collect sounds by their flat faces and funnel it toward their ears. It was one of the few things the old fool said worth hearing. Ever since then, I have considered owls the pinnacle of avian perfection. I take on the tawny owl form and silently fly back toward the druid lords.

I land atop the tor. The blanket of fog will hide me from their eyes and their ears.

". . . and what did Loris say?"

"Loris decided that the situation was too nuanced to decide from afar. That's why he sent me."

"So, he still avoids making decisions?"

"He is, as always, worried about the political ramifications."

"He's the head druid. Short of being challenged and defeated, he can't lose his spot."

"Still, he has decided to have another make the decision once that wise individual is finished collecting information."

"So, I must wait for some lapdog of Loris to decide?" Boswen asks, laughter in his voice.

"A lapdog, am I? Why is it that your insults were rare when I was your student, but now that I am your equal you give me nothing else?"

"When you were a student you needed to have your confidence boosted. Now that you are older, you need to have your humility encouraged."

"Age has done plenty of that, I assure you." Caradoc rotates his left arm in circles, grimacing as he holds onto his shoulder. "I don't recall an abundance of praise when I was at your knee."

"So, your mind has gone as soft as your stomach."

Caradoc laughs off the insult before he turns serious and changes the topic. "And what did Eghan say?"

They must be talking about Lord Eghan, another of Boswen's former students. He's known far and wide as the preeminent healer on Pretanni; hence he is the protector of the healing hot springs.

"He agreed with my assessment." The air is gusting from behind me. For them, the tor is acting as a windbreak. For me, the chill in the air is undeniable. My feathers rise to trap in more body heat. Still, I wouldn't leave this perch now for anything less than freezing rain.

"How much time?"

"A couple of months, maybe a bit more."

"Will he be ready?"

"He's ready now."

"And you are still going forward with your plan?" Caradoc stirs up the fire before adding the last of their kindling.

"Yes."

"He will never forgive you for this," Caradoc says.

"He will, once you use your rhetorical flourishes on my behalf."

"He will feel betrayed, and that is not something that can be explained away with a few sympathetic words."

"Even if you're right, I'm committed to my plan. He is a rare talent; the best at his craft since Bodmin."

Caradoc rolls his head back and his shoulders follow. "Must I hear about your ancestor again?"

"The old stories of Bodmin are all true. He was the greatest animorph this isle has ever produced."

"And he abandoned his brethren," Caradoc says, exasperated, "multiple times."

Bodmin was a famous druid from centuries ago, but everyone invokes his name with either anger or sadness. Who is he talking about being nearly as good as Bodmin? I'd love to see this druid embarrass Arthyen in an animal duel.

"You know the old stories as well as I do. Did he have much choice?"

"It was a sad time, no doubt," Caradoc says agreeably, if only to stave off a Boswen ramble.

My mentor idly inspects one of the multitude of spots on his robe. "So, I assume that Loris has not taken my warning about the Obsidian Lord of Solent Keep seriously."

"He has his doubts. He's not heard of any such calamities occurring on the mainland."

"Ah, yes, the mainland again, why did the man leave there if he's so fond of it?" Boswen asks.

"One suspects that they were not sufficiently deferential to his august presence."

Boswen stirs the fire. "Does anyone think that after the Obsidian Lord led the Sorim of Ynys Luko to take over Solent Keep that he would be content to rule a single city? That mage has bigger plans. Mark my words."

"And his plans revolve around obtaining a silly flower?" Caradoc asks.

"Have you ever seen one before?"

"No."

"The scarcity is a sign of its power."

"Loris was not the least bit concerned about this."

Boswen lowers his head into his hands. "Why did we let Loris become our leader?"

"It could have been yours, if—"

"I won't re-argue the decision." Boswen waves away Caradoc's scolding. "We needed more time and more knowledge if we were to make a better choice, and we had neither available to us."

"Or an ally in possession of a backbone."

"Don't start now. Hedred has always desired consensus and he's right. A divided Nine would be worse in the long run."

Hedred must be the Protector of the Caves of Ogof Cawr. Everyone agrees he's a strange one. But I guess you'd have to be if you choose to live your entire life underground. Apparently, he's the waffling type, too.

"Forgive me," Caradoc says in a flat voice. "I'll have to remember to count our blessings that we have a self-aggrandizing fool as our leader and not you."

Startled, I let out a soft hoot without thinking. Boswen was in line to be the next head druid? And he turned it down? I adjust my head left and right to make sure I heard correctly.

The wind changes direction and it begins to bite the druids below. Boswen stands and stretches. "I for one do not wish to sit here in the cold and listen to two old men complain about past injustices. Come; let's rejoin Grahme before idleness causes him to do something unfortunate."

The two druid lords kick dirt on the fire and I quickly take flight. It would never do for them to find out that I've been eavesdropping.

3

The Revelation

The Twelfth Dark Day of Elembiu, 819

Events from Lughnasa in Llanmelin are forever planted in my memory. The Silures have long been known for the most raucous celebrations on Pretanni. Usually, the three days before the Lughnasa festival are the wildest, but the Silures keep it going through the three days after the festival as well. This harvest festival was no exception.

Leaving Ysella was the hardest thing I've ever had to do. Why couldn't I have met her at the start of the celebration instead of the second to last day? It's been two days and all I can think about is meeting her again during the druid council at Kantom Lijanks Kuros. Then we can meet again at Beltane in late spring. Seeing her at the fertility festival, I can't help but get excited. But that's an eternity from now.

Had Boswen not unexpectantly left as soon as I returned, I surely would have tasted his wrath. I have been unable to focus on any of my studies.

I've had the camp to myself and my bedroll is nice and warm. I allow myself this little indulgence of not rising with the sun.

"Grahme," Boswen calls out, "Please come here."

I nearly fall out of bed at the sound of his voice. When did he get back to camp? I slide into my robe and grab my mantle as I exit. Boswen and Caradoc are standing near the fire pit, waiting for me.

Caradoc is here? What kind of trouble am I in now?

I throw on my wool mantle to hide my confusion before joining the two lords. It's as if I'm five again and Father is about to scold me for not doing my chores. By the cold ashes, the fire hasn't been tended since I let it burn out last night.

"Lord Caradoc has not come here for merely a social visit this time," Boswen says as he directs me to sit at the fire.

"I find myself overly warm, so I will stand if it pleases you," I lie. I don't know why, but I sense trouble has found me once again. I force my shoulders back and my hands to hang motionless at my sides. Whatever it is, I won't give any indication of my anxiety.

Boswen extends his hand in a placating gesture. "As you wish."

I must be in trouble.

"It seems that Master Arthyen is still unhappy about you remaining in our order. And he has once again gone around me by bringing up your instruction directly with Loris."

"But I thought Lord Caradoc ruled on this two months ago, right after the summer solstice," I say.

Caradoc looks to Boswen, who flashes a subtle smile. Deflated, I realize they are silently noting my impertinence.

"Any responsible head druid would have quashed this nonsense at once. Loris has decided to resolve this issue during the gathering at Kantom following the autumn equinox."

I freeze in place. Rarely have I caused Boswen to lose his temper over the past five months. I inhale slowly. Whatever he is going to tell me next will affect the rest of my life.

"How has your instruction been going?" Caradoc asks.

What is he doing, making small talk? "I spend my time practicing weather magic and learning whatever else I am able from Lord Boswen," I say a little too sharply.

"And he has done well," Boswen says, cutting me off before I can explode at Caradoc. "Arthyen took the unusual step of meeting with Loris over this past harvest festival. Caradoc can fill you in on what transpired."

I'm covered in a nervous sweat. I rub my arms for warmth and to comfort myself.

Caradoc clears his throat. "I was made aware of Arthyen's trip to the sacred grove of Ynys Mona. Knowing Arthyen as I do, I assumed he was going to cause trouble for Boswen so I hurried to Nemeton Dywyll Derw myself. It was three days before Lughnasa. Loris does not like to hear petitions from anyone, including his druids. Being the first day of the seven day festival, he refused to hear any petitions until after Lughnasa was over."

I can feel it all slipping away. My throat constricts so much that I worry if I'll be able to breathe. I have been a good student since I joined Boswen in the spring.

"My goal was to irritate Loris before Arthyen could speak to him so that whatever Arthyen might ask for would be refused. I asked to be allowed to take on more students for training. Ogmios must have been working through me, for my eloquence found a friendly ear and Loris granted my request. After me, Loris was well disposed to Arthyen's complaints." He throws his arms up at the unlikely event. "Of course, I reminded Loris that I ruled as his proxy a scant few months ago, but it was to no avail."

Boswen retakes the lead. "Arthyen showed some initiative for a change, and had Master Gwalather join him. Their comments about

28

you were one-sided. They claimed that Caradoc had not considered the issues you had with your previous masters." His hands tremble as he tries to rein in his emotions.

A cold shiver goes down my back. Once his jaw healed, Gwalather threatened to poison me if he ever saw me again. It took all his skill to heal his partially detached tongue. Though secretly I hold the incident as one of my proudest moments, I dare not utter the thought aloud.

Boswen keeps his lips sealed tightly, not trusting himself to speak. Caradoc breaks the silence and continues the narrative. "I agreed to personally bring Loris' decision on whether or not your instruction should continue."

I freeze in place. Caradoc waves his hand, unsuccessfully trying to banish my deepest fear.

"But I feinted a need to return to my people at the Tomb of the All King first," Caradoc says. "I promised Loris to deliver his message by the end of the fifth day after Lughnasa."

"That's today." I blurt. My eyes switch back and forth between the two lords, imploring someone to tell me what it all means. Neither is willing to put me out of my agony.

"Come, let us view the moor ponies," Boswen says.

He changes into a raven and is off to the northern end of the moor, just like that. Caradoc shrugs at me before following Boswen's lead.

"What in the abyss has happened?" I ask the empty camp, before hurrying to catch up.

The two druids stand upon Black Tor, overlooking a stallion and his harem of moor ponies. Is this aptly named outcrop to be where my dream of becoming a druid is ripped from me once and for all?

"I never tire of watching them," Boswen says, eyes unfocused.

"Excuse me, lords, but can you tell me of my future?" I say without whining. I definitely do not whine.

Should I have interrupted the lords? *How can I not?* Will my presumption turn them against me? My life is spinning out of control and I am powerless to stop it.

Boswen raises a hand to silence me. "Please, Grahme, I know you're anxious, but I have a significant decision to make."

What decision? It's my future in the balance. *Must he decide on what's for dinner?* My head is about to explode. I ball my fists and release them over and over to bleed off the tension.

"You have done well these past few months," Boswen says, distracted.

"I'm afraid that is as close to a compliment that you are likely to receive from him," Caradoc says to me. "Trust me, I should know."

I can barely control the urge to strike out at both of them. *Clench and release, clench and release.* My hands ache but I continue anyway.

Caradoc says gently to Boswen, "It's not like you to hesitate, old friend."

"I must beg your indulgence, Grahme, please leave me be for now; I will call when I'm ready."

I stare at the bare, grassy plain and wonder what I am to do. I dare not go far, but I can't stay on the tor, hovering over the lords.

I see a young foal darting about the high moor, without a care in the world. How I wish I could feel that way. I take the form of a tawny owl and land in front of it. He lowers his head to sniff me and I change into a foal myself. He lets out a surprised squeal and his mother eases over toward us. I break into a canter and circle my new friend. He sprints after me and a game of chase ensues.

I start to get hungry, but I know better than to fill my stomach with grass. My human body will not appreciate that. I animorph back to myself and manage to spook several of the mares nearby, causing the stallion to investigate. I broadcast feelings of calm to him and his harem. The foal walks to my side, declaring his friendship.

Mollified, the adults return to feeding.

"Grahme," Boswen calls from the base of the tor.

I change back into a tawny owl and return to hear my fate. Delighted by this new game, the foal gives chase. I botch my landing by turning back into human form too early and too far from the ground. I land on my knees. Staring at Boswen's feet is quickly becoming my signature move. I spring up at once. "Yes?"

Boswen extends a gentle hand to my new equine friend. "Go, little one, back to your mother." He takes his place next to Caradoc.

I alternate my gaze between them, silently urging one of them to speak.

"Very well," Boswen says softly. "I will speak with you both again back at camp, before nightfall. Grahme, you will be given your quest."

4

The Quest

The Twelfth Dark Day of Elembiu, 819

S taring endlessly into the flames at camp has drained me of all energy. Too exhausted to contemplate my future anymore, I glance at the fiery orb in the sky, the god Belenos, as he sinks toward the horizon. I return my gaze to the fire. The day's end is nearly upon us.

Caradoc begins to pace. "Where are you, Boswen?" he mutters.

"Behind you, old friend."

Caradoc spins and places his hands on his hips. "Cutting it close, aren't we?"

"It was a weighty matter I had to mull over. And, if I explained the quest at midday, Grahme would still be pestering me with questions."

I stand and formally bow to my mentor.

"Lord Caradoc has some important information he must officially tell me by sundown. If I see you between then and the completion of your quest, it could affect your status in our order. Do I make myself clear?"

"Yes, Lord Boswen." Absolutely not, but I can't say that.

"It is my belief that you are ready for greater responsibilities in the community of druids."

I'm awash in sweat, and my heart is racing fast enough that it may fail at any moment.

"Yes, I believe you possess the skill and discipline to take your place in our society of druids. Therefore, the time for your quest is nigh."

I rub my palms together to burn off some energy. Why must he repeat his previous statements?

"I most fervently hope that you prove my assumptions correct."

"My quest?" I prompt.

Boswen flashes a telling smile, but he does quicken his pace. "You will find in my hut a newly woven white robe. I wish you to put it on and return for your instructions."

I run to his hut. *Why couldn't he have mentioned this at midday?* It's lying on top of his bed. No time to change, I drop my mantle and swap the new robe for my brown novice's attire. I make it back to the fire before Caradoc can start yammering.

What were the requirements to start a proper quest? I'd always thought this would be a happy occasion, but all I can do is think of how it could all be invalidated.

"I-I was led to believe that I must pass a test before the quest is g-given," I stammer.

Caradoc preens in delight. "Yes, it seems in your dotage, old friend that you have forgotten about the test."

Their inane banter grates on my nerves.

Boswen rolls his eyes. "Any teacher who has to quiz his student to determine whether the common knowledge is retained

33

should not be in charge of instruction. But to assuage you both, I will test Grahme's knowledge. What are our nine places of power?"

"The Nemeton Dywyll Derw of Ynys Mona is the gift of the elves. The Men Meur Kov Keigh is the gift of the giants. Men-an-Tol is the whimsical gift of the pixies. Ardri Bryn Cadwy is the Tomb of the All King." Caradoc nods his head appreciatively, but I don't dare slow down to acknowledge it.

"Brenin Cairn is the resting place of great druids in the past. The Gwanwyns of Sulis are to heal and enlighten. Ogof Cawr is an entire realm beneath our feet. Keynvor Daras is the gateway to Lir's watery expanse. And Tochar Briwa reminds us of the importance of working with nature."

"Very good. Now, what are the seven druidic masteries?"

I have known these answers for at least the last fifteen years.

"The seven druidic masteries started with herbology and runes. Animal lore and animal-morphing followed quickly after. The summoning of elements remains elusive to this day, and weather magic is the most difficult to master. Finally, the verse-making bards wield the power over the people's hearts and therefore they *claim* to be the most powerful of all," I rattle off.

Caradoc snorts. Damn. He's one of the premier bards of the land.

"What are the five forms of magic?" Boswen asks, increasing his verbal pace.

"The Demon Summoners call forth the hell spawn for their wretched ways. The Sorim addle men's thoughts and overcome their minds whether in trade or combat. The Wigesta create only destruction with their rune spells. The Shamanic peoples can peer into the future, so their council is often sought, though they answer

34

to no higher power. The druids alone fight for balance and protection of the land."

"What are the three rules of druid conduct?"

"Druids must not kill without cause. Druids must not favor one creature over others, including man. Druids must forswear the use of iron since its use is offensive to nature."

"Satisfied?" Boswen asks.

Caradoc nods slightly. "Time is getting short."

"At the summer solstice, Lord Caradoc informed a special session of the Council of Nine that the Obsidian Mage who rules Solent Keep had obtained a ghost orchid. This caused much consternation among the more learned of the council."

"Indeed, I was unsure if we would be able to get Master Hedred out of his cave once he heard the news," Caradoc deadpans.

Boswen raises his eyebrow. "Am I interrupting you? We can wait for you to finish your comments before I resume talking about this poor man's quest."

The camp has a partial view of the western sky, and the sun god's orb is touching the horizon. I barely stifle the urge to bang their heads together.

"I would hate for my humble words to interfere with your grand oratory," Caradoc says.

"You should watch your tongue. It will get you in more trouble than you can handle one day."

"I assure you that the only thing I accomplish by watching my tongue is entertaining children." Caradoc sticks out his tongue and stares down his pronounced nose at it.

Boswen smiles despite himself. I cough loudly to bring the attention back to me.

"Do you know what a ghost orchid is?" Boswen asks.

His first real question and I have no idea. "No, Master."

"Boswen, you're being cruel. Of course, he doesn't know what a ghost orchid is. We don't teach it; in fact, there were precious few druid *lords* who knew of it before this summer."

"Very well."

"Mark this date, Grahme; Boswen has admitted to being wrong. It is a first, I'm sure of it."

I force myself not to scream.

"If I may speak of the mind-controller who threatens the land and our hallowed ways," Boswen says grumpily. Silence takes over and he stops to straighten his splotchy robes rather than speak of my quest.

His voice takes on a formal tone. "The Obsidian Mage in control of Solent Keep has in his possession a ghost orchid. It is an exceedingly rare and powerful plant. We cannot idly wait for him to wield it against us. I am giving you the quest to bring one or more ghost orchids back to me here at Dartmoor before year's end."

"Must it come from Solent Keep?"

"I know of no others on the isle of Pretanni, but your quest is to return to me with a ghost orchid so that I may study it. If you wish to search the land instead, it is possible that you could find another one."

"Samhain is nearly three months away. Surely I will not need that long to retrieve it."

Boswen notes the setting sun.

"You must complete your quest before Samhain to take your place among us," Boswen says with great solemnity.

36

"I will start immediately, Master." I start for my hut as I mentally go over the contents in my bag.

"Wait, Grahme, I am not finished."

I freeze in my tracks, hanging on his next words.

"I have not described the flower to you. Do you perhaps want to know how to identify it?"

I hang my head in humiliation.

"The flower is only as long as the width between your outstretched thumb and little finger. It is leafless, it has a hollow, yellow stem and though usually there is only one flower, it is possible that it will have two or three. The flower itself possesses pale shades of pink, yellow, and white. It is not a pleasant flower to look upon, and I would advise you to handle it as little as possible."

"I understand."

"Before you obtain a flower, I require you to do the following. First, you must go south to your old home of Dinas Gwenenen and visit your eldest brother. While you are there, you must pay homage to your parents. You will be saying goodbye to that life and you should do so properly. Next, you must visit your other brother, Ferroth, the blacksmith, and make peace with him, if you can."

"Why would you ask that of me?" Ferroth has hated me for as long as I can remember. My happiest childhood day was when he left home for good.

"A druid must be able to remain in control of his or her emotions. Are we not called on to judge the people's complaints? If you cannot manage yourself, how can you discharge this duty?"

"As you say."

Most of Belenos' disk is below the horizon. There are precious few heartbeats left in the day.

Caradoc clears his throat.

Boswen gives me an apologetic shrug. "I meant to give you some time for some questions."

"Fly, Grahme!" Caradoc orders.

I can't even inspect my hut one last time. I change to a tawny owl and launch into the air.

"Boswen," Caradoc clears his throat, "you must cease any further instruction to your acolyte, Grahme, until the council can decide upon his future standing within our order."

I head west into the fading light. Once out of sight, I circle around and spy once again on the druid lords.

".. . been to see Gwalather for a second opinion?" Caradoc asks.

"Ha, I would eat a hedgehog, spines and all, rather than confer with that fat old louse."

All this time and not once did he reveal that he felt much the same as I do concerning Gwalather. I'm a little irked at my mentor.

"Will you make the gathering after the autumn equinox?" Caradoc asks.

"It depends. I dare not give any hint of my condition."

"Perhaps I can convince your old students to visit you here. It would be nice to get together without having to deal with that fraudulent Gaulish leader of ours."

"That sums him up quite well," Boswen says with a chuckle. "However, you are as addle-minded as always."

"'As addle-minded as always.' I must remember to put that in a verse."

"If the others come, you will be honor-bound to tell them about Grahme, and they will be honor-bound to stop him if they should encounter him. It will be best that neither of us speak to our friends until this is resolved."

"And why would Grahme go so far north as to come in contact with Eghan or Hedred?" Caradoc asks.

"I don't pretend to know the future. However, I wish for him not to be hindered in any way." Boswen throws dirt on the fire. "Now, if you don't mind, this old man is tired."

"I'll sleep in Grahme's quarters, then?"

"Yes, you snore horribly." Boswen looks up at me in my perch and winks at me before retiring for the night.

5

Family Reunion

The Fourth Light Day of Elembiu, 819

Seventy Days until Samhain

A honeybee gets his fill on wild carrot nectar and flies past me, going straight back to its hive. I follow the bee's line toward the wood's edge. Before the clearing, I see more bees heading for the old tree trunks still embedded in the single earthen wall outside Dinas Gwenenen. The city's name means "bee's gate" in the old tongue. Long ago, the city was inside the wall, but now the livestock is kept there instead. It is improbable that anything has changed in the five years I've been away. Dinas is a good place to grow up, but it's a better place to be from.

The long-memorized path from the animal pen gate to my childhood home has not changed at all. After Mother died, Father moved us out from the shadows of the ramparts and into the woods next to fallow fields. Over time, the trees were felled for fuel as our farmland slowly expanded. The woods I grew up in are now gentle rolling fields of wheat, barley, and oats.

Only the apple trees planted to mark the passing of our parents now stand near the homestead. Just as in life, Mother's tree dominates Father's. I spy Eseld tending the last of the spring wool, spinning it into thread. I wave in greeting and get a tepid response.

"Grahme, curse my failing eyes; I didn't recognize you at first." She closes the distance and gives me a cursory embrace. She backs away and takes note of my robes. "You're a druid after all," she says, surprised.

"It has been too long, Eseld. How are the farm's fortunes these days?"

"Thanks to all of our hard work and the benefactions of Sucellos, we have done well. Your brother is up in the hills checking on Kenwyn and our sheep. I suspect he will be back by supper time."

"Is all of this"—I wave my hand expansively—"yours?"

"It is," she replies, beaming. "Kenal must hire help to bring in the harvest now, and beyond that rise is a hut for our first tenants."

"And you have sheep as well?"

"We do, praise Brigantia."

"You'll be richer than Drustaus before long."

"From your mouth to the gods' ears," she says. "We've been asking permission to expand our holdings for years. It was only after Ferroth and his adorable wife, Conwenna, accompanied Kenal to see Drustaus that the request was granted."

There is nary a flinch from me when Ferroth's name is mentioned. He left a year before I did. So, it was I who abandoned Kenal and his young family. Looking at the state of the homestead, my guilt is firmly absolved.

Making Eseld sit idle and accompany me will only add to the distance between us. She has never been the warmest of people in any case.

"I know well that the work on a farmstead is never done. I'll see if the apples are ready yet."

Eseld tends the porridge from over the fire and ladles out three bowls. She unwraps a fresh loaf of bread from a linen cloth and we sit around the fire for our evening meal. Kenal tears off half the loaf for himself. Eseld and I split the rest. My brother sops up his vegetable soup with his hearty chunk of bread as he attacks the meal.

"It's been five years, Grahme; what brings you to our door now?" Kenal asks between gulps.

He and Eseld cast furtive glances at my white robes.

"At long last, a quest has been granted so that I may become a full druid."

"Masters Gwalather and Arthyen will be surprised," he says.

"Please, I would rather spend my visit without encountering either one of them."

"Is it true that you knocked Gwalather to the ground and pummeled him with a stone?" Eseld asks, a slight edge in her voice.

"Is that what he tells people? I struck him once, with my fist to his jaw. He did fall to the ground like a stone, though."

Kenal smiles at my response, but Eseld is not amused.

"He says he awoke to you trying to poison him," she accuses.

"My uppercut nearly caused him to bite off his tongue. I was attempting to apply white clay to stop the bleeding. When he awoke, he tried to shout, but couldn't. He pushed away from me and made loud, awkward noises. I offered him the remaining clay and he grabbed it from me."

"Is that all there is to tell?" Kenal asks.

"Well, I moved out of my hut while he tended himself. With him being a master at potions and all, I declined to stay with him and await his retribution."

Neither my brother nor his wife are moved by my defense. Each is content to quietly eat their food. Their rounded hut is neat, clean, and well provisioned for the coming winter. More than ever, I want to perform a kind gesture to repay them for their hospitality. Maybe they could even have a kind word to say about me when I leave.

"Well, brother, it seems that you were seen walking through the forest," Kenal says at last. "And Drustaus has requested to speak to any itinerant druids that might pass through."

"He never had many dealings with druids in the past. What does he want now?" I ask.

"It's true that he doesn't like your kind coming and rendering judgment against him. But he won't object to help when he needs it."

"Nothing ever changes here, does it?"

"Kenal has over doubled our holdings," Eseld says.

I nod. "Does anyone know that I'm here, at your home?"

"No one but us, why?" Kenal asks.

"I don't want to delay my quest." It's a true statement as far as it goes. I expect Eseld to be relieved, but her face is full of thunderclouds. Frankly, a druid's presence should be treated as a rare blessing, at least if the old ways still hold sway.

"Grahme, if you insult Drustaus by not visiting his hall, it will be us who pay the price. You cannot avoid paying your respects to our chieftain," she says.

Gwalather has always been close with Drustaus and regularly finds his way to Drustaus' table. I managed to impress Gwalather five years ago in the hall. That's what allowed me to become Gwalather's student. But if he went with Arthyen to see Loris during the Lughnasa festival, there's no way he could be back yet. He's atrocious at animorphing and too fat to ride a moor pony.

"You're right," I agree. "In fact, brother, let's go to his hall tonight and start all the tongues wagging."

"Really? This doesn't sound like the Grahme I knew."

"That was the old, undisciplined me. Lord Boswen has taught me to control my temper."

"Why then did Master Arthyen renounce you, if not due to your temper?" Eseld asks.

I flash an embarrassed smile and peer down into my lap. My seat feels uncomfortably hard all of a sudden. "Does no one here speak of anything other than my business?"

Kenal laughs. "What do we farmers have to talk about after our kids, our crops, and the weather?" You have become renowned, little brother."

"Infamous," Eseld corrects. Kenal leans over and kisses her softly. He also whispers something into her ear which she doesn't appreciate. She glares back at her husband.

"It's good that Kenwyn is shepherding our flock in the high pasture, or Eseld would never be able to sleep." Kenal puts his arm around his wife protectively. "She would be afraid your fantastic tales would lure him away from us."

"I would have liked to have seen him. He must be near the change into manhood now. When will he have younger siblings to boss around?"

Kenal clears his throat and glances nervously at his wife. "Are you ready to walk the path to Dinas Gwenenen? I'd like to return home earlier rather than later."

"You know me; I've never favored long nights in mead halls with drunken fools."

Kenal pushes himself away from the fire, kisses his wife, and leads me out into the night air. "Promise me that you will not drink too much and start fights like Ferroth did the last time he came here," Kenal begs once we are away from his home. "Nechtan and his wife still will not speak to me, thanks to our brother. There are precious few families here. I don't miss conversing with them myself, but Eseld would like to be able to find a good bride for Kenwyn when the time comes."

"Shouldn't Kenwyn be the one to do that?"

"You have much to learn about women."

"In any case, I promise to be on my best behavior tonight. Do you frequent Drustaus' hall often?" I ask.

"No," Kenal replies with a silly grin.

"Why?" I ask confused.

He laughs. "The D-D-Dinas Gwenenen stutterer forbid-id-id it."

My head sinks into my hands. He got me, even after all of these years. When I was little, I would put question after question to Father. He would answer each and every one with great solemnity. When he passed on, I couldn't very well approach Ferroth, so that left only Kenal. Unless my question pertained to the running of the farm, Kenal would give me this same old nonsense answer.

I sigh audibly. "It's good to be home, even if you still refuse to answer my questions."

"We'd be standing here until sunrise if I let you get warmed up."

The mead hall had seemed immense and filled with life when I was younger. Now I see a small and dank place in need of new roof thatching. Drustaus still sits at his table on a raised dais. His chair is still draped with the same old blotchy Auroch hide. As always, he sits in the double seat alone. For years, his queen refused to sit with him. Now she has passed on. I remember him as an energetic reveler, always drinking and competing with his men. Now he's more of a sad old man trying to drink away his memories.

I lean over to Kenal. "Is it the flickering firelight or is his beard more gray than black?"

"He pulls back his hair now to hide the gray. His new wife insists," Kenal says under his breath.

He needs to whisper; tombs are livelier than this place. Morose men stare into their mead as they stubbornly wait out their time in this life.

"His new wife avoids the hall," Kenal adds.

Drustaus half-heartedly throws morsels into his mouth. His scraggly beard collects more of the food than his mouth does.

What would possibly entice a lady to frequent here?

Kenal leans into me, "Not too long ago, Drustaus woke from where he sits now to a rat feasting on the food trapped in his beard."

"You're kidding."

"Kenal!" Drustaus shouts. "It has been a long time, and I see that you have encountered a druid as well." For a moment, his eyes show signs of life.

"Hail Chief Drustaus, it is I, Grahme, Kenwyn's son and brother to Kenal. I have come back to my place of birth. May you continue to have fine health."

"Why would I want that?" he mutters under his breath. He applies a fake grin. "I must say, I am surprised to see you dressed as you are."

"My Lord," Maedoc yells. "He's an impostor. Gwalather promised us all before he left that Grahme would never wear the white robes. We should seize him." He knocks his mead cup but manages to stop it before it falls to the packed earth floor.

A couple grunts from behind are our only warning before Kenal is sent sprawling to the ground. Two burly arms grab me in a bear hug and lift me off my feet.

"I've got him, Drustaus!" the hulking man behind me shouts. He's squeezing my chest, hard. I banish my rising fear and close my eyes. I envision a wolf and take its shape. I snarl and twist to face my stunned attacker. Startled, Bricus the Bear dumps me onto a drunkard's table. The man grabs his ale and flees.

Bricus was always Ferroth's partner in bar fights. He must have taken to Maedoc now. Retaking my human form, I point my finger up at his big round face. "You should be flogged for attacking a druid." I shout.

"And you should be killed for impersonating one," Maedoc cuts in.

The oversized simpleton smirks at me. "Come at me again as a wolf and see who wins." Bricus pulls out his hand ax and attempts a low crouch.

"Bricus!" Drustaus roars. "You know the penalty for bringing weapons into my hall."

"Your Highness, stay out of this. I'll take care of him. We can't let his impersonation go unpunished." Bricus looks up at his chief, oblivious that he is giving his superior orders.

He lunges at me with his ax dagger. I dodge easily. It's clear that the mead has brought him false confidence. He slashes wildly at me again and I slowly give ground. I reach the central fire pit and I continue to retreat around the fire.

"Bricus," Drustaus calls menacingly.

"I can take care of myself," I say.

Glancing up at Drustaus, I see him nod. I duck down and grab a good-sized branch from the fire's edge. I wield it in my left hand so our weapons are on the same side. He lunges at me again, ax held high. I jump back a step and his thrust doesn't even come close. I slam my burning club onto his overextended hand. The ax falls into the fire. He foolishly reaches for it and my next blow is to the back of his head. I grab his tunic in time and divert him from falling into the fire. He lands on his back and remains still.

Stooping down, I can smell his stinking breath. "He'll sleep for quite some time," I say.

The hall erupts in laughter. I bow to Drustaus and make my way to his table.

"Guards, drag him out of here," Drustaus says, pointing to Bricus, "and tell him to present himself to me tomorrow at midday for his flogging." The conversation around the hall grows louder with this new information.

"My Lord," I say, "I judge the man to be controlled by the mead in his blood and not by his head. I do not require any punishment for his feeble attack of me."

"That is well said, druid, and a fair judgment. However, everyone knows that weapons are forbidden in my hall and Bricus had no mead in him when he made that choice. It is for that reason that he will be punished tomorrow." He waves me to sit at his table. I motion for Kenal to join us. Two cups of mead appear from a serving woman as we sit.

Perhaps Kenal will have a positive story about me to tell his wife. The mead is sweet and powerful. I greedily finish mine only to see a full one replace it.

"I am known far and wide for my hospitality," Drustaus says with a smug smile.

Kenal is more deliberate with his drink.

"Lord, you can't be sitting with that charlatan," Maedoc shouts over the din. "Masters Gwalather and Arthyen have both removed him from the order of druids. His wearing the white robe is a crime punishable by death."

Drustaus cocks his head inquisitively toward me.

"Lord Boswen, Protector of Men-an-Tol and Keeper of the Laws for Land's End, has seen fit to give me a quest to demonstrate my worthiness. If you doubt me, then please interrupt Lord Boswen, and check on the veracity of my words," I call back to Maedoc.

"I hate the moorlands," Drustaus says, speaking up. "And I doubt you could drag your brother into my hall if this is all a deception."

It's clear that Maedoc is not satisfied, but he has enough sense to tread carefully, unlike his lumbering friend. "I have a question for our noble druid," he yells. "What good is your lot to us farmers? You take food from our tables, mete out heavy punishments, and never blister your hands. What do you do for us?"

49

The hall grows quiet awaiting my response.

I stand up and straighten my robe. "How would you fare if there was no one to intercede with the gods on your behalf? To heal the sick, be they man or livestock? Who counsels kings and judges complaints fairly? All of this is given freely. All we ask is for some bread when you have plenty. Who else would do these things for an ungrateful lout such as yourself?"

"Just as I thought," he calls back. "We work and you mumble meaningless words." He wiggles his fingers as he laughs at me.

I nod my head slightly and smile back at him. A demonstration is clearly needed. "Is your drinking mug empty?"

He tilts his head back and finishes his drink in two large gulps. "It is," he calls back. The men around him cheer him on.

"Then hold it out in front of you and I will fill it."

He does as I ask while encouraging the crowd's laughter with a mocking grin. I close my eyes and concentrate, calling on some friends nearby. I've never tried to be this precise before. The little black rats that always inhabit this type of place emerge from the shadows.

"He's fallen asleep." Maedoc calls.

The rising tide of laughter tells me my time is running out. I add extra emphasis to my summons before opening my eyes. The rats leap at Maedoc and start scaling his trousers.

Maedoc turns wildly to and fro, trying to slap at them with his free hand. Still more rats come running from the shadows, each racing frenetically to Maedoc as he whirls in panic.

"It seems you're not the only rat among us," I say.

There are over a dozen rats climbing up him now and at least a dozen more trying to gain purchase. I look at Drustaus; he's laughing heartily at the spectacle before him.

"Unbelievable," Kenal says in amazement.

There is a rustling noise coming from outside the hall. The guard slams the door and braces his shoulder against it.

"What is it?" Drustaus calls, but the man is too scared to respond. Multiple thumps hit the door. Chirping noises rise up the walls of the structure. In no time, scraping claws reach the old thatch roof above us.

Everyone is frozen in wonder or fear of what will come next. The only noise comes from Maedoc's shouts and wild spins knocking over benches. Finally, a rat dives into the empty cup. I punch Kenal playfully on the shoulder and point to it.

"I told him I'd fill his cup," I say with a smirk.

He looks at me as if I'm daft.

The roof starts to sag in places with small noses poking through. Several brown rats start falling from the ceiling. One poor creature falls into the fire. The flaming rat screeches in pain and darts under a wooden bench. The drunks grab their drinks and clumsily hop up on their seats. One of the men makes a run for the door. As he opens it, a wave of rats knocks him to the ground as they flood over him.

Maedoc runs toward other patrons, but wherever he goes, the crowd melts away. Drustaus starts panting as he sits frozen in fear. Only his eyes move as they dart around the hall following the horde of rats. One drops onto the table in front of the petrified chieftain. He waves his arms wildly as he falls backward on the dais. Scrambling to his feet, he runs for his private exit.

Part of the roof collapses from the weight of the rats and the fire greedily consumes the old thatch. Roused from their astonishment, the patrons sprint for the exits, each dodging falling rats as they go. In short order, only the incoherent Maedoc, Kenal, and I remain.

"Make them stop!" Kenal shouts as he jumps up onto the king's table.

Embarrassed that I didn't think to do it sooner, I thank the little ones and release them. They quit the blazing hall as fast as the men. Maedoc hurls his cup, runs through a partially consumed wall, and goes screaming into the night. Thick black smoke is billowing up, obscuring the stars as it drifts into the night's sky. I leap down and retrieve Maedoc's cup.

The village folk have been wakened from their slumber and they race out to watch the dancing flames. I hand my brother the cup. "Here's something to remember this night by." He draws his hands away as if I were offering poison.

"Do you realize what you did?" Kenal asks, incredulous. He grabs my robe and pulls me away from the village center.

"It's only what he deserved," I say defensively as I knock his hand off.

"And what will Drustaus say tomorrow when he sees his only mead hall burned to the ground?

"Oh," my exuberance leaves me at once. "I am sorry, brother."

Kenal quickens his pace before calling back to me. "It's good that you were on your best behavior." He tries to hide it, but his giggling is unmistakable.

We stop twenty paces into the woods and watch as the rest of the walls give way.

"That is an impressive bonfire," Kenal says.

"Should I apologize to him tomorrow?"

"If you show up tomorrow, you're as likely to be flogged as Bricus is."

I sigh heavily. "I had planned on spending more than one night with you, brother, but that doesn't seem like such a good idea now."

Kenal lets loose with a belly laugh in the cool night air. "You've guaranteed that the people here will never lose interest in you, little brother."

"I am so sorry for this. What will happen to you?"

"No one was seriously injured, so that's to the good. I will go see Drustaus in the morning and remind him that it is Maedoc and Bricus who are ultimately responsible. With luck, he'll agree with me."

"Just in case, I'll sleep in the woods behind your house tonight. You can tell him I fled in disgrace."

At sunrise, Kenal and Eseld meet me at the wood's edge.

"I had wished to stay longer, but perhaps I should be moving on." I can't manage a straight face, no matter how hard I try.

Eseld is not in a laughing mood, however. "We are simple farmers here; we honor the gods and obey our leader. Before your arrival, it was only a handful that spoke ill of your kind. Now you have destroyed Dinas Gwenenen's mead hall. I hardly see anything to laugh about."

Kenal's face has turned serious. We shake hands. "Brother, I hope that you will suffer no ill effects from my actions. Please blame me for everything and tell the king that you forbade me from entry to your property after last night."

Kenal hands me a pouch. "I had Eseld prepare food for your journey."

I take the pack; it's much heavier than I anticipated. I tie a quick knot around my belt with the drawstrings.

"I will leave you now. Perhaps more nights spent at home will lead to having more children." I grin at my brother.

He and Eseld stare back, stone-faced.

"I'm sorry; it seems I'm a walking disaster. I did not mean to upset you."

"We have been unlucky for some time now," Kenal says as he refuses to meet my eyes.

"Right." My druid training takes over. "I have not the time to investigate properly, so I will tell you this. On the sixth day after the full moon, take fresh mistletoe from an oak tree and crush the leaves. Add three leaves to each of your mugs of ale and drink them down. This is the surest way I know to solve your problem."

They let the comment hang for a few moments.

"Thank you, Grahme. If you are right, we will consider your visit as our good fortune," Kenal says. The tension melts away from my brother's face. Eseld, well, at least she doesn't strike me.

"It is good that you named your eldest after our father. I would ask that you name one of your future boys after me, but Drustaus may take offense."

My brother smiles once Eseld turns for their cottage.

"What a tale I have to tell, if only I could find an audience," Kenal says.

We laugh until we're both in tears.

"Did you see Drustaus' eyes?" I ask. "The horror on his face . . ." We start laughing again.

"Are you waiting for Drustaus and his men to arrive?" Eseld calls back at us.

That successfully kills the moment.

"Good fortune to you, especially if you still plan on visiting Ferroth," Kenal says.

I bob my head. "It can't go any worse, can it? Stay well, brother."

"Ferroth's wife is very kind," Kenal calls out to me. "She has dulled many of his sharp edges."

The River Fowey is east of the family farm. It marks the border between settled land and the unspoiled Arden, the great southern forest. I cross the river and peer back at my former home. Surprised, I must blink back a sudden tear and turn into the ancient forest. Literally, I am turning my back on my previous life.

6

Hammering Out the Differences

The Tenth Light Day of Elembiu, 819

Sixty-four Days until Samhain

Being in no hurry to see Ferroth, I explore the great old forest. Rare is the tree that is less than a hundred years old. Often quoted elvish wisdom says that it takes an oak three hundred years to grow, three hundred years to stand, and three hundred years to die. Walking in this hallowed forest, I can see the evidence of that statement all around me.

Farther in, a stand of beech trees stretches onward for nearly a league. The white wood and deep shadows are the domain of Fagus, god of beech trees. The stillness of the air is oppressive, so I don't linger for long. I stash readily available nuts in one pouch and dried leaves in another as I hurry along. This is the dream of many a druid. Red squirrels dash up and down the trees in a frenzy. Though signs of deer and elk are everywhere, they are keen to keep their distance from me.

My last night in the forest is at the wood's end and only a short walk to Mai Dun. The forest has been cleared for over a league around the great hillfort. Somehow the pastureland and fields of grain feel wrong. So much of Cernunnos' wild lands has been taken from him. But Sucellos, the god of cultivation and the people of Mai Dun are the claimants to this land now.

The early morning sun has little warmth, but it does illuminate a flock of brown-coated sheep grazing peacefully. Their wool is what is used for a druid acolyte's robe. Mine itched whenever I sweated; I won't miss it. Curious but shy, the sheep pause from their foraging and eye me warily as I pass their enclosure. Tiny horns peek out from even the ewes. The shepherd and his dog must still out foraging, for there's no one watching the sheep.

The great hill on which Mai Dun sits emerges from the flat lands and black, billowing smoke can be seen rising above it. Most likely Ferroth and his forge are the ones polluting the air. I must trust that Boswen is right in this like he is in most things. My feet drag me ever closer, despite my reluctance.

Six concentric earthen walls climb the slopes of the hill, protecting the citizens from any invaders. Each wall is thrice the height of a man and each ditch between them is half as deep. To enter, one must follow the walkways through the ditches to each of the offset gates. The circuitous route to the top of the hill makes it easy for only a few defenders and their slings to decimate any force foolish enough to attack. A massive wooden gate stands at the last earthen wall as a final immovable obstacle. The timber could have only come from the ancient trees of the Arden.

People come and go under the watchful eye of an old gatekeeper. This will be the man who knows the town gossip, who is coming and going and at what time. His sharp eyes no doubt give him access to secrets never voiced in the wind. He greets me with a smile that lacks several teeth. His meager mantle gives dubious protection from the cold and his battered cloak pin is further testament to his lowly station.

"The rutting season begins in another month," he says. "So, you should be glad that your travels led you here when they did, Honored One."

"It might have been preferable. I'm seeking my brother Ferroth, the blacksmith, and my guess is that we will butt heads at least as hard as the rams."

"I knew not that Ferroth had a brother. He has never spoken of family in my hearing."

It seems a little harsh that even Kenal has never been acknowledged. Ferroth has blamed me for Mother's death since I was five and he twelve summers old. Now that I have renounced iron, it's understandable, though not mandatory, that he dislikes me.

"You should hear the clanging well enough, but I would recommend finding the scamp Figol instead. He's Ferroth's stepson. You'll know him by his red hair, cropped short so that none can grab him by it. He'll be the loudest if there is a group," he says without malice.

"Could I have your name, good sir?"

"I am Lowen, Revered One." He bows his head again in deference to me.

"You are a credit to your town, Lowen. May your days be blessed by the gods."

"High praise for one as low as me."

There's no sense in delaying the necessary. I enter the city. The pounding of hot iron rings out clearly, guiding me onward to my unwanted reunion. On the corner of the central square, the roiling black smoke blows into the face of the other members of the city. Opposite the forge, a wooden statue of the god Sucellos sits amid harvested grains. It has been a good harvest by the offerings. Mai Dun's mead hall is three times the size of the one at Dinas

58

Gwenenen and it is but one of several. I think it best to avoid the drinking halls this time.

"Keep the flow even," is bellowed out between ringing strikes. I sigh. I recognize my tormentor's voice from childhood.

The shop is dark and sweltering despite the cool weather. With only the glow of the charcoal visible through the smoke, I stand several paces away and wait for Ferroth to notice me. He glares at me before he removes the red-hot metal from his forge. He strikes the metal with impressive force and sparks fly everywhere. *Why must he always try to intimidate?*

Finally, he is done hammering. He places the sword into the embers until it is glowing red hot. He grabs the blade with metal tongs and plunges it into a barrel of oil. A loud ting comes from the barrel and my brother pulls the blade out at once. The oil on the sword ignites and Ferroth blows ferociously at the flames. He inspects the still glowing metal and throws it down in disgust. The warped sword lands on loose straw, igniting the tinder. The red-haired kid drops the bellows, grabs the incandescent metal with another set of tongs and places the blade back atop the anvil to cool. Without a second thought, he takes off the leather apron and smothers the fire. Ferroth watches in silence until the fire is out, then he turns to face me. The forge has made my brother more chiseled. He wipes his brow and flings his sweat in my direction.

"You've cost me plenty of time by surprising me here. This accident will set me behind schedule."

"It is good to see you, too, Ferroth." I know better than to get defensive. "Is there a better time to see you?"

"Come to my hut an shortly before nightfall. That will give us the time to say whatever needs to be said and for you to find lodging elsewhere. Figol, show him our hut, then the common area for shepherds and animals." He eyes my robes. "Perhaps your uncle will deign to help bring up our sheep for the night."

He walks out of the shop, making sure to drive his shoulder into me on his way out. I ball my fists but think better of it. Boswen told me that I must conquer my own emotions before I can be a leader of men. I focus on the muscular young lad.

"I am your Uncle Grahme, and you must be Figol."

"Sorry about Father, he got angry all at once."

"He didn't strike me, so it went better than I expected. Now, what do you need to do in this shop before you can show me the city?"

I study the boy; he can't be older than seventeen. Despite being four years younger, he's nearly as tall as I am. What must it be like, growing up with Ferroth as a stand-in for his father?

Ferroth impregnated the old blacksmith's daughter nearly six years ago and it was a lucky break for him. Being twenty, he never would have started so late in this profession without that accident.

"The shop is easy; it's the sheep that take forever," Figol complains.

"I'll help you with the shop, then you can show me the city. We'll get to the sheep last."

The square is filled with market stalls, although they give the smithy a wide berth. Tanners, shamans, bakers, and potters flout their wares and services. The dirt is firm underfoot, even in the low spots, so there has been no rain for nearly ten days. I sniff the air.

"There will be rain late tonight, so don't be too quick to let the sheep out tomorrow. The damp cold of the early morning can lead to sickness."

"How do you know that?" Figol asks.

"I did not become a druid without picking up some knowledge of the weather."

"Father said that you would never become a druid. He said, many, um, well, *things* about you."

I shake my head. "I won't speak ill of your father, but this is not surprising to me."

"He's not my real father, so I won't take offense," he assures me.

Already, the flat, grassless plaza makes me uncomfortable. "Is there any more of the city worth seeing?"

"Only the brothels."

"Do you have a favorite lady there?"

His face turns as red as his hair. I chuckle at his discomfort. "I have no need to see the brothels. Follow me and I will show you what it's like to walk with nature."

We pass Lowen at the gate and climb to the topmost earthen wall. I bid Figol to point to the field with his sheep. One by one, I compel the sheep to hop the woven willow fence and make their way up the windy path and through the gates. The youth shepherding the sheep in the field looks on in awe. Once they arrive, I have them follow Figol to my brother's pen. Figol laughs in delight. At least I have some family happy to see me. We return to the central plaza as the other children are struggling to lead their livestock to the pens.

"When are you expected to return home?" I ask.

"Dinner is not for a little bit. Father asked you to visit after then, so you will have to find your own."

"It was not unexpected. Who in this city is still attuned to the old ways?"

"Isla is the one to see. She and her ladies will be happy to see you. She may even ask you to stay with her through the night."

"You seem to know a lot about the brothels," I say to make him blush again. "A simple meal is all I seek; I will lodge somewhere else."

Figol leads me to Isla's place. The ladies begin their catcalls of poor Figol. He and his very red face leave me almost at once.

I ask for only a simple meal, as is my due, and give honest thanks. Metal is anathema to druids, so I have no coin for her other services. It's early yet, so the women aren't busy. I speak with them about the town gossip until the disk of Belenos is low in the sky. I wrap up the loaf of fresh bread and bid Isla and her ladies a good evening. There is no sense delaying my visit any longer.

The door to his home is open. "Good evening, brother," I say as I approach.

His wife greets me. "I am Conwenna. In my country, the door is left open when guests are expected. It is an invitation for friends to enter."

My sister-in-law is nearing the end of child-bearing age. Despite this, only a few shallow worry lines are etched on her otherwise smooth face.

"Conwenna, you are as gracious as a hostess could be." I kiss her on the cheek before she escorts me inside.

There are three small girls sitting quietly on a heavy blanket near the fire. The youngest two are avid crawlers. The oldest of the girls must be about five. She throws a finely wrought bone comb at me. A small piece breaks loose. The white orb has subtle streaks of color flittering across it as it catches the light.

"Is this an oyster rock?" I ask. "I have never seen one before."

"It is," Conwenna says as she quickly takes the fine stone from me. She turns to her daughter. "Berga, I told you not to touch my comb."

"But I want to be beautiful like you," her daughter says in a petulant voice.

I grin foolishly at the girls.

"Why are you here?" Ferroth demands.

So much for getting to know my nieces.

I straighten up and ready myself for what's to come. "I have been sent on a quest by my mentor and he has insisted that I see my family in case it ends badly for me."

Why did I say that? I know better than to expect sympathy from Ferroth.

"I'm not buying it. What do you want?"

"Ferroth, give him a chance, please," his wife urges. She goes to his side and gently rubs his back.

He scowls at her before facing me again. "Conwenna doesn't know you as I do."

"You have the prettiest blue eyes," she says, interrupting her husband. "They are so bright, I can get lost in them."

"Thank you. They are like our mother's, or so I've been told."

Ferroth slams his drink down.

Conwenna deftly changes the topic. "Where does this quest take you?"

"My next stop is Solent Keep; I know not where I will go after that."

"The Sorim are in charge now and they don't like your kind," Ferroth says, smiling maliciously. "They are an enlightened folk."

"I aim to go there nonetheless."

"No matter what trouble you cause, I will not come to your aid."

"I wouldn't want you to do that, dear brother. This quest is for me to accomplish alone." Speaking to Ferroth just makes me weary.

"Then this is goodbye, perhaps for the final time?" he asks, hopefully.

"Ferroth, he's your brother," Conwenna scolds. "Don't go wishing ill fate upon him."

I could have told her it's no use. His head is as hard as his anvil.

"I did not come to fight, or to beg. I came simply because I will become a druid and I don't know when I may see you again. The only request I will make of you is to share news of the road to Solent Keep, if you have any." I keep any hint of disappointment out of my voice. I would have liked to have gotten to know my nieces and nephew, but that is obviously not going to happen.

"The road is fine since the coming of the Obsidian Mage. He's cleared out the petty brigands and now anyone can travel the road without fear of assault. He has been a blessing for the surrounding area."

"The Obsidian Order has invaded our lands and enslaved our people with their mind control," I say with more heat than I expected. "You would trade safe roads for thousands of our people becoming slaves to a foreign power?"

"Who exactly are 'our people'? Do they include the cutthroats who preyed on innocent travelers?" Ferroth asks. "Do they include the hardly civilized Silures, Ordivices, or Atrebates? The Obsidian Lord can take over all of Southern Pretanni for all I care. He has been hiring out all the blacksmiths he can find to make quality swords and ax heads. With luck, he'll rule the entire south within a few years."

I don't even try to hide my revulsion. Disagreeableness I expect from Ferroth, but never did I think he would abandon the land and set his lot with a soulless invader.

"Can I go with Uncle Grahme?" Figol asks. "I can show him the way to the city."

"You're needed in the smithy," Ferroth says, quashing his son's excitement.

Conwenna hugs my brother and leans her head on his shoulder. "We could get by for a day, don't you think?" She casts her deep brown eyes up at Ferroth. "He's performed well as your apprentice, you said so yourself at supper yesterday."

My brother gazes into his wife's eyes, as if enchanted. "Figol can escort my brother far away from here, for all I care." He points his finger at his son. "As long as you're back before nightfall."

Figol is giddy in his thanks. Oddly, no one has bothered me for my opinion on the matter. I could flatly refuse and throw it back in my brother's face, but then I would be injuring my nephew as well.

"Find me at sunrise, Figol. I will be staying with someone who still respects the old ways."

Ferroth finds mirth in my statement. It would be like him to try to bait me into a fight. Few could contend with his impressive strength.

"I have slowly been learning your ways," Conwenna says. "Were all of you raised with this devotion?"

"It was Mother who instilled it in us."

Ferroth goes rigid and glares at me with hatred in his eyes. "I'm going to the mead hall." He makes straight for the door. I retreat a few steps out of his way and let the angry fool pass.

"Goodbye, brother," I say to his back. I tried. I even managed to keep myself calm and not rise to my brother's barbs.

"Figol, watch your sisters. I wish to show Grahme our fair city." She extends her arm and I clasp it gently. Once clear of the house, she guides us to the statue of Sucellos in the central plaza.

"You will take Figol with you tomorrow, won't you? He is not cut out to be a blade smith and he never gets to leave this city."

"I would welcome his company, even if only for a short time."

Conwenna relaxes now that her son has a chance to leave. "I have to be sure you really mean this, and you aren't just agreeing to aggravate your brother."

"Your son will be welcome to join me."

I don't know my sister-in-law at all and I'm afraid I might be overstepping, but I can't remain quiet. "Would it be possible for Figol to go to his real father?"

"No," she says quickly. "That is not an option." She glances sideways toward the hall. "We shouldn't linger here. Silly men may start wagging their tongues about us, even though we are in the middle of the town."

I don't envy her dealing with the angry drunk that Ferroth is no doubt on his way to becoming tonight. We slowly stroll back to the house.

"Don't worry about your brother," she says. "I can handle him. I only took us out of the house in case you were to refuse Figol's company. He would have been crushed had you said no."

"Are you sure you and the children will be safe tonight?"

She waves away my concerns. "Ferroth is tired these days. The Obsidian Mage keeps all the blacksmiths of the area *very* busy."

I nod slightly to show I understand her warning. The Nine will have to be made aware of this at once. The Obsidian Mage is preparing for war. "You don't need to make apologies; he is my kin and I know him too well to be surprised."

Back at their door, I nod. "Goodnight, Conwenna."

"Please," she says as she grabs my hand. She reaches inside the door and hands me a loaf of bread and a small leather bag that jingles in her hand. "I ask that you take this, if not from him, then from me."

"The bread I will gladly accept, my lady, but not your coin. Metal is distasteful to druids and that is one of the many reasons why Ferroth and I will never be close."

"Please take it, Grahme; you will need it when you enter the city. It is little enough, and it will keep you from drawing suspicion." She places her hand tentatively on my arm and my resolve fails me at once. She slips the small bag of coins into my hand and presses my fingers closed. "My family comes from the Ynys Luko, so I can sense that you are looking for trouble in the city. The mage's power is among the greatest of my people. You must avoid his attention at all cost." Her big, earnest eyes stop my protestations before I can even make them. "I wish you success," she whispers.

Leaving my brother's house, I feel as if his wife and I had shared a moment as intimate as any I have experienced. My desire to gloat is instantly met with shame. I don't know what it is about Conwenna, but she makes me feel like raw dough in her hands. She could stretch, knead, or knot my will in any way she desires. I shake my head to clear it of the confusing but not unpleasant experience.

7

The Road Less Traveled

The Eleventh Light Day of Elembiu, 819

Sixty-three Days until Samhain.

Lowen and I break our fasts at first light with the loaf of bread from Ferroth's home. I offer him Conwenna's coin as thanks for the place to rest. There's no sign of Figol. It's probably for the best; Ferroth would be unhappy for days if his son left with me. No need for Figol to suffer any more than he must. I make my way down between the ramparts to start my quest in earnest.

"Wait for me, Uncle!" comes ringing off the top of Mai Dun's earthen walls. Figol is running with exaggerated strides and his sheep are following closely behind. The thought of a man running from a pack of vicious sheep pops into my head and brings a smile to my face. The redheaded leader and his obedient, brown-fleeced flock appear briefly at each descending gate; only to disappear as the path takes them through the ditches between earthen ramparts. He arrives, gasping for breath. Clearly, blacksmithing does not require much in the way of running. The sheep all crowd around Figol expectantly.

"Perhaps I overdid it last night," I say. "I told them to follow you. Silly animals, they took it too seriously." I close my eyes and reach out to the sheep: "You are not to look to Figol as being your leader, only a friend of the flock," I say aloud for Figol's benefit.

The stupid animals stare mindlessly back at me.

"Father has agreed to allow me to show you the way to Solent Keep," he reminds me.

"I heard him say it, but that still doesn't sound like the brother I know."

"Mother may have persuaded him," Figol says softly.

We start northward on the tamped earth road. "What way do you plan to take us?" I ask.

"We'll take the Mai Dun Road north until it meets the Great Londinjon Road. From there, we'll head east until we reach the Solent Road. We'll take that south into the city." He acts as if this will clear it all up.

"I am not familiar with the Great Londinjon Road."

"What? It connects every major city in the southern part of Pretanni. It starts at Dubr along the east coast and meets up with the Camulodunon Road at Londinjon. They merge and run westward to Venta, then Sarum. From there, the road runs west until it hits the Druid Ditch Road." Figol gives me a furtive glance. "Father says that the Druid Ditch Road leads from one dead end to another."

"The road leads to Dinas Gwenenen, the place where your father grew up."

"He tells everyone that we are Sorim."

I shake my head, not trying to hide my disgust.

"Father says that the moors are hellish places where no man can survive for long. And that there are great creatures, like giant

69

black cats, that will hunt anyone foolish enough to find themselves there."

"Aye, many say that Bodmin patrols his moor as a great black cat, but I've met none who make a believable claim of seeing him. However, I've lived on top of Dartmoor with my mentor for nearly a year."

"But how?" he asks in wonder.

"It is cold, damp, and nearly treeless. The wind only stops when the frigid air has settled to make life even more miserable. But all in all, I quite liked it."

"Well, Londinjon Road is mostly straight and flat, so it will give us no trouble."

"That sounds boring. I have a better idea. Have you ever seen Keynvor Daras?" I ask.

"I've never heard of it."

"In the common tongue it is called the Sea Stone Door."

"Dad always says to stay far away from there. It's dangerous."

"The Holy Site or the sea in general? Never mind, either would challenge Ferroth's way of thinking, and that would surely be considered dangerous. Come with me; I'll introduce you to one of the nine druid holy sites which is practically on your doorstep."

I angle us off the road toward the forest.

Figol tugs at my arm. "There are wolves in there."

"Aye, and cave bears, too. Hopefully, we'll get to see them."

"But I have only my knife and you have only your staff."

"And our wits," I add cheerfully as I quicken my stride. Whether due to fear or a sense of adventure, Figol quickly catches up to me.

The woods are cool and dark. Precious little sunlight lands on the forest floor. The chilly air is perfect for traveling. If only I didn't have to slow my gait, but Figol manages to find every raised root as he stumbles his way through the forest.

"Are you not familiar with woods-craft?" I ask.

"I'm a blacksmith apprentice."

"So, you never go into the forest?"

"We hunt deer at dusk as they leave the forest."

"I propose we play a game. I'll point out signs of animals and you try to identify it. If you're right, I'll give you more insight to any animal of your choosing."

He was not lying about avoiding the forest. He knows no animal tracks, scat, or even bird calls. At long last, he's able to identify deer hooves pressed in the moist loam.

"Very good," I say, staying upbeat. "Now, what animal would you like to learn more about?"

"The cave bear," he replies immediately.

"Very well, continue ten paces and then stop."

Once he turns to face me, I transform. Rising to twice the height of a man, I bask in the awesome power these creatures have. Blood has drained from Figol's face as he stands petrified. Only the twitch in his left hand differentiates him from a statue. I let out a monstrous bellow and crash to the ground with my forelimbs. It's too much for my nephew. He turns and runs headlong into an eighty-year-old oak. Blood begins to trickle from his forehead.

"Perhaps we should find a creek so you can clean up."

His head swivels in all directions before focusing on my smiling face. One emotion after another flashes across his face. He settles on amazement.

"That was you?" he exclaims.

"You wanted to know about cave bears," I reply with a smile. "A creek should be over this hill. Wash it well while I find some hazel leaves to stop the bleeding."

The forest goes quiet except for Figol, who is oblivious to the change. No birds are singing and even the squirrels have stopped foraging.

"Figol, do you trust me?"

He stops and shoots me a confused look. "I guess so."

"No guessing allowed today. Either come stand next to me or climb up that oak."

"Why?"

"Make your decision, and quickly," I urge.

Confusion and fear lead him to freeze in place again.

"Decide, right now," I hiss.

He walks slowly to me as an impressive gray-and-black wolf comes out of the brush behind him. It is primed for an attack, its head and tail held low. I clutch Figol's hand before turning my attention to the leader of the pack. Figol follows my gaze and panics. I tighten my grip before he can run.

"If you run, you're inviting them to hunt you down."

"Them? There's more?"

"You chose to trust me and it's too late to change your mind now. Be still."

I lower my head and avoid direct eye contact. Mentally, I project our peaceful intentions. The lead male relaxes and the eight other wolves surrounding us reveal themselves.

72

"Do not stare at any of them unless you plan to challenge them."

Figol is trembling with fear but he holds his ground. I converse with the alpha. Figol slowly edges behind me. It's exactly what a cub would do. The leader sees the retreat and the tension in his muscles eases. I project my apology for startling the pack with my cave bear roar. The pack has eaten last night, and they wish only to rest this day.

"You're in for a treat," I say to Figol. "Make no loud noises or sudden movements and follow me." We follow the creek to its headwaters, a natural spring. I spot the den and start yipping. First one, then four more wolf kits exit the den.

"They heard my cave bear roar and smelled your blood. They were ready to defend their den to the death, if necessary."

"Then we should leave."

The rest of the pack assembles around us. There are eighteen in all. "I have allayed the alpha's fear."

The queen of the pack snarls her dislike for us.

"Is that one going to attack?" Figol asks, voice trembling.

"She does not like you."

Figol takes a hard gulp.

"Your clothes reek of smoke and iron, both of which the wolves fear."

"Maybe we should leave." Figol's eyes never leave the spot directly in front of the queen. His iron grip is turning my fingers white. The longer we stay here, the better the chance for Figol to lose his nerve.

"You may be right. Let's go before there's a misunderstanding."

73

I send my apologies once more to the leader and his queen. We slowly move off to the south and east. Figol stays close, checking behind us often for the next couple of leagues.

"Figol," I say finally, "listen to the noise of the forest. If predators were still following us, this place would be silent."

After another league, Figol resumes his carefree, stumbling way.

"When you became that beast . . ." Figol starts.

"Yes."

"Did you become that animal or was it a projection?"

"It was not an illusion; I had all the strength and power of the great bear."

"But what about your mind? You were there, and then your mind disappeared and a bear was roaring at me."

"The animal mind assumes primacy. My human mind is still there, in the background, but I have all the senses and motivations of the animal. The human mind is like a rudder. It can steer the animal but only crudely."

He nods as if that explains everything.

"How is it that you can tell that my mind had receded?"

Figol freezes as if he's just been caught thieving.

"Is that how your mother was able to convince Ferroth to let you be my guide? When your mother said she was from the Ynys Luko, the Black Isle, that wasn't all of it, was it?"

"How else would he have allowed me to leave?" he asks, dejected.

"How else indeed. Does this mean you can read my mind?"

"My . . . power is not that strong, and I have only a fraction of my mother's talents. If a thought or emotion is very strong, then I can sense it whether I want to or not. I can also distinguish people by their mental patterns when they're near me. But mostly I nudge others to agree with me and shield my mind from those more powerful."

I smile despite myself. "Is this why I have such warm feelings from my encounter with your mother?"

"Mum always says that if you start meetings off on the right foot, you'll have fewer stumbles."

I clap my hands in delight. "I will hold your mother in high regard, then. I was wondering how Ferroth and I managed to avoid trading blows."

"Whatever you do, you can't let Dad know about Mum or me."

"You saw us last night," I say. "I will gladly take this secret to my grave and get enjoyment from keeping it all the while."

Relieved, he loosens up. "What other animals can you take the shape of?"

"Any animal I'm familiar with."

"Can you become a bird?"

"Yes."

"A fish?"

"I draw the line at fish. They are cold and empty-headed creatures."

"Do you have a favorite?"

I realize that the questions are unlikely to end any time soon.

"This is my favorite, so follow me, and try to keep up."

I transform into a tawny owl and take off into the canopy above. I spiral back down lazily to the height of the lower branches before leading the way through the woods. Now I know why Boswen did this to me so often. But surely, I never pestered him this much.

At last, we make it to the wood's edge and the salt air and crashing waves are unmistakable. I change back to myself to walk through the marram grass on the sandy rise. The ground falls away before us to a smooth, sandy beach and the churning sea below. On the isthmus in front of us stands Keynvor Daras, the gateway to the watery expanse of Lir and Melusine.

"Can you feel the energy?" Despite our trek, I feel energized and ready for anything. Figol is staring at the salt spray and the great arch extending out into the sea. Pride swells within me for giving my nephew an experience he will never forget. The waves pass under the stone archway and crash restlessly onto the sandy shore.

"Uncle, I want to become a druid." he shouts over the sea.

I let his declaration go. Now is not the time for arguments. "Come, we must make a sacrifice."

"I have nothing to give," Figol answers, confused.

"The gods expect us to give something of value. If you have no possessions of value, the gift of blood will do."

The path to Keynvor Daras is well worn. With any luck, fellow druids will see the offering and come greet us. We walk out on the arch as the waves batter the stone beneath us. At the edge, I break my staff over my knee. The place makes me feel insignificant by comparison.

"Please accept this offering, Lir, from your humble servant." I hurl half of my staff as far into the turbulent sea as I can. I walk back to Figol. "The gift is to show respect, not to flatter, so a few drops will do."

Figol slices his palm and lets some of his blood mingle with the sea. On the other end of the monolith, we repeat our gestures to Melusine.

"Who are these deities?" Figol asks.

"Lir is the Lord of the Sea. Melusine is the Goddess of the Merfolk."

"There's no such thing as mermaids."

"There are, but they left our shores over eight hundred years ago, along with the elves, giants, and pixies."

"That's all make-believe," Figol counters.

"What year is it?"

It's eight hundred nineteen."

"What do you think happened eight hundred nineteen years ago? All the elder races, except the centaurs, sailed into the endless sea. Branok the Burly started the Emerald druids of Eriu and my order, the Protectors of Pretanni, on that day. He swore that he and his druids would protect the land for the next thousand years."

"What happens when they return?"

"With any luck, our souls will be reborn during that time and we'll find out. Now come, I have brothers and sisters to greet." I point to the five druids standing atop the adjacent grassy knoll and wave in greeting. They change into sea fowl and join us as we descend the path to the beach. I bow and spread my hands wide to the woman in the center. I do not know her, but she radiates authority.

"I am Meraud, Protector of Keynvor Daras," she says solemnly. "Who might you be?"

"I am Grahme, the questing acolyte of Boswen, Protector of Men-an-Tol. This is my nephew, Figol, born of strong and proud parents. He is accompanying me to Solent Keep."

"Boswen has taught you well. You give proper offerings to the gods of the sea. Will the young man Figol of strong and proud stock consent to catching us dinner with my charges so that we may speak?" Her robust smile belies her true feelings about formal speech.

"Of course, m-my lady," Figol stutters.

"Lord," I correct him.

"But she's a woman."

"I am sure Lord Meraud is aware. When you speak to one of the nine great druids, you call them lord."

"Sorry, my lord," he says to me. He blushes and turns to Meraud. "Sorry, my lord lady."

She wishes him good fishing with a genuine smile and extends her hand toward her druids. They surround him and excitedly introduce themselves. One of her students gives Figol a reed basket before she and her cohorts change into pelicans and begin their fishing. I sit patiently, waiting for Meraud to focus her attention on me rather than the Southern Sea. The druids begin dropping fish into Figol's basket. The simple joy on his face as he awaits the next catch makes my pride swell up as if I was his parent.

"I will know of your quest, and speak plainly. No lords, ladies or masters, please."

"As you wish." I tell her about my quest.

Her countenance darkens as I speak, but she doesn't interrupt me.

"Tell me of you relation with Boswen."

78

Knowing that Boswen shared all my failings with Caradoc, I must assume all the Nine know about my past. I admit to the worst of my previous transgressions before I can be asked.

"Interesting, and when did Boswen give you this quest?"

"It was very sudden. He gave it just as the fifth day of Lughnasa ended at sundown."

She studies the vast expanse of water. "And was Caradoc present?" she asks, giving me a sidelong glance.

How can she know so much? I'm too shocked to speak. I nod.

Amused, she continues. "Now more than ever I wish to know, is Boswen fond of you or not?"

"I don't know how to answer that. He has rarely had reason to fault my skills."

"Perhaps it was an unfair question. Boswen keeps himself distant, even from his closest compatriots. I ask because this quest he gave you speaks loudly, and I wish to know what it is saying. Either he dislikes you and set you up to fail or he believes strongly in your abilities. Whichever it may be, he has sent you upon the most difficult quest of which I have ever heard."

I pause before "my lord" comes stumbling out of my mouth. "It is only one flower."

She gazes at me, inhales deeply, and mentally makes up her mind. "I will say no more other than to implore you to keep your wits about you at all times. Boswen has always been inscrutable to me even at the best of times."

8

Entering the Obsidian City

The Fourteenth Light Day of Elembiu, 819

Sixty-One Days until Samhain

Being among fellow druids is a treat for me. Meraud has a total of eight students. *Surely Boswen could handle more than one druid at a time.* I appreciate that her students rise early, gather wood, and catch and fix our morning meal. These were all my duties alone under Boswen.

Figol is still sleeping soundly as Belenos rises in the east. He was supposed to be home by nightfall. I don't envy him for his father's response for tardiness. I watch the students with a twinge of embarrassment.

I begin to second-guess myself. *Shouldn't I be helping?* Meraud motions with her head to join her and I feel instant relief. Being part of the cleaning brigade is past me now.

"Your nephew tells my students of his strong desire to become a druid. I think he has the mind for it and right temperament as well."

"My brother is a blacksmith and has no love of me or our order. He would never allow it."

"A pity. Will you send him back to Mai Dun then?"

"I doubt he could find his way through the forest. I will take him to the Londinjon Road and part company there."

"My students have it well in hand, follow me." She transforms into a red deer and scampers into the forest.

I hate changing into deer. Once I change back, my muscles are all tense and I jump at shadows for days. I choose a tawny owl, instead. She makes her way to a secluded, grassy meadow. Only the forest behind us and Lir's watery domain are visible.

"Who else knows of your quest?" she asks.

"Only Lord Caradoc knows the details. Masters Gwalather and Arthyen will soon know that I am questing, but only that."

"If only it was Caradoc alone." She pauses and her eyes go distant. "Why are my thoughts as cloudy as the sky?"

I wait patiently for a question I can answer.

"Tell me, Grahme, if I were to give you an order of secrecy, what would it take for you to disregard my order?"

Is this a test? I'm tempted to blurt out that nothing could cause me to do that, but I catch myself. "If a lord were to give me such an order, it would take the majority of the council to release me from that charge."

"You have been instructed well. I will give you an order then, though I hope that it neither helps nor hinders your quest. It is this: Do not tell anyone else the details of your quest. Tell them neither of what you seek nor where your quest takes you, unless the knowledge is already known to them. You are going into the very heart of the mind-controllers. Above all else, tell no one in Solent Keep of your true business."

"I understand."

81

She pats my hand with motherly affection. "We mustn't speak of this any further or we'll be late for our meal."

Are all the members of the Nine like Boswen? One cryptic statement followed by an order to get moving.

"Like most younger druids, I'm sure you would rather transform into a bird and fly back to camp, but do show an aging lady respect and walk back with me."

"Yes, my lord." I take her raised arm and escort her back to camp.

Meraud's students have all changed into swifts and are chasing each other throughout the forest. Entranced, Figol tries to watch all of them at once. Upon Meraud's arrival, the acolytes retake their human forms and gather in front of us. Meraud dispenses the daily duties to her charges.

"I wish to someday be able to do that," Figol says.

Meraud raises her eyebrow before deftly stepping away, allowing us privacy.

"First things first," I say, turning to Figol. "You were supposed to return by nightfall. As it is, you will be returning a day late."

Figol frowns.

"We'll go north to the Londinjon Road and part company. I dare say you can make your way back from there."

"I don't want to return to Mai Dun."

"And I don't wish to have Ferroth drop his anvil on my head while I sleep. Your father already dislikes me. I will not steal his son from him, especially when the terms of this trip were agreed upon by everyone."

After the meal, we make our way north through the forest. Figol has taken the rejection well. I had expected him to harangue me the whole way.

"Can you at least teach me some of the basics as we make our way to the road?"

I smile. "Of course. What do you want to learn first?" He really is a good kid, and his attitude is infectious. After a spell of walking due north, I realize my error. "To get to Solent Keep, we must chase the rising sun."

"Then lead the way," Figol says, smiling.

Keeping his head down, Figol studies the ground as I change course to the east. Once we're pointed in the right direction, Figol opens up and asks me a never-ending series of questions.

"Tell me, how did your mother come by the bone comb with the oyster rocks."

"Mum has always loved those stones. She has a necklace filled with them, though she doesn't wear it anymore."

"A necklace? I'm not an expert, but that must be expensive."

"I think Mum was important back at Ynys Luko, but she doesn't talk about it much."

Over our two-day walk through the old forest, Figol is bright and cheerful the whole way. He compliments me often on my teaching of woodcraft. The more I think about it the more I agree with Meraud. Figol should be a druid. Something is bothering me, though. I don't know what it is, but it feels as if I overlooked something.

"What kind of lodgings do you want in Solent Keep?" Figol asks.

"I have no coin, so whatever the good people of the city will allow us."

"You have no money? What happened to the coins Mother gave you?"

"I gave them to Lowen. It is customary for druids to forswear metal. Never have I been refused a night indoors or a simple meal."

"You've never been in a city, then."

"I've been in Mai Dun."

"That doesn't count. Mai Dun is a Silurian community of farmers and a few tradesmen. Solent Keep is a trading city. It's entirely different. Most of the people there have never planted crops or tended animals in their lives. Everything they eat has to be bought at the market, so no one is likely to waste their money feeding us."

"It will be Helghores Loor tomorrow."

Figol motions me to explain more.

"The Hunter's Moon."

He shrugs at me.

"By now, no doubt, the vegetables have all been harvested and will be quite scarce, but we'll make do with what we can find," I assure him.

"Uncle, you have no idea what awaits us at Solent Keep. The Sorim are known for their warriors, the Obsidian Order, and their traders, the Tyrians. The city never runs out of fresh vegetables. There are ships from all over the mainland and beyond, arriving in the harbor. Mother says they have fruits that most people of Pretanni have never heard of before, much less tasted."

"Close ties to the mainland? I like them less and less all the time."

Figol shakes his head at me. I let it go, amused that he thinks himself so worldly.

"Uncle, you never explained what Helghores Loor is."

"The last day of Elembiu is known as the Hunter's Moon. With the harvest taken in, the farmers can now hunt for fattened deer under the full moon. The first kill is usually a squirrel, and it is offered up to Cocidius, the goddess of the hunt."

"I've never heard of it, but then few in Mai Dun are hunters. We mostly buy our meat from the woodsmen."

"Do you know any of the high festivals?"

"I know Samhain is the start of the New Year."

"Yes, and it's when the realms of the living and the dead are quite close to one another."

"The idea really scares me. Why can't the dead stay dead?"

"Would you still say that if one of your parents had passed on? Or would you like to be in their presence this one time each year?"

"I guess, but my parents aren't going to die for at least thirty more years."

I raise an eyebrow at him. "You are not distracting me that easily. What are the rest of the holy days?"

"Imbolc takes place near the end of winter and it is in honor of Brigantia, the goddess of fertility and prosperity. It also coincides with lambing season."

"I suppose you would be aware of that one," I say grudgingly.

"It's also near my birthday. I don't think it's fair to have to take care of the sheep on my birthday."

I let that go.

"The next festival is Beltane, in honor of Belenos. It is in late spring and his warming rays make life pleasant. Everyone is happy at Beltane, and the adults tend to get drunk."

I nod. "The planting is complete so everyone can rest, unless they're active in the fertility festival."

"It's also the start of warring season. Well, some people start earlier, but after Beltane everyone is fighting. Dad and I are busy making weapons up until that time. After that, it's more repairing farming equipment."

"Do you celebrate Godhvos Gras?"

"Mother tries to celebrate it. She's a Sorim who wants to fit in. Father and I are still really busy at the forge, though. And Father wants us to become good Sorim folk. He thinks it will get us more work."

"And which do you wish to be?"

"Do I have to choose? I would like to be both."

"Then you should celebrate Godhvos Gras with your mother. It is the one day for families to come together and give thanks for what they have."

"Uh-huh." He rolls his eyes at me.

"Enjoy the family gatherings while you have them. If you become a druid, it will be years before you see your family again." I give him the final holyday. "The final festival is Lughnasa, the harvest festival. The crops are taken in and there is time for the farmers to improve their holdings."

"And it marks the end of the warring season."

"It is in honor of Sucellos," I chide. "You mustn't forget the gods on their festival days." I try to keep my voice stern, but the thought of Lughnasa causes Ysella's form to pop into my head.

"If it's in honor of Sucellos, why is it called Lughnasa?"

"Lugh is the ancient name for the god of the harvest and wine. Before you ask, I don't know why or how a god's name can change."

"The Sorim have many more festivals, but they're usually only one day, not seven. Are there no more druid holidays?"

"The Albans are holy to we druids, so we observe them, though the common farmers and such do not."

"What are those?"

"Alban Arthuan and Alban Heruin are the winter and summer solstices. They are a time for us to recheck our records so that the days and months do not run out of their proper seasons. They are my least favorite since we must pay homage to the Hooded Ones and Camulos. I like none of them."

"I know Camulos is the god of war, but who are the Hooded Ones?"

"They are the oracle gods. You must sacrifice an animal to them to receive their words. I find that to be a poor excuse to kill an animal."

He nods.

"Albans Eiler and Elved are the spring and autumn equinoxes," I say, more upbeat.

"What are they?"

"They are the days when Belenos and Aine rule the sky for the same amount of time. Five days after each of the equinoxes, the Council of Nine convenes their meetings. Alban Eiler is held at the sacred grove of the druids and only the Nine are present, but Alban Elved is held at Kantom Lijanks Kuros, the hundred stone circle, and most of the druids and their students attend the meeting."

"What do you do there?"

"In truth, I don't know. I have never been, but I hope to attend it this year. It's only a month away. Now tell me about this city and its infamous Keep."

"Well, I haven't been there since I was little, but Mother has told me a lot about it."

"Where should we go to find shelter?"

"Without coin, we're not likely to find any."

"Then we'll have to stop for now and find a solution."

"Uncle, you can't wear those white robes into the city, at least if you trying to *not* be noticed."

I grudgingly have to agree with him. "Can you lead us into the city once we're on the road?"

"The road doesn't go anywhere else."

"Then you will lead the way tomorrow."

As a hunting dog, I catch three squirrels before we leave the forest. We might as well enter the city with something to sell. I bark when a group of local farmers appear on the road. We wait for them to approach before Figol makes for the eldest of the group.

"Do you mind if I join you?" Figol asks.

"Aye, it's not far now," the gray-haired man says. "We haven't seen you around here before. My name is Estus," he says with an easy-going air.

"I'm Osgar of Tottem and I've been teaching my hound to hunt tree dogs. I mean to sell them at the market."

"I don't like tree dogs. Once you remove the fuzzy tail, there's nothing left, but I doubt you'll have much trouble finding a buyer."

A limping man quickens his pace from the back to walk beside Figol. "And why do you smell of smoke if you're coming from the forest?"

"We spent the night by the wood's edge and whichever place I sat, the wind changed and blew the smoke into my face."

"We? Who was with you?"

"My dog, of course."

The limping man gives him a hard look. Despite his limp, he's keeping up with his neighbors.

"That is a fine dog you have there," he says brightly.

"He's never failed me," Figol responds.

"Well, he will eventually, they all do. When the time comes, he'll fill up a stew pot all by himself."

I resist the urge to growl. Figol deftly walks to the side of the road and bends down to pet my chest. "Uncle, you need to lower your hackles."

Irked by the man's talk of cooking me, I dart off into the woods and return with another squirrel—or tree dog as they're called around here. The limping man continues on at his quick pace.

The city walls in the distance slowly come into view. A two-story, black, stone arch greets all newcomers instead of traditional wooden gates. The rest of the walls are earthen, as they should be.

"Mark my words; the Obsidian Lord will have us all building a wall out of black stone now that the harvest is done. He no doubt means to have a ring of stone around the whole city to match the Keep," Estus says.

"Aye, and we'll all be safer for it," the limping man replies.

"Easy for you to say; your limp will keep you from the backbreaking work."

"But I'll drink ale in honor of you and everyone else for all the hard work."

"After the wall, the lord will want to expand his Keep," Estus complains. "Then the town will be too cramped, so he'll want to move the wall farther out. We'll be hauling stones for him 'til we draw our last breath."

"Does he pay well?" Figol asks.

"Hah," Estus replies. "Not a single coin."

"Why do you do the work, then?" Figol asks, confused.

Estus stops and scratches his chin. "I'm not real sure. We just do."

The soldiers atop the walls on either side of the arched gate idly survey the surrounding fields. The guards down at our level lean up against the stonework, lazily waving everyone through. One picks at his red tunic while the other polishes his large metal shield emblazoned with an all-seeing eye above two crossed spears.

The market is located just inside the gate. The tree dogs are sold before we can even push our way through. Once we're alone again, Figol assures me that it will be enough for a couple nights of lodging. His collection of coins is meager, but I have no choice except to trust his judgment.

I find a spot out of view of the market and change back to my old self.

Figol rushes over to me, and whispers, "You can't be seen here in druid robes."

"It's the only clothing I own."

"Well, change back into a hound. I'll find something else for you to wear."

I choose the form of an emaciated, wheaten-coated dog that I knew from my childhood. The light-colored fur highlights my protruding ribs. No one is likely to pay me any attention.

My canine nose alerts me to the benign smell of horse manure. The stables are likely the only place in this whole city where I'll feel comfortable. I head straight for it, ignoring Figol's yells from behind.

I send a feeling of calmness to the horses so they don't try to kick at me. Unlike the moor ponies, these horses are huge. Figol scrunches up his nose as he enters. I would laugh if I could. He wants to be a druid, but he can't stand the smell of animals? Breaking off in a trot, I inspect each horse as I pass. The final stall is twice the size of any other. Off by himself is the single largest horse I have ever seen. A gray-coated stallion stands majestically with a long, fine tail reaching below the knees. The top of Figol's head only comes up to the horse's shoulder. Though I send a mental greeting, it stands aloof.

Figol catches up with me. "Uncle, what are you doing? We can't stay here."

A guard sees Figol and starts yelling at him. Two more guards come in quick succession. Figol throws his hands up as the men approach. "Sorry, sir, I was just chasing my dog. He has a nasty habit of going where he's not supposed to go."

I slink along the wall and give the guards my big, pitiful eyes. The leader walks past Figol and checks on the great gray horse.

"Regis is undisturbed," he says, relief evident in his voice.

The nearest guard slaps Figol hard on the side of his head. Figol raises his arms to ward off more blows. Two well-dressed youths enter the stables.

"Dairthi, where's my horse?" the boy asks the first guard. He's about Figol's age, but his tone is like a reproving parent.

Figol makes for the door with some urgency.

"Sorry, young lord. We had to remove some vermin." He eyes Figol. "Come back again and you'll get much worse."

"My riding time is supposed to start now. If this happens again, I will have to let my father know," the boy says.

"No need for that, young lord, I assure you," Dairthi says.

Figol glowers as he waits for me to exit. He heads straight for the inn opposite the stables. Figol reaches down to pet me. "Being next to the horse stalls, this inn will be the cheapest in the city. He reaches for the door. "Remember Uncle, you're supposed to be quiet and unseen."

I turn myself in a circle. There's no one watching us. I change into a brindle-coated dog. I'll blend into the shadows much better in this form. Figol jerks his head back and forth in alarm. Finally, he shakes his head in disapproval and pushes the door open.

The sunlight causes several dour patrons to shield their eyes. "Close the door!"

Figol hurries past the men to the barkeep. The man has a plump face with deep laugh lines.

He looks down his bulbous nose. "You're a bit young to be in here, aren't you, boy?"

"I've got coin. Do you have a room?"

"Show me your coin, then," the man says idly.

"I can get more if I need to."

"I don't care where you filch your money from, little thief," the man banters with a smile, "as long as it's not from me. You can have the room at the end of the hall for two nights. After that, you're out on your ass unless you can pay up."

Figol stares directly into the man's eyes. "So, I'm paid up for five days?" Figol asks in a steady voice.

The barkeep shakes his head once before agreeing.

Once the door to our room closes, I bite Figol's leg hard enough to draw a drop of blood.

"What was that for?"

I change back to myself. "You used your mental powers on that barkeep, and on me."

"No, I didn't," he says reflexively.

"Remember how you were going straight back to Mai Dun that first night and again once we reached the Londinjon Road?"

At least he blushes when he's caught in his lie. "I wouldn't have stayed, back at Mai Dun, that is. I would have kept nudging Father until he agreed to let me go. And this trip with you, it's opened my eyes to the ways of the druids. I have never wanted something so much in all my life."

"You're seventeen. By spring you'll be intoxicated by the girls of Mai Dun. Becoming a druid is only the latest new thing in your life."

"You're wrong, Uncle. As soon as I saw you change back from the bear, I knew what I wanted to do with my life."

"Your other talent"—I tap the side of my head—"will not be tolerated by my fellow druids. The Sorim fight us for our land; we would be foolish to enlist one of them in our midst."

"Most Sorim don't care. It's the Obsidian Order that covets power. Besides, I can always stop using it."

"Can you? If so, why have you been manipulating me since we first met? You need to leave and go back to your parents. What I'm going to do, it's not . . . safe."

Figol falls backward, headfirst, on to the bed.

How very dramatic. I should send him back now. I don't care about Ferroth's anger, but I do regret not following through on my word. I have the room for five days, so I should have all the time I need.

"Uncle, if I'm not here, you'll only get the room for two nights. And you can't walk around the city in your white robes."

I glare at him. "You said you couldn't read thoughts."

"Only sometimes," he says. "Let me stay, please? I can help you."

Perhaps I could let him do some scouting, from a distance, of course. I wouldn't let him get anywhere close to the Keep. Besides, he can't make it home before the day ends.

Figol stares at me expectantly.

He has been very useful so far, and I do enjoy his company.

No, I can't endanger him. And Meraud commanded me not to share the nature of my quest with anyone in this city. That includes Figol.

Figol closes his eyes, as if he has something significant to ponder.

If nothing else, he could get me a new robe so I can walk about town without being the center of attention. He also knows the customs much better than I do. He could be a great asset while I'm here in town.

Figol's lips are upturned ever so slightly into a smirk. As if he has some great secret.

"I have some business in this city. But after I'm finished, we will go straight back to your parents and I will speak to them about you becoming a druid." *And no doubt get drubbed by Ferroth.* Who am I to deny him the opportunity to become a druid?

"Really?"

"Yes, but only if you stay out of trouble while we're here."

Figol jumps in the air and voices his excitement until the other residents yell for silence through the thin wooden walls. Chastened, he grins at me before putting both hands over his mouth.

"Your father will never like me, but I worry about what your mother will think. If she becomes angry at me—"

"She knows I'm all right."

"Does she now?"

"She does. Once we know someone's mind, we can seek them out and . . . connect."

"You can talk with her?"

"Not talk, but you do pick up on how they are feeling. And since I haven't been scared or injured since the wolves, she knows that I'm all right."

"You haven't made me feel any better. Your mother could very well take her anger out on me."

"Mother is not like that. She wants everyone to get along. Besides, she has her hands full with my little sisters. The power favors the female line in our family. Berga is nearly as strong as me and she's only five. Mother has to make sure she doesn't use her powers on Father when she throws one of her tantrums. Why are you smiling?"

"The idea of Ferroth being ordered around by a five-year-old girl will delight me for a very long time."

9

Solent Keep

The Fourth Dark Day of Edrin, 819

Fifty-five Days until Samhain

Our room is small, dark, and depressing. The only light is from a single candle that I suspect Figol filched in the market. I've summoned a couple of rats for companionship. They notice the light from under the door disappear and they scramble for cover.

Figol bursts into the room dressed like the noble boys from the stables. "The guards of the palace don't have mental powers."

"First things first, where did you get those clothes?"

"Oh, these? I may have been around the stables when those rich kids returned from riding," he says innocently. "And the main one may have commented on my clothes smelling like ash."

"What did you do?"

"I nudged him a little, mentally that is, and he decided to give me his purse rather than create trouble for him and his friends."

"You intimidated three rich fops, all by yourself?"

"Not exactly, they didn't realize that working in a smithy builds strength. The first one I sent sprawling with a punch to the head. After that, they were more than willing to part with a few coins."

"That doesn't explain your clothes."

"I didn't want to keep wearing my old woolen clothes. Most people here wear linen and if he sends guards out looking for me . . ."

"That was smart."

"After I got proper attire, I entered the Keep."

"What?"

"I just acted like a rich noble's son and no one tried to stop me."

"Why didn't you get me nobleman's clothes as well?"

"Well, Uncle, I didn't think you could pull it off. So, I got you this. It's a slave's tunic." He pulls out a smock made with ratty linen fibers. He raises a hand to keep me from lashing out. "Before you say anything, this will allow you to walk about the city unnoticed."

I hold the garment at arm's length. "Is this held together by the stains?" I mull the situation over before finally accepting the dirty rag. "It makes sense, I guess. I can accompany you into the Keep with this."

"Yes, but we won't get far. The Obsidian Lord has guards posted throughout it."

"Can't you just make them *not* notice us?"

"For people like me who can nudge other's minds, the extremely gifted and the dimwitted are the hardest to manage. The gifted have layers upon layers of thoughts. The slower people, well, they don't have much going on other than basic survival. The Black Mage employs only the dimmest of guards around his hall."

"Still, isn't this good news?"

"They lack the imagination to interpret their orders as anything other than what is stated, so we can't fool them into leaving their posts. I bluffed my way into the Keep, but I could feel the Black Lord's mind everywhere. I've never encountered such power. If I use my skills, he'd notice me."

"Damn. We need to find a way inside. I assume the night will have less people to manage," I say.

"I did overhear some of the house staff making fun of the night guard of the treasury. His name is Jory, and he's about as simple as they come. So even if we could get you into the Keep unnoticed, which we can't, I wouldn't be able to manipulate him, anyway."

"There has to be a way."

"The treasury is on the second floor, overlooking the harbor. The only other way would be to scale up the wall. The night watch from both the harbor and the Keep would likely spot us."

"Then we will have to go through the front gate."

Figol throws his hands up in despair. "This is what I'm trying to tell you, even if we could get in the front gate, what then?"

I inspect the slave's tunic. "It reminds me of what I used to wear as an acolyte. I bet it itches horribly."

None of the buildings in Solent Keep have smooth, daubed walls. They all have harsh, square corners and are made of wood or stone. The paths are covered in gravel and trampled down by the thousands of residents. Even one simple weed would be a welcome sight in this barren place.

The southern end of the city comes to a point, with the River Itchen on the east meeting the River Test on the west before rolling into the Southern Sea. The wharf sits at the southern-most tip. A crowded fish market reeking of decay is next to it. The people are packed so tight, it makes me wonder how half of them don't get elbowed into the water. An empty plaza stretches out from the docks, enclosed by huge storage houses to the east and the dark, threatening Keep to the west. A white stoned building with high walls forms the final barrier. It's the temple for some Sorim god. Not content to displace honest Pretanni, now they seek to supplant our gods as well. *What god is pleased by such an ugly building?*

Despite the bright white stonework, the temple is even more uninviting than the Keep. Staring down onto the square is a disapproving, stone-faced god. He's bracketed by a ship and a dye pot, for whatever that is supposed to symbolize. A long tunnel beneath the stern god is made with more white brick, but it remains forever cast in shadow. It is more fitting as a portal to the underworld of Dubnos than to a living god of the land.

A humorless man sits next to the entrance. I watch as a shopkeeper approaches and pays the man for admittance to the temple. This is what happens when merchants start a religion.

Desperation hangs in the air as heavily as the stench of dead fish and salt air. Poor Ancasta, her River Itchen is polluted by these heathens and sell swords. I take out my bone knife and cut my hand, letting my blood spill into her waters as a sacrifice. Men are scuttling about as a new ship is coming into port. Thick ropes are thrown over the ship's hull to the huge iron rings on the dock. Gangs of slaves slowly pull the ship closer.

"You! Slave, come here and help my men," a barrel-chested man yells.

I continue my walk away from the oppressive noise. A meaty hand wrenches my left shoulder and spins me around. "I said to go and help my men," he sputters.

"I am not your slave."

"You are a slave, and that means you do what freemen tell you to do." He grabs the back of my neck and propels me toward the wharf.

I face him, defiant. "I am not yours to command."

"Get over there and help my men or I'll see you flogged for your insolence."

I hold my ground, defiant.

With a roar he takes out his mace and rushes me.

I lean forward, hands on knees and wait for his approach. He holds his club out wide, winding up his blow. I launch myself upward, hitting his chin with my head. His head snaps back and his mace goes sailing off behind me. I kick the inside of his knee and hear a satisfactory pop. He crumples to the ground, holding his useless leg. In one precise movement, I kick the side of his head, knocking him unconscious. It's better than he deserved—now he's unaware of his pain.

All goes silent, save the lapping of gentle river waves and the calls of seabirds. I turn slowly toward the docks and into the faces of stunned slaves and dockworkers alike.

"Get him!"

Pandemonium ensues. A few slaves dare to cheer me on as dozens of men flock toward me. The east end of the square is full of large warehouses. Several men give chase, but I'm able to lose them after a couple random turns. By the smell of it, I'm near the latrines. I slip into a narrow alley. It curves gradually to the right before it reaches a dead end. With nothing but closed doors and puddles from emptied chamber pots, I'm cornered. The shouts of the guards announce the beginning of an organized search. I close my eyes and transform into my emaciated tan-colored dog. "Fan out; we're not stopping until we find that slave."

I plop down against a door and give my best look of quiet desperation.

The door opens inward, causing me to roll onto my back. Getting to my feet at once, I scurry out of the doorway before turning back at the owner. He's as surprised as I am. Leaning against the opposite wall, I give him my biggest, saddest eyes.

He goes down on one knee and beckons me to him. "Here puppy, puppy."

The guileless man produces a small piece of bread. I slowly make my way to him; stopping and starting several times. I let his kind voice coax me toward him. Finally, I gingerly extend my neck and accept the offered breakfast.

"You're new around here, aren't you?"

He scratches behind my ears and I enjoy it, despite myself.

"You look worse than Cryton did, but that is not a worry; Jory is here now to take care of you."

My ears perk up. I can't help myself.

"What's got your attention now? I better give you some more bread before you decide to run off." He offers me more and pats me solidly on my ribs.

Doesn't he know that it's hard to swallow when the wind is being knocked out of you?

"Jory is here now. Don't worry."

A simple man named Jory? Surely Ancasta is repaying my homage to her. I lean into Jory's legs and lift my half-closed eyes toward his face. My tongue flops out the side of my mouth.

"That's a good boy. You could be mistaken for a half-starved cur, if not for that silly grin. I'll call you Buddy, since you'll make a good one. I have no doubt." He holds more bread just out of reach. "Follow me, Buddy, and let's meet Cryton."

Stale bread is all Jory has. I can't help but feel guilty as I accept a sizable portion of the man's meal. He leads me inside his ramshackle one-room home. I catch Cryton's scent, and I know immediately that he is old and frail. His life is likely measured in days. There are no other people or animals in the room and barely any possessions. Cryton wags his tail up and down, thumping the dirt floor, but he doesn't rise. I send a calming assurance to him. Before long we're lying back-to-back near the small central fire.

I spot Jory's guard uniform along with his spear and polished helmet on a small table next to the door. Jory busies himself tending the fire and petting Cryton and me for an eternity or more. I'm eager to get back to Figol and tell him I have the beginning of a plan. At long last Jory's stomach starts talking. He's forced to focus on more than the fire, Cryton, and me. He grabs a small change pouch from the table with his uniform.

"I think I can splurge and get some day-old fish for us all." He smiles back at us.

My conscience won't let me accept any more of the man's food. Once the door is opened, I dart out between his legs.

"Buddy, come back."

I scamper along the city wall until I'm almost to the market at the main northern gate. At last, I feel safe enough to change back to myself. I keep my head down and walk with a purpose back to the tavern. As luck would have it, Figol is out. I plop on the thin bedding and await his return.

"He's leaving the city!" Figol shouts as he enters our room.

"Who?"

Figol closes the door and rushes over to me. "The Obsidian Mage," he says softly. "He's leaving the city as we speak."

"Why?"

"No idea, but it's definitely him, there's no way you could mistake that power for anyone else. He's taking some druid woman and eight guards."

"A druid woman? Are you sure?"

"She was dressed in a white robe like yours. But who cares. Don't you see? If they are leaving this late after midday, they are bound to be gone at least one night."

"Then we're going tonight."

"But the guards . . .?"

"I have news of my own about the treasury guard."

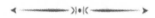

"I caught wind of a slave ruthlessly attacking the dock master today," Figol says. "It seems he is still at large in the city. We can't have that happen again."

I wag my tail in broad strokes to signal my happiness.

Figol reaches down and scratches my side. "You're as dumb as they come, Uncle Grahme."

I'm aware of the slight but a dog's instinct is strong, so I lean into him and start kicking my hind leg.

We watch as Jory nods to the guards and enters the Keep. Cryton is following behind him. The guards laugh and pet Cryton. Jory sends him on his way back home, something he must do nightly. Cryton retreats around the corner and lies down, waiting for his master to return. Once the watches are resumed and the commotion dies down, Figol walks confidently to the entrance.

I hate to admit it, but I'm in awe of the building. Only the Elder races built in stone and few, if any, were three stories tall. My tail starts short, anxious strokes and I'm thankful to be in canine form. My nervous afflictions would never go unnoticed as my human self.

"I'm here to see the lord," Figol announces.

"The lord is not within the Keep, Young Master . . .?" The guard looks at Figol for an answer.

"You will not delay me any further," Figol says. "I have given you my sworn testament, now let me through."

Confused, the guards part. I follow closely behind Figol.

"Sir, what of the dog?"

"Do you want to make that your business, also?" Figol asks ominously.

"Very good, sir."

We enter the foyer; Figol takes a wax candle from his tunic and dips it into the fire. I smell his fear before I see the sweat beading up on his forehead. "I think it best if you take the form of my slave now."

I change back. "Why are you sweating?"

"That took all of my skill to pull off. In the end, I think it was my attitude that got us through."

"Are you able to do this?" I ask.

"Will we ever get another chance?"

"Lead the way."

The corridor is lined with smooth, black stone. The unadorned passages intensify the oppressive feel. I rub my hands together for warmth and to hide my nerves. I have never felt so cut off from nature in my life.

"Remember, one aggressive move by you and we'll be discovered," Figol whispers. "Even more so than outside, slaves are at the mercy of everyone they encounter within these walls."

The walls feel as if they are closing in on me. My throat begins to tighten and I'm on the balls of my feet, desperate to hear where the next threat is coming from. I'm not sure what Figol just said, but I nod my head anyway.

"What are you doing?" Figol asks. "You act like you're about to run. Keep your head down and your hands inside your smock. No one is going to see your tanned skin and believe you work indoors."

I do as I'm told and Figol places his candle in a holder. He struts around the corner as if he is the ruler here. An iron gate allowing entry to the stairs is open. Two guards sit idly at a table. They've been throwing dice by the look of it. Figol strides forth confidently. The surprised guards rise as they grab their spears.

"I have a gift for the lord, Figol announces. "I don't have time to waste; let me through."

"Who are you?" He demands.

"If you were important, you would know. Now step aside," Figol says with all the self-importance he can muster. A noble would have his slave carry the light. I meekly approach Figol and take the candleholder.

"What is the nature of your gift?" the guard asks, still suspicious. He doesn't even acknowledge me. "We must inspect everyone before they may pass."

"I am not in the habit of telling every lackey my business with the Black Lord."

"If you are so important," the guard says with a patronizing smile, "then you would know that the lord is away from the Keep this night."

"Of course, he is, fool. I have been sent over hither and yon to discover a new source so he can complete his plans. I will not be questioned by every insignificant servant I pass." Figol brusquely pushes past the guards and jerks his arm for me to follow. "Come along."

I keep my head down and follow. He strides confidently up the stairs before halting.

"I need a new torch," Figol demands.

"Didn't your slave bring more tapers with him?" the guard asks.

"Well?" Figol turns to me.

"I don't . . . . Forgive me, sir, I have forgotten them."

"I will beat you senseless once I have the time to do it properly." Figol hits me upside the head hard enough that my vision clouds for an instant. I stifle the instinct to strike back and bow my head, instead. "Don't just stand there. Get a torch from those men and be quick."

The guards are watching gleefully. No doubt they're entertained by Figol's ire. I bow and turn to follow orders.

"Move!" Figol kicks me in the ass with the bottom of his foot.

I manage to grab the corner of the wall to keep myself from tumbling down the stairs.

The guards are too busy laughing at me to notice my tanned hands. I keep my head buried as I pass the guards. I grab two candles and scurry back to my master. They smirk at me as I pass between them.

"Keep your head up, slave, and hold the torch high. No amount of groveling will save you from your beating."

I raise the torch and see Figol is wiping the sweat off his brow. I follow behind him as we turn the corner.

"That was close," Figol says as he exhales. "I dare not use any more of my power than that. There are still powerful mages in the Keep."

"Do you plan on beating me more tonight?"

"Sorry, Uncle Grahme, I wasn't sure I could fake a blow."

I let it go.

"Do you need to rest?" I ask.

"No, there should only be one other guard between us and the treasury."

"I'll take care of Jory. Are you sure you know where we are?"

"I was able to read several guards' minds yesterday and it seems that this level spirals to the right from the stairs and has four large rooms, each the size of my parent's house. At the end of the hall are stairs going up to the third floor. The first room is the gaol, and the last is the treasury."

"The other two?"

"The second is the armory. None of the guards I came across have ever entered the third room."

"What's on the third floor?"

"The Black Lord's private rooms, I would guess."

"Right, let's avoid those at all costs."

There are reed torches on either end of the prison cell. The prisoners lie motionless as we pass.

"It's as if they're dead," I say under my breath. We hurry past the cell.

Figol stations himself at the corner and peers into the next corridor. He silently waves me on. The room at the center of the corridor has a thick oak door with the Obsidian Lord's insignia carved in the center. A single, all-seeing eye floats above two crossed spears. We stop to try the armory door. It's locked. Good, locked doors mean no chance of a surprise. We advance around the spiral corridor to the next door.

"We're going to have to leave the torch here, or else Jory will see us coming," I say.

Figol nods. We inch our way along the hall, stopping at the oak door midway down. I push against the door and it gives slightly.

"This is our place for cover if we need it," I say.

Figol risks a quick peek around the corner and scurries back to me. "The simpleton is at his post. I can't hope to control him with my power."

"His name is Jory, and he is a good man." I can't help but come to his defense. "Go back to the third door and let me take care of this."

I transform into Buddy and hobble around the corner and out of the shadows.

"Buddy? How did you get in here?" Jory asks, confused.

I whimper as I limp toward him. He reaches down to pet me and I jump as if I've heard a loud noise. I tuck my tail between my legs and slink off past the treasury, to the third-floor stairs. Jory whispers urgently for me to return. The man will not leave his post, even a handful of steps. I place my front paw on the first step and yelp in pain.

"Buddy," Jory whispers. "Come here. I can't leave this spot."

After a few agonizing moments, Jory leans his spear and shield against the wall and tiptoes over to me. He bends over to scratch my chest.

Thwack! I animorph back into human form and land a blow to his temple. He collapses to the ground. Feeling his pulse, I know he'll recover. I pat him gently on the shoulder. "I'm truly sorry for this." Searching his person, I find a single key. "Got it," I whisper as loud as I dare.

Figol waits for me at the treasury door.

The key opens the door to piles of coins, jewels, and several ornate daggers.

"Uncle, this dagger has a wooden hilt and an obsidian blade. You could use this one instead of your bone knife."

"Leave it be. I want nothing but what I've come for."

I turn a blind eye as Figol takes some of the silver coins. I scrupulously examine every table, but the ghost orchid is nowhere to be found.

My shoulders sink. "It's not here."

"What are you looking for?"

"A flower, about this long," I extend my thumb and pinky finger. "It should have a whitish-green stem and pale purple and yellow flowers."

"What?" Figol says, as if I was the one struck in the head.

"It's the whole reason I was sent here."

"We broke into the Black Lord's treasury so you could take a stupid flower?"

"We'll have to check the other rooms."

Figol mumbles something about flowers and unbelievable, but it is hard to hear over all the coins clinking together in his pouches.

10

Escape from Solent Keep

The Fifth Dark Day of Edrin, 819

Fifty-one Days until Samhain

Figol quietly closes the treasury door.

"The armory is locked; the only place left to check is the third room." Figol retrieves his candle while I check on Jory one last time. The third door creaks open, followed by silence. As I round the corner, Figol stands motionless inside the door.

"What are you doing here?" he asks in a small voice.

"You come in as well, druid," a voice calls from within.

I glance down the corridor to the treasury and Jory's spear. It's a mere seven paces away.

"You'd never make it to the spear," the voice calls.

I'm forced to enter the room. Figol is sweating profusely as he props himself up against the doorframe. He drops his torch and makes no effort to retrieve it. Figol's eyes are closed and he's muttering some sort of chant.

"And done," the voice says triumphantly as he snaps his fingers. Figol's chant ceases.

I turn to face . . . the limping man from our entrance into the city.

"You?"

"Did you think the Black Lord controls this city all by himself?"

"What did you do to Figol?"

"What you saw was our mental duel. He . . . tried." There's still a steady pulse in Figol's neck. "Impressive. You two made it farther than anyone else ever has. But no one will ever know, will they?"

I throw Figol's reed torch at him and it flies through his chest. The illusion dissipates and our only light hits the back wall.

"Tell me, did you know that was an aura or were you just angry?" He steps out from behind a curtain and kicks the torch into the corner where there is nothing to catch fire. "It took forever to tame Seisyll's anger."

I back up slowly toward the door.

"That won't do," he says. "Close the door."

I stare down in disbelief as my limbs obey another master. The door closes with a resounding thud.

"You can tell me what you hoped to accomplish here, or I can root around in your mind until I find it, your choice."

I focus on the image of a bear and will myself to take its shape.

"None of that, either. The silly druidess was forever trying to turn into a bird, or a squirrel, or a toad. You can't hope to perform any of your magic. I'm in your mind and I can stop you with ease." He sighs. "It took forever to re-sculpt her mind away from those druid tricks. I don't have the time for that. So, if you would rather I do this—"

The image of me being intimate with Ysella at Lughnasa is pulled up in my mind. I relive every sound, every physical touch as faithfully as the night it happened. I can feel the warmth of her body and my arousal. Then the memory goes blank, and I'm nearly overcome with exhaustion.

"Interesting," he says with a condescending smile. "Now, would you like me to pick out other memories that are not at the top of your mind, and are of a more painful nature, or will you answer my very simple question?"

I start recalling all the healing herbs and their seasons that Gwalather made me memorize. Thousand leaf in the fall for divination, mead wort in the summer for a well-flavored ale, lovage leaves in the spring for digestion . . . .

"I see we will have to do this the hard way."

My spine starts tingling. Whether it is from my fear or his control, I can't say. I send out a mental plea for help.

"And who do you think is going to come to your aid?"

"What have you done to Figol?" I stall for time.

"He'll recover shortly. My lord insists I don't kill intruders. He likes to save that pleasure for himself." He leers at me.

"How did you know we would be here tonight?"

"Boy, my job is to identify petty threats like you and observe your actions. I know that you two have been staying at the flea trap of a tavern by the horse stalls. I know it was you who assaulted the dock master. I've been following you two for the last four days as you tripped your way all over the city. Young Figol's tampering with the barkeep's mind was enough to bring both of you in, but I waited to see your whole pitiful plan unfold. Once the lord left on his errand, I was reasonably sure that we would meet here tonight."

I open the door behind me.

In a tired voice he says, "And still you would resist me."

I take a couple steps back into the doorway before my body goes rigid.

"Silly druid." He draws a knife from under his robe and taps the dull side of the blade in his left hand. "Should I take an eye or an ear?" He cocks his head sideways to ponder his decision.

"The Obsidian Lord will not be pleased, but I think it's worth facing a bit of his ire." My body as immovable as a stone, I watch as the knife eases closer and closer to my left eye.

I hear labored breathing coming from the stairs.

"What do you want with a ghost orchid?" I shout.

"Thank you for telling me what you were seeking here. If you would have told me sooner . . . ."

"No, not my eye," I beg. His cruel grin expands. He giggles softly, intoxicated by my fear.

"I'm sorry!" I scream.

Five stones of canine fury bound through the door from behind me and digs its teeth into the limping man's shin. He screams out in pain as Cryton starts to thrash his head side-to-side. The man drops down to the ground, frantically trying to dislodge Cryton. I grab the druid's staff set next to the doorway and connect with the limping man's head. The room falls silent except for Cryton's panting. Shallow breaths let me know my attacker is alive, for now. Cryton is wheezing as he releases his bite. He lies on his side, whimpering anxiously.

I gently pat Cryton on his chest before stepping over him. I slam the end of the staff with all my might against the limping man's neck. He will never attack anyone again. I drop to one knee and check on my canine friend. Cryton is trying to rise but his legs can't seem to gain purchase. His tail starts nervously slamming into the floor. I scratch his chest as I pay attention to his breathing. The pace and force of his tail hitting the floor lessens, but it is not because of my affection. His breath is wet and labored.

"Easy, Cryton," I coo. "You are the best friend a man could ask for." I gently stroke his patchy coat. "Rest now, and take a break from your aches and pains. Easy now, let the great sleep take you." I mentally project peace and calm to him.

He exhales and his chest fails to rise again. I peer into his big, sad eyes and know that my friend, my savior, has passed on.

I close his eyes and sit puzzled. I know of no prayers for animals when they make the passing. If ever there was an animal who earned another life . . . I must ask Boswen for direction when I return to the moor.

Grabbing the limping man's torch, I check on my nephew. Figol grunts and his eyes twitch sporadically. I slap him a couple times on the cheek and call his name. He's moving, but not very well.

The room has the same feel as Master Gwalather's cottage, right down to the organization of the ingredients and the mortar and pestle made from oak heartwood.

What is a druid's study doing here?

I crush some mint leaves and place them under Figol's nose. I scan the pots for wolf's bane and jimson weed. I crush them together in water and add some dried wild onion. I pour the mixture down Figol's throat. It only takes a few heartbeats before he is roused from his stupor. I search the room while he coughs and sputters.

All the desks are filled with herbs except one. It has a petrified ghost orchid sitting in the center and three symbols scribbled in the dust. "Flower," and "below," I say, reading the first two symbols. The flower must be referring to the ghost orchid. I check beneath the desk. Nothing. There is another sigil written in the dust, but I don't recognize it. I upend all the other desks. No sign of the orchid.

Figol struggles to get to his feet, leaning on the wall for support. "Is Venta where the Dark Lord is going?"

"What?"

"That's the city symbol for Venta." He points at my undeciphered sigil. "I have no idea what the other two mean, but that's definitely Venta." With an uneven gait, he walks over to me.

"How do you know that?"

"Before the agents of the Black Lord came, Father would make swords for clan and city leaders from all over Southern Pretanni. I had to learn the symbols for all the cities around us."

Flower, below, Venta; what does this mean?

"That solves one mystery." I grab the stone flower and erase the symbols from the desk. "Can you walk?"

"Do I have a choice?"

I offer my shoulder for support. He surveys the room, keying on Cryton and the limping man.

"What happened?"

"I'll fill you in later. Can you get us past the guards at the bottom of the stairs?"

Figol's eyes flutter and he inhales deeply. "No. I feel . . . empty."

We stumble toward the steps.

"Wait. Maybe they can help us get out of here." He points to the prison door.

"It can't hurt to find out," I say.

I leave him leaning up against the opposite wall. The cell is dark and there's little sign of life from within.

"Is there anyone who wants out?" I ask.

"Who are you?" a short man with a stubby beard asks.

"I'm willing to release you if you can get us past the guards at the bottom of the stairs."

"Why bother? The Dark Lord's second will stop us dead in our tracks. If I pray to Melqart, perhaps I can die in this cell."

"Is that man the one with the limp?" I ask.

"Yes, and he's never far away."

"You're right, only this time, he's dead."

The man's eyes become unfocused as he grabs hold of the bars.

"I can't sense him," he says excitedly. "Where did you see him last?"

"He is lying two rooms over, with a broken neck."

The man perks up at once. "Open the door and I will happily take care of all the guards we meet personally."

"No killing," I say. "We can't arouse the watch."

He pauses for a moment. "Agreed."

"What is your name?"

"Alfswich, at your service," he says with a slight bow.

I search in vain for a lock. Frustrated, I ram the door with my shoulder and stumble inside. "The door wasn't secured. You were always free to go."

"To what end? The limping one was always nearby. This door meant protection from him. As long as you didn't draw attention, he usually didn't punish you."

"Well, come out quietly and bring whoever is able."

Alfswich exits by himself and inches himself to the top of the stairs. The guards are absorbed in their game of dice. He clenches his jaw and shuts his eyes for a moment. "The guards won't cause us any problems."

I let my disbelief show. He claps repeatedly and gets no response. I peek around the wall to see the guards sitting motionless below.

"They won't cause us any trouble."

"How long do we have?" I ask.

"A good while, I'll get the rest of the prisoners."

I retrieve Figol and we shamble to the stairs. I can spot no physical injury. At the bottom of the stairs, the motionless guards stare motionlessly at the dice. Time creeps by as we wait for the prisoners to emerge. The clinking of coins alerts me to Alfswich's true mission. He issues a low curse as a gemstone hits the ground and tumbles down the stairs.

I catch it with my free hand and hold it at arm's length as Alfswich descends. He stuffs it into a hole in his shirt.

"I've got pockets everywhere," he says.

Figol inspects the guards. "The waking sleep," he says with grudging approval.

"Can you walk on your own?" I ask.

"For a little while."

"Good, we'll have to ditch the master and slave act. Take a torch and walk in front of us." Figol shambles on ahead, with each step becoming more sure-footed than the last. Alfswich takes out a huge golden torc from his pouch and lingers behind as he admires it.

"Alfswich, are you coming?"

"One moment," he says. He puts the torc away and grabs something else from his bag.

One of the guards collapses to the ground with a thud. Alfswich spins and plunges his dagger into the second guard's chest as well. He falls out of his chair with the same vacant eyes and bleeding chest.

"The whole Keep will be looking for us at the next changing of the guards."

"Did you think no one would notice that the lord's second is dead?" Alfswich replies. "Now follow me and keep quiet." He strides past me, humming a pleasant tune to himself.

Thanks to Alfswich's bravado and mental abilities, we make it out of the Keep.

"The gate will be closed at this time of night, so we'll have to lie low somewhere in the city," Figol says.

"Can you trade one of your gems for lodging?" I ask Figol.

Alfswich grabs Figol's hand before he can withdraw one of them. He sneers at us. "If you want to announce yourselves as the thieves of the Keep, then by all means spend the Obsidian Mage's fortune in his own city." He shakes his head. "Good luck to you both. I'm going to go it alone from here."

We watch Alfswich circle around to the wharf. "No doubt some poor fisherman is going to be missing his boat," Figol says.

"We need to get to the animal stalls."

Figol creases his eyebrows in confusion.

"It's best we not be seen entering the inn after the guards have been killed. It might lead to uncomfortable questions."

I project calm to the animals before we even arrive. The huge empty stall in the back is empty.

"We need to be out at first light. The stall keeper won't be so kind if he sees us here again," Figol whispers. "Now tell me what happened back there and why you took that stupid stone flower and nothing else?"

"When a druid has finished his training, he is given his white robe and a quest he must fulfill. This is my quest."

Figol waits for me to say more. After a long silence, he shakes his head in disgust and drops to the floor in the corner of the stall. He falls asleep at once. I transform back into the brindle-coated dog and melt into the shadows. Once the city settles in for the night, I sneak into the inn and retrieve my pack and our original clothes.

Before Belenos rises, I lick Figol's face until he wakes. His eyes grow big and his mouth opens. I lick his tongue and the top of his mouth. He sputters and lurches his head away from me. I straddle his body and resume my tongue work.

"Why?" he demands. "What makes you think this is a good idea?" He pushes me away and sits up while scraping his tongue with his front teeth. My tail swishes back and forth. He scowls at me, but he's collected his wits.

He replaces his nobleman's clothes with his Mai Dun attire. "Stay in that form, Uncle. The guards may want to question the young lord and his slave from last night, but no one will think twice about a boy in unkempt clothing and his dog leaving the city." He stands and stretches. "Let's get moving." I playfully nip at his leather shoes as we make our way to the main gate, much to Figol's consternation.

A large, agitated crowd has amassed in front of us. "What's happening?" Figol asks.

"The gate's been sealed. Prisoners escaped last night, and the city guard must round them up before anyone is to leave."

"How can prisoners escape?" Figol asks. "Can't the Black Lord just mind-control them back into the prison?"

The man smiles at Figol shrewdly. "You ask good questions, young lord. . . ."

"Osgar of Totten is my name," Figol responds.

"Well, Osgar, if I were you, I would go back to your inn and secure another night's lodging. I wager no one is leaving the city today."

We walk through the deserted market, putting a good distance between us and the gate. Figol gives the Keep a wide berth and we end up near Jory's home. I can't help but feel guilty. I change back into human form.

"Figol, give me a couple of your silver coins." He squints at me as he complies. I hand him my pack before I dash down the alley and slide the coins underneath Jory's door. Figol starts to ask a question but thinks better of it.

"It is only fair," I explain.

"You need to remain a dog for the rest of the day."

The fish market is bustling, and we find ourselves in the thick of it almost immediately. Figol keeps one hand on his money pouch as we wander aimlessly.

"If you want to leave the city, follow me," Alfswich says as he materializes behind us.

I let out a low growl to voice my displeasure.

"Quiet, druid," Alfswich commands. He leads us to the lower docks. "They are concentrating their search in the north of the city for now. Most prisoners would run straight for the north gate and would be easily captured. It will be awhile yet before they inspect everyone in the crowd. Then they'll move the search down here."

"And why should we trust you?" Figol asks. "You broke your promise not to hurt the guards and you ran from us once we were free of the Keep."

"Because we will all be sent to the King's Mark if they capture us." He looks at Figol. "Can you convince a boater to give us a ride across the river?"

"I don't think so," Figol responds sullenly.

"Then I will provide our escape." Alfswich smirks at me. "And this means that *you* are now in my debt."

"Why did you wait until now to take a boat?" Figol asks.

"The half-moon still gives off too much light. The watch would have noticed a boat leaving and I'd be riddled with arrows. Come, we have to hurry if we're going to make the tide."

Once on board the simple fisherman's boat, Alfswich turns to us. "Do you know what the King's Mark is?"

"No."

"The Dark Lord first did this to the old ruler of the city, King Mark. Now it's the name of the most heinous punishment that can be meted out. First, he compels you to walk to the gallows and spill your own guts in front of the whole city. It's mandatory; everyone must come out or answer to the maniac. And of course, he can tell if you're lying, so no one chances it. Anyway, you are made to toss your intestines over the scaffold and wrap another part around your neck. Finally, he mentally nudges you to jump off the platform and strangle yourself."

"But won't the intestines rip?" Figol asks.

"Aye, they usually do. Then you're left for the dogs." He picks this moment to scratch me behind my ears.

Once the boatman turns his boat back toward the city, I transform back to myself. "Figol, leave your nobleman's tunic here with my slave's smock. If we should be stopped, we don't want to have these on our person."

"If you have no use for those, I will gladly take them," Alfswich says.

"Take it, in payment of my debt to you," I say.

"You put so little value on our escape?"

"With luck, we will never meet again."

Alfswich mockingly bows to me. "May your next spoils be more substantial." He breaks off into the woods at a trot.

"Uncle, check your bag."

The stone flower is gone.

"Leave him be, uncle," Figol says. "He'd only mind-control you when you get close and I'm in no shape to give chase.

11

Visit to Venta

The Sixth Dark Day of Edrin, 819

Fifty Days until Samhain

We begin our trek north well after sunrise. Figol shambles along behind me, incurious of his surroundings. We reach the crossing of a woodsman's path with the road. There's nothing physically wrong with him, but he tires fast.

"Uncle, where are we going?" he asks.

"I don't know," I sigh. We stop in the middle of the road. "Where can I find an orchid that is so rare that most druids are unaware that it even exists?"

"I don't know anything about plants, but the sigil for Venta was written in the dust back at the Keep."

"Yes, but what does that mean? Is that where the Obsidian Lord rode off to yesterday? Do we want to go where he is going to be?"

Figol drops to the ground and sits cross-legged. "I'm going to get comfortable while you try to make up your mind."

Belenos is rising ever higher in the sky and standing in the middle of a crossing achieves nothing. "Can you get us to Venta?"

"Yes, Uncle; we continue north until we hit the Londinjon Road. We go toward the rising sun from there."

"Then we have our plan. After Venta I must go north to warn the plains druids that the Dark Lord is preparing for war." It was my duty.

What will I do if I can't find another ghost orchid? I'll be cast out of the druids. What will I do, become a laborer on my brother's farm? I can't be a simple farmer.

"There is nothing wrong with a farmer's life," Figol says.

"I see you have recovered your ability to enter my mind uninvited." In truth, I think it a good sign.

I give Figol my hand to pull him up, but Figol releases it and collapses into a fetal position. He cradles his head, puffing his cheeks as if he's in pain.

"Figol?" I scan for threats, but the road is clear.

He shakes his head and extends his arm upward to me. "Didn't you feel that?"

I stare at him blankly.

"Some very powerful person is flailing around in the mental spaces, screaming out for another." Figol massages his temples. "I told you how Mother and I can sense how each other is feeling, even when we're far away. She was searching for me since I was attacked by the limping man. It wasn't until this morning that I could make contact with her."

"So, this wasn't your mother, then?"

"No, I recognize Mother's gentle touch. This person possesses undeniable strength and is unconcerned about how it affects others."

"The Obsidian Mage?" I ask.

"Who else could it be? He is probably trying to reestablish a link with the limping man."

"Perhaps we should get off the road."

There's a thicket of hemlock bushes close to the road. There is a cloud of dust to the north. We get deep in the bushes and wait to see who is galloping south on the road.

The huge gray steed from the stalls mounts the hill. It must be the Obsidian Mage leading the way. Decked in all black, his scabbard gleams brilliant silver. A shiny black stone adorns the pommel.

"That's one of Father's blades," Figol says. "The obsidian took forever to be mounted."

Eight men and a druidess follow behind him.

"Treacherous whore! She has betrayed her own kind." I take a step forward, wanting to confront her, but Figol holds me back.

"You heard the limping man," Figol says. "They have overwhelmed her mind. She can't help it."

The limping man may have controlled my body, but never did I surrender my mind.

I know he's right, but it still infuriates me. "Where were they and what were they doing?" I demand.

"Maybe he was searching for another flower?" Figol says. "Since the only flower we found was turned to stone."

I chuckle. "I hope you're right, because I have no idea where else to search for the stupid flower."

"Do you think they found another orchid, or are they rushing back because he couldn't contact the limping man?"

"Only one way to find out."

"Greetings, Gatekeeper," I yell.

Venta's hillfort is up a steep incline, and the heat is sweltering, at least to me.

"State your name and come no closer."

Figol and I look at each other, confused.

"I am Grahme, a questing druid from the west. This is my nephew." Despite his order, we close the distance to the city gate.

"We've not had a druid in these parts for two years, and now we get two in two days? How do I know you're actually a druid?"

There is a woodpecker off to my left. I can't see it, but I call it forth anyway as I lift up my arm. A mottled brown and white bird with a bright red head flies over and lands on my arm.

"It is a juvenile green woodpecker," I say to Figol. "It will lose the brown feathers, the breast will become bright white and the wings will turn green, like moss." I thank the bird and send it back to the forest.

"Pardon my tone, but I wanted to be sure you weren't a fraud."

"It does you credit to be cautious," I say. "Tell me, what did my fellow druid want?"

"It was not a druid, but a druidess."

I feint surprise. Lonely gatekeepers are easy to befriend. "I would be well pleased if you could tell me why my peer was here, but first, please, give me your name." I give him a head nod as a sign of respect.

"I am called Lougha and I have watched this gate for twelve years. Never have I had anyone ask where the elven graves could be found. As a rule, men leave them alone. But she wished to harvest whatever Elven Tears she and her party could find. Just this morning, she and her group left without even a thanks."

"Elven Tears?"

"Aye, it is a small flower that only grows in deep shade near elven burial mounds. We see our share, since we have four mounds inside our walls and another seven outside."

"Can you show me these mounds?"

Lougha is uneasy. "I can't be leaving my post."

"I will be glad to keep watch while you two visit the tombs," Figol says. He gives me a wink.

"Come this way, then," Lougha says happily. He limps due to his left foot being turned outward from his body.

"I hope whoever tried to heal your leg decided to become a butcher rather than a healer."

"Funny you should say that. The man was my father, and he was the town's butcher. But that was long ago; I can get by well enough."

"At least you can be thankful for that."

"There are never any Elven Tears within our village; the trees have long since been cut down. But I will take you to the tombs outside the walls so that you can see what yesterday's party was interested in."

The inner gate opens onto the village and the bowl barrows of elven warriors fill the enclosed grassy area in the center of their town.

"Have these tombs been left undisturbed?"

"They have, but no Elven Tears grow near these anymore."

We pass a wooden statue of Brigantia, surrounded by votive offerings. *Do they think they can buy the good will of a goddess?*

"This is our shrine to Brigantia," Lougha says proudly.

"There are many offerings. Do you not send them to the bottom of the river?"

"Why would we do that? The offerings are made when Aine refuses to climb into the sky. Once she has regained her full glory, the offerings are taken back until the next time."

"The gifts are not permanent?"

"If Brigantia requires them, she will take what she wishes. What's left is for our own use."

"Has the goddess ever taken an offering?"

"No. This is how we know that she showers goodwill upon us."

Or she will have nothing to do with you.

I must tell Boswen of this when I return. When the Wigesta invaded the eastern lands, they brought this habit of building statues to the gods. That it has traveled this far west is concerning. The old ways are being forgotten.

We reach the far side of the hillfort and the west gate. A stout oaken door is hidden within the rampart. Lougha turns his key, and the door opens to the remnants of a forest.

"I come out here in the morning and search for mushrooms before the main gate is opened."

There are four shaded mounds below the entrance. Lougha scampers down the dirt path to the mound farthest from the city.

"It was over there, in the deep shadows. I saw a single Elven Tears flower yesterday." He points to a hole in the ground. "By my reckoning, this is grave theft. What use is such a small flower?"

"In truth, I do not know. I only know that I must bring one back to my master." My shoulders sag, "It seems I have failed."

"Poor Lougha understands little of you forest folk, but you have been more than kind to me. For this reason, I will share with you the location of a much larger elven cemetery. Perhaps you will find your flower there. It is a good walk, five leagues from here and off the main road to boot."

I grab his hand tightly, too tightly. "I will be in your debt, Lougha," I say with a grateful smile.

"The Flowerdown Cemetery is the largest of its kind in these parts. If there are any more Elven Tears, that would be the place."

"Flowerdown?" The female druid must have known of its existence, too. *Those sigils drawn on her table, they meant Flowerdown, not orchid below.* I hit my forehead for being so stupid. Lougha gives me a curious look.

"Did the druidess ask of Flowerdown?" I ask urgently.

"She demanded directions from me, but I played dumb. I did not care for her tone. She sounded... hollow." He gives me a questioning look. "Did I do right?"

The barrows atop the Flowerdown Ridge are easy to spot in the light of the setting sun. Each barrow resembles an upturned green bowl from a distance. Once we arrive within the burial grounds, we find more than two score barrows. The trees along the edge of the ridge were once the northern boundary of the Arden. Now they are a dwindling reminder of better days. There are many trees beyond, but they are young and supple still, not like the commanding exemplars of the south.

"Why do only some of the mounds have a small ditch and rampart around them?" Figol asks.

"I suspect no one alive today knows that answer. When the elves return in our future lives, we can ask them."

Figol meanders around the graves. I make for the forest's edge. There is a stately oak whose thick branches leave much of the ground in shadow. It had been split early in its life, which is why it still stands.

If I were an elf, I would stand under this tree to mourn the fallen. Only the oak has a chance of outliving an elf, as the saying goes. I change into a squirrel and run up the tree.

"Uncle, are these the silly flowers you're seeking?" Figol is in the deepest shadows of the forest where scarcely any light penetrates. I dash from limb to limb until I'm over top of my nephew. I run down the tree and transform as soon as my feet touch the ground.

"Thank the nameless gods of the elves." Five delicate yellow-and-pink flowers have emerged from five even less substantial stems. "How could you see these in such darkness?"

"I don't know. I looked down and there they were. They aren't very impressive, are they?"

"The elves are an understated race. They were never ones to flaunt themselves like the giants, or at least that's what the ballads claim." I cut the flowers even with the ground using my bone knife.

"I can make you a real bladed knife with a leather grip so that you don't have to touch the metal," Figol offers.

"It's not as if I would break out with infections if I touch iron. This bone knife came from nature and it will go back to nature." I cut the last stem. "And it performs rather well."

131

"Why didn't you dig them up, like the Black Lord did?"

"As a druid, I seek to do as little as possible to disturb nature. And with any luck, no trace of them will be found if the Obsidian Mage and his druid come searching here."

12

Sallying Forth to Sarum

The Seventh Dark Day of Edrin, 819

Forty-nine Days until Samhain

Figol should never have been exposed to all of this. Once we reach the hillfort of Sarum, I must send him back to his parents. It's best for him and I don't want my brother chasing me all over Southern Pretanni as I try to fulfill my quest.

The Londinjon Road extends from Venta to the unending hills of the southern plains. Packed earth from wagon tracks makes up the meandering westward road. Lore says that the giants felled any number of trees from the Arden to create this expanse. There are no clouds in the sky, leaving us to the unrelenting warmth of Belenos. Each step is monotonously repeated over the rolling hills of grass.

A lone merchant with a brightly dyed cart nearly overtakes us before we're even aware of him. For the life of me, I can't imagine how we didn't hear him coming. The curious man with a hooked nose makes a florid bow from his perch as his two sturdy ponies draw him down the road. The gray streaks in his otherwise jet-black hair leap out under the post midday sun.

"Greetings, noble druid. Would you and your student like to take a load off your feet and join me?" His honest face and excessive gestures make me like him immediately.

"Thank you, good merchant. Where are you headed?"

He places his hand over top his eyes with an exaggerated gesture and faces behind him. He swings his head dramatically in the opposite direction to the road before him. "I'm headed westward, it would seem."

I can't help but smile at his foolishness. "Then we will be happy to rest our weary feet."

He leans down, and with a firm grip he pulls me up on to the two-man bench. Figol jumps into the back of the cart. The red and yellow dyed Auroch hide stretches taut above it. The deep shadows obscure the man's wares. Figol makes his way through the barely visible crates and stuffed leather bags until he's right behind us. With a flick of his wrists, our benefactor asks his ponies to quicken their pace to a trot.

In a nasally voice, he says, "My friends call me Blachstenius, and I am a friend to every honest traveler and trader."

"Then you must have many travelers and few traders as friends."

He chuckles good naturedly. "I always ask about the roads and the cities they connect. I currently have the finest linen garments in all of Pretanni with me from the Atrebates. So where might you be going to and is there profit in me going there?"

He reaches back next to Figol and hands me a fine linen robe. I inspect it closely. Mother made finer tunics, but my tired feet keep me from sharing the insight.

"The Atrebates continue to ask when the druids will return to their lands."

"What?"

"The druids left for the west and none have returned. The Wigesta have begun to ferry more men to the eastern coast from the mainland and your druid folk have left the war chiefs to fight alone."

"Never! The druids are caretakers of all Pretanni."

"I mean no disrespect, but as I said, the druids have been recalled to the sacred isle of Ynys Mona."

"I have heard nothing of this. Surely there is an explanation." My head spins. Which is more concerning, that the druids have left or that this common trader knows that Nemeton Dywyll Derw, our most sacred and secret site, is on Ynys Mona?

"For now, the Wigesta and the Sorim are fighting for control of Londinjon. Each maintains control of one shore of the great trading city. Unless one side foolishly decides to escalate the conflict by attacking rival trading ships, the sides will settle down to an uneasy truce again. When that time comes, they will begin taking more Atrebates and Silurian land."

"This is too strange to be believed, though I sense no falsehood in you. I must bring word of this to my master."

"Even now some of the Sorim use their power indiscriminately." He glances back in the cart but Figol refuses to meet his eye. "The disrespect for the common folk among some of the Sorim is the ugliest of failings. Some feel no shame about controlling others simply because they can."

"Are the Sorim our biggest threat?" I ask. Boswen rarely spoke of the wider issues, and never in depth.

"The Wigesta may fight for land, but at least they still respect druids. On the mainland, druids are advisors to kings, not the protectors of nature. Power is what they strive for. Either side would put Pretanni under the yoke if they can, but the Sorim would make you believe it is for the best."

"Then we have two enemies to contend with," I say, dejected.

Blachstenius grimaces. "I'm afraid you have three. The demon summoners, the Tusci as they call themselves, are the vilest of people. Their numbers are always small, since they fight amongst themselves for prestige and rank. They believe themselves greater than the common man, so they think it proper to enslave the weak. I have seen one demon duel and I never wish to see another." He shudders at the recollection.

"Aye, the demon lords are hard for us to battle since iron is anathema to us, yet it is the weapon most deadly to demons. But in the time of Bodmin, all the tribes of Pretanni united and the demon summoners were driven from our land."

Blachstenius nods. "They were driven back, but they are still a menace that— Stop!" Blachstenius roars. He lets the reins go slack.

"Did I offend?" I ask, bewildered.

"Pardon me, I was focused elsewhere," he says, distracted. "You are right to worry about the Sorim for now. The undisciplined can cause havoc." He keeps his gaze locked in front of us, his jaw set.

I scan the rolling grassland but see no one within leagues of us. I turn to Figol, but he's unconscious and drooling from the corner of his mouth.

"I apologize for doing that to your charge, but he would not refrain from using his mental powers. He will be out for a good while."

"Do you also have the mental gift?" I ask.

136

"I do, though I only use it to protect myself. It is something the young master would be wise to practice."

"Has he been manipulating us this whole time?"

"Not us, you."

I'd already forgotten about splitting from him at Sarum. I clench my jaw. How am I supposed to recommend him to become a druid when he spends his time on his other magic?

Blachstenius rests his hand on my knee. "It is not the worst offense to want to stick with you. He admires you greatly. Still, always bending another's will for your own can lead one down a dark path." He looks me square in the eye. "What do you plan to do, now that you are not being nudged in any particular direction?"

"He was only to show me the road to Solent Keep. Yet he is still with me half a month later." I knew that he would scan my mind, but I had nothing to hide from him so I didn't worry, but to be manipulated the whole time? "I need to send Figol back to my brother at Mai Dun. Then I will go north to Sarum."

"A druid who frequents cities? You have managed to surprise me," Blachstenius says. He glances at me from head to toe. "I would guess that you are a newly minted druid. Your robe is so very clean that I suspect you are on your initial quest."

"You're using your powers."

"No, I'm just observant. I avoid over-relying on my mental gifts. Paying close attention to those around you often tells more than my powers can. How do you think I've remained safe all these years on my own?"

I stand up to better see the road ahead of us. I long to be under a lush canopy of trees. I feel exposed on this road with nothing but grassy hills surrounding me.

Blachstenius clears his throat. "If I may comment on what I've observed? You do not have the bearing of a plains druid. I would think you are from the west or even the far southwest. Why do you not go there?"

It is rare for me to trust someone so quickly, but I can detect no deception in this trader. "The Obsidian Mage of Solent Keep has taken an interest in me. I'd rather have Sarum and its high walls between the Dark Lord and me."

"The Dark Lord? Indeed." He scratches his beard. "Why would Rhunior take an interest with a questing druid?"

"Rhunior? You know the name of the Lord of Solent Keep?"

"When you have traveled as long and far as I have, you learn things that others would prefer you not know."

There is a jagged tree line two hills in front of us. It can only mean that a river is present. The plains are too dry for trees otherwise. "Is that Sarum up ahead?" I point to an unnaturally flat-topped hill to the north.

"It is. If memory serves, we will need to pass the Solent-Sarum road. About a league farther, we'll leave the road and ford the river at the shallows. No one maintains the Solent-Sarum Bridge any longer."

"Are you sure about the bridge?"

"I am. And even if it was only in need of minor repair, you druids still forgo the use of iron, yes?"

"Yes."

He looks back at the sleeping Figol. "Then these old bones would be stuck doing most of the work. That doesn't hold much appeal for me."

The grass is trampled as we reach the ford. The muddy slope makes the horses nervous. I'm forced to lead the horses at a gentle walk.

"If there is this much movement, you would think someone would fix the bridge. The bank is not far from becoming a muddy disaster," I say

"Yes, it does seem as if there has been a large uptick in travel between the two cities. . . ." His voice trails off and he tries to make sense of what he sees. "Grahme, look at the tracks in the mud. What do you see?"

I walk among the muddy slope on our side of the river. "I see feet, both man and horse, mostly going north. I don't see any cart tracks though."

"Traders always have carts." Blachstenius squints at the evening sun. "We could push on to Sarum before nightfall, but I think it better to camp off the road for the night and see what the morning brings. Let's ford the river and make our camp in the woods a bit."

Figol wakes after the camp is set up and our dinner prepared. A touch groggy perhaps, but otherwise he looks fine.

"Grahme will be departing us for Sarum in the morning. What are your plans?" Blachstenius asks.

"I'm staying with my family." Figol moves next to me at the fire. Blachstenius lets the declaration go unchallenged.

"This is my quest, Figol," I say softly. "Your part was essential to my success, but it is over."

"No, you can't mean that," he sputters. "Who will protect you from mental attacks?" His eyes dart over to Blachstenius and back.

"I mean to go north and speak with my brethren about what we learned of Solent Keep. You were only to show me the road to that city, after all. Your father will never forget this."

"But I want to become a druid, not a blacksmith."

Blachstenius stares off in the distance, feigning disinterest.

"Figol, will you help me collect the skins and refill them with fresh water?" I ask.

Once we are out of earshot, Figol tries a different approach.

"Uncle, he is a very powerful mage. If I were to leave you, he could mess with your thoughts at will."

"Like you have been doing this whole trip?"

"That was different, we're family. I was only doing it because I knew you would need my help."

Maybe one of us believes that.

"Figol, I am going north tomorrow and you and Blachstenius are going west. If you stay with him, he will take you to the heart of the druid land." I put up a finger to stop his protests before they start. "I am going north, away from anyone who might tamper with my thoughts."

He turns away from my gaze. "Then tell me how I can become a druid?"

"I will see if our friend is willing to take you to Lord Boswen or Lord Caradoc. Tell them of your desire and tell them of your other gift. They are druid lords. Do not try to use your power to influence them. If you're caught, I honestly do not know how far their anger would go. I can give you no more guidance than that."

"I'm worried for you."

"If I am unable to take care of myself by now, it's better that my essence leaves the world for a time and tries again in a future body."

He stomps off back to camp. At least he knows when to stop arguing.

13

Disturbance at Sarum

The Eighth Dark Day of Edrin, 819

Forty-eight Days until Samhain

Old Sarum stands out among hillforts because of the height of its walls. Mai Dun has six ramparts, but it is not as tall as Sarum and its two. The earthworks reach higher into the insubstantial air than even the ancient oaks of the Arden. Below the man-shaped mound is a sprawling market that spreads well out from the main gate. From this distance, the rush of activity looks like a colony of ants scurrying about their anthill. A massive wooden gate rests at ground level at the only cut in the packed clay walls. Adventurous sheep dot the steep hills, searching out elusive grasses.

The outskirts of the market are filled with tanners and shoemakers, based on the stench. Hundreds of deer and ox hides are stretched on racks to dry in the sun. As I get closer, the fine linen and wool merchants take over. The farmers with their produce are closest to the gates.

"You'll need a fine woolen robe come winter, I'd guess," a merchant woman shouts at me. Her ample body is barely restrained by her own smock.

"And how do you know that I don't already possess such a garment?"

"The young never plan ahead," she chuckles. "As a druid, you refuse to carry coin, don't you?"

"You are correct, dear merchant. So, I have nothing to give you for such fine wares."

"Come closer to Ol' Dorit," she leers. "I'll whisper to you what I will require." She cackles in devious delight. I bow slightly and try the other side of the stalls. Her coarse laughter turns into a hacking, coughing fit.

"She's a lustful woman in need of a man," a disapproving voice says.

I turn to see a jumpy little bald man obsessively refolding his wares as he scans the crowd.

"Everyone knows that it's better to have a warm wool straight cloth. It can be used as a blanket or a cloak. I can even throw in a cloak pin if you don't have one."

"Alas, I carry no coin. So how are we to reach an agreement?" I ask.

He leans forward before cocking his head sideways to check on Ol' Dorit. "If you could make me a potion to send her affections my way . . . ."

I stand up straight. "I have studied under the master alchemist Gwalather of Land's End and I can assure you that no working love potion has ever been devised."

"But not more than seven days ago a merchant offered one to me. I've been cross with myself for not buying it ever since."

"Take solace in the fact that you were not swindled. I would offer you some advice though, for free."

"Oh?" His eyes grow big in anticipation.

"If you were to march over there and let her know that you have the experience to please her in ways the young men have never imagined, I bet you would get better results than from some worthless potion." I smile knowingly.

He flashes a wolfish grin. It seems I will make two people happy today.

"You have done me a great service, noble one, so I will try to repay the favor." He surveys the crowd again. "You should leave now, and not return," he whispers.

"But I've just arrived."

"Things aren't the same here of late." He motions me to keep my voice down. "The armed men have doubled here in the last few months and honest townsfolk like me are no longer allowed up top." He hides his finger from the guards as he points toward the hillfort. "Even to give payment to Brigantia."

"Too many people look to the goddess of prosperity for all their desires. Perhaps you should go to the plains, start a bonfire, and make offerings to Artaius. It is his protection over the sheep that allow you to sell you wool cloaks."

"But prosperity is what matters most to a merchant." The funny little man shakes his head in disgust. "Before the soldiers changed, it was easier to pay the priestess to intercede on my behalf."

"Then you're wasting your coin. We druids tend the relationship with the gods and never would we accept payment."

"The priestess only deals with Brigantia, so I trust that she knows what the goddess desires from us. But I tell you, something is not right up there. I have a friend in the guard who I've known since childhood. He would come join me in the tavern whenever he could, until two months ago. Now that a new leader is in charge, my friend acts as if he doesn't know me. The demands on we poor merchants keep increasing. Would they even let us into the fort if attacked?" He shakes his head, answering his own question. "These are bad times, druid."

"Perhaps I should go up top and see what I can find out."

"'Tis better for you to leave before trouble finds you." He nods his head at the pounded earth ramp. A large man with four spearmen in tow is descending from the fort. "Mark my words, they are coming for you."

The common folk spend their lives living in fear. They fear their kings and the armies; they fear the weather and they fear sickness. Every season brings a new dread. Once you learn to listen to nature and live with her, those fears melt away. I stand in the middle of the road, awaiting my escort.

It's not long before the mountain of a man steps in front of his spearmen and bows his head to me. The market has gone silent around us. "Druid friend, would you please accompany us to the top?" His great baritone voice fills the area. "Our war leader wishes to speak with you."

"Please, lead the way." I catch Ol' Dorit's smug face. She quickly breaks eye contact and resumes heckling potential customers. The din of commerce restarts as we retreat from the market. The four guards surround me, forming an honor guard as we follow the barrel-chested commander.

"Who is the war leader here?" The soldiers march in step with one another, eyes straight ahead. No one acknowledges my question.

The leader signals ahead and the massive wooden gates creak open. A narrow path cuts through the earthwork and ascends

145

upward. Moor ponies on either side of the doors are ordered to reverse their course and the gates boom closed behind us.

The path leads us through the first rampart and between the forests of sharpened branches pointing downward. We descend to the second gate protecting the only excavated path up along the higher earthen wall. Smaller and less grand than the bottom gate, it serves as a platform for archers.

"This is an impressive fortress," I say. The burly leader grunts and continues his pace. The four men around me stare impassively forward, not a single talker among them.

The path cuts another narrow opening between the towering embankments. The canyon-like earthen walls deaden nearly all sound, making the procession feel like a funeral march. The gray clouds overhead only enhance the mood. The third gate is more akin to the first, monumental, imposing and closed. The leader signals a stop before approaching the gate alone. After a brief conversation, the man returns.

The final gate creaks open. A square, wooden building sits a mere ten paces from the gate, obscuring the view of camp. A life-sized depiction of a raven-haired woman and her cauldron are scrawled upon the front of the building. I can only assume that this blighted construction is the alleged temple of Brigantia—as if a goddess so powerful would be bound to such a paltry construct.

Our non-communicative leader reports to another man, who has his own four guards, swordsmen this time, standing behind him. Unlike the rest of his pockmarked men, he wears no armor or weapon. His smooth, baby face is a clear indication of a life free of disease or hardship.

"We will escort him from here." He raises his fist above his shoulder and one of his men produces iron shackles.

146

"What's this?" I raise my staff in a defensive posture.

"My apologies, good druid," Babyface says. "But before we can take you to see the war chief, we must make sure that you will be unable to harm him. So please, surrender your staff and allow us to place these on your wrists."

"Everyone must be so bound?" Never have I heard of a druid being treated as such.

"It is unsettling, I admit. Common folk are merely disarmed; however, as a druid, we require the iron manacles to ensure that your formidable powers are also restrained."

"Who so fears druids that he must bind them as if they are serious criminals?"

His men all share the same blank expression.

"We are living in strange times," he says apologetically.

Sensing no choice, I comply. "I will speak to your leader about this treatment."

The burly man and his guards depart and Babyface's men escort me around the temple. The camp is bustling with activity. Men are advancing in rows during mock battles instead of the screaming, reckless charge that so intimidates the opponent.

"We are changing the way in which we fight," Babyface says. "It is my contribution." The obvious pride in his voice makes me want to laugh out loud. Living a life of ease, he has clearly never experienced a crazed, blood-lusting charge so common on this island.

There is an island of sorts in the center of the camp. A ditch thrice the height of a man, and equally wide, surrounds a stout wooden building. The construction is clearly superior to the disgrace of a hut they erected for Brigantia. *This war chief must be the suspicious type.* The bridge to the commander's hut consists of two halves, each pointing upward to the sky.

Upon a signal by Babyface, the guards unbind each half. The sections meet in the center, perfectly connecting above the dry moat. We don't even change our gait as we march across.

One of the soldiers takes a key from around his neck and unlocks the door. Everyone stares at me expectantly. *Now that I'm chained, they wish to show me deference?* I stride forward confidently into the darkened building.

A guard shoves me from behind and I end up sprawled on the floor. A knee is driven between my shoulder blades and at once the men are claiming all my possessions, save my robe and shoes.

"Rise," Babyface says after the thievery is complete.

I jump to my feet and see the four guards, swords drawn, between me and Babyface. "Into the cell, prisoner, or my men will skewer you for sport."

Words fail me. The men lower their swords in unison and advance.

"You're Sorim."

Babyface smirks at me.

Afraid to turn my back on the entranced guards, I steadily give ground until I'm forced into a cell. The iron grate slams shut.

Babyface comes to the cell, filled with glee. "The Obsidian Mage of Solent Keep has an interest in druids, for some reason. I will be well rewarded for capturing another of your kind."

"You serve the Black Lord?" My knees start to buckle. If Sarum has fallen, there is nothing to stop the Obsidian Mage from over-running the plains and capturing Men Meur Kov Keigh. "How could you betray your own kind?"

He smiles at me. "It's best to serve on the winning side." He and his men depart, leaving me with only my despair.

14

Escape by Moonlight

The Eleventh Light Day of Edrin, 819

Thirty-two Days until Samhain

Having thrown my shoes at the guards days ago, I have nothing but my robe and manacles left. My plan to rush the first guard that enters my cell is a source of self-derision now. No one has entered my cell. No one has asked me any questions. Twice a day guards wordlessly place bread and a waterskin inside my cell. I crave eye contact or some other small acknowledgment of my existence. If not for one tiny opening in the wall below the thatch roof, I would be totally cut off from nature. I let the morning light hit my eyes. I barely have time to pray before Belenos is lost from view until the next day.

The bridge to my cell slams together. It's not time for the second meal of the day. *Have they finally come to interrogate me?* My heart starts racing as the door creaks open, flooding the building with beautiful, blinding light. A man is being dragged into my dismal home, but I can't make out more. I stand at the front of the cell, allowing the light to strike my whole body. For the moment, I feel alive again.

"Don't put me in with a filthy druid." The half-conscious man yells. He stirs a bit more and tries to break free of his captors. "They're cannibals! He'll kill me when I sleep. He'll eat me!"

"Would you prefer to go to the King's Mark?" Babyface asks.

His oily voice sends a shiver down my back.

"Please," the man says desperately. "Please, not with the druid."

Babyface smiles his malicious grin as he points the men in my direction. "Put him in with the druid."

"No, you can't do that to me!" The man makes himself hoarse as he is forced toward my cell. I step back without being told. I know that he'll be bodily thrown in once the door is opened. He lands face first on the ground as the door slams shut. The man freezes as the guards retreat. Once the door closes, he screams in his ragged voice until the guards are out of earshot.

He turns to face me. "You are Grahme, are you not?"

The thrill of having someone speak to me turns into suspicion. "How do you know my name?" The man is in a dirty servant's smock. His beard is unkempt, and he reeks of ale.

"This is the second time we've met at a jail of the Obsidian Lord."

"Alfswich?"

He smiles at me. "At your service. I must say, I don't like your old clothes."

"Why are you here?"

"Much like you, I wager, I thought this was in Silures hands. I came to sell some of the gemstones I acquired from Solent Keep."

"Why the servant's robes and why the ale? It's not even midday."

"The ale is worn, not consumed and it's to make the buyer overconfident. As for the robes, they were supposed to protect me if I got caught. Being a servant, I could always pin the crime on a wealthy merchant."

I wasn't prepared for a mental duel so that fat child of a soldier struck at me first."

"I'm afraid your thieving days are over now. Just like my quest to become a druid is doomed to failure."

"Why haven't you turned into a bird and flown away?"

I raise my hands and show him my shackles. "Iron interferes with a druid's powers."

"Is that all? Why haven't you gotten out of the manacles and left before now?"

"Because I can't use my powers." *His mind must still be fuzzy.*

His white teeth gleam in the darkness. "I think we can find a common cause once more."

Belenos and his fiery chariot signal morning has arrived. I slip in through a crack in the prison wall. I change back into human form and Alfswich slams the manacles back on me.

"Cutting it close, aren't we?" Alfswich asks.

I cut off his banter. "The Obsidian Lord is coming here tomorrow."

Alfswich's smile fades. He tugs on his mustache. "By the gods, I'm dead." He stares at me with horror.

"I think there is a way out for us both."

"You believe there is a way, do you? You have a way out for *both* of us?"

152

"I swore to tell you the truth. I wish you wouldn't—"

The bridge slams down. Our morning meal is arriving. We separate to opposite corners. I fix Alfswich with a hateful stare.

The door opens and the sunlight blinds us. "They're both still breathing, so neither of us wins today," one of the guards says.

"They'll wish they had taken care of each other before long."

They both chuckle. The short guard throws a loaf of bread in the middle of the cell. They have been trying to get us to fight over food since Alfswich's arrival. We eye each other warily but neither of us makes a move for the bread. Irritated, the guard unties the waterskin and drops it just inside the bars. Alfswich throws a handful of dirt at me and dives for the water. I make for the bread and we continue to glare at each other.

"I don't believe either of them knows how to fight," the fat guard says. In disgust, they turn and leave.

Once the door closes, we come together and share our meal.

"It's not fair that they never strike you with the bottom of their spears," I say. The water is always left closer to me, but I take a beating when I go for it.

"You're right and it's not likely to ever happen." Alfswich taps the side of his head. He takes a huge bite out of his half of the bread. "And you have to go for it; otherwise, they'll wonder how you can survive without water."

"So, you're fine with them striking me?"

Alfswich shrugs.

I hold my arms up and Alfswich deftly picks the locks. I drop to the floor and sketch out the camp in the dirt. "They still have five guards around the dry moat at all times, two to man the bridge to the west and three archers on the sides and back of the building."

"That's not going to change tonight."

"No, and you are going to have to use your mind magic to get off this prison island."

"They're not all in a direct line of sight and they're spread out too much. I can't control all five of them at once."

I wave away his objections for now. "The men have erected a low wooden wall to keep the townspeople from entering the camp. The guards are going to be stationed behind the wall in case the crowd gets too excited. The townspeople are allowed up at dusk to perform their blasphemous two-day rites to Brigantia. The equinox belongs to no god, so any such invocation is nonsensical. It is only we druids who mark this day."

I stop and take a breath to keep myself from ranting. *Focus on what you need to do.* "At nightfall, the day before the autumnal equinox begins and everyone will be focused on the meaningless rituals. Most of the guards will have their backs to us, so we'll use that time to escape."

"That must eat you up, that the common folk are communing directly with the gods."

"If it allows us to live, then I will find one redeeming factor in this city's impiety."

"So how are we getting out of here?" Alfswich asks.

I kneel down next to where our one tiny ray of sunlight hits the floor and I draw my plan in the dirt. "At sunset, everyone will be gathered around the temple to celebrate the equinox festival." I draw a box to mark the temple. "I'll be in bat form, so you'll have to slip out between the wall and thatch on the north wall and shimmy into the dry moat without being seen. The noise from the crowd will mask any noise you make, hopefully."

"Is that all?"

"No." I flash an apologetic grin. "You'll have to take care not to be seen by the archers on either side, at the same time you're mentally controlling the rear archer . . . you're going to climb up the ditch directly underneath his feet."

"Oh, I really don't like this part. I'll never see the kill shot that's coming for me."

I shrug. If we had more time, we could come up with a better plan. "Everyone should be at the ceremony, so I'll turn back to human and release the animals from their pens as an added distraction."

"A distraction doesn't do us any good if we can't leave the hillfort."

"I'm getting to that. I will meet you at the treasury, between the war leader's house and the warriors' camp."

"What then? You fly away and leave me to fend off the whole fort?"

"No," I say with exaggerated patience. "We'll use the escape tunnel next to the warriors' camp."

"What escape tunnel?"

"I spotted it early last night, but I couldn't check it out until right before daybreak. There's a drop of two to three times my height, then a tunnel that goes underneath both ramparts and exits on the western side of this place."

"The war leader has a bolt hole?" Alfswich pumps his fists in the air. "So, we will make it out of here alive."

I give him his moment of celebration before I finish my plan. "There are a couple problems we have to overcome first."

Aine is well up in the sky as Belenos takes his leave. Her bright glow will make our escape that much harder. Her next rise will be special, Aine at her full brilliance on the equinox. One would be lucky to see it happen three times in their life.

I flutter out of the small opening between the stone wall and thatch roof and scout the area. Bats have terrible sight, but they have a magic all their own for navigating at night. A tall bonfire sends tendrils of flame above the temple edifice. The chanting of *priests* and the cheers from the crowd feed off one another. I fly right in front of the rear guard's face; he doesn't even flinch. So far, the plan is going smoothly.

Alfswich drops down from the newly enlarged opening and slides into the ditch. He freezes, waiting for the kill shot. His brown robe stands in stark contrast to the chalky dirt walls. When it's clear no arrows are loosed, he begins his slow climb up the trench. Covered in sweat, he reaches the top at the feet of the frozen guard. Alfswich rises to his feet and with an air of confidence signals me to proceed to the next job.

The animal pen is not deserted as it had been the previous two nights. A soldier and a local woman have discovered the privacy the space offers and are busy shedding their clothes, his is a full uniform, so he must be on duty. I land on the gate post. If I open the gate, the guard will be forced to call the alarm. We may not even make it to the tunnel before the base is alerted. I let out a small chirp of annoyance and hope this will be the only part of our plan that goes awry.

The torchlight in the treasury tells me that Alfswich has made it safely to cover. I regain my human form and enter the room. Alfswich greets me with a jeweled dagger ready to throw at my head. He exhales and refocuses on the valuables in front of him. I hadn't considered the possibility of him killing me and escaping alone. Silently, his deft fingers spread out the baubles and the ones that meet his fancy go into his bag.

"Are you going to stand there or are you going to collect your booty?" He holds up a thick golden torc with a smoky yellow gemstone at each end.

"Right, I need to get my possessions."

"This was King Mark's." He shows me the torc from Solent Keep's treasury. "I was caught trying to sell it in the marketplace below. I should have been suspicious when Ol' Dorit led me to a buyer as soon as she saw it."

In the sack it goes, along with a lot of other coins and trifles.

"Will you be able to run with all that?"

"If not, I'll start dropping some as we go. I've never seen a soldier who wouldn't pause a pursuit to pick up treasure."

I scanned the room and spot my pack. Opening it, I see that the orchids are badly damaged. I spread them out on the table as neatly as I can. I utter a simple restoration spell. The orchids glimmer for an instant before the brilliance ripples from the bottom to the top, reconnecting the plant tissue. Once whole again, the flowers pulse with a dim white light. A second ripple begins at the bottom and I gasp in horror as the flowers all turn to stone. A drop of water is released from the center of each stone flower.

"More stone flowers? Stop staring and grab what you need."

Deflated, I realize that I have failed my quest. I scoop up the stone flowers and put them in my pouch. Maybe Boswen will be lenient for once. And maybe the tides will halt their rhythms, too.

I scan the camp and carefully take my first step out of the building.

Alfswich grabs my arm. "Can't do that, if anyone sees you, they'll know you're guilty of something. Walk purposefully to the bolt hole."

I feel exposed, but I do as he says. Not daring to speak, I point to our exit. Alfswich scoffs as he flips over the wooden cover and his first whiff reveals the unpleasantness of my plan.

"This is a latrine."

"No, well, yes, it is at times. The tunnel goes all the way to the base of the hillfort, but apparently the warriors do use it as an extra latrine, too."

His moonlit face shows his disgust for my plan. After a moment, he shrugs. "At least my smock is brown. You're pretty white robe is about to be badly soiled." He smirks at me before splashing in the dirty puddle below. I drop a reed light down to him. He uses his sparking stones and lights the reed easily.

I scan the camp thoroughly. No one has sounded the alarm. I give silent thanks to Brigantia and Aine before I transform into a bat and fly into the tunnel. *My robes will not be getting badly soiled.*

The reed light is bouncing up and down ahead of me. Alfswich didn't bother to wait for me. I continue my flight until I'm right on his shoulder, then I retake my human form.

"You can be very stealthy," he says without breaking his stride. "I didn't hear you approach."

I fall in beside him. The tunnel opens up to a grassy slope ending at the burbling River Avon. There is nary a tree to provide cover and Aine's light feels so very harsh to my eyes.

"Your white robe will give us away in this moonlight."

"Make for those trees," I point north of the river. "I'll meet you there."

I wait for him to cross the fields and make it to safety before I become a bat once more and join him.

"Neat trick," he says grudgingly. "What now?"

"We go into the River Avon. If they do find our trail, they'll lose it again where we enter the river."

"And we can clean this filth off of us." The shit has splattered all over his legs and smock. He looks me up and down. "Why don't you have any shit on you?"

"I took the bat form to enter the tunnel and avoided your fate." I don't even try to keep the smugness out of my voice.

"Then how did you put the lid back to cover our escape?"

"I hadn't thought of that." I shrug. "They will most likely assume that the last person to use it as a latrine didn't replace the lid."

"And if they happen to see my footprints below? Do you think they'll ignore that, too? You've pointed them in the very direction that we're fleeing."

"Keep your voice down," I urge. "I hadn't thought of that, but there's nothing to be done about it now. It's all the more reason to get moving."

Alfswich clenches his jaw in anger and closes his eyes.

"One last thing before we go," I add.

"What?"

"Can I see that dagger you readied to throw at me when I entered the treasury?"

He opens his sack and retrieves the dagger. "I thought you druids forswore the use of metal."

"We have."

He hands it and the sheath to me. The embroidery on the leather is impressive. I see the oyster rock embedded in the base of the handle. I draw the blade and note the keen edge.

"A princely gift."

"Indeed."

"Thank you, Aine and thank you, Brigantia, please accept our offering." I fling the dagger as far downriver as I can.

Alfswich curses me in low tones. He takes a step toward me, his fists balled. "What the hell was that?"

"We must give thanks to the goddesses who aided us in our escape. I have nothing to give, so I asked for something that I knew was not yours to begin with."

"What about those stone flowers you took?"

I didn't realize he'd noticed. "I must keep them . . . for a different purpose for which I may not speak."

We follow the river north. After only a league or so, Alfswich declares us safe.

"Give me your waterskin; I'll fill them both up," he says.

"Thanks, I couldn't find my stave in the treasure room; I'll look for one now."

I return with a stout oak branch, but Alfswich is missing. I search and find my pack by the shore. He didn't even leave me a waterskin.

"I guess our partnership is over once again."

I must go north and warn the plains druids that Sarum has fallen. This news is more important than my quest. I hang my head, knowing that I continue to get further and further away from completing my quest, but it cannot be helped.

I grab my gear and realize that my pack is very light. The five stone flowers have vanished, like my future with the druids.

15

The Battle at the Giant's Choir

The Equinox, Last Day of Edrin, 819

Thirty Days until Samhain

I could have spent days walking aimlessly on these plain searching for the Giant's Choir, but I calmed my mind and sensed the subtle pull of the holy site. By midday, I stand in awe of Men Meur Kov Keigh, as it's called in the old language.

The massive standing stones form a great circle topped by equally heavy lintels. It could only have been constructed by giants. The lore tells us on the equinoxes and solstices the giants would stand between the stones and sing as one powerful voice to their gods. No one alive today can name those gods; they left this land with the giants to their new home, across the Endless Sea.

The main path to the stone circle is lined by earthen banks and shallow ditches. The air has a charge to it and the very ground pulses with energy. The animals must sense the thrumming power of the holy site, for the hills are empty of creatures great and small.

Why *haven't the plains druids assembled here on this most auspicious of days?* I scale the central trilithon and search the sky in vain for any druids in avian form. How could they pass on a day with a full moon and the equinox?

A group of horsemen approach from the grassy path leading to the circle. A man in black is astride a great gray horse leading a group of mounted warriors. I've seen that horse before. A chill runs down my spine. The Obsidian Mage is here. Next to him is the female druid.

My heart begins to race. Scanning the horizon, I see only a few tendrils of black smoke off to the west. I am all that stands between the Dark Mage and the Giant's Choir. I don't know what the mage's plans are, but I dare not allow him to enter this ring. *But how can I stop him?* The evening sky grows darker as Aine begins her rise in the east. The druidess rides forward and points me out to the mage. They stop their advance. There is only a shallow dip between us. They could cover the ground and reach the stone circle in only a score of heartbeats at full gallop.

Time stretches stretch by as neither they nor I move.

The man in black nods his head toward me and the warriors take out their bows in unison. The group advances. First their steeds, then their bodies disappear from view as they near the bottom of the depression. I scan the sky nervously once again hoping in vain for aid. Even Belenos is retreating from the sky. I am all alone.

Their heads reappear as they make the last climb. Anger and fear cause my whole body to tighten. The breeze alerts me to the cold sweat all over me.

I know not if it is the retreating Belenos or the ascending Aine who quiets my mind. With perfect clarity, I know my purpose. *They will not take this place while I still breathe.*

I raise my arms and start the rain chant, biting off each syllable with a cold fury. The wind picks up behind me and it whispers through the stones. The clouds heed my call, and they race to me from the southwest.

"Continue, if you dare," I shout before resuming my chants.

The warriors march on with a slow, methodical pace.

Fat raindrops splatter on the stones around me. I take courage in every drop and compel the storm to intensify. The cold rain begins streaking down now, causing me to go numb. The intruders are barely visible at fifty paces as the rain falls in frigid sheets. The horses become nervous, but the men are able to control their mounts.

The druidess dismounts, lays a calming hand on her horse and walks forward a few strides. I can feel her counter-chanting, sapping the fury from the storm. I bark out the holy words over the thumping of the rain until my voice becomes ragged. The clouds collide and I can feel the hair on my arms stand up. Godsfire begins to flash from cloud to cloud. I know what my next command must be. At last, the power of the storm has been fully manifested.

I point to the counter-chanter, and scream "Strike!" with what voice I still have.

Thunder booms as the flash of light blinds us all. The horses trumpet their fear, and I can hear riders grunting as they hit the ground. The pounding of hooves recedes as the horses wisely run from my wrath. I blink away the lightning's afterimage from my eyes. The rain pours down and when I at last can see the field before me, there is but one rider left on his horse. Still as a stone, his eyes are locked on to me.

How dare anyone brave this onslaught. The wind picks up around me, pressing my soaked robe tight against my back and my legs. The front of my robe whips and snaps in the wind. The rain flies straight into the black rider's unflinching face. I urge the storm on until tiny hailstones start pelting the ground around the stone circle. Still, the man in black and his massive gray warhorse remain calm before my wrath.

I choke out "Strike!" with the last of my voice.

The wrath of the gods descends with such ferocity that the ground itself is thrown up in all directions.

The heavy clouds have obscured the remaining rays of Belenos. It is only with the storm's sporadic lightning that I can see the battlefield clearly. Tiny tendrils of smoke attempt to rise from the newly formed crater.

I lower my arms and whisper prayers of thanks to whichever of the gods came out to aid me this night. The rain eases, settling into a soft, steady patter. The field before me is free of enemies.

I leave my perch to survey the damage. The druidess and her charred horse lay hopelessly broken in the grass. Her entire left side is barely recognizable. The pungent smell of burned meat nearly causes me to puke. I gently touch her right shoulder and say a prayer for her soul's safe travel.

Several paces behind the druid, I inspect the scorched grass around the hole. There are no remnants of either the mage or his mount. Peering at the hole, only the beginning of a muddy puddle is within. *Strange; godsfire may burn, but it does not consume entirely.*

There is precious little I can do now, so I choose to attend my brethren. I check her possessions, making sure there is no iron upon her skin. Only heretics and traitors are given iron in death.

The druidess' saddlebag contains only one bit of cloth, rolled up tight. Grabbing the end of the cloth, I pull it upward and let it unroll. As the last of the cloth is exposed, a ghost orchid falls into my outstretched hand.

I fall backward, laughing at the unlikeliest of objects. The rain mixes with my tears of joy. It's not until the rain has slowed to a misty drizzle that I collect myself. My arms feel ponderously heavy, but I can't give in to my exhaustion yet. I reroll the flower and stuff it into my sack. Looking into her lifeless eyes, I feel shame at laughing next to a fallen druid. I straighten out her legs and set her hands upon her stomach as best I can. I respectfully search her person for more clues.

"Back away from her now or I will brain you." A voice rings out from behind me. Standing above me is a druid, staff raised, ready to strike.

"I am merely searching for answers," I say.

"Back away."

I raise my hands and retreat several steps away from him. My own staff is still within the stone circle, not that it matters. I am too drained to defend myself.

A red kite with a man-sized wingspan lands behind the belligerent druid. In an instant, the bird has morphed into his human form.

"Hold, he's one of us," the man calls.

"I saw him looting Seisyll's body," the first answers, still ready to strike.

Three more red kites land and take their human forms. "We'll sort this out, I promise you," the second druid says. Clearly, he is the one in charge.

"Now, give me your name," he says.

I demand my legs to stop swaying, but they are not up to the task. I spread out my arms to secure my balance. "Forgive me; I'm a bit unsteady on my feet, it seems."

The one in charge clamps his hand on my shoulder, steadying me. He stares intently into my eyes. "Ysella," he says without moving his head, "Find Arthmael. We have need of his healing arts."

Ysella?

Before I can confirm that it is the Ysella from my memory, the man has his nose nearly touching mine. He lifts up my eyelids and studies my eyes from all angles. "Yes, you've severely overextended yourself."

Blinking is all I can manage as a reply.

"You were the one who called that storm, then?" He doesn't wait for me to answer. "You're lucky to be able to stand."

"It was my lightning." I try to sound proud, but it comes out flat. My head starts to fall to the side, and I decide to follow it down. Before I know it, I'm lying on the ground again, next to the druidess I killed.

A third man is kneeling next to me now. He's not belligerent like the first, or bossy like the second. "Not bossy, bossy," I murmur. "He's comforting." He looks at me with a kind drink as he prepares some faces for me to herb.

Why is he so worried? He checks my eyes again and again.

"Drink this," he says.

"I drink it all up and down my throat." I giggle at my own cleverness. The ground feels cool; this would be a good place for a nap.

Funny face slaps me on my cheek. "Drink this first," he says with some urgency.

I sit up and grab the cup with both hands. Funny face won't let go of the cup, though. Why can't I hold the cup by myself?

"Hey," the bossy man claps to get my attention. "Can you tell me your name?"

"I taste peppermint and chamomile. Those are good for stomach ailments and to help one sleep. Why wouldn't you include

167

stinging nettle for energy and the common bladderwrack to . . . augment . . . the . . . ."

"Hey! Not yet, tell me your name first."

"His name is Grahme," the girl druid says.

"You know him?"

"We met at the . . . during Lughnasa."

I smile to myself. It is my friend, Ysella . . . .

16

Dark Days Begin

First Dark Day of Cantl, 819

Twenty-nine Days until Samhain

I t's well past first light and I have no idea where I am. The night's moisture is dripping from the crude lean-to. Several druids are rushing back and forth on their errands. *What happened?* I hear unhurried footsteps getting closer.

"Ah, you are awake?" a middle-aged druid asks. "Sorry our hospitality is so poor, but we have been chasing the Black Mage's men across these hills for the last half month."

The man is familiar, but I can't place him. I scrunch my eyes and blink a few times in an effort to wake up my mind.

"You are still at Men Meur Kov Keigh," he says. "What do you remember from last night?"

"I remember the men approaching on horseback and my calling of the storm . . . it was the Black Mage and his men. I called down lightning. Then I remember being made to drink some misconcocted brew."

The old druid chuckles. "You will no doubt recover your wits with a little more rest. The magic you summoned was as impressive as I have ever seen."

I nod at the compliment.

"It was a reckless thing to do." His countenance grows stern. "On any normal night it would have consumed you."

"I didn't have time to consider the implications."

"Raise your arms for me."

I try, but more than a hand's width from by body, they tremble violently.

"You have been completely drained. You won't be able to summon any power for quite a few days and if you have any sense, you will wait a month or more to fully recover your vitality."

I lower my arms and try to think how I will complete my quest now. If I had an orchid . . . I remember holding a ghost orchid last night. Was that real or a delusion?

"I don't mean to scold," he says, more kindly. "I have no doubt now that this place was the Black Mage's ultimate goal all along. His men were used to draw us away on diversions. We were fortunate that you were here when he approached."

Despite his kind words, I struggle to keep my eyes open.

He pats me on the shoulder as he rises. "Rest a while longer and we'll talk when you have regained your strength. I will ask Ysella to watch you in the meantime." He starts to rise. "And I will keep Arthmael focused on other duties."

"Thank you, Master. Have we met before?"

"I am Cynbel, the leader of the plains druids."

A flash of panic hits me. *The Protector of Men Meur Kov Keigh and member of the Nine.* I try to rise up at least to my elbows. He gestures me to stop.

"No need for all of that. Rest up and we'll speak again after you eat."

Eat? My stomach starts pitching and rolling at the thought. He gives me an amicable smile before leaving.

I sit up and wait for my head to stop spinning. I feel around for my pack, but it's not here. *Where is the orchid?* I jerk my head this way and that.

"Where's my pack?" I call out, trying to keep the fear out of my voice.

"It's here, Grahme," Ysella says from behind the lean-to. "Now relax and let your mind and body recover."

I crane my neck to see from where the voice is coming, just in time to see my leather pouch come flying over. It lands with a thud, barely within reach. I stretch along the ground, grab it, and pull it close to me. No one can see what I'm doing, so I take inventory of my sole possession. Relieved, I toss my bag behind me and lie back down.

Ysella rounds the shelter. "Wake up Grahme," she calls out much louder than needed. She is even more beautiful than I remember. "Arthmael is beside himself because of you," she says with a wicked giggle.

"Why? What did I do?"

"You criticized his restorative—correctly, I might add—and gave a better recipe before falling into unconsciousness."

"I vaguely remember drinking something last night," I say, exhausted.

"You need to get the blood moving if you want to heal. Take my hands."

She pulls me up and practically carries me to a small cooking fire. She ladles an herb and mushroom soup into a wooden bowl and hands it to me. She sits down next to me and I catch a whiff of lavender. I subtly straighten my moustache. I'm simultaneously relieved and appalled that she doesn't notice. Her eyes are glued on the magnificent stone circle instead.

"Arthmael has floundered ever since Seisyll went missing," she says. "He desperately wants to be an herbalist and she was the only one with that kind of knowledge here on the plains. Now she's dead and Arthmael has no one to teach him."

"I studied under a master herbalist for a time; perhaps I can help him."

Ysella snorts. "He's been muttering all night about how his next potion for you will have hemlock in it."

"I should apologize."

"You should stay clear of him if you want to keep your teeth."

"I'm just glad the Obsidian Lord is dead."

The silence stretches out, uncomfortably so.

"Why do you say that?" Ysella asks in a neutral voice.

"When I summoned the storm, he stood there all alone on his horse staring at me. I called down lightning and killed him."

"There were two people killed last night, but Seisyll was the only one killed by lightning. There was a rider who broke his neck when his horse threw him."

"What? I saw the dirt under him fly every which way. There is no way he could have survived that."

Lord Cynbel sees us at the fire and heads back over to us. "Grahme, it's good to see you up and about," he says as he takes a seat on the opposite side of the fire from us. "I only have a few moments before I'm off again."

I hold the bowl with both hands and slowly sip my soup. I struggle to keep even this down. There is something he wishes to say to me, but he doesn't know how.

"You are a bit of a mystery, Grahme," Cynbel says at last. "You wear the white of a druid, yet I am the Caller of the Nine, and I have never called your name to join the ranks of the druids; so, you must be on your druid quest. However, you appear to be rather old to be questing. What am I to make of you?"

"I have not had the straightest of paths." I cough uncomfortably. "I was a student of both Masters Gwalather and Arthyen, but I have finished my studies with Lord Boswen. As you surmised, it has taken longer than normal for me to get to this place."

Cynbel nods, as if I confirmed what he already knew. "So, tell me of your quest."

I set the bowl down and lower my gaze to the base of the fire. "I am unable to speak of it."

Cynbel and Ysella exchange surprised glances.

"Lord, I do not wish to sound impertinent, but how is it that none of your people were here for the conjunction of the full moon and the equinox?"

"Indeed, it was. In any normal year we would have been here honoring the gods and goddesses in grand fashion. However, the Black Mage has been sending multiple raiding parties into the plains for days now. They have been looting and burning whatever unlucky homesteads they find and then fleeing before we can engage them. In fact, it was your storm that finally quenched the last of the fires."

Ysella squeezes my hand again. "We managed to save a family of four because of the rain you caused." She leans in close and rests her head on my shoulder. I can smell lavender again as she gets close.

"I'm glad I was able to do some good."

"So, tell us about last night," Cynbel asks.

"I saw them coming up the grassy path to the Giant's Choir. One or more gods interceded, and I was compelled to bar them from entrance within the circle."

"The gods speak directly to you, do they?" Ysella asks curtly.

I ignore her. "The soldiers drew their bows but approached too cautiously. That allowed me to call the storm before they were within range. One of their number dismounted and started counter-chanting me." I look directly at Cynbel. "I had no other way to stop her, so, so I . . . called down a—"

"I understand, Grahme," he says, his voice full of remorse. "You had no other choice. Seisyll was a strong-willed woman. No doubt somewhere in her mind she screamed in horror at what she was being forced to do. Your action gave her a release."

My hands start to shake. Even as Cynbel gives me absolution, the immensity of what I've done is made clear. "I tried to honor her. I straightened her body and prayed for her soul's safe journey." Tears well up in my eyes and my breath becomes haggard. *You have to pull yourself together.*

"She was the first person you have had to kill?" Cynbel asks.

I think of the limping man. He entered my mind so easily. I glance at Ysella and feel the shame from when the memory of us was *inspected* by him. I clench and release my fist. *How can I possibly explain?*

"Do you know why the Black Mage brought Seisyll to the Giant's Choir?"

"I do not."

Ysella pats my knee. "It's fine, Grahme, you are among friends."

"I do not know." A wave of emotion rolls over me and I'm unable to say more. My eyes plead with Cynbel to take this guilt away from me, but I realize no one can grant me absolution.

"It's all right," Cynbel says. "We have located the Black Mage's men; soon we will overtake and capture them. Perhaps we'll get something out of them."

"What of the Dark One?" I ask.

"There's been no sign of him, though I have sent out scouts."

I smile inside. Perhaps I did kill him.

Ysella rubs my knee affectionately. "Judoc said he saw you take something from Seisyll, something small. Is it in your pouch? Show us what you have."

I try to stand up and regret it immediately. My head is swimming, but I don't ask for any help. "I can say nothing further."

"I'll see what's in it for myself, then." Ysella's voice turns hard. She stands and faces me. Her eyes follow mine toward my pack. *Are we going to race for it?* Even if I won, I couldn't stop her from taking it from me.

"Ysella, sit down." Cynbel says calmly, but it is an undeniable command. "This is not how we show hospitality to one of our own."

"I'm sorry, Lord," she says tightly. "I must see to a personal matter." Her nose flares and I am certain that our discussion will be revisited.

Cynbel smiles ruefully at me. "So far, Grahme, Judoc has accused you of theft and wants to challenge you to a duel, Arthmael hints of

175

attempting to poison you, Ysella feels embarrassed, and you refuse to answer my questions. If I didn't already know that Boswen was your mentor, I would surely have guessed it by now."

"Angering people is a specialty of mine." I dump out the remaining cold soup. I've eaten as much as I can.

"There is nothing that can't be fixed," he reassures me. "We have granted you our hospitality, so none of my people will open your pouch, on that you have my word."

"Thank you, Lord Cynbel."

"I know that Boswen can be difficult even at the best of times. The man is never truly happy unless he's being unnecessarily cryptic," he complains. "Only he would command you to keep your questing secret. I would ask this of you: would he want you to withhold your information from me and my men with the situation being what it is now? The Black Mage has never dared to send men this far north, much less come this far himself. Nor has he ever attempted to come so far himself. I am not just a fellow druid, but the protector of this holy place. Would Boswen want one of the Nine, his peer, to fight this battle blindly? I know you have been compelled to silence, but Boswen is not aware of all that has happened since. So, it is now in your hands. Will you support your fellow druids, or will you let us flounder?"

My body feels cold and gutted, like a fish. I was sent to retrieve a stupid flower. I was never meant to be in the middle of a power struggle. I close my eyes and take a deep breath. I'm desperate for a solution, but it's like grabbing at smoke. I hang my head to avert his gaze.

"I'm sorry, Lord Cynbel. I made a vow."

Cynbel exhales as he stands. "I can tarry no longer; my men and I are leaving to capture the riders from last night. But consider this, we will interrogate them closely. Is there anything you wish to say before we hear from them?"

"No, Lord."

"I pray that you have been acting in good faith with me."

17

Reversal of Fortune

First Dark Day of Cantl, 819

Twenty-nine Days until Samhain

The rest of the plains druids have left. Only Ysella and Arthmael remain behind to escort me to their summer camp.

Ysella waves her arm expansively. "Behold, *Hen Fawen Doer Chi*, in the old tongue."

"Ancient Beech Earth House?" I ask, not sure if I translated correctly.

"Very good. The beech trees are over the next rise, by the river." She points over the hill and the tops of the trees are barely visible. "We've carved out our homes under the hills."

I can only see a few of the well-hidden doors within the three rolling hills. The communal fire pit in the central area is the only other hint of occupation.

Everyone had heard the legends of the plains druids and how they vanished into the hills. "I can't remember the number of times Father threatened to hide my favorite toys here if I didn't behave," I say.

"It's the favorite threat of parents throughout the isle," Ysella says. "My parents did the same."

Only as we approach the closest of the hills do the moss-covered doors come into focus. "The dwellings seem nice, but how do you keep people from stumbling upon you?"

"We have sentries on the surrounding hills to spot travelers and steer them away from us. And when we break camp, we pile dirt on our doors and seed it with grass."

"So, your homes really do disappear into the hills."

Arthmael plops down in front of one of the doorways. His animosity is unspoken but clear none the less.

"You've recovered your strength quite quickly," Ysella says, ignoring Arthmael.

"Boswen taught me that when you're overextended, you also lose your appetite. The best way to regain strength is to eat as much as you can."

"I would not have believed that you would make the entire walk without a break, if I had not seen it for myself," Ysella says.

"And what I find amazing is that neither of you so much as flinched when we encountered the aurochs," I say.

"The giants may have left, but their cattle still remain," Ysella says.

"They should have retreated as soon as they saw us," Arthmael says, irritated. "We'll have to start our mock hunts again."

Only I see Ysella as she rolls her eyes. "We want them to stand their ground when they see humans. Why else would we go to great length to tell tales of the dangers of being near the beasts?"

"They're too tame. They won't scare anyone."

"Arthmael, we may have some injured druids returning," Ysella says in a clipped tone. "Do you have what you need to treat them?"

"I should be there fighting with Cynbel and the others," he responds.

"Our lord asked us to make the camp ready, instead. Now, are you going to sit there sulking or are you going to do your duty?"

"If you will let me be of use," I say humbly, "I will gladly harvest some thousand leaf for staunching any bleeding."

Arthmael looks at me closely, as if trying to decide if he should trust me or not.

"Is that what Master Gwalather taught you?" Ysella asks.

"It was, at least before he cast me out. Now he would most likely want to feed me unripe elderberries . . . or worse." Thank the gods for Ysella. Anyone wishing to be a healer will know of Gwalather.

"You two get the thousand leaf and I'll harvest some stinging nettle," he replies.

"I will only slow Ysella down since I can't animorph. Would you rather I start the fire so you can better extract the herbs' essences once you return?" It's a common practice, if you've been properly trained. I hope he knows this much at least.

"Um, yes, you do that," Arthmael mumbles.

The poor fellow, he isn't even well drilled with the basics and now there's no one left to train him.

Ysella returns first with the thousand leaf plants. After soaking them in water, I crush them to a fine green paste. Arthmael returns with the stinging nettle. Scalding it removes the stingers and I repeat the crushing process.

"Do you have any mead? Or at least some ale?" I ask.

"Celebrating, are we?" Ysella asks.

"The mead will help purify any wounds while the thousand leaf and nettle slurry will stop the bleeding and improve the constitution."

"I have some mead," Arthmael says, perking up. "I wondered why Cynbel gave it to me."

The first couple men from Cynbel's party land in the middle of the camp. They remain in avian form for a couple breaths before changing to their true forms.

"What news?" Ysella asks.

"No one was seriously hurt, on our side at least. We caught up with seven of the men. Three were on horseback and they tried to run, leaving their fellow soldiers to their fate." His scowl tells us what he thinks of the riders. "We dove at them repeatedly until the horses were spooked and tossed the men. All told, three of the soldiers died rather than be taken. The two are unconscious and the last two were fighting back-to-back and giving no quarter."

"They were the ones to die, then?" Ysella asks.

"No; all of a sudden they stopped fighting, dropped their swords and surrendered to us. They were confused about how they got there. They've been blindfolded and are being brought back here."

"In that case," Arthmael says, "we'll keep the mead to celebrate with our brothers and the prisoners can make do with the healing paste."

"A great idea, Arthmael," Cynbel says from behind us. None of us had even heard him land.

"How long until the rest of the men are back?" Ysella asks.

"It will be a half day," Cynbel responds. "The men we captured were all from Sarum."

"No!" Ysella and Arthmael say in unison.

Cynbel purses his lips. "One of the men who died fighting was Ayden."

"The leader of the guards?" Arthmael asks.

"Yes. I sent Judoc to scout Sarum, but I'm afraid that it can only have fallen to the Black Mage."

"It has!" I blurt out. "I was imprisoned there until the night before the equinox." All eyes stare back at me. "It's only now that I remembered it," I add lamely.

"You knew of this?" Cynbel says in barely a whisper. Only his white knuckles hint at his frustration.

"I hadn't . . . I mean, I didn't, I didn't even think about it until you mentioned the city." *Another thing I screwed up.* "I'm sorry, but my mind was still addled this morning."

"You just now tell us that Sarum has fallen to the Dark Lord?" Cynbel booms. "What else are you holding back from me?" he asks in a dangerous tone.

"Nothing, Lord, I am truly sorry." I hang my head, waiting for a damning pronouncement.

"Once the men have all returned, we will discuss your recent movements *in great detail.*" He turns to Ysella and Arthmael. "For now, he is our guest, but do not let him out of your sight and do not let him leave. Am I understood?"

"Yes, Lord," Ysella and Arthmael intone together.

"Yes, Lord," I repeat.

◄ ————)|●|(———— ►

The druids and their prisoners march into camp at dusk with much laughter and good will. Never have I seen prisoners in such good spirits.

Ysella sees my confusion. "The men are well known to us. They were compelled by the Dark Lord to do his bidding. Once his hold over them was broken, they returned to the stout men we are accustomed to. I need to help Arthmael attend them, so you're coming, too."

"Lead the way."

The men are singing old ditties and swaying back and forth.

"The soldiers have partaken in liberal doses of medicinal mead," Arthmael informs us.

"What will happen to those men?" I ask.

"They will be given protection from the Black Lord and sent to other hillforts, likely Fynbardun or Idendun. Though without Sarum, the successful defense of the plains is unlikely."

Ysella keeps wrapping and unwrapping her hair around her pinky finger. It dawns on me that she must be nervous about something. "What's the matter?"

"It's Judoc," she says. "He's long overdue."

"Could you have missed his arrival?"

"Not likely. He has been courting me for the last several months. If he got here, even if he had to sneak in for some reason, he would report to Cynbel and then find me straightaway."

"Oh."

"Lord Cynbel requests everyone's presence," a breathless young acolyte stammers as he approaches the prisoners, "And he has his hand harp!"

"Have you heard Lord Cynbel perform before?" Ysella asks.

"I have not."

"On clear nights like tonight, with Aine shining down on us, Lord Cynbel will sing the ballads for both us and the stars."

We descend the hill to the campfire below. Cynbel waves us over.

"Grahme, you and I are going to have a very open and honest discussion tomorrow morning." He puts up a hand to forestall my response. "You must decide if you will be a friend of the plains druids or not. But that is for you to think about tonight. Now, I wish to give you a glance of what it means to be our friend, so please sit." He points to a single chair facing the rest of the druids. "I wish to properly introduce you to my people."

Cynbel waits for me to take my seat before mingling with the crowd. He makes his way through his men, complimenting each one on their service in the past few days. The man is a natural leader. What would it have been like if any of my mentors had taken this approach in training? At last, he disengages and stands before the fire.

"We have business that we must attend to before I begin," Cynbel announces. "First the good news, Judoc has at long last made it back from his scouting mission at Sarum."

The crowd stirs at this news. Ysella gives herself a soothing embrace as she waits for Cynbel to say more.

"He was shot through the wing, but he should be fine by Samhain. But he will be unable to lead the staff-fighting exercises for a good while."

A couple druids give a mock cheer and others rumble their approval. Ysella is scanning the camp for any sign of Judoc. My hands ball up into fists as I watch her. Cynbel smiles at his band's good humor. As the conversations start to die down, he raises his hand for quiet.

"Judoc received his wound while he was flying over Sarum. The hillfort has been taken by the Dark Lord's men." A hush falls over the crowd.

"Fynbardun and Idendun are indeed still loyal to us and they have been alerted our *temporary* loss of Sarum."

The only noise comes from the gentle breeze.

"I can say no more about Sarum until after the upcoming moot at Kantom, but rest assured this setback will not stand. The people of Sarum are as always, our friends. It is only the hillfort that the Dark Lord controls and even that he controls only by way of a few well-place mind-controllers." He lets his words be absorbed by his men. "As you all know by now, Seisyll passed last night. It sits ill with several of you and with me as well, the lack of honor shown to our fallen compatriot last night. In times of duress, ceremonies cannot always be properly performed. But we all knew Seisyll, and we have all seen her 'rest her eyes' during our ceremonies and sometimes she even managed to snore as well."

The troop chuckles.

"So, I think it only fitting that Seisyll's burial did not become a long and drawn-out affair. She died at the Giant's Choir as the Dark Lord was approaching. What his aims were, we do not yet know. However, there was one druid there last night, standing on the very stones of Men Meur Kov Keigh and defending our holy site from the Obsidian Mage. He sits here now, in our midst."

185

There are some animated discussions and lots of pointing at me.

"I realize that not everyone is aware of what happened last night, so I am prepared to give a short accounting," Cynbel says.

He strums his hand harp and the commotion ceases. "It's still a work in progress, but I give you: The Ballad of Grahme Fairweather."

The Cursed's chase is for naught

After Grahme he has fought

Lightning crashing

Thunder bashing

The angry storm did cause his flight

His men dispersing

Without rehearsing

At Giant's Choir, dead of night

Pursuit on horses they did come

Two and eight, a nasty scrum

Enemies vaunted

Grahme undaunted

Chose to stand at Giant's Choir

Mighty powers

More than showers

Stone topped, his voice rose higher

Riders tossed, horses scattered

The Dark One's plans a'shattered

On Grahme's demanding

Hail is landing

Pummeling foes left and right

Plans defeated

Feeling cheated

Dark One broke and took to flight

Alone and open in clear sight

Only Grahme to show his might

Storm clouds summoned

The air a'humming

Godsfire is Black Mage bound

Standing below

A shadow's glow

Grahme's wrath touched only ground

The Cursed's chase is for naught

After Grahme he has fought

Lightning crashing

Thunder bashing

The angry storm did cause his flight

His men dispersing

Without rehearsing

At Giant's Choir, dead of night

Cynbel strums his last chord and lets the harp fall silent. After a pause, the men respond with raucous calls of "Grahme" and "once more." Everyone feels compelled to shake my hand and admire my feat.

I was frightened and backed into a corner. I am not a hero. I smile and thank my well-wishers, all the while I desperately look for a hiding spot. At least when under attack, I can silence my foes.

Cynbel calls the druids to order, after an eon or two. "I bid you all good night. We will finish up our reaping tomorrow before we depart for Kantom Lijanks Kuros." The gathering finally breaks up and my pounding heart can relax. Dried reeds are dipped into the fire as everyone retreats to their own places to rest.

"No need to act so scared," Ysella says with a chuckle. "I promise you no one is going to attack you here."

"All the same, I'm glad that everyone has stopped staring at me. What did Cynbel mean by reaping?"

"We grow flax in various patches across the plains. We harvest it and take it to Sarum for trade with the townspeople."

"What do you trade for?"

"Mostly information and the people's good will." She grabs my hand and leads me to her hill-cut home.

"It's too bad you can't see this place when the flax is in flower. The fields make the very sky jealous of their rich blue color. And the fragrance is never so strong to be pungent, but the nutty aroma is intoxicating.

Three-foot walls of earth bend away from the entrance to her hill home. In Aine's light I can see the image of flax flowers forming a Y on her door. I trace the flower with my finger for luck.

"You must be tired," she says

"I have never desired to sleep more strongly in my life."

She pushes on my chest to halt my motion. "I was going to offer you my home, but if it's only sleep that you desire, you can spend the night with Arthmael."

18

From Guest to Captive

Second Dark Day of Cantl, 819

Twenty-eight Days until Samhain

Ysella sticks her lit reed torch into the kindling of her central hearth. The flame starts to spread at once. She walks over next to the door and without word slips off her robe and hangs it on a peg. Her lithe body is adorned only by a rowan-wood necklace with the protection knot carved deeply into it.

"You need no adornment," I say as I pull my own robe off over my head.

Ysella stares at me in horror? Revulsion? I scan my body, searching for what would make her react so. Everything is ready to go.

"Where is your charm?" She demands.

"What?" Didn't I just tell her she was beautiful?

"Where is your protection amulet?"

"I don't have one."

"Cynbel," she shouts. She grabs her robe and is out in the night air, raising the alarm. I grab my robe and run after her. In no time, two owls land in front of us and transform into druids.

Ysella pauses only long enough to slip back into her robe before thrusting her finger at me. "He wears no amulet!"

The sentries lower their staves. I raise my hands to halt any blow. A slight gust of wind alerts me that my robe is still in my hand. A third owl appears and morphs into Cynbel. I use the distraction to don my own robe. He glares at me and my misaligned garment and then at Ysella. Before I can pronounce my innocence, Ysella shouts loud enough for the whole plain to hear.

"He does not wear a protection amulet." she says as she points her accusing finger at me again.

I look at her as if she's lost her mind. Druids are streaming from within the hills now, brandishing torches and staves in equal number. I turn to Cynbel for some explanation with my hands out wide.

"Where is your amulet?" he demands.

"What amulet?"

"The rowan amulet that protects us from the mind-controllers."

It sounds as if Cynbel is talking to a simpleton or a child. "I have never heard of this."

Cynbel closes his eyes and collects himself. "If the Black Lord has taken note of you, and we can be sure that he has after the equinox, he can mentally home in on your mind and know your general location. If he gets close enough, he can overwhelm the sentries and take control of their minds and bodies."

"I told you he stole something from Seisyll's body. He's working with the Dark Lord!" Judoc interjects. His right arm is bound in a sling or else he would no doubt be pointing at me as well.

"He defeated and tried to kill the Dark Lord last night," Cynbel says patiently. "I doubt that was some devious plan hatched by the Black Mage."

"He's doing the Cursed One's bidding since their encounter. He's given away the location of our summer camp."

"That may in fact be true," Cynbel agrees. He clicks his tongue for a moment. "Ysella, you have not been south since Lughnasa, correct?"

"Correct, Lord Cynbel."

"Then give Grahme your amulet for now. I'll have the acolytes make more amulets in the morning. We will leave after the reaping tomorrow."

Ysella takes off her amulet and throws it in my face.

"Does it have to be in contact with the skin?" I ask.

"It's always better, since it is less likely to fall off *unexpectedly*," Cynbel replies. "You will sleep with the men from Sarum. If you try to flee, my men will stop you, even if they must kill you."

I stare at Cynbel, Ysella, anyone for an explanation. No one has anything but hostility to offer.

"Everyone, get your rest," Cynbel calls out. "We will have to collect whatever of the harvest we can tomorrow, then leave this camp."

"I'll escort him to the other prisoners," Judoc says. The crowd disperses, leaving only me and Ysella's rival suitor.

"I have you to thank for this injury." He flexes his hand on his injured right arm. "No worries, though, I can still best you using my staff with my off arm."

"I mean no harm to anyone."

"Except Seisyll. You killed her and looted her still-warm body."

I dare not respond. Instead, I bow my head and walk up the hill to the other prisoners.

"Nothing would please me more than to see you run for it." Judoc pokes me in the back a couple times, but I don't take the bait.

"What's all the commotion?" the druid on duty asks.

"We have one more who has been compelled by the Dark Lord for you to watch."

One of the guards from Sarum rises and points at me. "He's the one that killed two of our men on the night the Obsidian Lord arrived at Sarum. He's why I was forced to join the Dark One's party."

"I didn't kill anyone. I turned into a bat and escaped through a hole in the roof of my jail."

"Aye, then you came back and killed Cadyrn while we were on guard, so your thief friend could escape." He turns to Judoc. "He killed Caome as well and left Drest for dead, too."

"I had no weapon to do such things. Killing guards would only draw attention to our escape. Any killing must have been by Alfswich's hand."

"Alfswich? Judoc asks. "The mind-reading thief who has been banned from the plains under pain of death? Is that your friend and accomplice?"

"He certainly is not my friend, but we were imprisoned together, and we knew the Obsidian Mage was coming that night. I warned the damned fool not to kill anyone."

"So, you only knew him from jail in Sarum? Is that the story you're going with?"

"He's a liar," the beardless fool says. "Alfswich told us he was a killer. It's only because we caught him trying to sell stolen jewelry that we locked them up together. So, they had to know each other before Sarum."

Triumph is in Judoc's eyes. He allows a small smile as he awaits my answer.

"Because of my vow, I cannot respond to any of these accusations except to say that they have been unfairly represented."

"Don't say another word." Judoc is smiling from ear to ear now. "You will confess to Lord Cynbel tomorrow or you will be treated as the criminal you are. Either way, I will enjoy your fall." He turns to the druid guards. "Don't let him escape or you will face Cynbel's wrath."

Cynbel and Judoc are seated around the morning's fire while Ysella and Arthmael escort me to my captors. My pouch sits between them, unopened as far as I can tell. The gray clouds overhead refuse to let even a single ray of sunlight reach the ground. Only Belenos and Aine are witnesses to what happened. But neither will show themselves today.

"Sit," Cynbel says as he gestures toward a stump. "Before you start with your excuses about your vow, I want you to listen to me."

Ysella and Arthmael take up stations behind me.

"Yes, Lord."

Judoc's smirking face gives me a clue of how bad this is going to be.

"This is what we know of your story. You were given a quest by Boswen, even though the Council of the Nine had forbidden it.

My guess is that Caradoc was in on this as well, though I am not sure about your level of knowledge."

"But, Lord—"

"Silence! Your chance to tell this tale has passed."

I swallow hard. It is going to be even worse than I feared.

"Boswen coerced a vow of silence from you in return for your illegal quest. You set off for Solent Keep with a known mind-controlling thief. You robbed the Black Lord and somehow managed to flee his city. You and Alfswich were captured in Sarum, selling jewelry and trinkets in the market. You were imprisoned together. Before the Black Lord arrived, the two of you killed two, maybe three, guards and made good your escape." He halts his story and stares at me expectantly. "Have I told the story truly?"

"No, Lord."

"Very well, I'm willing to give you this opportunity to correct the record. What did I get wrong?"

I hang my head. "I cannot say."

"Right, the vow of course, how convenient. We'll continue with my version, then. Alfswich knows that to enter the plains would mean death to him. So, with or without your knowledge, he left you soon after the escape from Sarum.

"Presumably, you are still questing, so why would you choose to go north instead of southwest back to Boswen?"

"I came north to warn you of the fall of Sarum."

Cynbel lets loose a barking laugh. "Of course you did, but you forgot to tell us until after we discovered it for ourselves." He waits a moment for me to say more. I hang my head, knowing my silence will only assert my guilt.

"Stranger still, you seem to have known the Black Lord's plans and waited for him at the Giant's Choir where you thwarted him. You killed Seisyll during the battle and stole something from her person soon afterward."

"No, Lord, that's not right."

He pauses for me to correct the record. Once again, I hang my head in silence.

"You have consorted with mind readers at every stage of your quest, yet you say you are unaware of the rowan protection amulet. You have potentially given away the location of our summer base; a base that has not been discovered by anyone outside the druids in over four hundred years. And now you sit here before me and take advantage of my offer of hospitality by not revealing what you possess in this pack that is so vital to you.

"You are either working for the Black Lord or you are his very useful fool. Is there anything you would like to correct about my version?"

I raise my head to meet his eyes. "Lord Cynbel, I journeyed to Solent City with my nephew. We became entangled with Alfswich and had to flee the city with him. I had never met him before then."

"So, it is coincidence that the two of you were reunited at Sarum, in the same cell? And what became of this nephew?"

"My nephew and I met Blachstenius the Trader after we parted ways with Alfswich. I left my nephew in his care since Blachstenius was bound for the west."

"Blachstenius is known to us. In fact, he is the one who warned us of Alfswich's thieving. So why did you join with a mind-controlling petty thief in the Obsidian Lord's city?"

"I cannot say."

"So, you were not overpowered by Alfswich's mental powers and forced to enact his plan?"

"No, Lord Cynbel." I realize he's trying to give me a way to escape culpability, but I can't lie to him.

"And how can you be so sure? You say you were unaware of the protection amulet."

I try to exhale all of the air from my chest, to avoid what I must say. "Because, Lord, my nephew also possesses the mind-controlling talent."

There is an explosive shout from Judoc. I hang my head, knowing that I have denied Figol his chance to become a druid. Cynbel lets out a humorless chuckle.

"For someone who is unaware of our protection from the mind benders, you certainly do consort with a good many of them."

"I have no explanation for that."

"And yet your family members are mind-controllers as well?"

"It is my brother's wife who has that . . . talent."

"You realize that it is our best estimate that there are no more than one hundred people on all of Pretanni who possess the mind-bending ability? And yet you have managed to encounter"—he ticks off a finger for each—"your brother's wife, your nephew, Alfswich, Blachstenius, and the Black Lord. This is all coincidence?"

I stare into the fire. I dare not mention the limping man.

"Judoc, get the message out to all of the plains druids, I would like to have Grahme's nephew brought to me."

"Yes, Lord."

"Now, my story is a good one and pretty close to the mark, I would guess. But I still have a few questions. First, what or who made you turn north from Sarum?"

197

"I came north to inform you that Sarum had fallen under the sway of the Black Lord."

"Sticking with that, are you? And yet you did no such thing until after we had discovered it for ourselves." He pauses. "Let's back up then. Why did you go north from Solent Keep to Sarum?"

"Lord, we came to Sarum from the east. I thought it would be a safe place to stop for the night on my way back to Land's End."

"So, you, Alfswich, and your nephew were in the east?" he asks with strained patience.

"No, Lord, my nephew, Figol, Blachstenius, and I were coming from the east. Alfswich never chooses to stay in my company once the benefit to him is gone."

"Where in the east were you coming from?"

I dare not mention Venta and the Elven Tears. I shake my head, declining to answer yet again.

"Interesting," is all he says. He rises and turns his head skyward as he stretches to full height. "Now at last we have come to the big reveal. Would you like to tell us what is inside this pack? You have nervously guarded it since you arrived among your druid friends."

"You know that I cannot, Lord."

"Not once in the five years that I have led this proud group of druids have I rescinded an offer of hospitality." In a defeated tone he says, "You have forced me to do so." The disappointment in his eyes says more than any words could. "Judoc, open up his pack."

"No." I reach out for my pack until I feel two staves pressing against the front of my neck. Ysella and Arthmael firmly force me to sit back.

Judoc opens the pack and takes out the leather wrap. With a bounce of the wrist, the wrap unrolls and the ghost orchid lands unceremoniously on the ground.

"What is it, Lord?" Judoc asks. "Besides a small, beat up flower, I mean."

"It's hard to say in this condition. Would you be so good as to cast a restoration spell upon it?"

"No!" I scream. This time I refuse to lean back, despite the staves at my throat.

Cynbel shakes his head and the pressure on my neck is released. "You can either tell us what it is, or Judoc will cast his restoration spell."

My eyes implore him to reconsider, but Lord Cynbel is unmoved. I shake my head. "I can't; you know I can't."

"Very well," Cynbel says. He waves Judoc to perform the necessary spell.

I make several strangled noises before the taste of failure settles into my gut. "It is a ghost orchid," I blurt out, knowing any chance of becoming a druid is irretrievably lost.

Cynbel stretches out his hand. "Hold, Judoc."

In my moment of shame, I can't bear to see Judoc's gloating or Ysella's disappointment. The small fire crackles on in its own merry little way, undisturbed by my demise.

After a few moments, Cynbel sighs. "I do not sense this man to be a traitor. A fool of the first rank perhaps, but he has not the guile to be traitor."

"But Lord," Judoc says.

"Repack the flower in Grahme's pouch and give it to him."

"Lord?"

"Then I want you to get the iron manacles."

"Yes." Judoc shoots me a look of triumph and hurriedly repacks the flower. He tosses my pack at me and he's gone before Cynbel can change his mind.

"We only possess the irons because the Obsidian Order has sent turned druids into our ranks before. Never did I think they would be used in any other way." Cynbel says, in case I'm still unaware of his disappointment in me.

19

Walk of Shame

Third Dark Day of Cantl, 819

Twenty-seven Days until Samhain

Cynbel has not asked to speak to me again, and though I am surrounded by druids, I have never been more alone. Cynbel's people have been given their tasks, so no one is left to voice their hostility toward me. Only Arthmael, Ysella, and I are left at camp.

Judoc leads a pack of horses into camp. The horses walk right in front of us and rear up. The flax from their backs fall to the ground as each changes back into a druid.

"Just because you two have to watch him doesn't mean you can't store these bundles," Judoc says. "No need to be idle while everyone else works." He stretches his hurt arm and makes fake faces of being in pain. To my astonishment, Ysella buys the act. I turn away from them before I retch. Arthmael is starring daggers at me.

"You can do this part, as well," he says.

"I would, but you have locked my arms in iron, and true druids like me have vowed to avoid using the cursed metal."

"You're horrible," Ysella says as she pulls away from Judoc.

He shoots me a small triumphant smile before ordering his druids back to the fields. As one, they change into red kites and soar off to the east.

"I at least take my vows seriously."

"Watch him while I open up the storage room," Ysella says, stomping up the hill.

"Feel free to try to run; I need to practice for the gwary at the moot."

"You need to practice against an unarmed and bound opponent? Your chances don't sound all that promising to me."

I plop down across from him and stare at the yellow seed pods on still-green stalks.

Ysella returns and they spend the rest of the morning stuffing the bundles in orderly rows.

"Clear out your homes," Cynbel announces after lunch. "We leave as soon as the flax is safely stored."

My brethren mill about in this happy time, waiting for Cynbel to give the word to seal up the camp. *What is it like, having that camaraderie?* Cynbel and Judoc take their places in front of the druids, facing the now-empty homes underneath the hills.

They begin intoning in the guttural old tongue. The ground beneath us begins to quiver, as if awakening. The other druids in the camp all stare rapturously at their lord. Great swaths of earth rise up behind the pair and start walking toward the collection of druids.

Elementals! I've never seen such huge animates.

"Arthmael, you may have the honor," Cynbel calls.

Arthmael's smile is the first I've seen from him. Cynbel directs his elemental to the first of the homes under the hill. Arthmael takes three massive swings at the shoulder of the elemental with his staff, causing its arm to drop in front of the door. It lumbers over to the next door and again Arthmael severs a hunk of dirt. As the doors are covered, the owners scurry over and mold the dirt into a believable hill slope. After the two elementals are dispatched and the doorways hidden, the druids sprinkle the slopes with clover seeds. Cynbel and Judoc now call forth a wind and water elemental and as they collide, the water gently sprinkles the hillside.

"So that is how your homes have remained hidden for all these years," I say in amazement.

"Yes, and we're fortunate that the Dark Lord didn't find us this year," Ysella responds.

"Why would he want to? Your hospitality is lacking." I raise my arms high enough for the manacles to slide down, revealing my rashes from the rusty irons.

"Are you looking for sympathy?"

"Better than one of Arthmael's concoctions. I'm likely to become violently ill and have the shits."

"Cynbel wants to see you," Arthmael says in a flat voice from behind me.

I drop my head. "I'm sorry, Arthmael."

He walks past me without breaking his stride.

Ysella shakes her head at me. "Some guests aren't worth having."

"Pray that we will find our camp undisturbed when we return next year," Cynbel says. It is a simple way to end the ceremony. "Now, let's make our way northward to Kantom."

Once again, I am headed away from Boswen and the completion of my quest. Not that it matters anymore. The Nine are as likely as not to expel me from their order. For the first time, I consider what I will become if not a druid.

Cynbel and I are the last to leave camp, save for Arthmael and Ysella. Cynbel motions them to join the rest of his band. Once they are out of earshot, Cynbel motions me to him.

"I see you still wear the amulet."

"I could hardly take it off without your guards noticing."

"I mean only that this is a good indication of your intent," Cynbel says agreeably.

I remain silent and keep my eyes on the wagon in front of me. *He locks me in irons and then tries to act like we're friends?*

"Have you ever been to a council meeting before?"

"No."

"Last year, Loris was elected as our head druid. Boswen could have very easily had the top spot; we were practically begging him to take it. But your mentor has always chosen to be unknowable, even when there is no cause for it."

He glances at me sideways, waiting for me to say something. I continue our leisurely pace. *Friends do not place another in rusty iron shackles.*

"Perhaps age has caught up with him at last and he has started to go daft like all the old ones eventually do."

"That is an interesting tale, master bard," I say in a flat voice.

He sizes me up again as if to determine what tactic to try next. "Has Boswen taught you the druid laws?"

"He didn't have to. I've known them long before I was a man."

"Then you know that if the council votes for it, any oath sworn to another druid, even if it is sworn to one of the Nine, can be set aside."

"Yes."

"When we arrive, I will ask Boswen to release you from your oath. If he declines, the Nine will vote on whether you should keep crucial information from us. I doubt that even Caradoc will support his old mentor in this. So you see, it is not a question of if, but when you will tell me what I need to know. Tell me now, the irons will come off and you will enter as a druid in good standing. If you refuse, you will force the Nine to act and you will be disgraced." He places a hand on my chest, stopping us both. "You are still very young. You have great power, and you could go very far in our order. Your choice of when to speak will decide your future."

"The three rules of the druids as set down by Branok the Burley are one, not to kill without cause; two, to favor no one creature over another, even humans; and three, not to use iron, for it causes a blight upon the earth."

"So, you do know the rules."

"I am a respectable druid, and I can prove it."

"How?"

I raise my forearms up again to reveal the abrasions on my skin. Several spots are becoming infected. "I bear the blight from the irons upon my skin. When did *you* stop being a druid? Be gone, betrayer of oaths."

Cynbel jerks his head, signaling my jailers to resume their duties.

"Cynbel is a very reasonable man," Ysella says. "How can you upset him so quickly?"

"Talent."

Well before sunset, we encounter a war band of sixty white-haired Coritani moving south along the road. Their hair treated with chalk and lime-water can only mean that they are off to battle. Relieved that the attention will not be focused on me for once, I angle my walk to within earshot of Cynbel.

"Gurthcid, what are you doing so far south?" he asks.

"I want to add more heads to my collection."

Gurthcid is a hulking brute astride a miserable-looking moor pony. He wears a long sword at his side and a woad-colored long shield strapped to his back. His hair resembling a white hedgehog. There are three heads tied around the horse's neck. Two are aged, but well-preserved. The third is much more recent.

"Is that your Uncle Soran's head?" Cynbel asks, disappointed.

"Soran was always very clever. It was important that I be gifted with his cunning."

"You stopped killing the Ordivices only to turn on your own kin?"

"They are kin no longer. My men and I have been expelled from the clan."

"So, you have come south to avoid your family?"

"We Coritani do not run like scared rabbits. We aim to kill black wizards. I am fearsome with weapons and now I must strengthen my mind."

"Morinn, bring whatever spare amulets you have," Cynbel calls.

A nervous blond-haired kid comes running to Cynbel's side. "Here they are," he says as he displays his three amulets.

"Gurthcid, the Black Lord and his minions can control yours and your men's minds. Make more amulets like these from the rowan tree. Once everyone in your band has one, you can attack, but not before."

Gurthcid laughs. "Funny druid. Most of my men have at least one other mind, see." He draws his hand back toward his men and their trophy heads. "If the wizards come into our heads, we can jump to one of our other minds."

"It doesn't work that way, Gurthcid. Take the amulets and heed my warning."

Gurthcid takes the amulets and hands them off to his woman. "The druids spend all their time playing as animals. The Black Lord will be surprised when he encounters us. We'll play with his head after the battle."

"Promise me, Gurthcid, you will have one made for everyone in you band."

"Yes, yes, let the druids flee and Gurthcid's raiders will set things right."

Cynbel swallows whatever his next directive was going to be. "Good hunting." He motions for us to clear the road and let the war band pass.

Arthmael morphs into a raven and soars into the sky. He is back in no time with the amulets in hand. "They dropped these in the grass as soon as they were out of sight."

Cynbel leads us up into the hills. Arthmael, Ysella, and I are the last in the procession. No one wants to be near me and my sour mood. These iron manacles represent Cynbel's shame, not my own, I repeat to myself.

I swore to uphold my vows. I don't think Cynbel is a bad man. He fights for the druid cause, but he expects me to roll over and submit to his authority. I wish to be a druid because the cause is right; but I refuse to become another man's pawn.

I raise my arms to move the rusty iron off my rashes.

"Are your arms bothering you?" Ysella says from behind.

I have no idea how she managed to close the distance between us without me hearing her. "No, only the iron causes problems, not my arms."

"Grahme, I don't want to fight."

"Good, because you'd have a distinct advantage over me." She doesn't take the bait. I swallow my anger. "Sorry, I'm a little frustrated."

"Well, you could solve this whole— You know what? I said I didn't want to fight and I'm tired of fighting with those who are on the same side as me."

"Yeah, I'm sorry, too. I'm just a little—"

"—frustrated," she finishes. She smiles at me. "That's the Grahme I remember from Lughnasa."

"I doubt this next gathering is going to be as much fun."

"It's a shame. The druid moot is my favorite."

"I've never been to one."

"Don't get me wrong, I like Beltane, Lughnasa, and the rest well enough, but this is the only gathering of druids for druids. There's none of the: 'Pardon, Miss Druid, can you bless this or heal that?'"

"Wow, you're a terrible person, hating those hard-working farmers. I used to be one of them, you know?"

"That explains why you were so grabby."

"What?" For the first time in ages there is playful banter. The time melts away as I get to talk to a friend instead of bearing the weight of the world.

"We should probably stop smiling so much," Ysella says.

"Why in the name of all the gods would we do that?"

Ysella purses her lips. "Because you've disappointed Arthmael again."

"I've been in irons. How could I have possibly done anything to him?"

"He was all excited for the druid gwary, since Judoc can't compete."

"What is it?"

"That's right, you've never experienced a moot before," she says.

"Gwalather was too lazy to attend and Arthyen didn't like me from the start."

"Well," she says as if she's the authority on this, "the top acolytes from each of the nine lords compete in a combat of staves in the Olmhnin Circle. The winner, by tradition, is promoted to a journeyman druid without having to complete a quest. Last year, Judoc made it to the final against Eosiah from Caradoc's group. It was the most amazing duel in memory, with Eosiah barely able to outlast Judoc."

"And now Judoc is hurt and can't compete. So, I know why he hates me."

"We both know there's more to it than that." She rolls her pretty green eyes at me. "Arthmael is the next best in single combat. With Judoc out, this year the tournament is wide open."

"So Arthmael should be thanking me?"

"Arthmael asked about the gwary, but Cynbel won't release him from his duty of watching you."

I throw my hands up. "This is not my fault."

"I didn't say it was. But if you were Arthmael, would you blame your mentor or the man who has been nothing but trouble since he arrived?"

"Where is he anyway?"

"I told him I'd watch you while he scouted ahead. Speaking of which"—she points at a red kite heading toward us—"I believe that is him now."

Arthmael lands in front of us. He takes a few awkward steps before he morphs into his human form. Animorphing is definitely not his specialty. I could teach him animorphing and herbal remedies if he weren't so set against me.

"It's as I thought, that's Milk Hill," he says.

"We'll get there before sundown," Ysella says, excited.

Arthmael returns the smile. I wait for someone to explain the significance.

At last, Ysella sees my confusion. "We always camp at the top of Milk Hill on the night prior to the moot. We enter the Kantom Lijanks Kuros complex the next day at first light."

"Complex?"

Ysella ignores my question. "Cynbel always times it so we don't get to camp until after dusk. For newcomers, their first view is always with the sun's rise," Ysella says.

I look up at Belenos. "We'll crest that hill well before dark" I say. They nod.

"It's not like him to mis-time our trip," Arthmael says.

"I think he's got something else on his mind this time." I raise my manacles and kill the excitement. That's my specialty, the good mood assassin.

"See that white hill? Ysella asks. "That's Silbury Hill. It's blindingly white in the midday sun. Caradoc and his people camp there."

"I've never seen anything like it," I marvel. The hill has taken on a soft, dull white color in the evening sun.

"You can barely see the white interior walls of Kantom Lijanks Kuros, just north of Silbury."

"I see them." I can't help but get excited. Every boy dreams of being allowed here at some point.

"That's where Cynbel and the rest of the Nine will be for the next couple days. Of course, none of us are allowed in there, but that also means that they don't have time to give us orders."

"I see why you like this event so much."

Cynbel raises his voice. "Everyone, gather around." His back is to Kantom Lijanks Kuros.

"Since we don't have any first-timers this year, I figured we could arrive early for once."

Arthmael, Ysella, and I stand off to the side of the main group. Part of me wants to shout that this is my first time, to contradict Cynbel, but I hold my tongue.

As Belenos' fiery orb sets, the color of Silbury Hill changes every couple of breaths. What was white has faded into a yellow-white, through all the shades of orange and now it's moving steadily through the reds. Just before sunset, the hill takes on a gray sheen, almost like iron, before it surrenders to the darkness.

I shake my head and blink several times. I don't want to be called a wide-eyed farm boy. Casually, I look around me. Everyone else was just as caught up in the spectacle. I try to place my arm over Ysella's shoulder, until I'm reminded that it's bound with cold hard iron. For all the beauty, I'm still a prisoner.

"Perhaps I've been wrong all these years, arriving after dusk," Cynbel says in a contemplative tone. "No matter, we will still enter Kantom at first light, as always. Enjoy this night."

20

Kantom Lijanks Kuros

Twenty-six Days until Samhain

Twenty-six Days until Samhain

In the predawn, we march to the Kantom Lijanks Kuros campsite favored by the plains druids. The Sanctuary is a series of five concentric circles, alternating in makeup of wood and stone. Whatever their meaning was meant to be, it was lost centuries ago when the elder races left. From the riverside, a big grassy causeway leads up the hill to Kantom. The rosy false dawn illuminates Olmhnin Circle, where the gwary will take place.

The sun peaks over the eastern hills. As one, Cynbel's band pivots to the west and watches as the rays of light shine upon Silbury Hill. A fiery yellow brilliance races down the hill, replacing the warm pinkish hues.

"Welcome to Kantom," Cynbel says to me. He turns to Ysella and Arthmael. "Remove the irons."

Wordlessly, Arthmael produces the key. "It will be your duty to watch over Grahme, and when he is summoned, to ensure he makes it to the stone circles. Do you understand your charge?" Cynbel asks.

"Yes, Lord," Ysella and Arthmael say in unison.

He beckons Arthmael over to him and places his arm around Arthmael's drooping shoulders. "You may have won the tournament this year, but it would be best for you to study the herbal remedies one more year before you leave us. I believe this with all my heart. And if I am unable to attract another druid skilled in these arts, I will see to it that you may go to whomever you wish to master your craft."

"Yes, Lord," Arthmael mumbles.

Cynbel pats him on his back.

"We are the first to arrive, as usual," Cynbel says to his charges. "Let's prepare for the moot."

Bracketing the grassy path every ten paces up to Kantom Lijanks Kuros are immovable standing stones. This had to be the work of the giants in the forgotten past.

"The first group to arrive," Ysella says, "And that's always us, set the bridges over the ditch to the central stone circles."

"Circles?"

"You aren't even familiar with Kantom Lijanks Kuros?" Arthmael asks, disgusted.

"There are two circles, each slightly larger than Men Meur Kov Keigh, one to the north and one to the south. Around them is the largest circle in all the world; one hundred stones in all, which stand inside the inner earthen rampart." Ysella says, cutting off Arthmael.

"No druid save the Nine may enter any of the rings unless summoned," Arthmael smirks at me. "You'll be one of the rare ones called to stand in front of the Nine."

The impulse to blacken an eye on his overly smug face is strong. I stare down at the now pus-filled infections dotting each arm and calmly look away. I may be called to stand in front of the Nine, but I refuse to act the part of a drunken brawler as they deliberate my fate.

Ysella gives Arthmael a shot to the ribs and resumes her explanation. "The Nine debate in the southern ring. Once consensus is achieved on whatever topics they deem important, Cynbel, as the speaker for the Nine, approaches the northern ring alone. All the druids in the area flock outside the great circle and he announces the rulings of the council."

"He must be hoarse after that."

"No, he speaks into the Cove Stones of Ogmios, and the god of the bards amplifies Cynbel's voice so that all within the ramparts may hear the rulings as if in a private conversation."

"And we will find out what this precious secret of yours is," Arthmael says.

Ysella rolls her beautiful green eyes. "It won't be long before Cynbel starts assigning duties. You two need to follow me unless you want to be stuck digging the latrines."

Arthmael points to the west. "Is that Lord Caradoc and his flock of merlins?"

"It is," Ysella says. "He will go directly to see Cynbel, so we can still escape if we leave now."

"Let's go," Arthmael says.

"Wait, Caradoc is coming this way," I say. The first bird has a lazy upstroke. It dives straight at us, flaring its wings at the last moment. It becomes hazy to the eye for a moment. Caradoc's human form drops the last few inches to the ground. I can't help but smile at his theatrical landing.

"Greetings, druids," he says in his robust voice. He starts at Arthmael and continues his gaze until he comes to me. He cocks his head sideways. "Grahme?"

"Lord Caradoc." I bow.

"I did not expect to see you here. The last I heard from Boswen, neither he nor you would be attending this moot."

"He is not, as far as I know, Lord Caradoc. I arrived with Cynbel and his druids." I place my arms behind my back, once I'm sure Caradoc has seen the iron-rash upon my arms. "This is Ysella and Arthmael." As my jailers bow to Caradoc, he signals for me to be patient, or to stop talking, or something else entirely. I decide to let him direct the conversation.

"Curious. And what of your quest?"

"It is still in progress, Lord."

Caradoc narrows his eyes. Both Ysella and Arthmael are doing their best to be inconspicuous.

"I will find time to speak with you later today," he says carefully. "This is Eosiah, my second." He turns and invites his protégé to step forward and meet us. "I wish to have a quick word with him before I am off to greet Cynbel. If you don't mind, I would like to leave him in your company. Will that be acceptable?"

"Yes, Lord," Arthmael blurts.

Caradoc pulls Eosiah off to the side while Arthmael grins from ear to ear. The conversation is short lived and one sided. Eosiah nods his understanding before he returns to us.

"May you all have a prosperous moot," Caradoc says. He starts to trot toward Kantom Lijanks Kuros while flapping his arms. At last, he turns into a merlin and soars away.

"I keep telling him that's a ridiculous exit," Eosiah says. "But he's fixated on dramatic entrances and exits."

"You're *the* Eosiah?" Arthmael asks.

"My name is Eosiah, yes," he says, bemused by Arthmael's excitement.

"You defeated Judoc last year." Arthmael is staring wide-eyed. Apparently, the gwary champion rates higher than a druid lord to him.

"Judoc is the best staff fighter I have ever faced. Is he competing again this year?"

"No, he has an injured arm and cannot compete," Arthmael says.

"Let's go over to Hedred's spot," Ysella says, before Arthmael can recount Eosiah's entire match. "There is something happening that I don't want to miss."

"Hedred's? Do any of his people ever leave the underground?" Eosiah asks.

"They do, under the cover of night. They are staying at the giant's barrow west of the River Kennet. And you all should know that my sister, Katel, is one of them and I will remove teeth from your head if you say anything disparaging about her."

Her aggressive stance dares one of us to test her. None of us are that foolish.

The long barrow sits along a gentle slope with only the rustling of the wild grass to keep it company. A stone twice as tall as a man and equally wide anchors the front façade. Even with the rising sun at our backs, the entrance eludes us for a time. It is only when I hear the soft rumble of drums that the hidden side entrance is revealed.

Eosiah is next to me at once. He keeps his back to Ysella and Arthmael and speaks to me in a low tone. "Caradoc said to aid you in any way you see fit. We will speak later." He gestures to Ysella and Arthmael to hurry to us before confidently stepping in front of me and entering the barrow.

The drums are joined by many male voices chanting in some version of the ancient tongue. A short, bald druid runs breathlessly out of the tomb. "Come quickly and make no noise."

"Yes, Lord," Ysella whispers. She shepherds us into the darkened cave mouth.

That is a druid lord?

The large stones keep the entrance in shadow at sunrise, but we can see the rays of sunlight sinking along the face of the barrow. Belenos will peer within the cave in only a few heartbeats. Stumbling in the dark, we pass between two druids chanting into empty side chambers of the hall. Their cadence echoes back from the chambers, yielding a deep, powerful harmony. The sound echoes within and I can feel the vibrations through my bones. Deeper inside is another pair doing the same at the second pair of side rooms. We pass them and the bald druid shoves us against the walls of the final chamber.

The light of Belenos slowly penetrates deeper into the barrow. The baritone voices slowly drop off and the drumming tempo slows. The alto timber of a woman's choir fills the space. Their harmonies increase into a crescendo as the sunlight strikes the back of the central alcove. The darkness is replaced with blinding white light as the sunlight reflects off the white strike stone at the end of the barrow. We all must avert our eyes from the very presence of the gods.

One final shriek of exultation and the women's voices fall silent. The men begin spinning flat wooden disks attached to

218

strings. A deep, booming vibrato cascades through the chamber. It can be none other than the thunderous voice of the Earthmother speaking to her son, Belenos. My legs go weak as the goddess' presence vibrates through my chest. My heart pounds ever faster to keep pace with the goddess.

Only Hedred is unmoved by the spectacle. Following his eyes, I see symbols glowing from the walls around us. After a scant few moments, the light sinks off the strike stone to the dirt floor. Before I can gather my thoughts, the light from Belenos retreats from the barrow entirely. All are silent as we contemplate what we just experienced.

Somehow, the male singers manage to shake off their amazement and start a steady cadence. The female druids join us in the corridor and Hedred leads us into the daylight. The spell broken, Hedred's cave druids shield their eyes from the sun and scurry for the shadows. The bald man drops to his knees and draws the symbols from the walls in the dirt.

"Thank you, Lord Hedred, for allowing us to partake in this ritual," Ysella says. She's absolutely radiant, standing in the sunlight. Her curly blonde hair shines like fine strands of gold. Another woman who could be Ysella's twin, save for her chalky white skin and dark hair, ventures from the shadows and hugs Ysella.

"Everyone, this is my sister, Ysella," the pale druid says. "And this big strong man," she grabs a tall, awkward druid by the hand and drags him over to her, "is Sieffre. Ysella is with the plains druids and this guy studies under Eghan."

Sieffre is too busy studying the ground to acknowledge anyone. He's all knees and elbows. I don't know of another person who would call him strong.

"Hello, everyone," Ysella says.

Hedred waits for a moment to see if there are any more distractions. "Think on this blessing that the Earthmother has bestowed upon you this day. Only the most prosperous of men receive such a boon."

"Yes, Lord," his druids respond.

"It may be a bit unseemly, but I must leave you now. The other lords are no doubt grousing about my absence. When I return, I will give whatever guidance I can about this visitation. For now, keep darkness from your thoughts."

"The absence of light is nothing to fear," his charges reply in unison. In broad daylight, he animorphs into a bat, of all creatures, and flies off toward Kantom Lijanks Kuros.

Thanks to Eosiah's suggestion, we head for the stone circle south of Kantom. The rest of the druids are off to the east at the gwary.

"My secret," he says, "is that for several years I spent my time here practicing staff fighting instead of being an idle spectator."

We approach the stone circle and Eosiah winks at Ysella. "I know Arthmael and Ysella are good with the staff; why don't you show me your skills, Grahme?"

Why is everyone smiling so mischievously?

In no time, sweat is pouring off me as I try to keep up with Eosiah and his lightning quick strikes. I'm no match for his skills on my best days. His staff hits the back of my knees. I crumple to the ground yet again.

"I think Grahme has had enough for now," Eosiah says without a trace of smugness. He pulls me up from the ground.

"Your footwork is much better, and you hold the staff up higher, like you should. You have learned a lot today."

Easy for him to say when it's me who keeps ending up lying helpless on the ground.

"Arthmael, are you ready to spar?" Ysella asks.

"I'll go easy on you," he replies.

Ysella unleashes a wicked spin and has her staff down low. She sweeps Arthmael's feet, and he tumbles to the ground. "Thank you for the courtesy, but I don't think I will need it." She skips off to the ring of standing stones, grinning from ear to ear, waiting for his next move.

It doesn't take long before their cracking of staves can be heard across the valley. Ysella uses her quickness to dance away from Arthmael's fearsome barrage.

"Ysella, you have a lower center of balance, so you can take more chances. Stop fighting so defensively and go on the attack," Eosiah calls.

Ysella nods her head and starts taking the fight to Arthmael. The cracking of staves is joined by audible grunts and heavy breathing.

Katel and Sieffre, uninterested in dueling, stand deep in the shadows of the forest. He has fine blond hair and delicate features on his tall, thin frame. It's hard to believe that Sieffre is a druid, or even from Pretanni. Surely, he comes from some softer stock of people. Neither he nor Katel carry any weapon save a sling. They make a very strange pair, but I wonder who else could possibly be a match for either one of them.

"While your escorts are busy, we need to talk," Eosiah says. "Very soon, Arthmael will start dipping his weapon and Ysella will brain him. So tell me, what has happened since you left our lords?"

"I wish I could, but I have been sworn to tell no one else of my quest that is not already aware." I show him my arms. "Lord Cynbel took a dim view of my stance and slapped irons on me."

"He placed irons on a druid?" Eosiah says loudly.

Arthmael turns toward us and Ysella connects right behind his ear. Arthmael is tasting dirt in the blink of an eye.

"Now you'll talk?" Ysella says with menace in her voice.

"The treatment I received from the plains druids was not part of my quest," I shout back.

Ysella twirls her staff and lodges it under her left shoulder. She advances in a no-nonsense fashion toward us.

"Say one bad word, I dare you," she says to me.

"Ysella," Eosiah says, "I don't know what has transpired so I'm in no position to judge. But this man's arms are infected, and they need to be treated."

Ysella's eyes harden. "Anything else you'd like to add?"

I raise my hands up in supplication. At last, she concedes to not dent my head. Arthmael has managed to rise to his hands and knees. He's shaking his head and trying to remember his own name.

"Well, our only herbalist is busy organizing his thoughts. So why don't you tell me what you told him," Ysella says to me.

"I merely showed him my arms and the effect of your rusty irons on them. As for a cure, all we need is some honey to spread over the wounds."

"We should go and find some. The walk will help clear Arthmael's head as well," Eosiah says.

"Who's doing that?" Katel points to the north, over Kantom Lijanks Kuros, where, against the cloudy sky, a carrion crow is commanding the attention of everyone within a league. The constant diving and aerial acrobatics are not natural for that species or any other for that matter.

"I've never seen a crow do that before," Sieffre says.

Is he so dense to not realize that it's a druid who has taken on that creature's shape?

"Yeah, let's not lose focus on the honey. We'll know soon enough who is out to embarrass themselves in front of all the influential druids of Pretanni," Eosiah says. "Grahme, give me a hand getting Arthmael up and steadied."

21

Flight from Kantom

Fourth Dark Day of Cantl, 819

Twenty-six Days until Samhain

Eosiah tells me in a hushed voice, "Caradoc wants me to get you away from Kantom Lijanks Kuros as quickly as possible. The crow is undoubtedly Caradoc, but his meaning is unclear."

"It probably means they are summoning me."

"You think so?"

I show him my infected arms again.

"Right, we're leaving."

"Where to?"

"Caradoc didn't specify that. I assumed you had a location in mind."

"Cynbel charged Ysella and Arthmael to stick with me and deliver me to the council when they request my presence."

"All the more reason to leave."

"What of Ysella and Arthmael?"

"Leave them to me."

We collect Arthmael, and Eosiah waves the others to follow us as we trudge toward the tree-covered southern hills.

"So, who here can find a beehive in these woods?" Eosiah asks.

"I can," I reply.

"Nonsense, you're the patient. Can anyone else remember their basic woodcraft?"

"Sieffre and I are out," Katel says. "I spend my time underground and Sieffre is involved in much more important tasks."

"I guess that leaves you two," Eosiah says to Ysella and Arthmael.

"And what about you?" Ysella asks.

"I am a journeyman druid. I never have to prove my worth to anyone ever again."

Ysella looks suspiciously at me. "Lord Cynbel charged us to stay close to Grahme."

"I will take care of him, though he seems stout enough to my eye." Eosiah twirls his staff.

"I could tell them where the obvious spots are," I offer.

Ysella scowls at me.

"Find the cat's eye flowers; they're the only plants still in bloom. You can follow the bees back to their hive," I say anyway. They can take my advice, or they can flounder.

Ysella grabs Arthmael's elbow and drags him into the thickest part of the woods. It appears they've chosen to flounder. Good luck trying to stumble upon a beehive that way. Katel and Sieffre move off in the opposite direction to have their own private conversation.

"Have you managed to get the ghost orchid?" Eosiah asks.

Startled, I grab my pack. "Yes." I eye him cautiously.

"Then why aren't you back at Dartmoor?" he asks, bewildered.

"I discovered that the Black Lord's men had taken the hillfort at Sarum. I fled north to stay out of his reach and warn Cynbel. The plains druids found me and have kept asking me questions that I can't answer. So, I ended up in irons and was brought here."

"Let's change into merlins and leave here."

I hold out my arm, still shaky. "I can't, or at least I shouldn't. I fought the Obsidian Mage and his men at the Giant's Choir."

His eyes go wide. "By yourself?"

"That's why I'm drained. I'm not to use any magic for a month."

"Then why did they slap irons on you?"

"I think Cynbel was hoping I'd give in and tell him the details of my quest."

"Why didn't you?"

"I was sworn by one of the Nine not to share details of my quest with anyone unless they are already familiar."

"That's asinine. I'm afraid to ask, but was it your mentor or mine who told you that?"

"I cannot say."

He waits for me to say more. Finally, he shrugs. "Well, if we can't take off without them, then we're stuck walking the whole way. So, I guess we're going to have to convince them to come with us."

I smile at his naiveté. "How can we do that?"

"Leave it to me."

I wish I had his confidence.

He inspects my arms once more before shaking his head. "Fighting the best staff men of the druids was so much easier than your quest."

He looks around to see if we are being watched. Katel and Sieffre are deep in their own conversation. Ysella and Arthmael are out of sight.

"No doubt if Loris finds out you have the flower, he'll take it for himself."

"What does he want with it?"

"If he can turn it to stone, the flower will release an Elven Tear. We think he means to use it for some sort of magical rite, but he keeps his council to himself."

"So that's why the orchids are called Elven Tears."

Sieffre and Katel furtively glance over at us. We end up staring at them until they release our gaze and resume their own heated talks. What would a fight between these two fragile druids look like?

Whatever they were discussing, Sieffre must have capitulated. Katel gestures with her head and Sieffre sullenly marches over to us. He keeps his head facing the ground. Katel hits him on the back of his shoulder, and he nearly topples over.

"Ask them," she demands.

"I, well, we." He checks Katel, but her face is hard as stone. He swallows and continues, "We heard you mention Elven Tears. Do you have any on your person?"

His voice trembles like a scolded child. I want to laugh at the situation, but I'm afraid that might make him cry.

"No. Why do you ask?"

He flashes an "I told you so" look at Katel.

"We've gone this far, and they do mentor under Boswen and Caradoc," Katel says, but no amount of cajoling will force Sieffre to speak further.

Katel sighs. "What did you make of the ceremony this morning?"

"It was a powerful moment to hear the speech of the gods, even if I couldn't understand the message."

"The Earthmother speaks in a language all her own. One does not translate her speech. You need to let it flow through you and *feel* the message she is sending."

"I felt an impossible power enveloping me, but that's all."

"If you are not accustomed to these meetings, it is hard to discern the message," Katel says dismissively.

"What did you hear from the Earthmother?" I ask.

"That is what we are trying to determine."

"Oh." Thank the gods that Ysella is nothing like her sister.

"You probably only know her manifestations as the three sister goddesses. We cave druids are closer to her than any other, so we know her true being. Sieffre and Lord Eghan are protectors of the Gwanwyns of Sulis, so they know her manifestations very well."

"Thank you for enlightening us," Eosiah says, tonelessly.

"That's not all. We are also working on deciphering the writings of the elder races," Katel says.

Sieffre is wringing his hands and avoiding eye contact. He shifts his weight from foot to foot. It's only after he realizes that we are all staring at him that he stops.

"Tell them," Katel says.

"What if we're found out?" he asks.

"Tell them or I will. You are the expert so they should hear it from you." They lock eyes briefly before Sieffre submits.

"What I'm about to tell you could get us all ostracized from the druids, or worse."

If he was trying to dissuade me, he couldn't have been any less successful. "Go ahead."

"Loris has been kind of a disaster for us since he ascended to the head druid position last year. Lords Eghan and Hedred had hoped that his experience from living on the continent would help push the stodgier of the Nine into expanding our knowledge."

"How has he been a disaster? Boswen tells me nothing."

"In the east," Katel says, "the Wigesta have built temples of wood and stone and they worship our gods in these buildings."

"That's ridiculous, you can't hope to contain a god in a building, no matter what the walls are made of," Eosiah says.

"There was a temple at Solent City, and at Sarum," I say. "And neither of those cities are controlled by the Wigesta."

Katel and Sieffre exchange a wordless glance.

"The Wigesta started years ago, to undercut us as intercessors to the gods," Sieffre says.

"Why doesn't every druid know this?" Eosiah asks in outrage.

"It is Lord Eghan who tracks them, but Caradoc should be aware as well. They had hoped that Loris could persuade the council to unearth elven and giant burials so that we could learn of their rune magic."

"By looting the graves of the elder races?" I don't even try to hide my disgust.

229

"The druids of the mainland use the magic of the giant's runes already. By learning the runes and the elven script, we would be in a better position to defend Pretanni," Sieffre says.

"The ceremony today was to honor the Earthmother," Katel says. "But we also asked her to aid us in understanding the runes. Lord Hedred beseeched her to give us the name of the ice rune. In the last chamber where we druidesses were, the light shone upon *iss*, so now we must test this to confirm that this is the name of the ice-making rune."

"Why would we need that?" Eosiah asks.

"It is the scholars like Sieffre and Lord Eghan whose duty is to expand this knowledge," Katel says. "But Cynbel, Braden, Drustan, and Meraud believe this knowledge is forbidden. Loris was supposed to convince them to allow it; but he focuses only on glorifying himself."

"That's why we can't speak in front of Ysella or Arthmael; they answer to Cynbel," Sieffre adds. "The Elven Tears, if you were to get one, could be used to commune with the gods more readily. Without it, we must wait for beneficial alignments like this morning to speak with them."

"Thank you," I say. "At last, I understand why the stupid flower is so important to so many people."

A bear bursts out of the undergrowth, loping right for us. Sieffre lets out a yelp before freezing in place. Katel screams and runs the opposite direction. I roll my eyes. Together, they have demonstrated everything you shouldn't do when you encounter a bear. *And they are druids?*

"Relax," I call out. "Can't you tell that that's Arthmael in bear form?"

The bear slows his stride and trudges toward us, grunting as he approaches. Sieffre has fallen into a fetal position. I walk forward to greet Arthmael. He rears up and growls at me.

"It's no use, Arthmael. I know it's you."

Arthmael ponderously animorphs back into his human form. "How did you know?"

"Yeah, how can you tell it's a druid when they're in animal form?" Eosiah asks. He twirls the staff absentmindedly as he approaches.

"When Arthmael walks, he dips his left shoulder. The bear did also. No bear would live long with that clumsy of a gait. It could only be successful hunting deaf prey."

"Really? Can you pick out Ysella in animal form? Eosiah?" Arthmael challenges.

"It depends. If one of you is in bird form, then I couldn't tell by your distinctive walk. But I could probably guess. Flamboyant people tend to be flamboyant birds, just like I know without a doubt that the crow we saw before was Caradoc."

"Katel," Eosiah shouts, "It's safe to return."

The leaves rustle as Sieffre picks himself up off the ground. "I'll get her."

Arthmael gives me a questioning glance, but I can't explain why Sieffre or Katel do what they do.

"Did you find a hive?"

"I did, follow me." Arthmael turns and dips his left shoulder as he shows us the way. Eosiah smiles. He saw the telltale move. We go slowly so that Sieffre and Katel can find us.

"Can we find a path without so many leaves?" Katel asks for the thirteenth time.

"It's autumn," I say.

"What is the problem with the leaves?" Eosiah asks.

"Down below, when you hear the ground beneath you crackle, it means the stone beneath your feet isn't stable. You move quickly or you fall to your death. These cursed leaves sound just like it."

"But you can see they're only leaves," I say.

"We learn to use all of our senses down below. Sight is in many ways the most useless of them all, so I don't trust my eyes. Hence, a path that doesn't promise me death at every step would be easier on my nerves."

"Try keeping your feet skimming over top the ground and kick the leaves out of your way," Sieffre suggests.

She takes his advice for the rest of the hike. We are the noisiest group of druids to ever walk upon Pretanni.

Two jackdaws go streaking through the treetops to our right, calling out an alarm.

"What is it?" Sieffre asks nervously.

"Quiet," I say.

"Everyone," Eosiah says in a low voice, "let's move into that copse of trees. We have much to discuss."

Ysella looks at me, but I shrug. I don't have any answers. Well, nothing that I want to volunteer, at least. Katel and Sieffre gladly enter into the darkest shadows. Holding his finger to his mouth, Eosiah asks for silence while we all scan the sky. The eerie silence builds as we wait in vain.

Finally, Eosiah speaks up. "We have much to discuss and not much time to do it." He turns to face Ysella and Arthmael.

"Grahme may not be at liberty to say, but I am under no such restrictions. Grahme possesses a ghost orchid . . ."

"You mean the flower in his pack?" Arthmael asks.

"Yes."

"I knew it!" Sieffre shouts.

Eosiah stares him down.

"Sorry," Sieffre says.

"Why does anyone care about that little flower?" Ysella asks.

"The ghost orchid is a rare flower that is said to form only when an elf's tear hits the ground. Once sprouted, it will come back only under perfect conditions. As you may imagine, they are few these days."

"I've never heard of them."

"They possess an innate magic that is best left undisturbed. Grahme's quest was to bring one of these flowers back to Boswen."

"Why didn't you tell us that?" Ysella demands.

"I was commanded to remain silent."

Ysella shakes her head in disgust. "You are as bad as your mentor."

"If I may," Eosiah says. "Loris is aware of the magic within these flowers and if he were to find out Grahme has one, he would demand it be turned over to him. What that fat fool would do with it is anyone's guess."

"He's the head druid," Ysella scolds.

"My mentor and I hold him in low regard, I'm afraid. There are those among the druids who would like to study the flower and harness its magic for good. It is for this reason that we can't let Grahme be found and presented to the Council of Nine."

"That's what we were charged to do," Arthmael says.

"No," I say, "you were to make sure I show up when and if I receive a summons. No one has summoned me yet."

"Nice try, but I don't shirk the duties given to me by a member of the Nine, either," Ysella says.

"Then your choices are," Eosiah says, "you can fight Grahme and me and if you subdue us both, you can present him to the Nine. Or you can travel with us, and if we should be discovered, then you are free to do your duty. I promise not to interfere." Eosiah spins his staff idly.

Ysella sizes Eosiah up before turning to Arthmael, but it's clear that he wants no part in making a decision.

"Katel, you and Sieffre have been quiet. Where do you stand?"

"I won't fight," Sieffre blurts.

"I love you, sister, but we are with Eosiah."

Ysella stares open-mouthed, unable to express her disbelief.

"It turns out, our lords are working with Caradoc and Boswen," Katel adds.

Ysella turns to me, but I'm as surprised as she is. How is it that everyone knows as much or more than I do?

"Then the jackdaws?" Ysella asks.

"They answer to Caradoc. It is a signal to us and a way to flush all the birds to flight, covering our exit."

Ysella looks expectantly at Arthmael.

"My head is still ringing," he says. "I don't want to face Eosiah."

Ysella glares at her sister but Katel is busy humming to herself. Sieffre is staring at the ground.

"It seems I'm outnumbered," Ysella starts. "You give your word that when they find us and we're commanded to bring Grahme to see the council, you will not interfere?"

"I do," Eosiah says.

Exasperated, Ysella throws up her arms. "Then I guess I have no choice but to agree."

"Thank you, I did not wish to fight either of you," Eosiah says. "I suggest we all turn into jackdaws and scout for Grahme."

"I can't animorph," Sieffre says.

"And I can only change into a bat or an otter," Katel adds.

With exaggerated patience, Eosiah says, "That's all right; you don't have to come with us."

"Oh, no. Grahme has an Elven Tear; we're coming with you," Katel says.

"Then the three of us will scout," Eosiah says, "and you two can walk with Grahme."

"I think actively trying to avoid our lord would go against our orders," Ysella says, "so Arthmael and I won't be your scouts."

"Then we walk all the way to Land's End together," Eosiah says, defeated.

"We can't chance the Londinjon Road to Lord Eghan's camp; they're sure to check his camp first. We should cross south of the road and then head southwest. We should hit the Druid Ditch Road somewhere near the tor of Ynys Witrin."

"Because no one will think to check the only major road that heads into the Land's End peninsula," Ysella says sarcastically.

"Hopefully, by then I can change into a bird and fly the rest of the way home," I say.

"Fine, lead the way. We will be crossing the plains without seeing a tree or any other means of cover for a couple days," Ysella says.

"You and Arthmael know the way better than anyone else."

"Again, I'm not going to actively shirk my orders."

I shrug. "How many druids would expect us to be doing that?"

Eosiah extends his hand, inviting me to lead the way. I don't blame him. I don't really want to lead the group on a fruitless mission, either, but I can't really refuse.

22

A Long, Tough Slog

Fifth Dark Day of Cantl, 819

Twenty-five Days until Samhain

Adense blanket of fog covers the rolling hills. "The chance of us being spotted before midday is about nil," I say, unable to contain my glee.

"Before long, Belenos will burn off this fog and we'll be revealed to any druid that happens to fly over us," Ysella replies.

"I think not. Look to the west."

"The west? I can't see more than twenty feet in any direction."

"Exactly, see how dark it is? A storm is approaching."

Our cold, wet band trudges silently across the drenched hills. At last we spot a homestead. By unspoken agreement, we pick up our pace.

"Hello, good people," Eosiah calls. There is no reply.

"The door is still open," Arthmael says.

"Oh no," Ysella says.

Sieffre shouts out as he falls down. Katel rushes to his side.

"There's a dead woman over here," she says, alarmed.

We gather around the unfortunate woman while Eosiah sits on his heels to examine the body more closely. He turns her head to the left. "That would be the fatal blow," he says. "It's an ax wound. Not enough force to cleave her skull, so they might have wanted to keep her alive." My stomach churns at the thought that this woman might have been lucky.

"Spread out, there are likely to be more poor souls left where they fell."

"By the looks of her, she's been through childbirth several times," Katel says. If it was possible to increase our collective dread, that did it.

"This must be the husband," Ysella calls out from outside the opened doorway.

"That's a Coritani spear point," Eosiah says. "Have they been raiding this deep into Silures territory?"

"War season ended more than a month ago," Ysella says. "But we've been busy chasing raiders from Solent Keep across the hills for the last half month or more. It could have been a blood feud."

"Even still, I doubt the Silures could keep such a vicious feud from your notice. Perhaps this was a personal vendetta?"

"If it were a personal vendetta, the homestead would have been burned to the ground along with the offending family," Arthmael says.

"It's hard to start a fire in a downpour like we've had," I say. "Maybe the children were able to hide inside."

Nobody bothers to say how unlikely that is. I brace myself before going through the opened door. The children all lay around the fire, the infant still clutched in the oldest daughter's arms. The middle child, a boy, lies face down in his own sticky black blood.

"There's not much light left. We should bury them while we can," Ysella says.

As darkness falls, we've finished digging a shallow grave. The water puddles up around the resting bodies.

"Blessed Epona, please escort these poor souls through the beyond and grant a better life for them on the next turn of the wheel," I pray.

"Aye," the others answer.

"What I don't understand," Arthmael says, "is who would have done this?"

"Maybe it was marauding brigands?" Sieffre says.

"Unlikely. The clans would halt all but the most bitter blood feuds to take care of outlaws," Ysella says.

"Yeah, it's fine for their own to kill each other, but outsiders? They're more likely to find an ax in the head than they are to be interrogated," Arthmael says.

"The food stores are untouched," Katel says.

Under firelight, Eosiah and I kick dirt over the boy's spilled blood.

Arthmael throws a few more branches on the fire. "We don't have enough wood to last the night, so I'll cook enough for us for tonight and tomorrow morning."

As the cold wind batters the house, Katel and Sieffre withdraw to the darkest wall. I stake out my own place, sitting a good way apart from them. To my surprise, Ysella follows me wordlessly and lays her head on my chest. Drawing what support we can from each other, we drift off into a dreamless sleep.

At first light, we restart our stroll, as Ysella calls it. "Until such time that we are discovered," she adds.

It's a bright, crisp day, and the blue sky stretches on as far as the eye can see. All I can think about is how exposed we are. The only trees line the rivers and streams. At least the plains had changed into their fall colors. Six white robes would be even more obvious on a blanket of green grasses.

"I hope you make it back to your mentor and complete your quest," Ysella says in a low voice.

"You do?"

"Yes."

"Then you're willing to help me evade capture?"

She gives a rueful laugh. "Don't misunderstand me. If I am commanded to bring you back, I will, even if it means going through Eosiah. But I hope it doesn't come to that."

A smile flits across my face. Perhaps we can get back to how we were, after all. I take a deep breath. The grass seems more vibrant and the air purer. I take in the beauty of the plains until my eyes fall upon Arthmael's gloomy face.

"I will be glad when this quest is over. Then our lives can return to normal," I say.

Ysella chuckles. "I've known enough men to know that your idea of normal is the Lughnasa festival. Let me assure you, that was not normal either." She playfully runs her shoulder into my side. Pressed in close to me she says, "Arthmael is watching us. It's probably best for the group to not antagonize him."

I quicken my pace and catch up with Eosiah before she can start to lecture me about getting along with Arthmael.

"Any idea how far we've come?"

He looks sideways at me. "Are you hoping for several more nights with Ysella?"

"What?" I say, startled.

"It's fine by me, and it's obvious that you two have a connection. Now Arthmael, he'll just have to deal with that on his own. But to answer your original question, see how the southwest horizon is hazy?"

I follow where he's pointing.

"I suspect that is Ynys Witrin, the Isle of Glass. The fog comes and goes with the tide, which floods the marsh around the tor. The water is so calm; one could gaze at their reflections for as long as they can sit still. It's a narcissist's dream. The road can't be far now. We'll turn south and I suspect we'll reach the tor after midday."

"Sieffre!" Katel cries.

We turn back to our group to see that Sieffre has managed to fall, again.

"He's amazing at finding every underground burrow," Eosiah mutters.

"How is he a druid?" I ask.

"His talents are not suited for long quests."

"Or walking in general."

Arthmael and Katel help him up. He gingerly puts pressure on his left foot. "I'm fine. I can walk it off," he announces.

"You know what," I say, "I need to keep Arthmael on speaking terms if I can. I'm going to switch with him so he can talk with you."

"I'm not properly equipped to satisfy his desires," Eosiah says with a laugh.

"Talk to him about staff fighting. That's nearly as important to him."

I think I hear Arthmael mutter his thanks when I relieve him of his task. It's a start at least.

"I'm interested in learning more about what you two are doing," I say to Katel and Sieffre.

"We don't speak of it openly," Katel says.

"Katel, Boswen is his mentor. If we start doubting our own allies, then everything is lost," Sieffre says. He turns his attention to me. "The elves and giants each had their own symbols for capturing their thoughts in a physical form. These scripts allow them to leave their thoughts carved into a tree or stone for others to read, even hundreds of years after they are gone."

"So, these scripts are like silent bards? They can record the deeds of times past?"

"Yes," Sieffre says. "You understand. But these scripts do more than that, they also—"

"Watch, that's a rabbit burrow," I say.

Sieffre walks in a ridiculously wide circle around it. "Thanks, the last thing I need is to injure both ankles."

"I'll watch for you, tell me more about these scripts."

"The elven script is readily accessible. It seems that each letter corresponds to a specific type of tree and they went wild carving it into bark through the western forest. Most of those trees are dead now, naturally, but we know the name of each letter. Of course, that's about all we know. There are a few instances where the same several letters are in a row, but no one knows what they mean."

"What good are these marks, then?" I ask. "And why are there none to be found at Land's End?"

"That's because you live in the area of the pixies. The plains were the land of the giants and the Great Western Forest was the realm of the elves. I am from Marloes, on the far western edge of Pretanni. The very oldest trees in the forest have hundreds of these symbols. Now, the giants, on the other hand, they only left their runes carved in stone, and mostly in tombs."

"So that's what Hedred was doing in the dirt right after the Earthmother's presence."

"Yes, exactly. As you experienced in the long barrow, these are runes of power," Sieffre says. "The people of the mainland have been experimenting for centuries with these symbols. If we want to defend ourselves, we need to understand how to use them."

"Eosiah is waving for us," I say. "You'll have to tell me more about this when we have time."

Eosiah is on top of a hill overlooking the western road.

"See the smoke to the west, near Ynys Witrin?"

"Not another massacre," Katel says, horrified.

"I'm afraid so, but the fire is still raging," Eosiah says.

"So, we can confront these brigands," adds Arthmael.

"I could feel the drumming of horses when I reached the road," Eosiah says. "Whoever it is, they have a healthy number in their band, and they will reveal themselves shortly." Eosiah waves us to lie down in the tall grass.

"We can block the road," Arthmael says.

"Better to take stock of our enemy before we become surrounded by them," I reply.

Arthmael scowls at me, but the rumbling of hooves forestalls further discussion.

"That's Gurthcid!" Arthmael says.

"Quiet," Eosiah hisses. "And everybody stay down. By their white hair, they are still looking to do battle."

Once the war band passes, a wagon full of freshly slaughtered hogs follows. We watch them disappear over the hill before anyone dares to move. Eosiah upturns his hands, asking for an explanation.

"Gurthcid is a Coritani warrior we met while going to Kantom. He and his men said they were going south to hunt the Black Mage's men," Ysella says.

"He's unlikely to find any in this part of Silures territory," says Eosiah.

"There's no way a single homestead could keep that many hogs," I say.

"Did you notice that there are several bloodstains on the horses below the trophy heads?" Arthmael asks.

"Let's wait until we're sure they're clear. I don't want them to turn around and ride us down while we're stuck on the road," Eosiah says.

In truth, no one is in a hurry to inspect the latest carnage.

23

Finding the High Ground

Seventh Dark Day of Cantl, 819

Twenty-three Days until Samhain

The marsh village sits on top of three small hills near the great tor. Now, at low tide, a stone-lined walkway leads to the first and lowest of the hills. The walkway spirals around the hill on its way to the top. Smoldering Remnants of ten raised houses are all that remain. We wordlessly poke at the embers. The lone survivor is a dog, but he's too scared to come out from underneath the homes. As much as I would like to coax this poor animal out, we have a grim business to attend to.

The second hill, a man's height higher than the first, holds raised granaries and a small, now roofless gathering hall behind them. The hill is extra steep and there is no path up the side, only a pair of bridges, one to the ruined homes and one to the third hill. All the granaries have gouges near their bases and spilled seeds litter the ground. The thatch roof has collapsed into a smoking mess and the walls will no doubt follow soon. Not trusting the wrecked interior, our only option is to ease our way between the side of the hall and the hill's steep slope. There is barely a foot's clearance between the wall and a quick drop into the mucky fen below.

Arthmael is the first around and he quickly returns to us. "The mystery of the missing townspeople is solved." He puts up his hand to Ysella and Katel. "There's no need for you to see it."

"And why not?" Katel demands. She pushes past Arthmael before disappearing around the building. After a gasp, she asks the wind, "What would drive people to do this?"

We join her at the site of the massacre. Ysella hurries to her sister's side. "Come on, Katel. Arthmael meant to be kind. Come away from here."

"But why?" Katel wails.

We let Ysella escort her sister away from the fallen. Before us are fifteen men and three boys. All of the men are headless. Most are peppered with several arrows, but none of them were the killing blows.

"They shot arrows at these men for sport," Eosiah says. They were treated like forest beasts." He pulls out one of the arrows. "It's another Coritani point. But why would anyone do this?"

"So senseless," Sieffre says. "What's the motive?"

I squeeze his shoulder. "For food, or coin, or because the band was bored. Often there is no reason at all. It's just what war bands do."

"These villagers are Silures; Gurthcid and his men are Coritani," Arthmael adds.

"They're all from Pretanni," Sieffre says.

"If not for one tribe attacking another, this island would know peace, but that is not the way of it here," Eosiah says.

"But *why* do they fight each other?"

No one volunteers an answer for Sieffre.

"Gurthcid has always been quick with his weapons," Arthmael says, "but he yearns for wealth and fame. There is no honor in killing a bunch of homesteaders."

"The tide is starting to come back in," Katel announces.

Eosiah points to an old man lying face down behind the defending group. There is no blood coming from his corpse. Arthmael leans down and inspects the body. "Clubbed, only once, in the back of the head. His head must not have been worth taking."

From the smell, we are all aware the third island was where the pigs were kept.

"No doubt he was the last line to keep the marauders from getting to the women and children," I say.

"He failed," Arthmael says in a detached voice. "The bridge still spans the two hills."

The third hill has a packed earth ramp leading down into the marsh. It had been for the pigs to traverse to and from the mud puddles of low tide. The top of the hill holds the pens, now filled with more victims. The bodies of over two dozen women and children lie in the muck where they were slaughtered.

"Has anyone *ever* heard of tribes killing all the women and children instead of selling them into slavery?" I ask.

"Their death is a blessing," Ysella says.

"I don't dispute that," I say, "but why kill every last person only to steal their hogs? This is not what raiders do."

"Grahme's right. They should have taken the women for sport if nothing else," Arthmael says.

Katel shudders. "So, these people were fortunate?"

Eosiah looks up at Belenos. "The road out will be submerged well before nightfall. Let's say prayers to the gods for these poor souls and leave their bodies for the tides and the fish. We don't want to be trapped up here for the night."

"There's another bridge leading off to the great tor. Why did the women not run?" I ask.

Docile sheep graze undisturbed on the great tor of Ynys Witrin.

"They must have waited too long watching their men," Arthmael says.

"They should have taken the children and run at the first sign of danger," Ysella says.

"Easy to say when it's not your loved ones. In the end, they paid the ultimate price for their devotion," I say.

"Why would they take only the pigs and leave the sheep?" Sieffre asks.

"The sheep are protected from predators and they have plenty of grass to eat. Most likely they were left until the war band grows hungry again," I say.

"They're coming back?" Sieffre says, his voice cracking.

"We should scout out the area instead of blindly leaving this place," Ysella says.

"I'll go." Before anyone can say otherwise, Arthmael launches himself into the air and morphs into a red kite.

"Why do all of the plains druids choose the red kite?" I ask.

"Is there a more elegant bird?" Ysella responds. "It has long, powerful wings that can soar on the wind effortlessly."

I follow his flight path enviously. As a rule, birds lack the capacity for pity or remorse. After what we've witnessed, I wish that could have been me.

Arthmael returns. "Even if the women and children had fled to the great tor, they would have been surrounded by water. They should have kept coracles for their escape."

"It's all so sad," Ysella says.

"We can't linger or we'll be trapped here for the night. Let's tend to the deceased quickly and be on our way," Eosiah says.

"He must have been out hunting," Katel says, pointing at a rider dressed all in black at the opposite end of the paved marsh path.

The man is sitting on the same gray horse I saw at Men Meur Kov Keigh seven days ago.

The hair on my arms stands up. "Hold, that's the Obsidian Mage."

Sieffre runs to the edge of the mound, trying to get a better look.

The Black Lord makes his way down the path with a methodical pace. The water is starting to inch its way back into the marshes, but it's not enough to bother a trained horse. Arthmael lets out a yell. "This is for Seisyll!" as he starts a steady barrage of slung stones. One of the stones strike true, making contact with the Dark Lord's chest and the illusion vanishes into nothingness.

"Look, there on the trader's road," Eosiah says.

While he was distracting us, Gurthcid's war band had been forming up behind the last copse of trees.

"We're trapped," Ysella says.

The Coritani warriors methodically start down the path the apparition had taken.

"Why don't they charge?" I ask. "They chose the same approach at Men Meur Kov Keigh."

"It's meant to unnerve us," Arthmael says. "A frightened mind is easier to control."

"How long until high tide?" I ask.

"Well after dark," Katel responds. "What?" She asks defensively. "We keep very close watch on the tides. It's critical to know about them when you're underground. Flooded tunnels can turn into death traps."

I raise my hands to show I meant no offense.

"We'll have to hold them off until darkness and then try to make our escape," Eosiah says.

"How? Grahme and Sieffre can't animorph," Ysella asks.

"If it's life or death, I can animorph," I say. I extend my arm out in front of me. It's not much worse than the first day I started under Boswen's tutelage.

"If we don't do something to slow them down, we won't make it to nightfall," Arthmael says.

"I can help," Katel says.

I look at Ysella, silently questioning what her daft sister could possibly do. She shrugs.

Katel's eyes lock onto the land bridge as she enters into a trance. She speaks too fast in the ancient tongue for me to follow.

Small mounds of dirt pop up in front of the horses and water oozes out of them. In no time, the paved road is submerged, and the warriors halt their advance.

Gurthcid spurs his horse onward, though its tail is swishing side-to-side and it's jerking its head upward at the unnatural rise of water. The poor animal is one surprise from bolting away in fear. Gurthcid realizes this too. He calls for a halt and he and his men retreat back to the Dark Lord. It's frustrating. If only they were closer, we could have urged the horses into a panic.

Without a word, the men dismount and tie up their horses. The next advance is on foot. The path is ankle deep in water now. Katel's eyes are squeezed shut and sweat is running down her face. Her whitened knuckles match her robe. The water continues to rise, but not enough to hamper the Coritani's steady pace. Each of Gurthcid's men holds a bow above the rising water.

"Can you hold the water?" Sieffre asks.

"Yes, for a time at least," she says through clenched teeth.

"Then it's my turn." Sieffre stands next to Katel and starts mumbling the ancient words while making grand gestures with both of his arms. A column of water grows to three times the height of the men. The arms of the water elemental separate from the torso and it sloshes toward the warriors. They continue toward us, undaunted.

"They should have run away at first sight of the elemental," Eosiah says. "Magical displays always cause a panic."

"They are being controlled by the Obsidian Lord," I say. "We won't be able to scare them off."

The elemental pounds the first two men into the water. Both remain face down, and unmoving. The elemental moves ponderously over the path, drawing more water to it. The water is waist high around it and barely puddles elsewhere in the marsh. As one, the warriors put away their bows and draw their spears and axes. The band forms a semi-circle around the waterspout and lunge

251

forward. The elemental responds by downing another two men, but their attack has been successful. The twisting, watery force is now merely equal in height to its attackers.

"Their orders are to advance to our location. Putting the elemental directly in front of them will cause them to confront it. If you can attack them from the side, perhaps they will focus on moving forward instead, and your elemental will prove more deadly," Ysella says.

The elemental collapses back into the water. The Coritani wordlessly put away their weapons. The march resumes, oblivious to their fallen comrades. Sieffre, dripping in sweat, is standing next to a red-faced Katel. "I will try one more time." He wipes his brow and flicks the sweat away.

"Can you hold?" he yells to Katel.

"Not much longer."

He begins his mumbling and arm gestures again. A slightly smaller waterspout rises from the stagnant marsh and moves toward the single line of attackers, this time from the side.

Ten lay unconscious in the marsh and Sieffre and Katel will soon share the same fate if they keep expending themselves. Gurthcid raises his arm to halt. They retreat for yet another plan.

"That bought us some time," Eosiah says, upbeat.

"Sunset is still far off," Ysella reminds us all.

"Even when Belenos sinks, we must hold for true darkness to make good our escape," I say.

The paved pathway has been swallowed up by the tide, a minor change in our favor. One of Gurthcid's men breaks from the circle, draws his bow and shoots in our direction. It lands harmlessly in front of the first mound of the ruined town.

"Do they mean to hunt us as if we're game animals as well?" Eosiah asks, indignant.

"They're mind-controlled," I remind him, but he's still incensed.

"The arrow is for the hunting of beasts, not a weapon of war."

"I don't think he cares about the niceties of warfare."

Gurthcid and his men start their advance again. One glance and it's obvious that Katel and Sieffre are spent.

"What's the plan now?" I ask.

"We make their approach as slow as we can," Eosiah says. "From the high ground, our slings should be able to reach them before their arrows can reach us. Three of us will use slings, two of us will block any incoming arrows with our staves and one will make ready for our escape to the tor."

"Does everyone feel that confident with their staves?" I ask.

Eosiah, Ysella, and Arthmael all answer in the affirmative at once.

"Very well," Eosiah says. "You three will be our slingers."

Great, I've been lumped in with Katel and Sieffre.

"Arthmael, can you prepare the bridges?" Eosiah asks.

"I'm on it."

Now that action is required, Arthmael is filled with a raw energy. I can learn to like this version.

Eosiah eyes our enemies. "They're still a bit out of range. Grahme, why don't you try to talk through the process of animorphing to Sieffre while you have the chance? It may be our only way out of here."

"Right."

Sieffre eyes me nervously.

I start my lesson with all the optimism I can muster. "Watch the birds around us and try to see the world from their eyes. The songbirds keep a watch out for seeds, bugs, and predators in the sky. Once you open your mind, concentrate on your own skin and pull it into the new shape of the bird."

Sieffre looks like he's constipated.

"The hard part is the beginning," I assure him. "But once you surrender your mental humanness, you can adjust to thinking like and becoming another creature."

Sieffre hangs his head in shame.

"Sieffre, you are able to call forth elementals from non-living matter, something I have never been able to do. You can do this."

"Everyone has different abilities," he smiles ruefully. "But I will treat this as if it's life or death."

24

Giving Ground

Seventh Dark Day of Cantl, 819

Twenty-three Days until Samhain

The narrow sheep path to the top of the great tor is trickier than at first glance. Half buried rocks are hidden all along its length and with the wet grass, tripping will likely cause a quick drop to the marsh below.

"Come on Sieffre, keep up," Arthmael bellows.

We're escorting Katel and Sieffre to the top. The height will put them safely out of range of arrows, but they'll be able to sling stones. Sieffre clutches his bag and hunches over it like it's the most valuable object on all Pretanni. He slips again, but I'm ready for it. Once again, he's saved from falling down the tor to the enemy below.

"Do you want me to carry that bag?" I offer.

"No, once we're settled, this bag and I will slow down those animals."

We're halfway to the top. The closest arrows have landed well below us. Arthmael surveys the site. Eosiah and Ysella are chancing the mead hall on the second hill, trading slung stones for arrows.

"You can take it from here, Grahme," he says. Without waiting for a reply, Arthmael scampers down the slope before changing into a red kite and joining the others on the second hill.

"We can make it the rest of the way," Katel says. "You can rejoin the others as well."

"I have nowhere near the skill with the staff as those three do," I say. "And I'd like to know how that bag is going to help us."

Sieffre gives me a nervous smile. "You know the giant's runes we've been talking about?"

"Yes."

"I told you before that Lords Hedred and Eghan, or more accurately, Katel and I on their behalf, are gathering up these runes. If done properly, magic can be locked into common items, like stones, and released when the word of power is spoken."

I look down the slope at our comrades. My interest is waning fast. I should be helping, not listening to him prattle.

"That's great work," I say absently.

"I have several of them here with me," he says loudly. "And I know how to wield this magic."

"Show me." Maybe he can be of use to us after all.

Sieffre pulls out a smooth river rock with a strange inscription carved into it.

"Can you hit the bridge between the first and second hills from here?" he asks.

"Of course," I brag.

The three hills form a line jutting out to the east from the southern end of the tor. I grab my sling and wait for Sieffre to offer up his precious stone. He places it in the cradle of my sling but holds on to it with both hands. "After you launch it, yell out the word '*cweorth*' and you'll see what these stones can do."

Ysella and the others are pinned down behind the partially collapsed walls of the mead hall. It's only a matter of time before the warriors cross the bridge and take up positions behind the ruined granaries. There's no way to pull the bridge down between the first two hills without being riddled with arrows. They can't stay on the second hill much longer.

I don't see how this stone can knock the bridge off its moorings, but what do we have to lose? Two quick rotations and the stone is sent arcing downward.

"*Cweorth*! Say *cweorth*." Sieffre shouts at me.

"*Cweorth*," I say, feeling foolish.

The stone ignites in midair into a fiery ball streaking toward the target. The incendiary stone strikes the bridge, causing a sheet of fire to race across it at an unnatural speed. Only the dirt on either side halts the flames. In but a few heartbeats, the bridge supports weaken, and the remnants crash down into the muddy water below.

Eosiah lets out a whoop. "Awesome work, Grahme," he shouts before turning his attention back to the warriors.

"What else do you have in there?" I ask.

"I only brought seven runes. Had I known that we were going to be in a battle—"

"What can they do?"

"I have one more fire rune; you saw what that can do. Then I have two bow runes, they will launch a blast of energy. It's like shooting an arrow, but it always flies straight to the target."

"So, if I throw the stone as far as I can, when I say the word, it's like launching an arrow from where the stone is?"

"Yes."

"So, it doubles the range of a bow and it's always a true shot?"

"Yes."

"That will be useful. Save those for taking shots at the Obsidian Lord if he gets in range."

"I also have a sun rune, which will light up the sky as bright as Belenos' disk. The last two I have are newly deciphered; one is a stone rune, which turns earth into stone. The other is an earth rune; it does the opposite, turning stone into earth."

"Can you make more?"

"Each one requires a precise ritual. It's not really conducive to a battlefield."

"Save the sun for after nightfall. It would be good to blind them right before we make our escape. I'll let the others know about your surprises. Gather as many stones as you can. It's going to be a long evening."

"I learned a new one at the Kennet barrow," Sieffre says to my back. I change into a tawny owl and glide down to my friends, instead.

"You're not supposed to be using your powers," Ysella says as she swats an arrow out of the air.

"Sorry, it happened without me even thinking about it," I lie. The transformation was easy, and I don't feel dizzy. It's been seven days; do I really need to wait a month?

"It's good to know that you can animorph," Eosiah says. "That was an awesome trick you did from up there. How did you manage it?" He keeps his staff constantly twirling, speeding up only when an arrow needs to be broken in two.

"They're Sieffre's runes, but he only has a few of them."

258

Gurthcid and his men assemble a wall of tree bark shields in front of us. The center opens up and a post from one of the houses is tipped over the void between the first and second hills. Thunk. It makes contact with the second hill.

"Fall back to the third hill!" Eosiah roars. We begin our retreat, never taking our eyes off our attackers. The ruined mead hall obscures most of us from view. The bridge and the third hill, however, will give them clear shots.

"Let's make sure this time we pull the second bridge down before we're pushed back too far," Ysella says.

"I'll do it," Arthmael yells.

"We'll go over the bridge in groups," Eosiah says. "Grahme, you go first and Ysella will block any arrows that come your way."

I don't have time to protest. Already men are crossing over on the downed post. They're taking up positions behind the granaries.

"I'm going." I sprint across the bridge, keeping my head lowered as best I can. I grab the support post on the third island and spin myself around to see the attackers. Ysella's mouth is agape. For some reason she's still on the other end of the bridge.

Ysella, then Eosiah start crossing the bridge, never looking away from the archers. Each knocks down the arrows with ease.

"Why did you take off running like that?" Ysella asks.

"I thought that was the plan."

Eosiah joins us. "Grahme, it's awfully hard to swing a staff accurately while running full speed. But we all made it over, and that's what counts."

Arthmael pries the second support from the hillside and the bridge between the second and third hill goes crashing into the knee-high water.

"Hurry, Arthmael," Ysella shouts, pointing at the warriors inching their way along the outer mead hall wall.

"He'll be overrun," I say.

Arthmael squinches up his face before animorphing into a red kite. He launches himself away from Gurthcid's men and circles around behind us before landing.

"I didn't see where the Obsidian Mage is hiding," he says.

"Damn. Taking him out with Sieffre's arrow stone solves all of our problems," I say.

"We won't be able to hold this hill for long. We're too exposed," Eosiah says. "The only cover is the fencing for the pigs. Remember, we don't need to kill them, only to slow their advance and destroy as many arrows as we can. The real battle doesn't start until they try to overrun us on the tor."

I glance back at our last bridge. It is a good fifty paces long and totally exposed to arrow fire. Worse, the bridge is supported every seven paces. There's no way we'll be able to collapse all eight of the bridge sections while taking fire.

Ysella's staff skims by my nose and snaps an arrow in two. "Grahme, you need to pay attention to the guys shooting at you," she says, annoyed.

Gurthcid has five archers shooting arrows while another five shield them from the stones Katel and Sieffre are slinging.

We follow close along the pigpen's wooden fence. No one should ever have to dodge arrows while backpedaling in pig shit. If I fall, I will never be allowed to forget my clumsiness. We're still twenty paces from the final bridge. I duck as another arrow flies through where my head had been.

"It's better to break the arrows when you can," Ysella says. "We don't want them to pick it up and shoot it at us again."

Gurthcid and his men are forced to slow their pace under the onslaught of Katel and Sieffre's hail of stones. They take cover behind the walls of the mead hall.

"How do they manage any accuracy with slinging multiple stones at once?" I ask.

"Don't know," Eosiah says. "But the longer they are held back the better chance we have."

One of the attackers tries to make a dash for the bridge. He has just enough time to notice it is gone before a stone slams into his temple.

"They should be reforming a shield wall any time now. Once they manage to replace the bridge with another log, be prepared to give ground very quickly," Eosiah says.

His guess is accurate. Another post is stretched over hills two and three in short order. The men run across the beams to our hill without fear of being hit. The Obsidian Lord must be compelling them, but where is he?

"Get your slings ready and cover me," I say.

"Grahme, no," Ysella says.

I look up at Belenos. "We need to bleed away more time."

"What do you plan to do?" Eosiah demands.

Another thump alerts us to a second post being laid down. The warriors are coming over two at a time.

"Cover me."

I picture the majestic sedge elk from the great Arden Forest and take on the shape, complete with antlers as wide as my outstretched arms. I charge. The battlefield clamor ceases as neither

261

side is expecting this. I'm up to full speed in three strides and the ground between us is disappearing fast. I slam into the first half-dozen men and transfer my momentum to them. Their limbs flail in all directions as they sail into the muddy water below. I scratch the ground with my right front hoof before charging again. Now the shouts are coming from everywhere and the men are jumping down the slope to avoid my wrath.

Surprise can be devastating, but it doesn't last long. I race back to my comrades and change back into my human form. Already, Gurthcid is redirecting his archers. Like every able-bodied man of Pretanni, they know the kill zone for all the animals in the forest.

"I suggest we fall back now."

"Fall back!" Eosiah roars between laughs. "You are one crazy druid." With a flick of his wrists his staff starts rotating again as he covers our retreat.

The final bridge between the marsh village and the great tor of Ynys Witrin is fifty paces long. After we make our way past the midway point, Sieffre hurls another fire rune at the bridge. The fire races unnaturally fast across the bridge, making us sprint or be consumed in the fire.

The last among us, Eosiah pumps his legs with single-minded determination. The bridge is collapsing faster than he can move. The flames reach his heels and he leaps before the wood below him disintegrates. His toes barely touch solid ground. He waves his arms wildly to propel himself forward. For an awkward moment, his body teeters on the edge. I grab hold of his once white robe and yank until he falls on top of me. I'm rendered speechless as I try to regain my breath.

"This is no time to lie down, Grahme," he says, smiling. He helps me up on the tor's grassy slope. He slaps me on the back and my vision starts to narrow. I regain my sense with Eosiah now

262

holding me from tumbling into the marsh. We silently marvel at the rune's destruction.

Gurthcid has called a halt to the attack for now. No one could foresee the entire bridge burning down in but a few heartbeats. Katel and Sieffre descend to see the damage the rune stone has wrought.

"I only saw two ways up the tor when I was scouting from the air," Arthmael says. "The sides are too steep to chance climbing up. This front way is the steeper of the two, so we have the advantage in combat fighting, but we'll be totally exposed to archers. The other side has a longer, more gradual path and is totally exposed from the sides."

Eosiah nods. "I suspect they will try a frontal assault first, especially because the Dark Lord doesn't seem to care if he loses men. The four of us will defend the slope and Katel and Sieffre will continue slinging stones from on top."

"How long do we do this?" Arthmael asks.

"Until darkness can hide our escape."

"Assuming we get away cleanly"—Arthmael nods his head toward Sieffre—"it doesn't matter what direction we go; they have horses and they are bound to ride us down."

"Do you recommend leaving our comrades behind?" Eosiah asks.

"Of course not. But Grahme has shown that he can animorph, so we should split up and go in two or three different groups."

"And whatever group I get stuck in will be killed by the Dark Lord," Sieffre says. "Because they have horses and will find my trail."

"We're not leaving anyone behind," Ecsiah says.

"Sieffre," I cut in, "while we have time, come with me and I'll give you the next lesson in animorphing."

Ysella and Katel are sitting back-to-back, getting their rest in while they can. Eosiah stands by himself, watching to see what comes at us next.

"How are the lessons going?" Eosiah asks.

"Sieffre still lacks the confidence to try. What are Gurthcid and his men up to?"

"I believe the Dark Lord has joined them on the second hill, though I haven't been able to spot him."

"He can project images with his mind, so perhaps he can hide himself from our eyes as well," I say.

"Do those men still have use of their minds or are they empty shells for the Obsidian Mage to control?"

"In my *very* limited exposure, the men should still have their own thoughts. It depends on if he lets them access their battle experience."

"No matter what, they are going to have to wade through the water to get to us. Can Sieffre or Katel summon another water elemental?" Eosiah asks.

"I doubt it. Sieffre nearly passed out last time and we still have to get him able to change into some kind of bird if we want to escape this mound."

"Grahme, if everything falls apart, you need to make sure that you get back to Boswen. Leave the rest of us if you must."

"No."

"Grahme . . . ."

"No, Eosiah, I won't abandon my fellow druids in their time of need. Like you told Arthmael, we don't leave people behind."

Not caring for more of this conversation, I leave Eosiah and seek out Ysella. She and Katel are sitting quietly. Sieffre sits apart from the rest, with his head between his knees.

"Sieffre, when you were growing up, were there any birds that you took an interest in?"

Happy for any topic that didn't involve him being the reason we all end up dying, he smiles broadly. "Oh, yes. I grew up on the coast. Just off shore was a puffin island. I always found them to be such comical birds."

"I grew up too far south to see them regularly. What do they eat?"

"Smaller fish, mostly; herring, hake, those sorts of fish." He smiles at the thought. "I always liked watching them walk. They walk like they're drunk."

"So, could you mimic them?"

"Do we really have nothing better to do?"

"I think we are having a breakthrough. You know quite a bit about puffins. I bet you could animorph into one of them."

"You know I've had no luck at that."

"You were also trying to change into a red kite, an animal that you don't know very well."

"It's late in the fall, how do I know that if I do become a puffin that I won't fly out to sea for the winter?"

"It's not like that. Your mind sits on top of the animal's mind. You're not quite yourself, but you're not an animal, either."

"We've done very well so far," he says. "No one has even been hurt. I think we'll defeat the Dark Lord's forces when it all comes out."

I drop my jaw in response. His level of self-deceit is astounding.

"Grahme, why don't you go see what Eosiah wants us to do next," Katel says. "Let Sieffre and I have a little time to speak alone, please."

"All right."

"They're moving," Eosiah calls.

Ysella and Arthmael leap to their positions. I turn to Katel and Sieffre. "Battles are all about morale. If one tries to charge us, we'll take care of him. If a dozen decide to charge all at once, we're in trouble. Your job is to keep the seed of doubt in their heads so coordinated plans fall apart. It's made harder because the Obsidian Lord can control them to some extent. If you see them getting the upper hand, we're relying on you two to blunt their momentum. It's the only way we'll make it off this tor alive."

The Coritani are crossing the marsh, shields held high to protect against our slings. Ysella is taking her place next to Eosiah and Arthmael. I can't spare any more time away from the fray. I scramble down and join the others.

"What'd I miss?"

"They have their bows and quivers held tight against their shields. They mean to get a base at the bottom of the tor itself and saturate the air with arrows before their advance. Or at least that's what I would do."

"And what's our plan?"

Eosiah purses his lips. "We are going to make them pay a heavy price for every step they take."

"This doesn't sound like a winning strategy," I say.

Everyone is silent. At least no one down here is deluding themself.

"They come."

25

Terror at the Tor

Seventh Dark Day of Cantl, 819

Twenty-three Days until Samhain

The Coritani form up with a wall of shields planted into the ground. The second row of men set their shields on top of the first. No one has ever seen one of the clans try this strategy before. Usually, they let out blood-curdling screams and sprint at the enemy. I scan the hills for the Black Lord. This has to be his doing.

The second row of shields drop and a volley of arrows flood the sky. Eosiah steps in front of us and swats arrows out of the sky with inhuman precision. Ysella and Arthmael flank him to either side. If I advance, I'll get brained by one of their staves.

A guttural roar is loosed from below and the warriors abandon their newly constructed wall. The charge is upon us.

"Eosiah, move!" I change into an auroch and dig my hooves into the rocky soil, exploding down the slope. Eosiah dives out of my way, his foot glancing off my shoulder as I pass. The pounding of my hooves drowns out the warriors' battle cries. I lower my head and charge into the center of their line. The first two men go flying backward over their comrades. Two more are gored, one on each horn. I shake my head to dislodge them. The men in back run for the protection of their shield wall. The men on either side are sliding down the hill feet first into the marsh. How I wish aurochs could smile.

I lower my head and run through the shield wall, crushing men and shields alike. There is nothing but the downward slope into the muck before me. I change my direction and race up the hill at the remaining men. The few stragglers break before me, too scared to take a kill shot. I proudly prance up the empty battlefield to my fellow druids and transform back to myself.

Ysella and Arthmael are shouting their encouragement.

"A little more warning next time," says a grinning Eosiah, gently massaging his foot.

"There was no room to join you on the slope and I wasn't about to simply watch from behind."

"Your charges are amazing, but they are unlikely to keep working."

"I know. What do you think they'll do next?"

"They'll want to take the tor by nightfall," Eosiah says, clucking his tongue. "They won't want to risk us somehow slipping past them. My guess is that they'll either go for a more sustained advance with archers at the ready to shoot your next animal iteration or they'll split their forces up and make us defend both paths up the tor."

"How is it you know so much about tactics?" Arthmael asks.

"I am the eldest son of Armel, clan chief of the Ordivices. I was well trained in warfare."

"No wonder you won the gwary last year," Arthmael says.

"I've been practicing since I was four." He smiles.

"They're forming up again," Ysella says.

Just as Eosiah had suggested, the shields in front protect the archers in back. A quarter of the men break off and start marching along the eastern side, toward the rear path.

"You were right on both counts," I say.

The archers below us start to loose volleys at us.

"I guess they're not going to let us stand around and strategize," Eosiah says as he breaks another arrow in two. "Arthmael and Grahme, tell Katel and Sieffre that we will be attacked on both fronts, then you two"—he points to Arthmael and me—"man the northern side. We'll hold the south."

"How did they come by so many arrows?" Ysella complains.

"The lake people shoot fish with their bows," Arthmael says.

"And being on three small islands surrounded by a marsh, it would have been the best defense," Eosiah adds.

"I can help with the archers." I point back over my head at the fat rain clouds to the south. "They're coming our way, but I can nudge them along a bit."

Eosiah nods approvingly. "For the first time, I think we may survive this day. Tell Katel and Sieffre to focus on the archers. Let's take out as many as we can before they get to the path."

Ysella sees the rain clouds, too. "No, it's only been a few days since the equinox. You'll kill yourself."

"Is it any better if Gurthcid kills me instead?"

Arthmael and I reach a flat area where we'll make our stand. Katel and Sieffre both are frantically launching missiles at Ysella's side of the tor.

"They must be hard pressed," Arthmael says.

"And if we run to aid them, these warriors will be on Katel and Sieffre in no time."

Arthmael grunts. "I hate standing around being useless."

"Well, I'm going to need you to guard me while I pull those rainclouds over to us."

"Great, more standing."

I channel my will to the sky and pull the clouds forward, but there is nothing for me to grab. The clouds are too nebulous. Still, I can't give up. My shoulders start to go numb and my hands begin to tremble. Nothing happens. I refocus my will, straining with all my might to make some sort of difference.

A solid force hits me in the ribs, knocking me back. I scan the area for enemies, but only Arthmael is near me.

"You became unresponsive, so I had to break you out of your trance."

"I have to pull the rain over to us."

"You were about to pass out."

"I'm close, I know it," I lie.

"You're no good if you're unconscious." An arrow whizzes past his ear. He gives me a look as if it's my fault.

Brandishing our staves, we block the path and begin to knock down or dodge arrows from the fifteen men below. A stalemate develops as they seem content to keep up a steady stream of arrows and not advance. Not one stone has been slung at our attackers. I check on Sieffre and Katel. They are still launching stones at a frenetic pace in support of Eosiah and Ysella.

"These warriors are a diversion to pin us down. Ysella and Eosiah must be facing the main force."

271

At last the rain arrives on its own accord. Arthmael lets out a shout. "You did it, Grahme."

I'm such a fraud.

It doesn't take long before the bowstrings are waterlogged. First their accuracy leaves them, now the distance is only half what it was. Gurthcid's woman is leading this group and she calls a halt to the arrows.

"We made it through the first round unscathed," Arthmael says, not even breathing hard.

I'm trying not to shake in the cold rain. I feel weak as a newborn. I lean on my staff for support.

The warriors below us start beating on their shields and shouting in unison.

"The charge will come any moment," Arthmael says.

The front shields drop, and the all-out charge begins. Screaming with vengeance, the warriors expose their woad-colored torsos in the mad dash up the hill.

What good are our staves going to do us against a shield and spear?

I blank for a moment and realize that I am charging down the hill at the screaming Coritani. My claws are digging into the dirt, giving me good traction despite the wet grass. I slam full speed into the center of the shield wall and the men go flying backward. On either side, men race past me, then falter. They did not plan on having an angry cave bear in their midst. I turn and charge the men on my left. All but one manage to dive head first down the slope of the tor. He remains frozen in place. I swat him with my right paw and his head follows his comrades to the marsh below.

A stabbing pain in my right side alerts me that not everyone is paralyzed in fear. I spin and see five men holding spears at the ready. I circle them, giving them the high ground. Before they can rouse their courage, Arthmael strikes from behind and fells two of them. That's all the opening I need. I charge at the nearest man and make quick work of him. An arrow strikes me in the hip, and I turn to face my new attacker.

Gurthcid's woman pulls another arrow from her quiver. It's hard to miss from five paces away. I try to change back to human form, but the iron-tipped arrow keeps me from animorphing. Arthmael jumps in front of me and parries the next arrow. Reaching behind, he pulls the arrow out of my hide. The change back to human form is still a challenge. No time to wonder why, I grope for a weapon and cut myself on a spearhead. With a stomp, I snap off the metal point and spin my new staff. It has a good weight. The remaining men on the path form a defensive position as they try to protect their wounded.

"Do we charge?" I ask.

Arthmael smiles back at me. "That's the spirit, but no, two charging a crowd is not the best move."

We give ground until we're back to our spot. The warriors regroup as the cold rain continues. I can't stop myself from shivering. The marsh-bound attackers wind their way back to their comrades, but none too quickly. There are still eleven warriors from the original fifteen. Many are sporting injuries.

Arthmael is protecting his left shoulder. I inspect the wound. Without a word, I grab my sling and tie it around the wound. "You'll have less mobility, but you won't bleed to death." I say in a cheerful tone.

He laughs. "It's good to know that this wound won't be the fatal blow."

"It's close to sunset," I say. "How much longer do you think we have to keep this up?"

"As long as we must," Arthmael says. "Remember, Gurthcid had sixty men when we met him going south. Only fifteen have come to our side."

"That would explain why we've not received support from Katel and Sieffre."

"I assumed that it was because they don't like you." Arthmael tries to keep a straight face but can't.

"I told Lord Cynbel that I possess the unique talent of making people dislike me upon first meeting me."

"I don't think they like you, either," he says, pointing to the men below.

Their spear tips are in front of their shields this time, their leader calling out the steps in a slow cadence.

"Another animal charge doesn't look promising this time," Arthmael says.

"I doubt I have the energy left to do so. This would be the time for an all-out charge."

"Well, then, let's thank the gods that we find ourselves on this tor in this bitterly cold wind, facing a group of blood-crazed, non-charging Coritani."

"At least the rain has stopped," I say.

Arthmael lets loose an infectious laugh. Smiling, we face our attackers.

They continue their relentless advance. As the wait stretches out, I'm given time to think about how the two of us will be able to fight a dozen of them. My vision starts to tunnel.

Arthmael hits me on the shoulder. "You need to stay in the here and now." He gives me a nervous glance. "Wield your staff near the base. We have to keep a good distance between them and us or we'll be overwhelmed."

I nod. My staff is too heavy for my trembling arms to hold upright. I let the tip rest on the ground for now.

When they close to fifteen paces, Arthmael lowers his staff into a combat position. "Remember, you want to sweep side-to-side. We can't let anyone get around us."

"Right." I raise my staff upright and sway it back and forth. If I leave it still everyone will see how bad the tremors in my arms are.

They are close enough now that I can hear their ragged breath. Mentally, I take a note of the injured men.

"Why do they wait?" I ask.

"Probably to unnerve us into making the first move."

We glance sideways at each other.

"I thought it was because their stinking breath is being blown back in their faces," I call loudly.

"No," Arthmael says, "they're wanting the woman to lead the charge."

Two men scream as they advance toward us, quickly closing the distance. Arthmael takes a step forward as he swings in a wide arc. The crack of the man's neck tells everyone that he's been silenced permanently. The second man is charging me. I also take my swing, but he manages to duck under it. I continue my momentum so I'm not an easy target for his response. Arthmael steps between us and cracks several of the man's ribs. The man falls to one knee.

"Stay down," Arthmael yells.

The man starts to rise. Arthmael pokes the man in the newly broken ribs with the butt of his staff. He falls over backward. The rest of the warriors scream in unison and charge us. The downed man is lost in the crush of his comrades.

I sweep my staff in wide arcs, varying the height. The men stop just outside the arc and point their spears at me.

"Grahme, we are going to have to give ground, but do so grudgingly," Arthmael calls.

Katel gives off a celebratory cry, but I'm too pressed to see what has happened. I guard the edge of the slope so that no one can go around me. Several of them move toward the center of the path and then peel off to attack Arthmael. Only three remain engaged with me. *They have driven a wedge between us.* I manage to make contact with one of them. His head is at an unnatural angle as he slides down to become food for the fish. I lunge at the other two before spinning and taking out the knees of an attacker between us. He's quickly finished off with a parry from Arthmael. We give a little ground so that we can reunite.

Arthmael takes another wide swing, separating the attackers from us. "We can't get separated again," he manages through ragged breath.

The ground begins to rumble and buckle, causing the warriors to lose their footing. Between us, the earth elemental rises from the hillside. Towering above everyone, it stomps the man closest to it. Gurthcid's woman screams for her men to retreat. Tightly huddled, they know fear. Any moment and they will break. Grim faced, their bodies goes rigid. One by one, the rest of the warriors stiffen. They form up in a line, spear tips down and advance.

"The Dark Lord has taken control of these men," Arthmael says.

"This has to be the last encounter," I say. "I won't last much longer."

Spears are largely ineffective against the walking mass of dirt. They switch to axes and immediately start taking chunks off the elemental.

"Get back," Katel yells from above.

We retreat up the hill a dozen paces. At best this will give us time to catch our breath, but already the warriors are dodging and weaving between the mound-of-dirt's slow punches.

"*Stand!*" Katel cries as a rock hits the elemental's back. A creaking noise emanates from the strike point and streaks of gray travel outward until the elemental is remade into stone. It falls forward and crushes two warriors. *This is our chance.* We charge from either side of the newly made boulder and make quick work of the remaining four warriors.

Atop the hill stand the other four druids, gesturing wildly for us to hurry. We shamble up to join them.

"I told you we should have charged," I say, between gasps of breath.

Arthmael breaks into a broad grin. "I'll fight at your side any day."

He breaks into a trot and I follow, struggling to remain on his heels.

"This is our chance for escape," Ysella says.

"Head for the Gwanwyns of Sulis," Eosiah says. "It's the natural place for Sieffre to go, it's close, and Eghan is sympathetic to our cause."

Ysella wants to argue but thinks better of it.

We all face Sieffre. His ears redden and he gazes at his feet. "Leave me behind; I'll find my own way out."

"Give me a moment with him," I say.

The others survey Eosiah and Ysella's steep-sloped battlefield.

"Where did the ice come from?" Arthmael asks.

"Sieffre was able to make an ice rune during the battle," Katel says triumphantly.

"Sieffre, remember the puffins?"

"Yeah," he says miserably.

"Being a druid, you probably know those birds better than anyone else on this entire island."

"What good does that do?"

"Remember what I said: you have to understand the animal in order to take its shape. Focus your mind on a puffin and slowly visualize yourself contained within that body."

He shuts his eyes tight. "I-I can feel myself becoming immaterial." His eyes bolt open, scared of what is happening.

"That's good," I say to soothe him. "Keep doing what you're doing, and you'll take the puffin's shape."

"What if I can't turn back?"

"When you change, your mind is overlaid on top of a puffin's mind. As long as you don't keep the form too long, you'll be able to visualize yourself and change back."

"The ice is melting," Ysella says.

"Don't rush him," Katel says protectively.

"You can do this, can't you?" I say as more of a command than a question.

"I think so," Sieffre says.

"Everyone, let's get ready to go," I shout.

Ysella and Arthmael take the form of red kites, of course. Eosiah takes on the shape of a merlin. Katel chooses a bat and starts her metallic chirping at once.

"You can do it, Sieffre."

He squinches up his eyes and his constipated look returns. About a dozen warriors are below us, shields raised as they gingerly test the recently frozen ground before each step forward.

Sieffre's form starts to waver and become insubstantial. He's right on the cusp. I hold my breath. Gurthcid and his men are gaining more confidence. It won't be long before they break into an all-out sprint.

Finally, the puffin form becomes solid and Sieffre lets out a grunting call that I interpret as a successful shout. I take a breath to center myself. I choose my favorite form, the tawny owl, but I have trouble animorphing. I calm myself and focus my sluggish mind. Finally, I'm able to transform.

We all launch ourselves into the air; everyone but Sieffre, that is. He begins running away in the puffin's awkward gait and flapping his wings in circles. He lets out a growling sound of alarm, so I return to the tor. Changing back into myself, I lift Sieffre up. The body of the puffin is spot on, but the eyes; they're still Sieffre's brown eyes.

"Change back to human form," I say slowly as I set him down.

He reluctantly changes back to human form. "How am I supposed to fly?" he blurts out.

We can hear Gurthcid extorting his men to keep up the pace.

"When you were a puffin, you were holding on to your humanness too firmly. Release yourself into the puffin's body. It will naturally know how to fly."

The voices are getting closer. Sieffre can't help but repeatedly check for the Coritani.

"Block them out; if we die, it won't be because we stood frozen like a couple of deer waiting for the killing blow."

"Dead is still dead."

"Yes, but it is the final statement you make about this life. Do you want to end it cowering in fear or giving your all to survive?"

"Right," he says. "But first," he pulls out a smooth stone, "shield your eyes." He hurls it toward at the top of the tor. "*Sigel!*"

A brilliant light blooms; too bright to merely close my eyes, I'm forced to look away. Shouts of confusion and pain come from our besiegers.

I blink several times in an attempt to remove the white spots in my eyes. "Now focus on the puffin and start the changeover."

He manages to change into a puffin quicker this time. After several awkward steps, his wings start acting like wings should. He takes off to the west and circles around to the south; directly over top the heads of Gurthcid's men. An arrow pierces his left wing. Sieffre lets out another alarm growl and flies back to me. His landing is a disaster as he ends up touching down with his beak first.

I search around for a weapon. I have to give him time to take off again. All that I can find is one of the slings. I dig around urgently for a handful of rocks. It's all I'll need. I'll either escape or be killed by the time I use all of them.

I hear a puffin's grunting call behind me. Sieffre is wobbling down the slope as fast as his tiny puffin legs can take him. I turn back to see Gurthcid and his remaining men cresting the tor.

Eosiah's merlin flies into Gurthcid's face, searching for eyes with his razor-sharp talons. Gurthcid manages to dodge, avoiding the attack at the very last instant. Eosiah swoops around the warriors, flies past me, and grabs Sieffre's clumsy form. He tries to rise, but his merlin is too small for the task. A spear whizzes past my ear and skewers Eosiah through the chest. Both birds crash into the ground. The Coritani raise a cheer. I snake my way to my friends. There is nothing I can do for the dead avian form of Eosiah. Sieffre is crumpled into a ball and is shaking uncontrollably. Choosing an eagle owl's shape, I grab him and launch us into the air.

A red kite has returned and is harrying the attackers. I silently fly off into the darkness. Before I'm clear of the tor I hear an injured screech from the kite. I adjust my flight over the marsh so I can see the tor. The red kite is losing altitude and headed for the islands of the lake village. I can't carry two birds at once. I let the avian brain take over and I flee north to safety.

26

Rejuvenating Bath

The Tenth Light Day of Elembiu, 819

Shivering, I wake in near darkness. A single reed torch casts fitful rays of light across the dark stone walls. I tighten into a fetal ball to conserve my body heat.

"Good, you're awake," a male voice says. A middle-aged druid moves from against the wall to my side. "I suspect you would like to know where you are."

"That would be much appreciated. Is there any chance I could get some food, too?"

"Hares or mice?"

"What?"

"For the first five days you were here, that was all you would eat."

Is he daft? We do not eat hares, they're sacred.

He chuckles to himself. "I am Eghan, and you made it to Gwanwyn Sulis ten days ago."

Digging through my mind, the battle comes raging back to me. "Where are Ysella and the rest of my companions? Are they all right?"

"Relax, Grahme. There is a tale to be told, some of it is good and some bad. Let me see to a meal for you, then I will tell you what I know." He rises from his stool and takes the torch, my only source of light. As I lie alone in the dark, I probe my body to see if there is anything out of sorts. The arrow wound in my hip is tender, but clearly on the mend and the infections on my arms are gone. I haven't been in this good of shape since I left Solent Keep.

How much time do I have left before Samhain?

I must have dozed, for I awaken to the smell of roasted pig. "Ysella? Is that you?"

She springs from the shadows and embraces me in a fierce bear hug. Her hair cascades off her shoulder and into my face.

"Lavender," I say.

"Do you like it?" she asks, bashful.

"It's lovely. It reminds me of . . . better times."

Eghan is holding his reed torch close to the runes carved into the wall. At least he's giving us the illusion of privacy.

"Here, you have to eat," Ysella says.

She cuts a slice of the pig's leg and holds it as if to feed me. I debate for a moment before deciding that I'm not so weak that I can't feed myself. Taking the meat, I barely chew before I swallow it down. Reluctantly, she hands over the knife and plate. I sit up and eat with abandon.

"Ysella," Eghan says gently, "I'm going to fill Grahme in about what has transpired the last several days. Do you wish to stay?"

She looks me over, her eyes suddenly watery. "No, I don't think I will." A look passes between them that I can't fathom. In a hopelessly sad tone, she adds, "I'll check in on . . . the others."

"Tell Sieffre and Katel that they were stupendous," I say. "And tell Arthmael that I wouldn't be alive without his heroic deeds."

There's a catch in her breath as she runs from the room.

"Be careful in the dark," I call after her.

Eghan frowns as he watches her disappear into the darkness. "What is the last thing you remember?"

Taking myself back to that night, I remember the cold wind blowing from the west and the rotting smell of the marsh. I hadn't taken note of either during the fighting.

"I was standing over Sieffre, but not human Sieffre, him in puffin form. A bird . . . . The merlin was really Eosiah, and he was dead from an arrow through his chest." It feels just as real now as it did then. "The enemy had crested the tor and were about to overrun us. I grabbed Sieffre, but with my feet?" I stop my babbling and look to Eghan.

He nods slightly. "Yes, anything more?"

"No, and as crazy as it sounds, I can't be sure it was real and not a fever dream."

"Very well, my turn then. You turned into an eagle owl and you did indeed pick Sieffre up with your feet, or rather your talons. Ysella tells me that you had nearly depleted yourself at the equinox and against sage advice from Lord Cynbel, you drew upon your powers repeatedly that night."

"I had to; we would have been slain if I hadn't done so."

"You misunderstand me, I do not judge you; I merely speak the facts."

Relieved that a lecture is not forthcoming, I settle in to listen.

"You grabbed Sieffre's puffin form, and you had enough humanness left to fly here with Ysella and Katel instead of veering off and eating the puffin in your talons."

The thought of eating poor Sieffre has my stomach uneasy. Putting a restraining hand on my belly, I force myself to relax.

"You and poor Sieffre, however, were both at the limits of your powers and neither of you would change back to human form despite coaxing from your companions. We dipped each of you into the three holy springs, and with the aid of the Earthmother's three forms, you were finally able to change back to your natural self."

"And Sieffre? I can't wait to talk to him. He came through and made his first animorph under extreme pressure."

Eghan turns toward the wall. "Sieffre never made the change," he says with great sadness.

"I didn't crush him in my talons, did I?"

"No, you did not harm him in any significant way. I'm afraid he has not been able to turn back to human form and I have precious little hope that he ever will."

"He's still a puffin?"

"Yes. To have such a great mind diminished to that of a common animal." He looks away for a moment, his eyes tearing up.

Of course, Eghan was mentoring Sieffre.

Afraid of what I might hear, but needing to know, I blurt out, "What of the others?" Arthmael? Katel?"

"Katel has no physical injuries, but her broken heart consumes her at this time. Arthmael was last seen falling from the sky. We can only hope that his life ended on the fall and not in the hands of the Dark Lord."

My stomach starts contracting spasmodically. How could I have eaten so greedily when tragedy has befallen so many of my friends?

"This is probably a good time for another nap. You should regain your strength soon." He forestalls all of my objections with a stern wave of his finger. "We have more to discuss, but it can wait until tomorrow." He rises and grabs the torch from its sconce.

"Lord Eghan," I call. "What of my pouch?"

"It and the ghost orchid are fine. Sleep for now and we'll discuss it and your quest tomorrow."

My head spins. "How am I supposed to sleep now?" I ask, but the darkness has no answers for me.

As I wake, I'm holding my pack tight against my chest, as if it were a woman. The cave's tunnel is partially illuminated by sunlight. I open my pack and feel a limp stem and crushed flower. Boswen never said that it had to be pretty; only to get it to him in the allotted time.

Why am I in a cave? I've passed through Gwanwyn Sulis before. I saw only normal cottages and two mead-hall-sized buildings; one is for drinking and one for healing. So why am I not there? I make my way out of the darkness.

It's a bright autumn day and I'm forced to keep my head down and shade my eyes. "Belenos, I praise you every chance I get, but for once, I pray that the clouds may obscure your brilliance."

"You're likely to get your wish," Eghan says. "The clouds are ready to take roost until spring."

Despite his assurance, I head for the shade of the entrance stones and wait in the shadows.

"I judge we have time before prying eyes or ears return, so come with me and let me show you the Gwanwyn Sulis. It is there that you were granted the strength to change back to your human form."

The rising steam from the spring has led to green, mossy beards on the tree limbs around the pool. Each tree has its own distinct look as the water cools and drips slowly from their straggly locks. The mist hangs in the air and warms a person, even on the chilliest of days. In the middle of the spring sits a puffin with human-like brown eyes.

"Sieffre?"

"He has taken a liking to the spring. Imagine that, a puffin that prefers hot spring water to the cold ocean."

"I am so sorry, Sieffre. You never should have been traveling with me."

"He seems to like this place, almost as if it is home. I have never heard of a druid changing back after so long, but if Sieffre is going to be able to do so, it will be with Sulis' aid."

We stand in the healing mist and give silent thanks to Sulis for her healing ways.

"It took you five days before you were able to change back. And we had to keep you and your hungry eyes separated from Sieffre."

I'm filled with dread. "Did Sieffre not get placed in the spring until after I changed back?"

"Relax, we have three healing springs here. No one was without treatment."

At least I don't have to bear that burden.

"After satisfying your ravenous appetite, and plunking you in the spring repeatedly, you were able to regain human form."

"Why don't I remember this?"

"I gave you my most powerful sleeping draught that day and every day after, until yesterday."

"You drugged me?"

"It was imperative that you stop using your powers, so I took matters into my own hands."

"But my quest—"

"Your quest is why I stopped. I would have liked to keep you sedated for an entire month."

I grab his arm and squeeze. "What day is it?"

"It is the second dark day of Cantl. You have thirteen days left to fulfill your quest. That gives you more than enough time to *walk* back to Boswen." He gives me his best disapproving look.

"Yes, Lord Eghan."

"If you wish, I will get word to Boswen that you have brought the ghost orchid to me. That should satisfy your quest."

"I don't wish to contradict you, Lord, but I do not think Lord Boswen will accept anything other than completing the quest as stated."

Eghan thinks on that for a moment. "You may be right about that. Boswen can be quite the stickler for rules, especially his own. You should think about leaving soon in any case. It seems that Katel has decided to return to Hedred's underground realm in the morning, and Ysella wants to accompany her sister. Perhaps you could join them?"

I blink a couple of times. There's nothing holding me here. "Perhaps I should."

"It's not that I find you unlikeable, but your absence would make me breathe easier."

"Oh?"

"So, you're not aware. Loris, the pompous fool, summoned you to the center rings at Kantom Lijanks Kuros. When no one was able to find you, he went into a rage and demanded you be brought to him by any manner necessary."

"Me?"

"He even went as far as to offer a reward for your capture."

"Lord Eghan, you must be making sport at my expense. What reward would a free druid want? We walk with nature."

"Boswen has kept you too far from the wider world. Loris doles out favors to those who follow his orders. Don't you know that his staff is wrapped with a silver band from the butt to the head?"

"But how is he to produce magic if he is in contact with metals?"

"He believes that to be beneath him."

The head druid refuses to perform magic in defense of nature?

"But what does he want with me?"

"Cynbel told the council that you possess a ghost orchid. Such flowers are known on the mainland. Loris has fixated on the flower to the exclusion of any other business. He wants it and he wants to know where they can be found."

"Why?"

"He does not feel he needs to explain himself to anyone. Indeed, in so many words, he told us that as our head druid, we should mindlessly obey his whims. Mark my words; he will stop at nothing to get that flower from you. Hundreds of druids left

Kantom Lijanks Kuros searching for you. The number is most likely higher now. Apparently, none thought to look for you walking across the plains with nary a tree to hide you."

"This is madness."

"Oh, that it is. Several times druids have arrived here unannounced and searched the grounds for any sign of you. That is why once you were in human form, we moved you to the long barrow."

I stare at Eghan in disbelief. Words fail me.

"That long barrow is, by the way, where Sieffre and Katel first discovered the runes of the giants. If Katel will allow it, I would suggest that you leave with them and travel to Ogof Cawr. I doubt many would check in Hedred's subterranean abode."

"Yes, Lord." My head is throbbing, and my life is out of control.

Katel stabs at freshly killed deer steak and refuses to even look at me, though we all sit around Eghan's small table.

"Are you prepared for your trip?" Eghan asks to break up the awkward silence.

"We are," Ysella says with fake enthusiasm.

"I can't wait to leave," Katel says.

"I would ask you two to accept Grahme into your company as well."

Katel slams her knife down and fixes her hostile glare at Eghan. "Him? No. He should have been turned over to Loris for his crimes."

"Katel," her sister starts, "what happened was not his doing or his fault."

"Two of our companions are dead and poor Sieffre . . . ." Her words run together into incoherence. She snatches up her bone knife and storms out of Eghan's cottage.

"I'll get her," Ysella says.

"No. Stay here," Eghan says in a firm voice.

"Lord?"

"I love Katel dearly, but she is not a child. Running to her now will only reinforce her behavior."

Ysella's face is a riot of emotions. She looks down at her deer steak. "Yes, Lord," she says unhappily.

Once again awkward silence reigns supreme.

"Lord Eghan," Ysella begins, "what if Katel refuses to travel with Grahme?"

"Then I will order her to do so."

"But why?"

Eghan stares down Ysella until she redirects her attention back to the deer steak before her.

I feel guilty for all the hostility. "Lord Eghan . . . ."

"If you two don't stop with the 'Lord Eghans,' I will kick you both out of this community tonight without provisions."

"Forgive me," I catch myself before I can repeat his title.

He must have realized my near slip up. He gives me a disapproving glance.

"What is known of the giants' runes?"

He pauses for a bit before he responds. "Sieffre was the real expert, perhaps Katel, too, though I'm not sure how much she knows. He collected over twenty runes and he managed to decipher the meaning of seven of them."

"What kind of magic is it?"

"We don't fully know. I suppose Katel is the expert now. Which is why we need her to stop acting the victim, even if it is warranted," he says to forestall Ysella's protestations, "and continue on with their work."

"If you don't mind," Ysella says, "I would like to go to my sister now. Someone needs to worry about the person and not just her work."

Eghan sighs. "Remember that she is not a child and shouldn't be treated as such," he calls after her.

I doubt Ysella heard him.

"I don't envy you on this trip," he says to me.

"Hopefully, nothing will make it worse."

Eghan chuckles. "There's slim chance of anything else going awry. The journey to Ogof Cawr is not a long one."

If he only knew me better.

27

In a Hole

Fourth Light Day of Cantl, 819

Eleven Days until Samhain

Morning comes with unseasonably cold weather. Emerging from the long barrow, my misty breath fills the air in front of me. Through it, I see Ysella coiling rope.

"Shall we begin this journey, then?" Ysella asks.

"You will allow me to travel with you?"

Katel scowls. "Ysella thinks that helping you finish your quest will give meaning to Sieffre's sacrifice."

"We should begin." Ysella gestures me to remain quiet.

"Of course."

"It's a half-day's walk to Ogof Cawr, I know it well," Katel mutters as she pushes between us.

With a shrug of her shoulders, Ysella follows.

"You have gotten over your fear of walking on leaves?" I ask.

"In a life without Sieffre, why does it matter?" Katel starts crying again.

Ysella increases her pace and pushes me back. I don't dare join them. Only the gods know what calamity my proximity to Katel might cause.

Once I fall back, Katel becomes much more expressive to her sister. Let them have their sister time. At least we are headed south. I have a four day journey to Dartmoor there are hundreds of druids still between Boswen and me.

"You know what? I think we should take the falls entrance to Ogof Cawr. It's always fun." Katel gushes.

"But Grahme can't animorph," Ysella says.

"He sucks the marrow out of everything."

And that is why I should have kept even more distance between us.

"We can take the crystal entrance," Ysella suggests. "We should get there before nightfall and the columns glow so beautifully with the setting sun."

"How do the crystals glow when they're underground?"

Katel gives me a death glare. "There are several small light-tunnels in the cavern ceiling that let light enter from the west." Fourth Light Day of Cantl, 819 Fourth Light Day of Cantl, 819

"Now is the best time of year for it, too," Ysella says. "Let's go see it together." She shoots me a look that can only mean to keep quiet.

I've been relegated to being seen but not heard.

"I suppose. Will you stay with me once we're underground?" Katel asks.

"You know that I've been charged by Cynbel to stay close to Grahme."

"Must he take everything I treasure away from me?"

The wooded hills give way to a cultivated valley filled with small homesteaders. This land was cleared by the giants thousands of years ago, according to legend. Once again, I'm under the open sky and feeling exposed. We pass one homestead after another until at last we reach the base of the Mendip Hills. I can relax now that we're under a canopy of trees. After so many days of resting, my legs are not ready for this exertion. Katel pushes the pace, whether to reach her home faster or to punish me is anyone's guess. Halfway up the slope we reach a pool of water fed by a man-sized waterfall. Only a small amount of water trickles out of the pool, much less than what the waterfall provides.

"Behold, the mighty Mendip Falls," Ysella says, sweeping her arm in an exaggerated fashion. "The water runs down this slope until it collects in this pool and falls through a shaft to the caves below. This is the spring entrance. The crystal entrance is at the very top of the hills."

The sisters hold each other's hands and gaze wistfully at the pool. Ysella leans in and whispers something in Katel's ear. Katel leans her head on her big sister's shoulder.

After they have their moment, Ysella turns to me. "We'll follow this stream up to the basin where the stream begins. It's only a short walk from there to the next entrance."

"We'll have to crawl on our bellies for a bit," Katel says. "I hope you don't panic in tight, dark spaces." I look at one sister then the other. Both are much smaller than I am. If they find it a tight fit . . .

"The crystal columns at sunset more than make up for the discomfort, trust me," Ysella reassures me.

"I trust you."

"If we don't hurry, we won't reach it until nightfall and the view will be ruined," Katel says. She resumes the brutal pace, and it's not long before the sisters are well ahead of me.

I welcome the time apart. It all seems hopeless, me reaching Dartmoor. What choice do I have but to carry on? Clouds are rolling in from the west. Whatever this illuminated cavern is supposed to look like, it will be muted at best. That seems fitting.

I've lost track of Ysella and Katel. I redouble my pace, taking advantage of the gnarled tree roots as steps along the hillside. The lack of air flow beneath the crowded treetops is causing my sweat to cling to me. There's no time to rest; I can't be known as the druid who got lost in a forest. Leaning more heavily on my staff, I continue as best I can.

Above me, Katel is running toward me.

"Katel," I shout, waving my hand. She makes straight for me but doesn't slow. I grab her by the arm, firm enough to spin her around as she passes.

"Run!" Heedless of the fallen leaves, she rushes down the hill. I look at her, then up the hill.

"Where's Ysella?" I call.

"Grahme," she whispers loudly. "Gurthcid is up there. Follow me."

"But Ysella—"

"She's buying us time to get to the waterfall."

"Are you sure?"

"No time," she takes off back the way we came, heedless of me.

A bear roars from above and I can hear several horses squeal in surprise. Gurthcid's battle-hardened voice responds, urging his men to maintain control of the mounts. I tear down the hill after Katel.

Katel slips on something, leaves most likely, and tumbles headfirst into a copse of ash trees. Sitting up, she gingerly stretches her neck and right arm. The shield ferns nearly hide her from view.

"Are you all right? Let me help you," I say, breathless.

"Run, you fool! I can change into a bat if need be."

"You can't animorph if you knock yourself unconscious." Despite her order, I grab her good arm and pull her up.

"Ysella is risking her life for you. Must everyone die for you? Run, you miserable excuse of a druid." She pushes me away.

"You need to show me the way," I lie.

She shoots me a venomous look. "Keep up."

We find the soggy basin and follow the rivulet downward. We reach the waterfall and a crow cahs, getting our attention. It scans the woods for pursuers.

"At last," Ysella says once she retakes human form. "I've spooked several of their mounts, but it won't take them long to find us once they get them back."

"We have to enter here," Katel says. "There's no other entrance without going through them."

"I can't animorph."

We fall silent and listen for any sounds of the horsemen.

Finally, Ysella speaks. "Katel, take the rope and turn into an otter. At the first air pocket, tie it to the pointing finger rock and bring the other end back here. Grahme can pull himself along the rope to safety."

"What about you?" Katel asks.

297

"I'll stall them, if need be." Without waiting, Ysella returns to her crow form and flies off.

"Here," Katel says as she tosses me one end of the rope. She tosses the rest into the pool. "The rope isn't that long so you'll have to stand in the pool."

My foot touches the frigid water and I take a sharp intake of air. Katel changes into an otter and jumps in next to me. She grabs the other end of the rope in her mouth and swims into the darkest water.

The rope jerks tight. Planting my feet, I refuse to let go. Katel's otter re-emerges soon after and retakes her human form.

"It's no use, it's too short," she says.

"How long is it to the first air pocket?" I ask in between my chattering teeth.

"Too long to try for the first time while holding your breath, I'll have to lead you. Keep hold of the other end and dive down after me. Whatever you do, don't let go of the rope."

Hooves crunching leaves lets us know that we're out of time. Ysella caws quietly at us before flying off again. Katel's gaze follows her sister.

"Ysella knows what she's doing," I say.

Katel animorphs and dives to the bottom of the pool. She wriggles a bit, then she disappears into the darkness again. I inhale deeply and follow. Immediately, my shoulders get lodged in the shaft. I back out and probe with my feet to see what shape it takes. I discover it bends under the hilltop. Lowering myself feet first, I realize that the shaft is only the length of a man before it opens up wide. I take one last gulp of air and I descend into the dark, cold abyss. There's only a tiny ray of light visible through the opening. The rope jerks and I lose my grip on it. Flailing around, I can't find it. The pressure to breathe is growing more urgent. In the darkness, I only know one direction.

Up!

I head back to the light and wriggle into the shaft. My shoulders are too wide, and they get stuck. The urge to breathe is growing ever stronger. I stretch my arms out in front of me and kick frantically. At last, my head is through and I can see plenty of light above me. I push myself up and explode to the surface. I inhale deeply and rest my head against the rocky side. I reward myself with several long gasps of air.

Ysella is nowhere in sight. A deep, bitter cold is seeping into my skin. One way or another, I have to get out of this water soon.

I hear steps above me. I press against the wall of the pool. A bit of dirt falls into the water right in front of me. I slow my breathing and listen intently.

"Ignore the bird for now. It's a diversion. I last sensed them in this area."

"Yes, Lord," Gurthcid says. "Where are they now?"

"I do not know, but they can't be far away. Remember, I want to catch all of them alive if we can, but that male druid is the most important. If anyone should kill him, the penalty will be severe."

"Yes, Lord. I'll split up my men."

"And Gurthcid, have your best archer stay here with me."

"As you say."

I'm trapped and I'm out of time. No matter which way around the pool they go, I'll be clearly visible. Gurthcid has his men split up into two groups as they take the paths around the pool. I freeze in place, waiting for one of them to notice me.

An alarm call of the crow emanates from directly in front of me. Ysella is diving for the men, wind whistling through her wings.

"Fire," the Obsidian Mage says.

An arrow from above is loosed. Ysella's alarm calls give way to a startled *kraa* as the arrow tears into her wing. She crashes to the ground with the arrow still embedded in her shoulder.

"Get that one."

Three men run to Ysella's wounded form and pick up the bird. The crow pecks repeatedly at her captor's hand, but he holds on with inhuman patience. Gurthcid grabs the arrow's shaft.

"No, do not remove the arrow. As long as metal is touching them, they cannot transform. Bring it to me and we'll put our little druid into an iron cage."

I have no choice. The men with Ysella are coming this way. I can't fight them. I would rather be an otter forever than a prisoner of the Obsidian Lord. I focus my will and take the unfamiliar form of an otter. Silently, I dive to the shaft below. I hear Katel giving off underwater clicks. I respond and let her guide me to her. I emerge in the air pocket and take a breath of the stale air.

Katel starts clicking and whistling her confusion. Not being familiar with the finer points of otter communication, her meaning escapes me. She dives into the lightless stream and I'm forced to follow. Thanks to her constant clicks, I make it through several tight tunnels and emerge at a rocky, underground beach. Once my lungs are refilled with fresh air, I focus my scattered mind on my human form.

"I thought you couldn't animorph? Were you lying to us all along? Where's Ysella? Do we need to go back and get her?"

"Katel!" I shout louder than I want. The echoes reverberate off the walls, each causing a spectacular cascade of pain within my head.

"Ysella is not following us. She was injured while in her crow form." I hate myself for what I have to do next. "She won't be able to fly, but she should be able to take on the deer form and outrun the Dark Lord and his men. No doubt she will find another entrance to Ogof Cawr." Thankfully, the darkness conceals my shame.

Katel's voice trails away from me and I hear items scuffing on the cave floor. The light from a single rushlight illuminates the area. The shadows dance on the walls of the grayish-white chamber. The clear water rolls up onto the reddish-brown gravel beach in small waves, as if it has tides like the oceans above.

"She won't take the crystal column entrance, at least not by herself," Katel says. "She gets too scared with all that rock pressing down on her unless I'm there to calm her. The only other entrance she knows of is the river exit."

"So how do we get to there?"

"I'll take you to meet Ysella, but then you must be on your way," she says. "I don't want to see you again." She hands me three rushlights of my own. "I suppose you will need your own source of light." She leans her flame over and ignites one of the oil-soaked rushes in my hand. "They will have to do, so I would not waste the light by standing idle," she calls to me over her shoulder.

I hurry to catch up. "Thank you, Katel. I would offer to help, but I need to get back to Dartmoor by Samhain."

"If you're in such a hurry, we can turn back into otters and we'll swim out in before nightfall."

"I can't keep animorphing, remember? Changing back this time was almost more than—" I shut up, but too late.

301

She stops dead in her tracks and comes back to face me. "You're afraid you'll end up like Sieffre." She finishes the thought for me. "It's what you deserve."

"Katel, I didn't mean—"

"You didn't mean what? To have multiple druids die for you without ever knowing the reason why?"

I exhale heavily. "I never wished for anything like this. All I know is that the sacrifices made for me are more than I deserve."

"At least we can agree on that."

28

A Walk through Darkness

Third Light Day of Cantl, 819

Eleven Days until Samhain

Katel doesn't slow for any reason. No matter how uneven the path, she's unperturbed. If I had time to think, no doubt I would have been panicked. We've been going steadily down for quite a while. She comes to a fork in the featureless corridor, and she hesitates as if to consider her options. She frowns at me.

"Hedred always says that we must show off the best of our realm to you sun-starers, lest you remain ignorant of all of the Earthmother's beauty." She chooses the left path. "This room is called 'The Needles' and it is a place of delicate beauty, laid down in stone over the ages."

A steady drip of water into a pool can be heard from the left. Any sound other than my footsteps is a welcome treat. Water drips on me from above. I look to Katel in confusion. She raises her reed light high and majestic stone fingers above come forth from the shadows. Moisture bleeds right through the rock and it runs down hundreds of needles to this chamber. One drop after another creates circular waves on the pool's surface. I am awestruck by this place.

"The problems of men to the gods are as the tiny ripples to this pool," Katel says. "Usually, people breathe with their mouth closed. You wouldn't want a bat to take up residence in that gaping maw."

"It's beautiful."

"It is, but remember, you're in a hurry." She turns and walks past the Needles at a clipped pace. Worried that she won't wait, I reluctantly hurry past the hallowed place.

She leads me through an endless number of nondescript gray passages before emerging at someone's quarters. She takes off her pack and rummages through it.

"Here it is." She takes out a flat rectangular rock and inspects it closely. "Good, still flat on top and bottom." She walks up to several stacks of rocks and stares before choosing the left most stack. Katel waves me over and gives me her rushlight. The rock is placed two thirds of the way up the pyramidal stack.

She smiles. "I collect perfectly flat-faced rocks and I stack them by mineral type."

"Oh, that's so very interesting."

Still engrossed in her rocks, she misses my sarcasm.

"Is this on the way to the exit?" I ask.

"Really? A girl takes you to her bedroom and all you can think about is leaving?"

I make several attempts at speech but fail miserably.

She smiles viciously at me. "Relax, you're not my type," she says. "I like men who care about others." Katel takes a thick wool mantle from a peg and wraps it around herself. She closes it tightly around her with a wooden cloak pin. "This will keep the chill away." She looks at me. "You really should have brought a mantle of your own." She says offhandedly before grabbing her rushlight from me and exiting. "Let's get moving."

We pass through several tunnels that I think we've passed through before, but I can't be certain. They are all dark, lifeless things. She stops and motions me forward.

"I've decided to take us over the stone arch bridge, then past the dragon's ribs and the stone curtain. I can call my friends in the Great Meeting Room to come meet us. Come take a look at the bridge and then put the torch out."

I join her at the entrance of the next cavern and there are enormous rock cones hanging from the ceiling and reaching toward their upward facing counterparts. A hundred-year-old oak tree could fit inside this place. Between them is a rounded bridge cutting through the forest of stone.

"See, the path is straight. So put out that torch and sixty-one steps later you will be on the other side. Oops, that's sixty-one of my steps; I'm not sure how many it will take you. Just keep walking straight until you hit the wall, then you'll be safely across. Keep darkness from your thoughts."

"What?"

"You're supposed to reply 'the absence of light is nothing to fear.'"

I must have heard wrong. "Why would I put the torch out?"

"Because I'm deathly afraid of heights, if I look down, I'll lose my balance and fall. You have to put the torch out. I can't risk it."

"Hold on," I say. "Do you have a flint that I can use to relight this?"

"Don't be stupid, after the bridge you'll be fine as long as you remember to duck before you run into the stone curtain."

"I don't think you understand," I say. "I can't walk across that bridge in the dark. It's not even as wide as my shoulders."

"Well, I can't walk across it in the light." She's adamant.

We stare at each other, waiting for someone to give.

"You have to go back down the passage, past the last bend in the tunnel. After I'm across, I'll call and you can try not to lose your balance while staring at certain death below you."

"Thanks for that."

I retrace my steps and wonder if she will wait for me once she's across. For better or for worse, I've put my trust in her. My mind imagines every possible disaster scenario as I await her call.

Did she abandon me? I start breathing heavily, wondering what I will do next. I could die down here and never be found, and that's true even after I cross that death bridge. Whether she's across it or not, I can't wait any longer. The cavern is even more massive and the bridge even more narrow than I remember.

"I was wondering if you decided to take a nap or something," Katel calls.

"Remember the part about you telling me when you're across?"

"Will you hurry up and get across? Or fall, as long as it's quick," she adds in a whisper. The echoes are amazing in this chamber.

"I can hear you very clearly," I say.

Katel studies the stone columns, unconcerned. Normally, I have excellent balance. As I walk, I brace myself for whichever way the wind might blow, only to remind myself that there is no breeze down here. My hair is sticking to my face but I'm too afraid to shake my head and remove the sweat. I lower my head down even lower so the sweat won't roll into my eyes. I focus on my breathing and take it one step at a time. Katel is kicking pebbles over the ledge and down the chasm as she waits for me. I dare not take my eyes off the bridge. After a couple breaths, I hear the pebbles land somewhere far, far below. My chest starts to tighten. I close my eyes and find my center. I take several ragged breaths before I can continue my slow but sure pace.

"Finally," Katel says, exasperated.

If I weren't completely beholden to her, I would cause great harm to this silly druid.

"Let's keep moving," she says.

I wipe the sweat from my face and follow with failing patience.

"When acolytes are first brought down to the Earthmother's world, we take them past the dragon's ribs and tell them how the gorge was formed when the last two dragons laid down next to each other and willed themselves to become stone. Here is the proof." She extends her arms and I see twenty stone ribs protruding along the wall. "It's all nonsense, of course; there's no such thing as dragons, but it's a good way to get their attention."

Around the next corner is the stone curtain. Katel ducks slightly and avoids the collision. The ribbon of stone hangs down below my shoulders and around a blind turn. *She wanted me to make sure to duck when I came upon this without my torch?* I choke down my comments and continue to follow.

"Hello, it is Katel who approaches," she calls. "I bid good tidings to all." Her voice echoes throughout the caves. "We don't want to be seen as inconsiderate," she says to me in a low whisper.

We wait in silence for a response. Finally, Katel waves for me to follow her. "Normally, someone would have come out to greet us. The echoes here are all funneled to the Great Meeting Room.

Because the walls bounce sounds back into the meeting hall, it is hard to hear anything coming from there. That's why we call, and they come to greet us."

"Except now no one is coming," I say.

"The Great Room is never empty." Katel signals me once again to follow her.

We find the Great Meeting Room and it's deserted. Only a single torch remains lit. On closer inspection, the rest are all warm to the touch. We frown at each other and check to make sure we haven't missed some telltale sign.

A booming voice enters the room. "You must leave us."

"Lord Hedred? Where are you and—"

"You have brought the pariah within our midst. We will not choose sides in this dispute. You must take him away from here. Only then can you rejoin us."

Even in the dim light, I can see her eyes tearing up. I will be happy to leave this dark, hostile place.

"Please show me the way out," I say to Katel.

She sets her jaw, and says, "Follow me." Her pace is even more brutal than before. As the tunnels branch, she always chooses the path heading lower.

Truly, the weight of the world is upon me and it's only getting heavier. "Where are you going?"

"To get answers." Ahead there are lights flickering off the walls of the tunnel. We enter the chamber, and it is ablaze with a dozen oil-soaked cattails.

"I knew you would be here," Katel says.

The diminutive Lord Hedred stands up straight. "Katel, did I not make myself clear?"

"Lord Hedred, there is much that I need to tell you. Sieffre is . . . lost to us." Her jaw starts to quiver and she's unable to say more.

"Sieffre is dead?" Startled, he looks at Katel, then me.

"He is not dead," I say. "He turned into a puffin and Lord Eghan has been unable to get him to turn back to his human self."

"A puffin, you say?" He stares up at the cracks running along the ceiling. "If there is anyone who can help him, it will be Eghan. He's a very kind and patient man. How long has he been in that form?"

"Thirteen days," Katel blurts.

Hedred shakes his head as he inspects the floor. He approaches Katel, reaches up and rests his arm on her shoulder. She lowers her head into his chest to muffle her sobs.

He looks up at me. "Perhaps you should tell me what has happened."

Lord Hedred is quiet for a time. He absently strokes Katel's hair before turning his attention back to me. "I do not blame you for all of these troubles. No, I blame Boswen and his never-ending schemes. And I blame Loris for his greed. Be that as it may, Loris has sent druids down here looking for you twice already, so I shall not offer you any hospitality other than a quick exit. I hope you understand."

"I do, Lord. Time grows short for me, so there is nothing else for which I would ask."

He gently pries Katel's arms from around his chest. "Please sit down for a bit, dear. After you show Grahme out, come back here so that we may talk."

She nods as she collapses into his seat. Lord Hedred invites me over to a different table. "Have you ever been in a scriptorium before?"

"I have never heard of that word before. Is that what this place is?"

"Katel and . . ."—he coughs—"have been searching the isle for remnants of elvish and giant scripts. These scripts have power, if you know how to wield them."

"Yes, Lord. Sieffre"—we both glance at Katel—"used several runes in the battle at Ynys Witrin. All would have been lost if not for him."

He pats my chest several times. "If Boswen doesn't tear us all asunder, I hope we have the opportunity to speak again." He pats my hand affectionately. "Your face speaks clearly. You do not need words of encouragement from me." He pats my hand again as if he were a father comforting an upset child.

"Though I am Boswen's senior in years, I was his first pupil." His eyes brighten at my surprise. "I was a problem for the druid lords all those years ago. The leading druids of Eriu and Pretanni were once again trying to forge closer ties. It never seems to work, but every other generation fools themselves into thinking that *this* generation will get it right. It was agreed that they would swap a promising young student, and each would learn the other's ways. If I may say so, I have always had great skill in the druidic arts; however, it was dealing with people that I never could master. I imagine the elders on Eriu were rather pleased to send me off to Pretanni. It was hard for me to find my place in this strange land."

He leans against a shelf and strokes the topmost sheet of vellum. The sheet is filled with runes and small pictures. He holds it up to the light and I can see fine scratches that were made without ink.

"I was sent to several different druids to complete my training and all of them parted ways with me."

I smile. So, I am not the only one who has had these troubles.

"At the festival of Beltane, my teacher severed our relationship. The Nine were out of ideas. It is then that a young and brash druid boasted that he could have me ready before the year's end. With only six months left, no one believed it could be done. So Boswen and I formed a partnership and we showed each other the arts favored on Eriu and Pretanni. It was the most exhilarating time of my life."

I look directly at Lord Hedred. "Learning under Boswen has been trying at times, I admit, but it has always been rewarding. But if that is the most exhilarating time of my life, I will die a disappointed man."

He fondly taps the stack of vellum and chuckles.

"I was never cut out to be a staff-wielding druid, changing into some bird and flying from one adventure to another. When I became a journeyman druid, Boswen suggested I go underground and help the ailing Lord Olchan. Not six months later, Olchan passed on and I became the youngest member of the Nine."

"You became a member of the Nine after only six months?"

"You must understand: Ogof Cawr has never been a popular assignment. The solitude suits me, though, and I have never regretted the choice. Six months later, Boswen also joined the Nine, and the isle has never been the same."

The cunning old man managed to steer me to the exit of his study while he spoke of bygone days. "I believe our young friend here has collected herself enough that she can lead you to the exit now."

"Keep darkness from your thoughts, right Hedred?" Katel asks.

"The absence of light is nothing to fear," he responds automatically.

Katel wipes one last tear on her sleeve as she comes to us. "Follow me."

She leads me through more tunnels until my sense of direction is hopelessly confused. At last, we come to a small grotto with thick furs lying on the ground.

"I will come back and get you in the morning." Katel turns to go.

"Wait, didn't Hedred ask us to leave immediately?"

"He did, but it's after nightfall and I'm not prepared to leave quite yet."

She slips back into the tunnels and I'm left to grope in the dark.

29

Barely Staying Afloat

Fifth Light Day of Cantl, 819

Ten Days until Samhain

"Get up, it's nearly dawn," Katel demands. "How can you know that?" "Our water clock, how else?"

"What's that?"

"No time. Get moving."

Katel races through the caves again, never hesitating on which passage to take. I stop to light my last rush and I nearly lose her.

"I can hear running water to our left."

"I'd be worried if you didn't. The water filters through the Mendip Hills and into the cave parallel to us."

"It's getting louder."

"You're hearing the upper falls. Thanks to all the recent rain, the river is much higher than usual. Higher than I've ever seen it, in fact." She pulls a dried cattail from a pitcher and shakes the free oil from the seed head. "We get the flaxseed oil from the plains druids. Ysella brings it to us every year. These will stay lit for a quarter of a day, at least."

I engage in some safe conversation. "Everyone knows that Ouma Cawr is the sacred space, but everyone topside calls it Ogof Cawr. Is Ouma Cawr a discrete place within Ogof Cawr, or is the whole underground considered sacred?"

"Of course, it's a real place, and you have been there."

"I have? Was it the Needles?"

"You're just another silly sun-starer, always thinking in visual terms. Down here vision is the second or third most important sense. Sound is the queen of the senses."

I shake my head. Apparently, that's the closest I'm going to get to an answer.

"Why didn't we use cattails instead of rushes when we first arrived?"

"We only use them when we must."

"Like the dozen Hedred had lit in his scriptorium?"

"That is the most important work we do here. Now, quit complaining and help me with the boat."

"You have a coracle down here?"

"How else would we travel by river?" Katel says.

"But we're underground. How do you see?"

"That's why I have the burning cattail. Now put the strap across your shoulders and carry the boat to the river."

"Are you going to give me a torch?" I ask.

"Of course not; the hide has been rubbed with flaxseed oil. If this flame sees it, the whole thing will go up in no time."

"I can't walk in the dark. I've never been here before. So, you'll have to lead the way."

She shakes her head at me like I'm stupid. "Fine, but stay well back."

The boat is made from interlocking hazel wood branches. The weave is very open, with branches spaced more than a hand width apart. A deer hide is stretched over the frame and as promised, coated in oil.

"Why did you use hazel? Willow is much lighter."

"When we go to harvest hazelnuts, we cut down the wands for boat-making at the same time."

The boat is only twice as wide as my shoulders and almost equal to me in height. It's going to be a tight fit for the two of us.

Katel increases her pace. I do my best to keep up, but the boat is bulky. "Wait," I shout. The echoes go on and on. I will never get used to that.

Katel faces me from the other end of the passage and starts to giggle. She turns down a corridor and the light disappears with her. I'm left in utter blackness. The boat scrapes against one wall, then the other. I raise both arms to keep myself centered and the strap slides upward from the front of my shoulders to my throat. I fall backward at once to relieve the pressure. My head hits the thwart and the crack echoes down the passageway. I lay still and take a breath. I'll be all right, except that I'm well below the ground, in the dark, with walls closing in on me. I have only a crazed woman to rely upon, and she's left me.

A glimmer of light appears from behind me and Katel starts giggling again. "The seat is meant for your butt, not your head."

"Thanks. How about we don't run in narrow corridors and leave me stranded in the dark?"

"I'm just teasing you. We don't need to take any of these passages. The river chamber is right next to where we keep the boat."

"Katel," I say with exaggerated patience, "we are trying to look for your sister. How about we stop playing pranks, and focus on what matters?"

She shrugs before leading me around a wide bend to a narrow beach. "Put the boat in there." She grabs two paddles and joins me. "Get in and slide all the way to the left."

I set the boat down in the quick flowing water and slide over on the bench.

"Set your pack in the boat. I won't have room to sit if you leave it there at your side."

My pack goes beneath the wooden plank, against the wall of the boat.

"You can't be leaning that far to shore; we'll knock heads when I get it."

I straighten up, even as I feel the boat teetering toward the water.

"Slide over more, I don't want to touch you," she says as she pokes me with an oar.

I tumble into the frigid water, my muscles seizing up immediately. I surge out of the water as the boat topples over on me. My pack is the only thing I can think of in this icy darkness. I throw the boat onto the beach and start feeling with my hands and feet. It's not in the boat. From the shore, Katel is laughing. My foot kicks something soft and supple. I lunge for the object in the calf-deep stream. Water trickles from my leather pouch as I retreat onto the beach. I unroll the leather wrap. The orchid is in sad shape, but it is still in one piece.

Goosebumps line my soaking wet arms and legs. My teeth start to move, but I clamp my mouth shut before my teeth can chatter. I give Katel a dark look and grab a paddle from her. I set the boat back on the shore and get in. I wedge my pack between the wooden frame and deer hide. I drive my oar into the soft sand to keep the boat from tipping again.

Katel hums a nameless tune as she inserts a wooden pole into the hole in the center of the seat. The pole's top is even with my eyes. She places the cattail torch at the top of the pole.

"If you tip the boat over again, we'll lose our only source of light," Katel says primly.

I swallow the bile coming up my throat and free my oar from the river bottom.

"Have you boated on fast water before?"

Now she decides to ask? "No."

"Keep your weight low and your head over top your body at all times. Leaning out over the water can cause the boat to tip."

We push off and the current catches us.

"Now, paddle; easy strokes."

Once out in the middle of the water, we relax and let the river take us onward. A few turbulent waves are to the left.

"See how the center of the river has a long, flat tongue and the sides are choppier?"

"Yeah."

"We need to stay in the central area as we go through the rapids ahead."

"Rapids?" I turn to look at her.

"Don't rock the boat."

317

All I want is to distance myself from her, but I can't lean away. The water is churning angrily ahead. The single torch which seemed so bright when we were on the light sandy beach, fails to illuminate what's in front of us.

"Left!" she yells.

The light picks up the frothy water ahead as a cross wave enters our path from another passage.

"We can't let it push us against the wall. Paddle! Harder!"

The wave slams up against my side and for an instant it feels as if we're going to spin around. Water flows into our boat. I dig in with all I have, and we finally breach the wave and reach calmer water.

"How do we get this water out?"

"By flipping the boat."

"Won't that extinguish the flame?"

"Yes."

Setting my paddle down; I make a cup with my hands, removing what water I can.

"The other way was narrow and filled with stone fingers pointing down at head level."

"I'm glad we missed it."

"That's the regular route. Instead, we're going to take the lower falls."

"We're going over a waterfall?" I try not to sound panicked.

"It's only the height of two men."

"Two men?" My heart rises to the back of my throat.

"Hopefully, we won't lose our torch."

"Is that it?" I point my unsteady hand ahead. The water mounds up, obscuring whatever is behind it.

"No, that's just a wave. We can rest while we go over it."

We crest the wave, and I can touch the ceiling if I stretch.

"Get down, brace yourself."

A thick stone finger from the ceiling is racing toward my head. I throw myself back, but not fast enough. It punches my chest, knocking my breath from me. The boat drops from beneath us and I grab hold for dear life. A veil of white spray obscures the angry wall of wild water in front of us. The boat lists sideways, leaving Katel to face the wave. I lean away from the water as the boat hits a rock. Bouncing from the boat, I'm lost in an icy darkness.

The current tosses me wherever it will. Water forces its way into my mouth, nose, and ears. I dare not open my eyes. My head rises above the water and I yell for Katel. The current pulls my legs downward. I take one last breath with equal parts air and water before I'm spun around in the bitter cold current. I resurface and cough up the water in my chest. Once more, my feet are being pulled down. I close my mouth and eyes and sink again into the abyss. I can't feel my arms or legs as I wait for death's kiss on my numbed lips. My head pops up above the surface. I inhale at once and wait to be pulled under. I'm able to get another breath before I realize that I've made it to calmer water.

"Grahme?"

I hear Katel call from my right. My muscles begin to seize up again. Death is trying to claim me. I feebly kick my legs, propelling myself toward the sound of her voice.

"Katel?"

"I'm over here," she says in the total darkness.

I use every bit of strength I have left to get myself over to her. My hand strikes the boat hard, but I don't feel the pain. I lean into the boat and find my pack, still sitting snugly along the side. Rising to my feet, I get out of the water and lean against the smooth stone wall.

"What happened?" I ask.

"The boat tipped over when you went overboard."

My face is burning from the unwanted water intruding through every possible opening. My head aches and I feel as if I'm about to wretch my waterlogged guts out.

"Give me you oar," she says.

"My oar?" I feel all around my body, as if it's sticking to me and I'm not aware. "It's gone."

"I can't believe you'd do that."

"I'm lucky to be alive." Before I can say more, the water in my stomach hurls up through me and back into the river. "It doesn't matter," I say, teeth chattering. "I can't feel my fingers anyway so the oar would be no use."

"How do we get out of here?" I ask.

"Get back in the boat."

My teeth chatter so hard that I'm afraid I may break a tooth. I lock my jaw shut in the inky darkness. I grope for the thwart with my arm and manage to seat myself on it. I refuse to let Katel know how battered I am. We settle the boat on the shore once again and I sit down on the thwart. Numbly, I realize that my life depends entirely on Katel now. At least in this darkness she can't see the terror on my face.

We push off and the smooth, swift water carries us on our way.

"At least the water is calm now," I manage to say somewhat casually.

"Brace yourself, it doesn't last very long."

"What's up ahead?"

"Shhh. I'm listening."

Our pace quickens and we can hear a dull roar in the distance. I face Katel, but in the total darkness, sight is useless. I dig my fingernails into the wooden seat and lean my head between my legs. The roar is undeniable now.

"Brace yourself."

Time slows down as I wait for the next catastrophe to arrive. I dare to release the thwart only long enough to check on my pack.

The boat starts to spin, but Katel is able to counter. At least I think that's what's happening. The boat tips forward and I push off against the front of the boat with both feet. I lean back to keep from tumbling out of the boat. The boat goes entirely vertical before diving into the water. I choke on some spray, but the boat pops up and rights itself. It's only by force of will that I manage to keep my grip on the wooden bench.

"That was awesome," Katel says.

The boat sways from side-to-side and spins slowly to the left. I hear Katel's oar make contact with the water and the boat stops drifting. As the sound from the falls recedes, it's replaced by the thumping of my heart.

"That's the last of the difficulties. We should be out of the caves before long. You can stretch your legs out now."

"They've been straight this whole time," I say.

"You didn't keep them under the thwart like you're supposed to? No wonder you fell out."

With every bit of control that I have, I keep myself from throttling her. I force myself to think about anything other than our predicament.

"The Great Meeting Room," I shout. My voice echoes over and over again. "Sorry."

"What?"

"The Great Meeting Room is the Ouma Cawr. 'In the dark, vision is useless, and sound is king.' So, the most sacred place would be where all the sounds are collected."

"Sound is queen," she corrects me. "You're not as dumb as the typical topsider."

30

Death at the Gorge

Fifth Light Day of Cantl, 819

Ten Days until Samhain

It's still morning and Belenos is obscured by rain clouds. A light breeze kisses my face and I delight in the smell of wet leaves. It's the first smell I've noticed since . . . Ysella's lavender fragrance.

"She should be here by now," Katel says.

She guides the boat to the eastern side of the gorge. Nervously, she taps her hips underneath her wool mantle. "This is the side Ysella should approach from."

The raindrops feel warm compared to the river. I rub my soaked arms as I pace back and forth. I need to create some warmth. Katel scans the cliffs above, filled with worry. I'm disgusted with myself for withholding the truth.

She sees me shiver. "You can wait inside if you want. There are a few small stone slabs inside the entrance that always remain above the river," she says with compassion.

I hang my head, if she just remained crazy, I'd feel less bad about keeping my secret. Head down, I walk toward her. She deserves to know the truth.

"There, I can see movement." She is pointing a good distance back into the canyon along the eastern rim. I strain to see anything, but the rain is being driven from that direction.

"This rain will dampen the echoes, but I can still make it work." Katel cups her hands to her mouth. "Sella!" she screams into the western side of the gorge. Her voice is muted somewhat, but the echo travels. We listen carefully as the rain continues to pelt us. A raven alarm call reverberates back down the gorge.

"What does that mean?" Katel turns to me.

"It means she's in trouble." Relieved and alarmed all at once, I'm able to release my guilt. *Ysella is still alive.*

The alarm is repeated, followed by nothing but the falling rain. We scan the rim again. Neither of us is willing to put voice to our fears. Scree falls down on us.

"Hello, down there," a deep baritone calls to us.

Chills run down my spine that have nothing to do with the icy water behind me. The Obsidian Lord is peering over the precipice.

"Is this bird your property?" He extends his arm to show us a caged crow. He's about two mature oak trees above us. The escarpment here is much too steep for anything but climbing.

"Ysella?" Katel shouts.

The crow lets out a long, sorrowful caw.

"I'll offer you a deal. Come up here and fight me one-on-one. If you win, you get this caged druid, but if I win, you return my property."

"His property?" Katel turns to me.

"He means the ghost orchid."

"Did you steal it from him?"

"I reclaimed it."

Outraged, Katel spins on me. "This whole time he's been chasing you because you're a thief?" Her voice rises in anger. She scans the beachhead and finds a stout branch. She holds it as if ready for combat. "Will you go, or do I need to knock you unconscious and take the flower myself?"

"Katel, you can't believe his offer is real."

"What's real is that my sister has been captured because of you. I will gladly trade your worthless life for hers."

I raise my hands in supplication. "I am willing to do whatever it takes to get Ysella back."

"Then you'll fight him?"

"I will if that's the only choice." I touch my amulet. At least the river didn't take it. "Do you see another branch I can use as a staff?"

She turns to scan the beach and I lunge for her weapon. Tearing it from her water soaked hands, I take a couple steps back, in case I need to wield it against her.

She gives me a hateful stare as her body tenses. She crouches and circles me until I'm left facing the rain. I lower the staff into a defensive position.

"Do you have your protective amulet on?" I ask.

"What? The earth protects us from the mind-controllers."

"You're not underground now. And you weren't when we fought him at the tor. He's been homing in on you. That's how he keeps finding us."

"If you're not interested right now," the Black Lord interjects, "I can always have her turn back into human form and compel her to pleasure me."

325

"We have to free her," she beseeches me.

"In fact," The Obsidian Lord says, "I think I'll let her out to pleasure my men while you two resolve your differences." He laughs at us. Before he can reach for the latch, Katel transforms into a bat and is gamely trying to ascend in the rainstorm. I leap into the air, taking on the tawny owl form.

Katel is getting tossed by the wind and rain. Her tiny form is not made for weather like this. Ysella restarts her alarm call, but she's more strident this time. I veer off to the right, then continue my rise. Off to the side, I see Gurthcid and the remainder of his men, arrows notched and waiting for a target to appear. I dive back down below the ridge and snatch Katel from midair.

Outraged, she retakes her human form and grabs hold of my wing. We crash into the muddy bank and slide down to the river's edge.

"Katel, wait," I yell, not sure if she intends to go after me or the Black Lord. She picks up the staff again and I have my answer. "It's a trap. Gurthcid and his men are behind the bluff, ready to shoot us out of the sky."

"I would rather die than abandon my sister." She raises the staff high, ready to strike. I extend my arms in front of me as my only pitiful defense.

Ysella lets out an earsplitting caw. Katel stops.

"What is it?" Katel calls.

Ysella delivers a long, mournful caw before morphing back into her human shape. Her human body, too heavy for the Black Lord to hold, tumbles down the gorge. She comes to rest on the ledge above us. We scramble up the rock face.

Katel beats me to the ledge and falls to her knees over her sister. "No, no, no," she repeats over and over. I arrive and see part of the bird cage protruding from either side of Ysella's chest. She must have known that she was dead as soon as she transformed. Katel lets out a wail of sorrow that echoes through the canyon.

Above us, Gurthcid and his men are taking aim at us. I tackle Katel against the slope as the arrows rain down. Ysella's body takes several hits.

"Why did you do that?" she shrieks.

I point to the arrows. "We would be dead otherwise."

"I think I'd prefer that," she says before her words degenerate into sobs punctuated by hiccups.

"We can't stay here, out in the open." I say, but it's useless. Her balled fists pound my chest in futility. I try gently shaking her, but still get no response. I'm running out of options. "Katel, find Hedred, he'll know what to do."

She stops her bawling and stares blankly into my face.

"Hedred. Go get Hedred. He'll know what to do," I say in a slow and clear voice.

"We'll come back with twenty able fighters," she says with determination.

"Go! Someone must sound the alarm." I squeeze her arms.

She transforms into a bat and races back into the cave, leaving me with Ysella's lifeless form. At least everyone will not end up dead, or worse. Gurthcid barks out an order and his men withdraw from the edge.

I quickly dart out from cover to check on my attackers. No one is there. I risk another couple steps to confirm they are gone before I run back to Ysella's side. "I never told you, but I loved you from the first moment I saw you. I pray the gods allow us to meet again in our lives to come." I cradle Ysella's head and give her one last kiss goodbye.

It seems wrong to leave her body out here in the rain, but the Obsidian Mage is coming. I must leave her for Hedred and his charges to perform the proper rituals.

I shove off and paddle as if my life depends upon it. I welcome the stinging rain and the discomfort it brings me. I deserve much worse.

31

Downward Dive

Sixth Light Day of Cantl, 819

Ten Days until Samhain

The rushes along the banks make for poor cover. The river meanders south through gently rolling hills, making the likelihood of being seen all the greater. Where is the torrent we endured underground? I must rely on myself to generate any pace. The river turns west and I rest long enough to see if my hands still shake. There are still noticeable tremors, but how much is from chills and how much from drained powers? At least rowing will warm me up.

As I get some distance from the gorge, oaks and aspens start to appear along the banks. The occasional willow with its pendant branches skimming the water makes an appearance. At last, there is some cover.

Ahead is a larger, more powerful waterway that makes my river feel like a muddy little stream. My boat is thrown against the left bank. I angle into the wave and attack it, only to be spun around and tossed against the bank again. Finally, the river widens and I'm not so close to either bank. The river slows and I notice most of the trees on both banks have been felled. There must be a beaver dam ahead.

There's not much light left in the day, so I stop under one of the last untouched willows. It is a small tree, which is likely why it hasn't been taken yet, and it sits upon a small island within the beaver-dammed lake. I beach the boat and turn it upside-down. The deer hide should melt right into the shadows under this tree. At least it better, for the bank is only several steps away. I have nothing to eat, and I dare not start a fire. It's going to be a long night.

There's been no sign of the Obsidian Lord, but I know the water on the opposite side of the beaver dam will be sluggish. In direct sunlight, I'll be an easy target.

Belenos has almost retired when I hear horses trotting along the river road. I remain still as a stone, even as they move closer to me.

"He'll want to head south to Dartmoor, so have your men patrol the southern shore of the river," a low-pitched voice says.

"Yes, Lord," is Gurthcid's response.

I grab my protection amulet from around my neck and hold on to it with both hands. In the still air, any sound I make will travel. I dare not move and give away my location.

The horses continue their trot off to the west.

How did he know that I am going to Dartmoor?

After an eternity of waiting, I can no longer hear their presence. I peer out under the boat shell and confirm that I'm alone.

As Belenos rises, there are no clouds as far as the eye can see. I paddle myself to the northern side of the river before dawn, carry the boat around the dam and put in from there. I paddle at a steady pace, making sure not to be heard as I pass the dam.

I'm frightfully exposed once again, but I have no choice. The riverbanks squeeze closer together and the current picks up. At last, something is going right.

A huge willow grows on the southern bank, half in and half out of the river. I see movement from within the canopy and spot an arrow as it comes streaking at me. I dive into the water, flipping the boat on top of me. Two arrows in quick succession fly through the boat's frame.

Keeping my head down, I grab the boat and keep it between me and the southern shore. The occasional arrow hits the boat. I take a quick look. There are three men emerging from the tree. They mount up once I'm passed and keep pace with me on the south bank. An occasional arrow embeds itself into the boat, but it's only target practice for them. The warriors take off farther ahead. *This can't be good.*

There is a low, wooden bridge around the next bend spanning the river, and six Coritani archers are waiting for me. Going to either bank would mean fighting all six warriors with only a paddle. I get a read on the speed of the river and the distance to the bridge. There is turbulence on the north side of the river, creating foam on top of the water. So, there are rocks just beneath the surface. My only choice is between the rocks and hardened warriors. I dive under my overturned boat and gather my breath. The boat won't give adequate protection but showing my face again will surely be the last thing I do.

I hear the men joking amongst themselves. I have to be close. Taking one final breath, I dive and swim well below my boat. I kick with all my might and keep pace. My right hand slams into a rock and I grab it instinctively. The boat's shadow passes me. I ball my fist and give each stroke the desperation it deserves. My lungs burning, my head breaks the surface under the back end of the boat.

331

Greedily, I steal a fresh breath. The whole frame sinks a few inches before rocking back and forth. *What are they throwing at the boat?*

An ax breaks through the woven branches, letting sunlight shine through.

I'll never make it without the boat. I propel myself upward, into the right side of the boat. The boat tips over, sending my assailant into the river. I pull the boat against my exposed head and swim for the northern shore.

The man shouts out his distress. He doesn't know how to swim. The thrashing man is pulled farther and farther away. Behind me, the remaining men pepper my coracle with several arrows. Giving up the tactic, they mount their horses and once again keep pace with me on the southern shore. They leave their comrade to his watery grave.

The river is reasonably wide, so I should be protected from them for a while. I check the northern bank. Maybe I can land there and shake off my pursuers.

The Black Lord emerges through the brush to the northern bank ahead of me. I flip the boat over me once again to stay out of his direct sight. Fearing him more than the men, I move to the center of the river. He too is content to ride at pace with me. And why not? I have no way to escape. At some point I will have to choose between two very bad options.

I can smell salt in the air, so I know that my dilemma will end very soon. The river widens out and I'm far enough away that no more arrows are coming my way. It is nearly midday and there is no cover. This sorry little boat riddled with holes is definitely not seaworthy. To the north of me there are mud flats stretching off well into the distance. The low tide has left delicate undulations in the mud. If my life were not imperiled, I might find it pretty. The Black Lord won't be able to cross the flats, but neither will I. One possible avenue of escape for me is eliminated.

The Obsidian Lord pulls up short of the flats on a small rise and waits for his men to finish the job. The road south of the river turns away as the ground gets soft, giving me some distance from Gurthcid and his men. Ahead is a tor with steep cliffs jutting into the sea. The Strait of Eriu begins tossing my boat about. I won't be able to hang on to it for much longer. On the northern side of the tor, the scree looks scalable. I release the boat, and swim for the loose rocks.

I send plenty of rocks into the water, but I make the top of the tor. I've bought myself a little time, but only a little. I'm still trapped. A small fishing village sits on the western edge of the tor. Going that way will only result in more people being enslaved or killed. A cry of discovery lets me know that my pursuers have found a path to the top. With nowhere left to run, I wait for my doom.

One of the men takes aim at me. I stare down the arrow without flinching. Gurthcid slams his horse into the archer's mount and forcibly lowers the man's bow. There will be no easy way out for me.

My arms begin to tremble, and I lose my nerve. Breaking into a run, I head back to the northern edge. I stare down at the rocks below. Even now, I can't bring myself to jump. I scan the ground and laugh at my predicament; my only weapons are the loose rocks themselves.

Gurthcid's head rises above the tor and he smiles at me. He moves off the path and waits for the rest of his men. They have no reason to hurry. I close some of the distance between us, stepping in loose gravel as I go. If only I had a sling, I would at least have a chance. At some point, I lost my bone knife, so I can't cut a crude sling from my robe.

There will be no ballads sung about this meeting with the Obsidian Lord.

My thoughts become clear. I'm a dead man; I know this to be true. If nothing else, I have to make sure that the silly orchid I carry does not fall back into his hands. That is all I have left to fight for. I plant my feet in the rocky soil and await their approach.

Gurthcid signals his men to halt. There are no taunts; the silence is unnerving. I review my options again, hoping that I missed something. Behind me is a steep slope that abruptly drops off into sea rocks; I will find no escape there. Gurthcid and his men have blocked off any retreat. There is the village, but I would only bring death and destruction upon them as well. No, I didn't miss anything. Gurthcid draws his sword, and his men take to their axes.

I run as fast as I can to the sheer cliff behind me. Certain death awaits, but at least it will be quick.

The Obsidian Lord figures out my plan and he shouts for the warriors to spur their mounts to overtake me. I skid to a stop at the very edge of the cliff. I am just a step away from my certain death. Gurthcid and his men are galloping hard. They'll never stop in time. I jump for the rocks below before pulling up as my wings beat furiously.

I turn to hover in the air as I see six men on horses ride over the cliff and fall to the rocks below. The center man leaps from his steed in an effort to grab me. I dodge him easily. As he falls backward, his hand remains outstretched, reaching out for me. How odd.

The spilled blood from the humans and horses below begins to fill the air. It won't be long before many others will discover this easy meal.

I land on the rocks near the strange human. The back half of his head cratered, he stares out at nothing now. The eyes will make choice morsels. The word, *Gurthcid*, flits into my mind. What a strange word. I cock my head and ponder it for a moment. Gurthcid, I seem to know that word, somehow. A human in black shouts out his rage from the shore.

My human mind breaks through and gains ascendency. *But for how long?* I leap into the air and make for Dartmoor. Yes, the moor is to the south, I must go there and find my nest.

32

No Time for Healing

The Tenth Light Day of Elembiu, 819

I sit up and listen for clues to where I am, other than a small, dimly lit thatch hut. I can recall the bitter taste of the sleeping draught, but it is gone now. There are two other men and four empty pallets here. Both men are out cold and have grievous cuts all over.

The fire is down to its last embers. I have no recollection of arriving here. It's becoming a disturbing habit. A reed-thin man throws back the leather opening and blinds me with the brilliance of Belenos' evening rays. He stirs the embers and adds a couple of logs. I sit up a little more to catch his attention.

He turns to me and gives a genuine smile. "It's good to see you awake finally."

"Thank you, it's good to be awake. Can you tell me where this place is?"

"You are in the healing house of Tochar Briwa."

"Tochar Briwa?" A feeling of dread falls over me. Drustan is the Lord Protector of this place and one of Loris' closest allies.

"Yes, you are safe. No doubt you have been out searching for this Grahme for too long. You are not the first to have trouble transforming back to human."

"How did you know I was a druid if I was in bird form?"

"A kestrel that passes on several vole baits then suddenly pounces on a third? I know how to spot a druid who is losing himself to the animal."

"A kestrel?" *What is the last thing I remember?*

"You managed to elude my net the first time, but not the second. I must say, as a bird, you have an angry disposition." He shows me his hands filled with long scrapes and bruises.

"Is that all from me?" I ask, horrified.

He waves me off. "If I couldn't handle a peevish bird, then I have no business being a druid. Now, I'm going to get you some food, so try to stay awake until I get back. After your meal, you can sleep to your heart's content."

I feel safe for the first time in a month.

"I will try to stay awake," I say with mock seriousness.

"Good, I will take my dinner with you."

The man returns with two bowls of porridge and a loaf of bread. He hands me a bowl and then breaks the bread in half. We both notice my hand trembling as I reach for it. We lock eyes before I break away.

"I know what you're going to say."

"Do you?"

"You're going to tell me that I've pushed myself to the very edge of my powers and that I need to refrain from using them for the next month."

"My question then, is how many times have you heard and not heeded this advice? There is talk of a druid who not so many days

337

ago became a puffin and could not change back. Why anyone would choose that ridiculous animal is the question I would like to have answered." He throws a couple more logs on the fire.

I cast my gaze downward at my bread and take a bite. My stomach reawakens. I finish the bread and the porridge like a half-starved man. The healer offers me his meal.

"No, no, I can't take that. I am sorry, even the crudest churl would fault me for that."

"My arm is getting tired, so please, take this bowl. I can always get more for myself." We trade bowls and I force myself to talk while eating my second helping.

"I am doubly sorry, for I have not bothered to ask your name."

"Nor I yours, so don't go turning awkward. We are brothers of the land, after all. I am Andrilou and I am the healer for Drustan's camp."

A shiver goes down my spine. I had been trying very hard to convince myself that I had heard wrong. "And where are all of Drustan's men?" I ask in a conversational way, I hope.

Andrilou laughs an amused, nonthreatening laugh. "Do you expect me to tell you the spots my campmates have chosen to find this wayward Grahme? They want the promised reward from Loris as much as you do."

I give a relieved smile. "My pardons, I meant to ask if the whole camp was out searching for this errant brother."

"Errant? It's more than that I'm afraid. You must have been in kestrel form for a very long time. Drustan revealed to us last night that this Grahme is a messenger from Boswen, and they are scheming with other druids to foment a revolt. It was stressed to us over and over that we are not to kill him before the disloyal members of the Nine are uncovered."

"*Members* of the Nine?"

"Indeed."

"Which ones?"

"I am not in the habit of questioning my lord. Is that common in your group?"

"Lord Cynbel allows for some questions, but we know well who is in charge. I am called Arthmael. My apologies for not offering my name before."

Andrilou waves my apology away.

It's a shame we are on different sides.

"After this Grahme is captured and his information revealed, Drustan anticipates a move against Boswen. It is a sad day when druid must fight druid."

"Indeed."

"Now it is time for you to rest. I can share some good news, however. It seems that Master Gwalather has left Boswen's land. He is to join us here, and his aid will be most welcome.

"Master Gwalather? He's coming here?"

He mistakes my anxiety for excitement.

"I will have him look after you when he arrives, of course, but I assure you I have been more than adequate to the task."

"You have my most humble apology. I was simply shocked to hear Gwalather's name. Do you know when he will arrive?"

"Soon, I would imagine. But then, this whole ugly affair will be over soon. Gwalather promised to be with us by Samhain, so he can't be too long now." He rises and takes the second bowl from me. "I would love to stay longer, but I must help with the fire ceremony setup."

"Fire ceremony? What day is it?"

Andrilou whistles. "You have been in bird form for much too long. At dusk we start the second fire ceremony leading up to Samhain."

"Samhain is only two days away?"

"Two and a bit, dusk is not quite here," he says, amused at my reaction. "You will remain here for it, no doubt. There will be no more transforming for you for a very long time." He shakes his head. "Alas, I fear you will not be the one to discover this Grahme."

I lay my head back down on the pillow as if the news has hit me hard. *I'm so close.*

"I'm sorry to dash your hopes. I will leave you be."

I give Andrilou time to move on to other tasks. I can't risk Gwalather seeing me. My shaky knees manage to hold me up, though I have to brace one hand against the wall to steady myself. My pack is under the bed. I curse my luck for having to get down to my knees only to rise one more time. I wait for the lightheadedness to go away before I check for the orchid. It's in sad shape, almost as bad as me, but there is nothing to be done for it. I edge toward the door and listen for movement. The other two men still sleep like the dead. All is quiet. I peek out of the leather flap and still see no one. To move cautiously is to draw suspicion, so I throw the leather flap to the side and stride out confidently. The biting cold wind hits me at once. It's good to be back on the moors.

"Arthmael? Where are you going?"

Just my luck, Andrilou is directly across from me. I blink a couple times as if the light is bothersome. I need some sort of excuse. "I am going to relieve myself. But my knees are being disagreeable," I say. It's partially true.

"Here, take my staff." He rushes over to me, as if he's going to have to catch me from falling over. "I should have thought of that. Do you want me to guide you there?"

"No, thank you, I don't want to keep you from your other responsibilities."

"Go to the left of camp, toward those two oaks. You will be able to find it from there." Andrilou holds his nose to underscore the point.

"And if I have the strength, I would like to see the Tochar Steps, since I have never been here before. Can you point out that direction as well?"

"This is why I find the current latrine location so vexing. Continue on past the latrines and down the hill. Follow the River Barle for a short while then they will be to your right. But you must wait another day or two before attempting it. I know that your knees at least agree with me."

I smile and nod. Slowly turning toward the latrines, I resist the urge to hurry on my way. I note the camp is still empty, which means there are scores of druids out looking for me. Somehow, I must obtain commoners clothing for my walk to Dartmoor. We are meant to serve the people, not steal from them. Must I break another tenet of our order to become a druid? I hurry on my way, disgusted with myself.

Andrilou's finely hewn staff will be a dead giveaway that I'm a druid. Still, I doubt I could walk down the hill without it. I trace the lightly engraved knot work design as my hand slides down the well-oiled staff. It is unfortunate that art such as this must be discarded.

The River Barle is a sedate little river, and the need for a bridge is debatable. But when the bridge was laid down by the giants, few are willing to criticize. Huge, flat rocks rest upon equally-sized upright stones. The river is wide if not deep, and seventeen massive rocks are needed to span it.

It seems obscene to scuttle across this great edifice, but my situation is dire. Midway across, I decide that I must stay in the good graces of the gods at least. I throw Andrilou's staff into the river and watch it catch between two stone columns. Let this be my meager offering to the gods. Poor Andrilou, I have lied to him and now I use his staff to curry favor from the gods. The man deserves better. But then, everyone else who has helped me has fared much worse. No tree falls upon me when I cross the bridge. I take this as a sign that the gods at least, are not seeking vengeance.

Dusk is upon me. I collect leaves and find a spot protected from the late autumn wind. One way or another, my quest is nearly over.

33

Unexpected Aid

Full Moon of Cantl, 819

Samhain Eve

Andrilou will no doubt notice me missing and start a search. I can't tarry in my warm leaf bed. How I wish I could have another hot bowl of porridge, but it is not to be. The fog is still heavy this morning, but it will only blind me to the sharp-eyed and sharp-eared animal forms my druid pursuers.

I have no opportunity for strategy. It will take the rest of the day to reach Boswen's camp along the Druid Ditch Road. One way or another, this ordeal ends today.

Coming from the south, I hear the steady gait of ponies along the road. I doubt these men will be druids, but I am fairly well known in these parts, though for the wrong reasons. I'm this close to Dartmoor and if even one person recognizes me, it will all be over.

Through the interweaving branches, I can see that the cart is moving at a comfortable pace. I bow my head low and move to the side of the road. With luck, this farmer will leave me be. I step off the road as if to relieve myself. My back to the wagon, I close my eyes and await my fate.

"Ho, Grahme, when you're done pretending, I've been sent to find you," a cheerful voice says.

I release my robe and turn to see Blachstenius smiling down at me. Speechless, I walk toward him. "How . . .? Who . . .? What is going on here?"

"I see you have not mastered the bardic tradition. Hop aboard and I will fill you in while I take you to Boswen."

I pinch myself to confirm that I am indeed awake.

"Hurry along; there are scores of druids abusing every owl, bear or wolf from here to Dartmoor in hopes that it is you. I was about to turn back. Be quick now, time is short." He winks at me. "Here's hoping no druids find us."

I climb up and take a seat next to the trader. He flicks his wrists, and the ponies turn around in a broad circle.

"What do you know about the current situation?"

I repeat some of what Andrilou had told me and I hint at problems between the Nine.

Blachstenius nods his head slightly and says, "You know the heart of the matter. It is interesting to me that Loris hasn't mentioned the orchid to the common druids. This story of insurrection is sure to inflame passions, but he will have to deal with the backlash once the community finds out it was all over a silly flower. Speaking of which, you have the ghost orchid with you, do you not?"

"I do." I hastily grab my pack and open it to confirm my statement. I remove the sad little flower from my pack and show Blachstenius the object of my quest. Several friends are dead or worse. This flower is all I have to balance out the tragic losses.

"Put that away. The next person to see that should damned well be Boswen."

"If it's still recognizable."

"You need to stay in the present and not to wallow in self-pity. I know that your trip has been an ordeal, but I need you to not draw attention to yourself." He waggles his finger at me. "I know you can be a hothead, so let me handle anyone we come across."

"I can fight, if I must."

He taps his temple. "I have a better way available to me."

A falcon flies down from its perch and lands in front of us. It is in the late juvenile stage by the look of it and a very young druid replaces it soon after landing.

"Halt," he shouts. "I must know the name of the druid in your cart before you can proceed down this road." He manages to keep his voice from quivering too badly.

"Why, I have no druid with me. This is my nephew. We are just a couple of poor traders chasing after the elusive prosperity of Brigantia."

The young druid relaxes. "My apologies, the angle of the light made your nephew's clothes look white for a moment. Please continue on your way and beware, there is a rogue druid about and he is as dangerous as he is ruthless."

"Thank you for the warning. I think we'll chance a bit faster pace," Blachstenius says. "But master druid, if I may be so bold, may I ask a simple favor from you?"

"Of course," he says as he perks up.

"My nephew hurt his ankle while searching for flowers to impress a certain young lass. In his fall, he wrenched his ankle. Would you be able to lend him your staff, so he does not damage his leg further?"

The druid is all too eager to please. He comes over to my side and hands me his oaken staff.

I look at Blachstenius, but he stares off impassively.

"Thank you, honored druid, we are fortunate to have such noble people as yourself among us. May I have your name, good druid? When my ankle heals, where should I call to return this excellent staff?"

He throws out his chest. "I am Brehmne and I am a student of Lord Braden at Brenin Cairn. But you may keep this staff as a gift from me. It is nothing to make a new one."

"If you should see any of your fellow druids, tell them that Grahme has been captured and is being held at Drustan's camp," Blachstenius says.

A huge smile lights up his face. "This is great news! I'll let everyone I can find know at once."

"Good druid," I call, "it may be better to take an owl's form in this fog. They sense much better in this stuff than falcons."

The boy furrows his brow in confusion. Blachstenius has his eyes pressed shut and there is sweat forming at his temples. The boy takes the form of a short-eared owl and leaves us be.

Blachstenius grunts his displeasure.

"What?"

"Grahme," Blachstenius says with exaggerated patience, "would a common merchant advise druids on what bird form would be best for them in various situations?"

"I doubt it."

"Then act like a common merchant. My illusion was nearly ruined when you suggested an owl form. I had to permanently change his memory so that once in animal form he won't realize the truth about us."

"Sorry, it won't happen again."

He flicks his wrists and the ponies increase their pace to a trot. I have barely been able to get comfortable and already we've been stopped. *How many more altercations are before us?*

"What of Figol?" I ask, to change the subject.

"We stopped at Mai Dun before coming to Land's End. Figol and his family are all with your brother Kenal

"Ferroth is at Dinas Gwenenen as well?"

"As I said, the entire family, but that is a tale best left for another time."

I shake my head to make sure I heard right before I try another approach.

"Boswen declined to take Figol as a student?"

"He felt it best to keep everyone out of sight until the current commotion is over."

I nod, "A smart move."

In the lowlands between the moors, the temperature is warmer. The fog has burned away and despite my present circumstances, it is a pleasant day.

"Boswen has to allow Figol to become a druid. He would surely be better than that child we just encountered."

Blachstenius chuckles. "If you had yelled at the poor boy, I wager he would have wet himself."

I have to stick up for my fellow druids, even if they are aligned against me. "He was young, but he would have done his duty as he sees it, if he had to do so."

"I doubt it. He wants no part of Grahme the Weathermaster, who throws godsfire and calls forth hail on a whim."

"Now you mock me?" I ask.

"No, I merely relate the tales that are being told of late in these parts." He smiles sidelong at me, "And perhaps a little bit of mockery slipped in as well."

"I hope you know better than to believe these wild tales."

His eyes playful, he asks, "Did you really call forth a griffin from up north to defend yourself from my brother's men?"

"Your brother?"

"Yes, Rhunior, I told you that didn't I?"

"No, you most certainly did not."

"I guess we'll have to blame it on my advanced age, since unlike some, I can't use the excuse that all of druidom is chasing after me."

"Are you done mocking me yet?"

"For now, but know that these wild tales are being repeated and exaggerated daily."

"Even though storm clouds follow me wherever I go, I have not summoned them."

We ride on in silence as my eyelids grow heavy. The horse's hooves continue their monotonous clip-clop tune, and I can barely maintain my vigilance.

"I think it best if you get in the back of wagon and stay out of view. That young one was no doubt close to Tochar Steps because he thought it unlikely to meet you. The ones closer to Dartmoor are bound to be both more eager and more capable."

34

Questions at the Quest's End

Samhain, First Dark Day of Cuimon, 820

The wagon's soaked cover is dripping cold water on my face. The cart has stopped, and I can hear the hushed voices of men around a crackling fire. *The orchid!* I feel around for my pack in the dark. It's not where I left it. I double check every flat surface within the wagon. I brace myself for a confrontation with the men. I've come too far to lose the stupid flower now. I grab the young druid's staff and hop off the back of the wagon. I put on my menacing face and turn to face the thieves.

Blachstenius and Boswen are sitting around a small fire. Next to Boswen is my pack. The trader looks at my mentor and sheepishly says, "Grahme is awake now."

Boswen has a thick winter cloak wrapped around his shoulders and his head is nearly in the fire as he brews his winter restorative.

"It's a bit early for the wintertime herbs," I say, trying to ebb my anger.

"Oh, to have the vitality of youth," Blachstenius replies.

"Blachstenius has been telling me what he knows about your quest, but I suspect you have much more to tell," Boswen says as he invites me to sit at his fire. He tosses me my pack. "We should do this properly."

I'm too relieved to get annoyed at him. "Let me present you with the ghost orchid, the ultimate goal of my quest." I unwrap the battered little flower and gently hand it to Boswen.

He looks at it for a while in silence. At last, he turns to me. "What was your quest?"

Still the taskmaster. "I was to visit both of my brothers prior to obtaining a ghost orchid and present it to you by Samhain."

"And what day is it now?"

I had slept through the day in the back of Blachstenius' cart. "Since Belenos has set, it is Samhain."

"You have erred in your recital of the quest," Boswen says.

"Lord?"

"You were to return to Dartmoor and present me a ghost orchid before the year's end. Samhain is the start of the new year."

Goosebumps form on both arms as I stare wide-eyed at my mentor. "But—"

"While you slept, I have conversed with Blachstenius and he assures me that you did arrive upon the high moor before nightfall. Do you concur with this statement?"

"Lord, I cannot say. I was asleep nearly the whole trip." I look at Blachstenius to confirm my statement, but he makes no effort to join the conversation. Instead, he throws another log on the fire. Boswen doesn't chide him for the wastefulness. I would never have been so generous with the wood.

"In that case, I will accept the testimony of the good trader as fact. Since you were on Dartmoor before sundown and you possessed the ghost orchid, I will grant that you have successfully completed your quest."

"But Boswen, I didn't present it to you until just now, and it is clearly after sunset."

Boswen looks to Blachstenius. "You see what I mean. Even when he can claim victory, he still tries to undermine himself."

Blachstenius smiles contently.

Did Blachstenius alter Boswen's mind to allow me to achieve my quest? I can't accept the honor if I don't deserve it.

"Alas, I cannot stay for Grahme's summary. No doubt this will be a tale told many times in many places. I don't doubt that his whole adventure will be recited by the bards in only a few years. I, however, wish to be off the moor before this chill reaches all the way to my bones." Blachstenius nods at me, then gazes for a moment at Boswen. "You are committed to this path?"

Boswen nods once and pulls his cloak tighter.

"Farewell, dear friends," Blachstenius says with a solemn dignity. Boswen fixes his gaze to the fire.

"Blachstenius, may I speak with you for just a moment?"

"Later, perhaps," he says. "You should fill Lord Boswen in on your tale before the night's chill takes hold."

I nod. Whatever it was I was going to ask has already flitted out of my mind.

He winks at me before retaking his seat on the wagon's perch. "I don't envy your stay up here with what promises to be a cold night." A quick flick of the reins and his ponies hurry him off.

"Now, I wish to hear your tale from the beginning, but first, indulge an old man and tell me, did you really invoke a thunderstorm?"

"I pulled the clouds to me. I don't think it possible to create a storm from clear skies."

"And you summoned godsfire from this storm?"

"I did, and I also summoned hail," I inform him smugly.

"Hail, as well? Very impressive."

His outright praise throws me for a loop. "I was trapped and had no choice," I add before he can admonish me for being prideful. It feels good to be home.

Boswen listens with few interruptions to my story, only stopping me to ask about Katel lifting the water and Sieffre summoning the elementals.

"Poor Sieffre, I fear his transformation is permanent," he says.

The cold wind picks up and Boswen pulls his wool mantle a little tighter. He throws more kindling onto the fire. The flames shoot up higher and are whipped hither and yon by the wind. I have never seen Boswen squander branches so.

"Would you rather we go into your hut and continue our talk?" I ask, concerned.

"No, I wish to stare at the stars as they stare back at us." He tugs his mantle tight again. "We seem to take them for granted, though they watch us every chance they get."

We spend a few moments in silence gazing up at the sky. I bite my tongue so I can't ask for the hundredth time what the stars are made of. It's a game we play on most every clear night. I will ask, Boswen will put forth an answer and I will then poke holes in his reply until he grows frustrated with me and retires for the night. It strikes me as frivolous to act such on this night.

"I had counted on you arriving, though not quite so late. There is blood bread and porridge waiting for us in your hut. Please get them, will you?"

"Of course."

"Do you know why I asked you to return from your quest before the new year?"

"I do not."

"It was an old custom, now largely forgotten. Many years ago, all quests were timed to end at year's end. That way the successful druids could tell their families, both living and dead, of their success. But younger people rose in the ranks and the youth are always impatient. They assigned quests when they saw fit and the old ways lost favor."

Boswen sits quietly with his mantle, lost in his thoughts. I had expected him to be more excited about me completing my quest. I tend to the heating of the food and leave him be. It's clear that something is weighing on his mind, so I give him the option to speak or not.

I divvy up the food and consume my portion with relish. Boswen is more restrained. He eats his dark blood bread before starting on his porridge. I've seen him eat his food this way at every evening meal.

"Why do you always finish your bread before you start the porridge? My father used to do the same thing."

"It also is an old custom that is not much observed these days," he seems pleased to think about the old days.

"And?" I wait for an explanation. "What is this custom?"

"Just as our days, months, and years start in darkness, so too should the meal start with the darkest-colored food and progress to the lightest. Further, I eat my dark portion, then I eat a similar amount of lighter-colored food. Everything is to be in proportion, and always the darkness is followed by the light."

"Even your meals?"

"It is how I was taught." We lapse into silence again.

"I do have questions for you, Master. What am I to do now that I have finished my quest?"

Boswen lets out a long breath. "Let us put that aside for a moment." He is slow to stand up. "I, Boswen of the Nine, Protector of Men-an-Tol and the Land's End Peninsula, do hereby pronounce that Grahme *Fairweather* has completed his druid's quest successfully. Therefore, I do bestow upon him the status of journeyman druid within the Protectors of Pretanni. I congratulate you." He nods at me formally before the slightest of smiles reveals itself.

Long have I dreamed of this moment. Mentally, I'm too battered and bruised to scream out into the night. The best I can muster is a contented smile. I want nothing more than to spend the next decade or so tending my new duties in peace and obscurity. I have seen enough of the wider world and I like it not at all.

"It is typical for new initiates to smile or perhaps show even joyfulness upon completion of their quests."

"Perhaps in the morning I will have the energy to do so. Tonight, I wish only a good night's rest."

"Before you retire, please show me your hands."

I'm desperate to keep them steady, but the shakes will not be denied.

"Three times you came this close to the edge?"

I want to lie, but old habits still hold. "No, Master, each time it was worse. This is after spending several days at rest."

"I will not lecture you, for you had no choice each time."

"Thank you, Lord."

"Better than any living man, you know the limits of your power. I hope you never have reason to come so close to the edge again."

My desire to bask in my success is pitted against my need for sleep. Neither can gain supremacy. "Why are we not holding the fire for Samhain in some public space?"

"Alas, I was waiting for you. For this one year, the people can provide for themselves."

"But Boswen, that is what the Wigesta and Sorim preach. They tell our people that we druids are not necessary to intercede on their behalf. It is a disease we must excise from the land." He nods but is otherwise unmoved by my report.

"Grahme, please sit, I have some news of my own to report."

In my excitement, I rose to stand over top of my mentor. Never have I attempted that before. I return to my seat and regain a semblance of my composure. "Is your news about Loris? I forgot about him, in my excitement."

"He greatly desires the orchid because he thinks it adds to his grandeur. Now that I have the flower, his foolish pursuit will end. But my news is more ominous, and it is about Dartmoor itself."

I sit still and gird myself for the news.

"When I came here, I was charged by my master, Uffa Horselord, to care for his moor ponies. He spent many years breeding a stout beast that could thrive up here. Prior to your departure, I deduced that a new illness was befalling them."

"Is it bad?"

He sighs; once again I'm the student speaking out of turn. "I have spent this time tracking the illness and though it does no harm to the moorhens, they carry the pestilence. When the ponies come to drink at the marshes, it is passed from fowl to horse. I fear the disease will wipe out the ponies and I will fail at my charge, even after all these years. This is the reason why I sent you to retrieve this flower. It is a parasite, only able to take, which is why the Black Lord wants it. He would have used it to steal the power from Men Meur Kov Keigh, dealing us a crippling blow while strengthening himself. I, however, intend to use it to take the essence of the moorhens so that this blight will die with them."

"Of which moorhens do you speak? Where is the infected marsh?"

"We cannot be sure, and we cannot take the chance of leaving even one infected hen alive. So, I choose to cull all the moorhens of Dartmoor to ensure the safety of the ponies."

"All the moorhens?" I say, stupefied. "But you will ruin the natural balance of the moor."

"It cannot be helped."

"But we are sworn to favor no single creature over the others. You can't kill all the moorhens; it's against the second rule of the druids." I stare at him, mouth agape.

"Other moorhens will find a home and repopulate this place in time."

"What you're proposing is an attack on the natural order. It's counter to the will of the gods. Who dares to second-guess their ways?"

"I dare. Many years ago, my master charged me with a task. I refuse to fail now, even if it is near the end of my days."

"You can't do this."

"Perhaps you should go to Dinas Gwenenen tomorrow and tell your family of your success. It will leave me to my preparations."

I take a moment to compose myself. This must be one last test for me to pass. "Boswen, what you intend to do is obscene and I cannot stand by and let you destroy the natural order."

"I am the lord here."

I close my eyes, wishing this ruse would end. "Boswen, if you will not renounce your plans, then I must challenge you to a death duel." My brain whirls away faster than I can control. I'm too dizzy to stand, yet I challenge my mentor to a death duel?

"I accept your challenge," Boswen responds.

I stare at my mentor, mouth agape again. I see deep sadness in his face. I try to speak but my chest lacks the strength. I silently implore him to put an end to this madness.

"I will need my rest before we duel in the morning." He rises slowly, like an old man, grabs a burning branch, and shuffles into his hut. I watch him depart, debating with my heart and mind if what just happened was real.

35

Duel at Dartmoor

Samhain, First Dark Day of Cuimon, 820

efore dawn, Boswen is up and he has restarted the campfire. Unable to sleep, I join him. We wait in silence for Belenos to rise. I reject yet another way to initiate a conversation. For his part, Boswen moves closer to the fire and stares into its depths. If I don't find some way to stop this lunacy, I will be fighting my mentor to the death today.

He gazes up as the last of the wandering stars fade from the predawn sky. "I have given it much thought," Boswen says.

I close my eyes and soundlessly thank the gods.

"We will duel with staves today, and no magic of any kind will be allowed."

He can't mean to go through with this.

"I think Cawli Circle is the proper place for our duel; there are many yew trees around from which to make a pyre."

"Why?" is the only word my stunned mind can utter.

"I have decided on the weapons so it is of course your decision as to where the duel will take place. I merely suggest it as a fair and convenient location."

"You can't do this," I say.

"Will you retract your challenge and assist me with my duties?"

"You know I can't do that."

"Then I suggest you start for the standing stones soon. It is typical to start duels at midday."

Without another word Boswen morphs into a jackdaw and flies away to the south. As usual, he leaves before I can ask my questions.

I stare at the fire and ponder how this could have come to pass. I grind my teeth together at the betrayal by the man I once revered above all others. I don't know why Boswen has chosen this path, but I intend to stop him. It is my duty. I let loose a couple bitter tears before grasping my borrowed staff.

Cawli Circle rests on a gentle hilltop meadow. To the east is a forest with plenty of yews, just as Boswen claimed. From the south, there is a long line of standing stones, too many to count easily, which lead up to the circle. Boswen is busy preparing a bier of yew wood off to the side. He salutes me and takes a break from his task.

"So, you choose to go with an oaken staff."

"I was not given time to construct one of my own making."

Boswen smiles sadly. "Blachstenius promised to deliver you with a staff. I wish it had been one of your one making."

"Is Blachstenius behind this lunacy?"

"No." Boswen looks directly into my eyes. "He is not. You will have my word on it."

"But—"

"No time for seventy-eight questions." He reaches for my stave. "It is strong, but heavy as well. Make sure you keep your guard up."

He gives me dueling advice before we fight to the death?

"I have chosen an ash staff."

"Boswen, it's not too late. End this madness."

"You are free to leave without slight to your character."

"You know I cannot do that."

Without another word, he returns to the bier.

Still as a stone, I watch my mentor, knowing that I cannot reach him. To let this sickened version of him go on would be an insult to the mentor I once knew. I hang my head and silently fall in step with him to retrieve more branches.

"I trust by your cooperation in building the bier that we can agree that the victor shall burn the defeated according to the proper ways?"

I grunt and nod my head.

"Then I would request one final boon from you, though I freely admit that I have no right to expect it."

"What?" I challenge.

"If you should be victorious today, I ask that the ghost orchid be added to my pyre so that no further harm will come from that terrible creation."

"I would rather we burn it together," I say.

"Alas, that cannot come to pass," Boswen says with real chagrin.

I try to find words to reason with Boswen, but I cannot. We seamlessly resume constructing the bier. Boswen takes the time to point out the secrets of having a proper pyre. If I close my eyes, it feels like we have gone back in time before this madness overtook him.

It's midday, and our work on the bier is complete.

"If you will join me at the opposite end, we can walk the line of standing stones," Boswen says. "I've always felt it adds dignity to do so." He starts down the hill without waiting. Once we reach our destination, Boswen is out of breath. He leans against the first of the standing stones for support.

"We don't know much about the elder races," Boswen says. "We know that the elves stuck to their forests and the giants frolicked over the grassy plains with those aurochs of theirs. And we know that everyone talks down about the pixies. I think the pixies were perhaps the wisest of the elder races. They let others claim superiority while they settled here, at Land's End. They have forests, some plains, the sea on three sides and the moorlands above. I count myself lucky to have been the caretaker of their land all these years."

"What of the centaurs?"

"If the centaurs would ever stop shooting us at first sight, I would have an answer for you. All we know is that their land is the most primeval of them all. Jagged cliffs, fertile valleys, and crystal-clear lakes are all within their realm. I think it is the griffins which they must contend with that makes them so fractious. It's not as if they can climb up to the mountain eyries and smash the eggs of their enemies. No, the centaurs are a hard race because they inhabit a hard land."

Boswen stands up and stretches. "If we don't get started now, I'm likely to talk you to death. Remember, there are seventy-eight stones between us and the circle. You will have two hundred paces in which to reconsider."

"As will you."

The meadow is empty. There are no birds singing or small animals foraging. Even the wind has fled us. Boswen marches straight ahead, allowing his attention to fall only on the circle. He is using his staff for support. *Is this a ruse?* Much like the rest of my time with him, I'm a half step behind and trying to determine what the man is thinking.

Outside the circle, Boswen turns to me. "Please leave the orchid outside the circle."

I set it on top of the last standing stone in the line.

"Also, the amulet, it may prove a distraction to you, and it does hold magic of a sort."

My free hand goes to the rowan amulet at once. This is the only tangible reminder I have of Ysella. I search his face for any chance that he may relent. I kiss it once and place it on top of the orchid.

"Now, I have assumed much. Are you satisfied with the details of this duel? I would not want the duel to be unfair to you in any way."

"It is fine." I am numb to anger or pain.

"Then when you are ready, we shall enter the circle and accept our doom."

"There is no reason to wait."

Boswen rises and bows formally to me. "Know that you have been my finest student."

Is he trying to disorient me?

I close my eyes, exhale once, and enter the circle.

I start spinning my staff from hand to hand, my thumbs leading the way. Beads of sweat form at once and trail down my forehead before leaping from my nose.

Boswen watches the drops fall. "I regret that you are not at your best for this duel."

He seems sincere, but what of it?

"Did you spar with Lord Caradoc during your quest? He has always been infatuated with a twirling staff."

He holds his staff at the base, as if it's a sword. He swings a violent upper cut, timing his strike to follow after my twirling staff. I am fortunate to duck my head in time. He smiles at me like before. He has delivered a lesson without speaking a word. I cease the twirl and hold the middle third of my staff in a defensive position.

Boswen mimics my stance as we circle one another. I swing down at his left shoulder, which he blocks. I reverse my momentum and sweep at his feet. He dances out of the way and jabs me in the chest, but his lunge lacks power. I disengage and begin spinning my staff again. Boswen times his horizontal swing to when my staff is opposite, but I'm expecting it this time. I slap his staff down and bring the heel of my staff into his face. He spits out a tooth.

I double the cadence of my spin and I alternate my attacks, ascending, descending, right and left, but Boswen has an answer for each. I see an opening, so I lunge forward and connect the heel of my staff to his chest. He stumbles back, surprised.

He gingerly feels his rib and inhales in pain. "If you are not going to press your advantage, you might as well drop your staff and let me end this duel now."

"Why must we do this?" I lower my guard for a moment.

He begins to spin his staff and approaches fast. He brings multiple combinations, but he lacks the power to drive them home.

We circle each other again. I note that his footwork is getting sloppy. I swing downward at his head, but he manages to block it. I reverse my momentum and bring the heel of the staff up and into his ribs. He stumbles away.

Once more he holds the staff at the base and goes for an overhead strike. I barely block it in time.

He goes to sweep my feet and I land on his staff, knocking it from his hands. Surprise registers in his eyes as my staff connects with his ear. Lord Boswen, member of the Nine and Protector of Men-an-Tol, lies unconscious at my feet.

I check to see that he still breathes. I kick his staff away and sit on my heels a body length away. I'm too exhausted to be brought to tears again and I can't make the killing blow to my unconscious mentor. Perhaps now he'll forgo his irrational plan. I can only hope that he comes to his senses when he wakes.

Boswen starts to stir. He feels his rib and the side of his head. "I still live," he says.

"You've been beaten. Please, Master, renounce your plans."

"I will not." He rises to his knees and searches for his weapon. He moves like a frail old man, unsteady and unsure. He spots his staff several paces away.

"It is unbecoming to taunt your beaten foe. Be quick and end this now."

"But Master—"

"Now!" he roars, though the effort steals away his breath. He pauses and collects himself. "If I have taught you anything it is that a druid can never shirk his duty. Now strike."

With a ragged breath, I scream, "Yes, Master!"

My staff connects with his head and my revered mentor and friend falls to the ground, dead. I stand over him, exhausted, and unable to produce a single tear.

I close his unseeing eyes and lift his body up over my shoulder. I am surprised at how light he is. I carry him to the bier that we have constructed. I retrieve his ash staff and place it in his hands. The cursed orchid is laid upon his chest. Striking the sparking stones, I start the dried leaves burning. Soon the fire spreads and Boswen lies on a bed of flames. The wind picks up as the clouds roll across the moor. It's as if nature herself held her breath and is only now rushing to see the result.

As the flames reach ever higher, I toss Ysella's amulet into the fire. I have not had time to mourn her properly. I sit on the ground, my back up against a standing stone, and watch as every last vestige of my old life goes up in smoke.

I wake at some point nearly frozen to death. My sweat still sticks to me and has stolen away the heat from my body. The chill has reached my bones. I stir the embers of Boswen's pyre with my shaky hands, desperate to find any warmth.

I find my way back to my hut. I will need some fine pottery in which to place Boswen's ashes, this much I know. The man did not believe in luxury. The only suitable pot is a plain, unadorned white pot with a lid. I smile sadly. The pot suits the simple man and his white robe.

Now I wish I had asked him what to do afterward. The death of one of the Nine surely must be communicated, but to whom? And how? I walk back to the awful spot of our duel and fill the container with ashes.

What do I do with Boswen's ashes?

He left no instructions. Are the druids still scouring the land searching for me? What are my responsibilities now that I am a full druid? Surely, I need to inform someone of Boswen's death, but whom?

If Blachstenius had stayed, could he have stopped this madness from happening? Is this what life is supposed to be; a series of events of which you are given no warning and you have to make your way through it as best you can?

I clear my mind. When Boswen was pensive and needed to think, he would head for Black Tor. He always surrounded himself with moor ponies when he was deep in contemplation. A weight lifts from my shoulders. At least I am sure of what I will do next.

I will spread his ashes tomorrow into the meadow where his ponies graze. In time, the grass will consume the ashes and the ponies will consume the grass. He will become part of his beloved herd.

36

Time of Reckoning

Second Dark Day of Cuimon, 820

s I approach the tor, the foal I befriended so many months ago spots me and runs to my side. His head comes up to my chest now, though his body hasn't filled out yet. Being nuzzled by a colt will heal even the darkest of moods. I scratch his shoulder and attempt a smile. He keeps pressing into me, as if we can get closer than touching. I give him an energetic scratch on his chest before smacking his rump. He breaks into a trot toward his mother before stopping to feed.

Once I reach the top of Black Tor, I grab a handful of ashes and throw them up into the wind. Waiting for the wind to shift, as it always does, I throw several more handfuls into the air until I'm sure I've covered the entire field below.

To the north, I spy a lone horseman riding hard. He must be new to these parts if he thinks traveling over the moor is quicker than the Druid Ditch Road. This area is full of bogs and quick earth. It's dangerous to walk in these parts without a guide, much less ride at great speed. He disappears into a valley. The path should be obvious and take him to the west, where he'll find the main road.

The man and his large gray horse emerge from the valley and he's not taken the detour. The horse is much too large to be a moor pony and the rider is dressed in all black.

The hair stands up on my arms.

It can't be. The Obsidian Mage?

I reach for my amulet, only to remember it was consumed in the fire. I set Boswen's ashes down and close the lid securely. I can only hope that someone finds Boswen's ashes and gives them their proper due.

My stave and I are a poor match for a man on a warhorse. There are bogs off to my left, but I would be run down long before I could reach them. Once again, the Dark Lord has me trapped. I will have to make my stand here.

The Obsidian Mage slows to a trot. I'm trapped on this tor and we both know it. His horse is covered in a white, foamy lather. The poor beast is on the edge of exhaustion. He must have been ridden hard since I took off the amulet.

The Dark Lord stops twenty paces from the tor. "We finally get to talk, young Grahme."

"You're too late."

"Why don't you come down here, so we don't have to yell?"

I focus my mind on his horse. If I can get it to throw its rider—

"That's enough of that."

My head is flung back as if struck. I blink repeatedly, but I can only see white until slowly the Dark Mage comes back into view. He's halved the distance between us.

If I jumped, could I land on him?

"You will throw your staff on the ground before me," the Black Lord commands.

"No," I say, but to my amazement, my arms rise to do his bidding. I try to halt the movement, but it is as if my command is

369

hitting a wall and my arms are unaware of my true orders. My hands, even with my chest, hold the staff horizontally. With one easy thrust, my only weapon is flung to the ground at the feet of my enemy.

"If you make me work for what I want to know, I will have you dive off that ledge after your staff."

In my mind, I can see myself, no *feel* myself leaping headfirst. My legs are propelling me forward and exploding off the edge as I career headfirst to the rocky ground below. I feel the tensing of my muscles and I know the fear of racing toward death. Then it's gone and I once more stare down at the Dark Lord. My chest is heaving, and the breeze alerts me to the cold sweat covering my body.

"I hope I've made my point. Now, tell me where the ghost orchid is."

"It is gone, destroyed by fire last night. You're too late." I give him a defiant smile.

He closes his eyes, and I can feel his presence within my mind. He is rooting through my memories; and I am powerless to stop him.

"So, you tell the truth. No matter, you will be an excellent candidate for the next King's Mark. Now, come down from there at once."

I protest, but my legs do the Obsidian Mage's bidding. In the tiny corner of my mind where he has not invaded, I decide to stop fighting his commands. If I comply now, maybe he'll loosen his hold.

I reach the bottom of the tor and I stand helpless in front of him. I keep my head bowed and count the number of steps to get to his horse. If I could make contact with it, I'm sure I could get it to throw its rider, even in my weakened state.

"How pathetic, still refusing to admit defeat," the Dark Lord chides. "Even if you were somehow able to best me, what do you think your future would hold? You are considered a traitor and hunted by your own kind. If they were to find you, you would be stripped of your rank and ostracized from the order."

"I'll take my chances."

"Grahme, I've seen your memories. The only person who could vouch for you was killed by your own hand yesterday. And the orchid? You burned up your only evidence of success, along with your mentor. Do you really think they'd confer honors upon you for killing your Lord Protector?" The Black Lord dismounts and walks to me. "It's time you realized that you have failed. You could scarcely have hoped for this to turn out any other way." He looks down his nose and I'm devastated by his disappointment in me.

I have enough of my old self left to know that he is using his power to make me feel helpless, but it's all the more agonizing because I know he's right. My power is spent, I have no allies. What could I possibly hope to do?

From behind the Obsidian Mage, I see a red kite circling and coming in for a silent landing. Hope courses through my veins. I must hide my excitement. He's bound to notice unless I can distract him.

"You're a failure, Rhunior. You can't even manage a city, much less a kingdom." I shout.

"So, you have met my brother." He smiles coldly. "I believe he is calling himself Blachstenius these days. Mark my words; his days are numbered, as well."

I've done it. Cynbel has landed and animorphed without being heard. He locks his staff behind his head and sets his front foot to launch the killing blow.

"That will be enough of that, Lord Cynbel."

The Black Lord turns with his outstretched left hand toward Cynbel. The druid lord freezes mid-swing. Cynbel's arms shake as he tries to loose the killing blow. The flaring of his nostrils is all he is permitted to do.

I feel the Dark Lord's power loosening on me, but what can I possibly do? I can only pray that my death comes swiftly.

"I will enjoy going through every corner of your mind, Lord Cynbel. Ah, that is the location of your secret summer camp. And you only post three sentries? You will ride with me next summer and see the destruction of your camp. Then we will watch as the Giant's Choir is dismantled stone-by-stone by your own charges."

Cynbel's hatred shows through his eyes.

Searching the ground, I look for anything I can use as a weapon. I fix my gaze at the warhorse, which is nonchalantly eating grass. *Help*, I project. It continues eating. My power is truly drained.

"That will be enough of that." The Obsidian Mage flicks his wrist, and my vision goes to bright white again.

I shake my head and blink several times to regain my vision.

"Leave us," the Dark Lord says without a glance in my direction.

Head down in shame, I abandon the field. I am so insignificant that he doesn't even check to see my progress. I have failed Boswen, failed Cynbel, and failed myself. I have failed the druids, and I will live out my days knowing that I have brought ruin upon them. I was foolish to have entertained thoughts otherwise.

I struggle to raise my weary head. I see my only friend, the colt. He alone is unaware of my abject failure. I trudge over toward him, desperate for some undeserved affection. He sees me and starts meandering over to me. I reach out my hand to scratch his withers and it feels as if the fog in my head has lifted.

I look back to where the Dark Lord is. The tor stands between us. What did Katel say? The earth stops the powers of the mind-controllers. My overwhelming sense of failure is gone. *But what can I hope to do now that I have my own free will?*

The foal senses my dejection and lets out a woeful whinny of his own. His mother comes to investigate. I look around me and see the rest of the harem staring at me as well. The stallion snorts a challenge as he comes over to investigate.

Horses don't give up on their own kind. And I cannot give up on Cynbel. Tentatively, I call the rest of the horses to me. I have very little power but communicating with animals takes little effort. The horses encircle me and the colt. They start swishing their tails and flaring their nostrils. They're agitated. I touch the stallion and ask him to hold. He paws the ground but remains in place.

It may be the death of me, but I have only one choice. I round the tor to face my nemesis for the final time.

He smiles triumphantly as he takes the protection amulet off Cynbel's still frozen form.

"Rhunior!" I call, anger boiling up from my stomach.

"You managed to survive my lightning, now prepare for my thunder." I can feel him trying to enter my mind again.

I turn to face the horses. "Charge."

The stallion rears up and squeals out his challenge. Head down, he leads his eight mares in a gallop. The ground is quaking from the onrush. The pounding of their hooves reverberates off the tor. The little foal rears up and runs in circles behind the adults. He's too young to understand. But one day, like me, he will take his spot as a full member of his kind.

The Dark Lord draws his sword and holds it low. As the charging herd gets closer, he loses his nerve and runs for his steed, ten steps away. It might as well be a thousand.

The stallion is the first to reach him and he bites onto Rhunior's arm. The sword drops harmlessly, and he's flung around as if he were a child's doll. He stumbles but manages to keep his feet. The stallion releases him and lands a powerful rear kick to his head. The Black Lord goes down like a felled tree.

The herd snorts and stomps around him, working off their anger and waiting for any sign of movement. I come running up and thank the stallion for saving us. His work done, he leads his herd away from danger.

I stare down at the still form. His chest still rises, so he still lives.

"It seems that once again I am in your debt," Cynbel says.

"Lord Cynbel, It's still in the time of Samhain."

"Yes," he says, uncomprehending.

"The Obsidian Mage can be reborn as early as today unless he suffers the threefold death. I need to find a sharp rock so I can slit his throat."

Cynbel grabs my shoulder. "Here, use my bone knife." He hands me the weapon, handle first.

"Yes, Lord, this is exactly what we need."

"I don't know how you could have traveled as far as you did without one." He shakes his head in mock disapproval.

I kneel down next to the body, the knife poised above his neck. I've never killed a helpless man before. *Well, that's not entirely true.* The image of the limping man intrudes upon my thoughts. I look up to Cynbel for assurance.

"It must be done," he says.

I swallow hard. There is no other way. I close my eyes and settle my mind. With my left hand I feel the neck and with my right, I drag the blade across it. I feel warm, oozing blood and know that my cut is true. The blade continues around the side of the neck until it reaches the ground.

"That will do, Grahme. Wait here, I will find my men and have them gather vines and saplings for the wicker cage."

I give him a weak smile. As if I have the strength to go anywhere else today. "There are bogs," I say. "They're close by, off to the northwest." I point them out, as if a druid lord would not know which way northwest was. I feel the Dark Lord's life blood pooling around my knees. I pull away and make the mistake of looking upon the helpless form that I have bled out. The whole world starts to rotate around me. I raise my arms to steady myself. Cynbel is quick to seat me on a flat stone at the base of the tor.

"I saw the bogs, Grahme. We will appease Esus, Taranis, and Teutates before the day is over." He shakes my shoulders sternly. "When I return and you have regained some strength, you will tell me what your mentor is up to."

The colt interposes itself between us and forcefully nudges Cynbel away.

Startled, Cynbel rises to his feet. The colt gives his best menacing snort. Cynbel grins wide and bows to the horse. "Message received."

The Obsidian Lord's body is placed in a wicker cage and stuffed with thatching. The cage is leaned against the tor. Cynbel hands me the torch and I start the blaze. The thatch burns quickly, as does the wicker. The Dark Lord's smoking corpse falls forward once the fast-burning fuel is consumed.

"A little rushed, but I judge that Taranis has been satisfied by our offering," Cynbel says. "And you gave homage to Esus. Now all that is left is for the body to be drowned in accordance with Teutates' demands."

A rope is affixed around the Obsidian Mage's neck and Cynbel's druids pull the body to the bog. I have no recollection of when they arrived, but I'm too tired to ask. A heavy stone is placed on the smoldering corpse and it sinks slowly, never to be reborn.

"It is done," I say.

"A great evil has been eliminated," Cynbel agrees. "Now, my men tell me that Boswen is not at his camp, so there is the matter of Boswen's location that we must attend to."

"He is here," I say. "Or at least his remains are here, on top of the tor."

One of Cynbel's men retrieves Boswen's ashes.

"You have much to tell us," Cynbel says. "Noga, go send out the alarm call and gather up as many of our kind as you can find. The search is over. We will meet at Boswen's campsite this evening." He turns to Torsech, another of his druids. "And I would have you fly to Ardri Bryn Cadwy and escort Caradoc and his many *friends* to Boswen's camp as well."

"But, Lord, I know not where Boswen's camp is."

Cynbel lets out a chuckle. "When you tell Caradoc this news, be quick in your transformation or he will lose you in his haste."

376

37

A Full Accounting

Second Dark Day of Cuimon, 820

It has taken nearly all of the daylight, but Cynbel and I manage to stagger back to Boswen's camp. The effect of the Dark Lord laying waste to our minds creates a fatigue like I've never felt before. At last, we reach the sliver of moss-covered forest along the River Dart. On the final rise, I get chills. Boswen will never be there to greet me again.

"I always liked this camp," Cynbel says. "There are so few trees on the moor, yet Boswen managed to have his camp within them without evicting the wildlife."

"It's the only place I have thought of as home since I left my parent's house."

"Are you ready?"

"For what?"

The dangling curtains of moss on the trees look ominous, with only weak rays of light from Boswen's campfire to illuminate our way. As we round the dangling curtain of moss, five score druids wait patiently. A knowing smile from Cynbel is all I get as an explanation.

"Make way," he calls in his booming voice.

The crowd pulls back at our approach. Several extra stumps have been placed around the fire, and most have been claimed. Before us sit Lords Caradoc, Eghan, Meraud, Drustan, and even Hedred. The rest of the druids crowd around the campfire. I know from experience that those in the back will become very cold very fast once Belenos sinks below the horizon.

"Greetings, lords," Cynbel says in an expansive voice. "We are in for an interesting end of the day, it would seem. I present to you the elusive Grahme." He bows low to his fellow members of the Nine. "He has quite the tale to tell, though I dare say that not even he knows all of it. So, settle in and let us get to the bottom of this today."

Hedred approaches me. "I hope you don't hold a grudge against me."

"Why would I, Lord Hedred?"

"Well, I was a poor host just a few days prior."

"Lord Hedred, I was in a rush to complete my quest, so your actions were exactly what I needed."

"This is good of you. We must all be willing to forgive in order to move forward."

I am sure he is trying to tell me something important, but I can't fathom what it could be. I nod as if I understand and watch as the dumpy little man shuffles back to his seat.

Boswen's seat at the fire is the only place open. I can see Belenos framed between the boughs of only two yew trees. This was Boswen's secret way of marking time. From his perch, the branches are equally spaced from one another. By watching Belenos sink past each, Boswen could tell within a heartbeat or two of when the new day would begin. I was so proud when I discovered his secret. My eyes begin to water. I force a cough to get myself under control.

"Grahme," Caradoc says, "everyone's waiting for you to begin your tale."

For the first time in my life, there are two hundred eyes staring at me, expecting who-knows-what. I croak out "Water, please" and the crowd gives a low chuckle. I am given a wooden cup and I take a quick drink. They are all still staring at me.

"For my quest, Lord Boswen charged me with finding and bringing back a ghost orchid. I had never heard of such a plant before, and he told me that they are very rare. The only existing flower known to Boswen was being kept within Solent Keep."

There are murmurs of surprise rippling through the crowd. If nothing else, I've captured their attention.

"I must interject here," Caradoc says. "For those who do not know, the ghost orchid is an evil, parasitic flower which, if used properly, can defile the very sites we hold as most holy. I was present at the bestowing of the quest, and I can assure everyone that this information was not shared with Grahme. He had no idea why Boswen so urgently wanted this flower retrieved from the Obsidian Mage's Keep."

"Neither do the rest of us," Meraud says. She looks at Caradoc, waiting for further explanation. The crowd feeds on Meraud's confident gaze and calls for more to be said. Caradoc holds his hands up for silence.

"Indeed, Boswen thought it best not to reveal the magnitude of possibilities while it was in the Obsidian Lord's possession. I believe that only Boswen and I were privy to this information."

Drustan and Cynbel are demanding to know more from Caradoc. Once again, he raises his arms. "Before we lose our way, let's have Grahme finish his tale. Then you can tear into my hide, if you must."

"Before you continue," Cynbel interrupts, "did Boswen instruct Grahme not to share this information with anyone, including other members of the Nine?"

"Lord Boswen gave me no such order," I cut in.

"Then you lied about keeping all of this a secret?" he demands.

"I gave the command," Meraud says.

Caradoc draws away from her, as if he had been struck. Cynbel stares in stunned silence. The crowd laughs nervously. He waves his hands in a placating gesture for an explanation.

"When Grahme came to show the proper respects at Keynvor Daras, I asked him of his quest and I can vouch that what he has revealed so far is the same as he told me over a month ago. I knew of the orchid's possible use and it was clear that Grahme did not. I did not, and still do not know what strategy Boswen wished to employ, so I chose not to interfere. For Grahme's protection, I bid him to keep his quest secret from any not already familiar with it."

Drustan looks annoyed and Caradoc is studiously avoiding Meraud's gaze. Cynbel remains lost in his thoughts. Only Hedred and Eghan are patient, as if listening to a bardic tale.

All eyes are once again locked on me. I tell of being cornered by the limping man and how the dog Cryton sacrificed himself for me.

"That would be the Dark One's second," Cynbel says. He nods his approval. "You faced off against the two most powerful Obsidian Mages on Pretanni and lived to tell the tale. You lead a charmed life, it would seem."

Charmed? He should know the price that I have had to pay. But now is not the time, so I swallow my bitter rebuke. I take another drink of water to refocus my thoughts.

I skip over how the orchid was already turned to stone and the necessary side trip to Venta. Instead, I place the blame on Alfswich for stealing it from me.

"This Alfswich is a known thief and a mind-controller," Cynbel says. "I have standing orders to kill him if he should appear on the plains again."

I tell of fortuitously meeting Blachstenius while on the road to Sarum.

"Do you really think that was a happy accident?" Caradoc asks.

"Indeed," Cynbel chimes in, "I doubt the meeting was random."

I had not considered this possibility.

Of being jailed in Sarum, I tell them of my luck to be held with Alfswich once again. "When we escaped, I made sure to keep the orchid in my possession." It's not quite the truth, but I fear what would happen if everyone knew that I took the flower off of a dead druid's body.

I try to skip over Men Meur Kov Keigh, only to have Cynbel interrupt me and heap undo praise upon me for my weather-casting. I mention being totally drained of my vitality, but I skip over the iron manacles and the trip to Kantom Lijanks Kuros. Eghan and Hedred visibly relax when I avoid mentioning the ceremony at the long barrow and the giant's script.

"I need to speak again," Caradoc says. He jumps to his feet. It's clear that his craving for attention must be satisfied. "It was I who told Grahme to be ready to flee if the discussions among the Nine went badly. It was my man, Eosiah, and several other druids who were in Grahme's company and chose to flee with him."

"So, Loris was right to suspect you," Drustan exclaims.

"For subverting his will and doing good for the land? Always. All that talk about sedition was just the latest silliness coming from our incapable leader. Who but the daftest among us could have believed that?"

"I believed it and I still do," Braden says.

Caradoc rolls his eyes. "Too easy."

"That's enough," Hedred of all people says. He cuts off the heated name-calling that was brewing. Surprised by the diminutive man's outburst, Caradoc sits down and urges me to continue.

I linger over the details of Ynys Witrin so that my companions can have their heroic exploits memorialized. I tell of the terrible cost to Sieffre, Eosiah's true leadership, and Arthmael's doomed escape.

Eghan raises his hand. "I fear that Sieffre's change will be permanent. We will always try to work with him, but he has made precious little progress." A pall falls over the assembled.

"I have some good news to report," Cynbel announces. "Arthmael did not perish as you believe."

"He lives?" I exclaim.

"He does. In fact, I was speaking to him when a messenger from Tochar Briwa arrived and informed me that one from my group, named Arthmael had wandered off while receiving treatment and could not be found. As you may imagine, the two of us found this report to be rather humorous."

"Lord Cynbel," I say, more sharply than I should, "in all the time it took us to walk back here, you didn't think to tell me that Arthmael lives?"

Caradoc laughs his big, booming laugh. "Cynbel is a bard, Grahme. You don't tell the surprise in the beginning of your tale. You wait until the end."

The crowd chuckles and I'm forced to let my ire go.

Arthmael is alive. That's what is important.

"He speaks very highly of you, Grahme," Cynbel says. "You give yourself too little credit at the battle of the tor. I believe this is true of your entire tale, but that can wait for another time."

The thought of people congratulating me for my series of debacles is too uncomfortable to think about. I dive back into my story and briefly touch on the healing springs before a lump in my throat makes it impossible to continue. After another drink of water, it's still hard to go on.

"It's all right, lad," Hedred says.

I pace back and forth in front of the fire, vainly trying to recover my composure.

"It should be said that Grahme once again came dangerously close to overextending himself," Eghan says. "Once we were able to coax him back to his human form, I had him drugged for as many days as I dared so that he could recover."

I give a detailed accounting of how Ysella saved Katel and me at the pond and how she was captured for her efforts. I see a single tear is running down Cynbel's cheek as he nods at Ysella's bravery.

"There will be a ballad composed in her honor," he says. "She was one of my best students."

There are scores of druids present and the only noise comes from the crackling of the fire. It occurs to me that my words alone have caused this. It's intoxicating, knowing that you can make the crowd feel however you want with the properly chosen words.

I sense that now is the time to raise those spirits. I check to make sure Katel is not among us. I tell of the ride on the underground rapids, framing it in the most humorous way I can. There are several laughs and smiles all around.

I finally understand the power of the bard.

Though I don't want to relive it, the story has a life of its own and I must continue with what happened next. I speak of Ysella's second sacrifice, saving us from certain death. Cynbel's tears are there for all to see. Meraud is openly weeping as well.

I gloss over my river escape for fear that more praise will be heaped upon me. I only slow my tale to describe Gurthcid and his men galloping off the cliff and being broken by the rocks below.

Cynbel stands. "This is the menace that the Obsidian Order poses," Cynbel says in his husky voice. "None are more aware of this than we plains druids." He realizes that now is not the time for a call to action, so he sits again.

I speak in glowing terms of the care I received from Andrilou. I even confess to taking, then offering his staff to the gods as well as misleading him at every turn.

"Andrilou deserves much better," Drustan says.

"He does, Lord Drustan. And I wish to make it up to him if I am able."

"Your repayment for our healing is clear enough."

I sigh. It seems I am destined to collect powerful detractors no matter what I do.

"In these trying times," Hedred says, "it is best to forgive one another so that we may face our troubles together."

Drustan turns his whole body away from me and the fire.

"And now we get to the most curious part," Lord Cynbel says. "There were many, many druids ransacking this area for you. I fear the poor tawny owls around these parts have been harassed so often that they are likely to abandon this area for a time. How did you manage to get back here without being spotted by any of your brethren?"

I pause for a moment and make them wait. I slowly smile to my audience, waiting for the right moment. "It was Blachstenius." I wait a beat for the news to be absorbed. "Boswen had sent him to find me and with his ability to persuade," I tap my head a couple times, "no one paid the least bit of attention to us. I rode in his wagon down the Druid Ditch Road."

The crowd murmurs again, this time in disbelief.

"Indeed, Blachstenius even convinced one druid to give me his staff. I hold up the oaken training staff for all to see.

"That's my stave!" a voice from the back yells.

"Thank you for letting me use it. Please come and reclaim it."

The boy excitedly pushes through the crowd. Once he's clear, he notices the hundreds of eyes staring at him and freezes. Knowing that feeling all too well, I go to him and return the staff. Once he takes hold of it, I pull him in tight. In a low voice I tell him, "Respect this staff, for it has bested a member of the Nine." His eyes grow large, and he searches my face for any deceit. I nod once and release the staff. He quickly melts back into the crowd.

"When I arrived here yesterday, Lord Boswen accepted the ghost orchid and confirmed me as a druid." It's not the exact truth, but . . . . I face each of the lords in turn. If they do not dispute this point, then my status as a druid will stand.

"You have completed your quest," Caradoc confirms. "Now please finish your tale."

I don't want to continue. Despite how it ended, I don't wish to speak ill of Boswen. Caradoc must know why I am hesitating.

"Go on, Grahme."

"Lord Boswen told me of an illness that was killing the moor ponies. Further, he had divined that the disease was coming from the moorhens. He proposed to use the orchid to kill all the moorhens in order to save the ponies."

There's a collective gasp from the crowd. I am proud to know that I'm not the only one who knows and respects our ways. Multiple side conversations erupt.

"Silence!" Caradoc bellows. His bard training is obvious. He stretches out a hand to me. "Please continue."

"I had no choice but to challenge him to a duel."

There are more gasps from the crowd, but no one dares raise their voice now.

"You challenged a member of the Nine and your own mentor to a duel?" Drustan says what everyone is thinking.

"I did not have a choice."

Drustan has gone pale.

A moment of silence ensues, and I hurry to fill the void. Now that I'm committed to the tale, I want it over as soon as possible. "We spent the night here, both hoping the other would see the error of his way. Before first light, Lord Boswen left for Cawli Circle. He built a bier of yew, to be . . . to be used afterward." I cough to regain my composure once again. "Lord Boswen insisted that no magics be used during the duel. He even insisted that I remove my rowan protection amulet. Before we entered the stone circle, he asked a boon of me."

I can't stop my voice from getting shaky. Tears fall unheeded but I dare not stop now. "He asked that if I were victorious, that I place the ghost orchid on his chest and let it burn along with him on the pyre."

"My men have flown to Cawli Circle," Cynbel says softly, "and they can confirm that a pyre of yew has been recently burned."

I feel relief now. Thanks to Cynbel, I've been spared reliving the duel. The worst of my story is over, and I rush to finish the tale. "I knew only that my former life was over, and I was at a loss for what to do next. Ysella had given me the protection amulet, so I added it to the pyre, since I never got a chance to mourn her or the rest of my friends properly. This morning, I went to spread some of Boswen's ashes at Black Tor where I knew the moor ponies would be grazing. From there, I saw the Black Lord riding his horse hard toward me. I was trapped with no place to run or hide. No doubt my removal of the amulet allowed him to home in on me." I turn to Cynbel, "would you finish the tale from here?" I beseech him.

"No," he says with regret. "I am but a small part of your greater tale."

I exhale. This is harder than I thought. "He compelled me off the tor to gloat face-to-face. Lord Cynbel swooped down behind the Dark Lord, but he was unable to get close enough to strike. Once he had Lord Cynbel in his power, he forced me to believe that I had failed. My only option was to walk away and abandon Lord Cynbel to his fate."

There is not a sound to be heard. Indeed, it feels as if everyone is holding their breath to hear what comes next. "To my eternal shame, I turned my back on Cynbel and did as the Dark One bid. I left the field." Again, I stop and let the feeling set in. I have the crowd spellbound. "It was only divine providence from the goddess Epona that a colt of which I was familiar was nearby. Needing a friend, I went to him. The Obsidian Mage's grip on my mind faded once the tor was between us. I used what little power I had to assemble the lead stallion and his harem to charge the Cursed One."

Cynbel jumps to his feet. "The horses rounded the tor and the pounding of their hooves struck fear in the Black Mage. Frozen in place, he squandered valuable time and failed to reach his steed. The stallion ended the threat with a double kick to the head. Then Grahme, still with his wits about him, demanded we perform the threefold death so that this menace would never again plague our land."

The crowd explodes into resounding cheers. They jump and holler into the night. How could they misunderstand so profoundly? As the bodies of my fellow druids bounce up and down, I manage to catch a glimpse of Hedred, still sitting in his spot. He nods sympathetically at me as his eyes fill up with tears. Boswen is gone, forever. When this frenzy is over, everyone will realize the utter disaster that I have wreaked.

Cynbel calls for quiet. Like Caradoc, he has full command of his voice and can easily be heard over the crowd. "What our humble Grahme isn't telling you is far more than what he has revealed tonight, and it is all to his credit. However, I think we can call an end to this tale and allow the poor man some rest."

"Not quite yet," Caradoc interrupts. "The tale is not over."

Caradoc ushers me to my seat before walking to the center. I gladly take my seat next to Meraud.

"Always has to be the center of attention," she says softly, shaking her head.

"Boswen had misled poor Grahme, in more ways than one." He waits for everyone to settle down. I try to catch his eye, but he won't look at me. "Just over a year ago, Boswen diagnosed himself with the wasting disease. He sought Eghan's opinion, and I believe Eghan concurred."

Eghan nods.

"He was impressed by his final student's abilities, so he honed them as best he could in the short amount of time he had left. For many reasons best left unspoken here, he devised this quest for Grahme and the false story of the moor ponies when his protégé returned. His hope was that Grahme would display his awesome gifts while questing and take his place as a young leader of our society."

I want to feel something at these words, but I've become numb from my recital.

"Indeed, Boswen thought so highly of our hero that he wished for Grahme to take his place among the Nine."

The assembled druids are buzzing by this rhetorical flourish. No doubt Caradoc will be pleased with the reaction it caused.

"So, he gave his student no choice but to challenge him to a duel. By defeating one of the Nine in a fair duel, Grahme is to take his mentor's spot and ascend to the high council."

What? I must have heard wrong.

"This is outrageous," Drustan shouts the words that I am thinking. "This man is a criminal."

"You heard the same tale I did, Lord Drustan," Meraud says. "Of what crime did you hear? I heard none."

"He willfully flouted the will of Loris. He destroyed a powerful artifact. He killed one of us! How many more crimes do you need?" He stares incredulously at the other lords.

"Grahme," Caradoc calls. "Were you ever informed of the fat oaf's wish for you to present yourself to him?"

"Caradoc, show some respect," Meraud says.

"The old fool imprisoned me in my own camp for no cause that he could prove. When Loris accords his fellow members with the respect they are due, then I will be happy to reciprocate."

Meraud raises her head to the stars, knowing that further discussion is a lost cause.

"Second," Caradoc continues, "would you have preferred that Grahme ignore the rules of our order and agree to kill all the moorhens? Since when is it a crime to passionately follow the three basic tenets? With the choice Grahme was given, would any of us have acted differently?"

The crowd is silent as the drama unfolds before them.

"You'll never get the votes," Drustan says savagely.

"He doesn't need votes, you oaf. You can ascend to the Nine by defeating one of its members in a duel. It is only when a position is vacated that it is filled by the vote of the council. He defeated Boswen; he is of the same rank as you and me."

I stare at the assembled lords, trying to process what Caradoc has said.

"But I screwed up every step of the way. I can't be rewarded for my actions." *Did they not just hear my miserable tale?*

Caradoc puts his arm around me. "You are not being rewarded. You are one of the Nine." He pats me on the back and chuckles.

A red-faced Drustan stands up and points in Caradoc's face. "Loris will have him voted off the council."

"Loris is not a king," Caradoc shouts back. "He is one of the Nine like the rest of us. The only difference is that he gets to talk first at gatherings."

Drustan and Caradoc are in each other's face, screaming obscenities. It takes several men to pull each one back. Eghan is sitting, taking in the whole scene. Cynbel is off directing his men to act as heralds and tell everyone what has happened here.

It is Hedred who approaches me and grips my hand. "I dearly hope that Boswen knew what he was doing. I don't doubt you, but he has thrown you into deep and dangerous waters in hopes that you can swim."

"Ah, thank you, Lord?"

He pats my hand to reassure me.

"How is Katel?" I rush to ask before he can leave me.

"She is . . . recuperating." He looks up at me with his reddened eyes and I can see that he feels her pain as well. He pats my hand once more and heads off into the darkened woods.

"I question if Boswen has done you any favor in this," Meraud says from behind.

I turn to face her thoughtful eyes. "Hedred said much the same thing before he left us."

"In truth, he hates crowds. I was mildly surprised that he made it through the whole telling."

"You could say the same thing about me and my quest."

"Indeed."

"I wish he could have stayed." I look off into the trees.

"Oh, he hasn't left yet. There is one more thing we must accomplish before we can return to our homes."

38

New Beginnings at Land's End

Third Dark Day of Cuimon, 820

Third day of being a druid

The wind has turned brutally cold as it blows off the coast.

"Can we hurry and get this over with?" Caradoc asks.

"We must go by seniority, so Hedred is first," Meraud responds.

Eghan leans in close to me. "They can't help but argue whenever they're around each other. It's what draws them together and pushes them apart. Even the tides envy their consistency."

"It's outlandish that the other three haven't shown up for this," Caradoc says.

It was reported by Cynbel's man that Loris went into a flying rage when he heard that I had become one of the Nine. He forbade my promotion and even threatened to kick Caradoc and Meraud off the council. Braden also elected to skip this ceremony in fear of angering Loris further. Drustan simply left and as far as I know, no one has bothered to look for him.

Caradoc is quick to point out that the only way for someone to be removed from the council was to be defeated in a duel to the death. He added that he would welcome the challenge from Loris and make himself available at any time.

"Finally, we're ready. Be quick for a change, will you Hedred," Caradoc complains.

"I would like to see you hurry when you've entered your seventh decade of life," Hedred replies.

One by one, the druid lords touch the upright stone, walk to the central circular stone and as gracefully as possible, squeeze their way through the opening before walking to the opposite standing stone. Men-an-Tol is a senseless monument, but it was made by the pixies, so it is to be expected. First Hedred then Caradoc, Meraud, Eghan and finally Cynbel proceed. Now it is my turn. At least I won't be embarrassed if I fall. Three of the others have already done so while trying to get through my induction ceremony. I am now Protector of Men-an-Tol and Keeper of the Laws for Land's End. I have large shoes to fill.

"Hurry up will you, Grahme? If my teeth chatter any harder, I'll start to break them," Caradoc complains.

Here goes, my first act as one of the Nine.

Thanks for reading my book, I hope you enjoyed it.

If you would like to know more about me and my upcoming releases, please check out my website: **www.AuthorMikeMollman.com.**

You can sign up to my newsletter and get short stories and other exclusive content for free. You can sign up at: **www.subscribepage.com/becoming-a-druid**

As a self-published author, the most significant obstacle is having your voice heard. Reviews are the social proof that a product is worth buying. Please, tell your friends and consider leaving honest reviews at:

Amazon and **Goodreads**.

Pretanni Pantheon

Agrona Goddess of Battle & Slaughter

Acasta Local Goddess of the River Itchen

Aine The Moon Goddess, her day is Godhvos Gras (the first full moon after Beltane).

Andrasta War Goddess, Patron of the Iceni

Artaius God of livestock (His day is the Vernal Equinox)

Lir Lord of the Sea, one primary Merfolk gods

Belenos Sun God (Beltane is his festival)

Brigantia Fertility and Prosperity (Imbolc is her festival)

Camulos God of War. His day is the Summer Solstice.

Cernunnos Lord of the Wild Things. Called the Horned One, has antlers.

Cocidius Goddess of the Hunt, Helghores Loor is her day (first full moon after Lughnasa).

Epona Goddess of Horses, the primary goddess of the Centaurs

Fagus God of Beech Trees, one of the Elven gods.

Hooded Ones Gods of Mysteries and Oracles. Primary gods of the seers.

(Opposed to Belenos, their day is the Winter Solstice)

Melusine	Goddess of the Merfolk, Lir's wife.
Ogmios	God of Eloquence, Music and Poetry, Patron of the bards
Sucellos	God of Agriculture and alcoholic drinks (Lugh is ancient name for god and Lughnasa is his festival)
Coventina	Goddess of Rivers
Nemetona	Goddess of Sacred Groves
Sulis	Goddess of the Healing Springs

Together Coventina, Nemetona and Sulis make up the Earhmother and she is celebrated at Autumnal Equinox. Her symbol is the triskelion.

Esus	Husband of the Earthmother – Human offerings by hanging
Taranis	Storm God – Human offerings placed in wicker cage and burned
Tettates	God of Male Fertility and Wealth – Human offerings drowned in lakes

If person suffers all three deaths (in one body), their soul is killed and they will not reincarnate.

Acknowledgements

The path to writing a book is a long and winding one. While much of the work is done alone, no one can finish a book worth reading without a lot of help.

My editor, Theodora Bryant took my lump of a story and made it shine. I cannot recommend her highly enough. She can be found at: **www.book-editing.com/theodora-bryant**

The cover art was made by Dmitry Yakhovsky and the quality speaks for itself. You can find him at: **entaroart.com**

No fantasy novel is complete without a map, and Theodor Andrei exceeded every single expectation I had. You can find him at: **fiverr.com/theodorandrei.**

Then there are the people who provided me services without payment.

Ask Jeff Davidson how a character would react in any given situation and he will paint a picture of mayhem and destruction. I did my best executing his ideas for the Dinas Gwenenen mead hall scene. And no Jeff, my druids will never be able to control fire, because with your ideas, they'd turn Pretanni into a conflagration reminiscent of the domains of hell.

My brother Danny had to listen to my trials and tribulations almost nightly, so I would be remiss not to mention him here. He had an opinion for every question I'd put to him, and sometimes he was even helpful.

Wyatt Johnson Ph. D. once asked me why we are friends. I told him it's because he makes poor decisions. Not a fan of fantasy, he still read my first draft and patiently noted all the inconsistencies and gaping plot holes. First drafts are supposed to be lousy, and mine didn't disappoint(?). I should probably treat him better, but I won't.

Tim, my eldest brother, (his age is my definition of old, thereby keeping me forever five years away from that state) was also helpful . . . when I could get a hold of him. He's harder to find than a ghost orchid. We had several thoughtful discussions on world building and character motivations. My book is better for them.

About the Author

Mike Mollman is a charming individual graced with good looks, undeniable charisma and humility. These descriptions come straight from his keyboard, so they must be treated as unimpeachable facts. Mike lives in the Richmond, Virginia area. When he's not self-aggrandizing, he likes to spend time with his two dogs and the many voices in his head.

CPSIA information can be obtained
at www.ICGtesting.com
Printed in the USA
BVHW060823021021
617894BV00001B/2